IRREGULAR PEOPLE

A novel by **Yazo**

ISBN: 0615799280
ISBN 13: 9780615799285

- 1 -

The sound of a stretcher rolling and people whispering next door awoke Miri. Nurse Yun wasn't on the chair where she usually sat every night knitting away, keeping an eye on her to make sure she wouldn't wander around at night. She left the knitting tools in the basket next to the chair.

The moon, neither half nor full, was still high up in the sky. Miri got out of the bed, took a few steps to the door, and cracked it open and put her ear to the small opening. It sounded like a patient was being moved into the next room, which had been vacant up until now. She heard a man murmuring and stood at the door for a while until it went silent. She opened the door wider and poked her head out. Nurse Yun suddenly materialized in front of her. "What's going on?" she asked, as she was being pushed back into the room. Nurse Yun, squeezing her enormous face through the door, put her index finger on her lips and motioned for her to go back to bed. She then closed the door.

Sitting on her small bed tucked in the corner of the room, Miri rolled her head around in the dark, blinking as if she would find something that would kill the boredom. Before she was conscious of what she was doing, her feet helped themselves into the slippers once again. She squeezed the door-knob and clicked it open. Her left foot braved the first step out the door but immediately lost its will when faced with the owner of the huge head who was standing in the hallway under the dim light. With a white cap perched on a bird's nest hairdo and a large pair of thick, black-framed glasses that reflected the dull light from overhead, she was like a monster bug in a horror movie metamorphosing into a space mantis.

The space mantis held her shoulder and hissed in her ear, "Get back to bed, right this minute." At odds with the unfriendly hissing, she handled her shoulders gently and guided her back to bed. The smell of Ivory soap told her that it was Nurse Yun after all. She had no intention of agitating the space mantis and climbed up into the bed. Without a word, the nurse put herself in a chair, folded her stubby arms under her breasts, and started to stare at her. Miri pulled the cover up to her chin and shut her eyes tight, feeling a tad defeated. This had happened a few times before. Miri walked around at night. It was not a sleepwalk; she just wandered around at night, some nights. And Nurse Yun had been assigned to watch her at nights.

They stayed put in determined silence, one with her eyes closed, feeling the stinging stare of the other's in the dark. The silence seemed to be sucking up all the air in the room.

- 2 -

It was late spring in May of that year when all the college girls had their hair long and straight, parted in the middle fashioned after Olivia Hussey from the hit movie *Romeo and Juliet* and Ali MacGraw in *Love Story*, when Miri became a resident patient at the mental hospital. It was about two months before the summer break. She was a junior in an all-girls high school that she immensely loathed. Her bizarre behavior of night walking and fainting spells introduced her to the new world of the hospital right before the mid-term, for which she had been hardly prepared.

Her mother insisted on hospitalizing her immediately. When Dr. Min met her for the first time, he thought that the mother seemed more angry than worried about her daughter. By then, her eldest daughter, Sohee, had been Dr. Min's outpatient for some time. It took less than a minute for him to develop a strong dislike for the mother at the first meeting. Her stern expression, tightly pursed lips, and the way she talked, not with her lips but with her teeth, seemed to drop the room temperature by a few degrees. One would be frightened to witness a smile on a face like that. What she said about her child confirmed his initial impression of her. According to the mother, Miri should not have been born. "That such a thing came out of me makes me shudder. She's always been a weird creature, I tell you...and now this," she said in one breath. He wondered if she was talking to herself loudly in the presence of others.

Sohee was twelve years older than Miri. She was tall and thin with an elegance that demanded respect. This highly educated woman, a graduate of the most sought-after university, came to him one day with suicide on her mind.

She was married with an infant son whom she never included in the narration of her life. She described her life as a long stretch of injuries, mostly from her parents but also more or less from everybody. All her intelligence was useless under the tyranny of the angry child in her. She blamed her parents for anything and everything that turned out disagreeably in her life. The picture she described of her upbringing was bleak. She was highly sensitive to criticism even as she often criticized others herself. A powerful formula for self-destruction, Dr. Min thought. She couldn't do anything wrong in her own eyes. It was something or someone else that made her do wrong.

The same year she graduated from the university, she married a guy she had been dating for a few years. Her parents didn't stand in her way, and she believed that finally a sweet life awaited her. However, what she had previously viewed before marriage as her husband's gentle nature turned out to be timidity and lack of ambition. Money became the main problem. Her husband could not understand why her father who was loaded didn't support them. He himself came from an aristocratic family but had no money. Before long she began to loathe him and crawled back to her father for financial help. Her rich father helped her out but not without a good dose of humiliation. This angered her, and she became more and more demanding, justifying her entitlement to her father's wealth, because in her mind, they owed her for not loving her. But it was an uphill battle. A good portion of the money she received from her father went to designer clothes, generous tipping, and such. She decided to attach her self-worth to her maiden home that she hated so much. But the constant anxiety of waiting for the atonement of her parents exhausted her, sending her into a depression.

Dr. Min gained better understanding of her suffering when he met the mother. Throughout his career he had encountered some unfit parents, but this woman took the cake. It took only a few minutes for him to realize this, for what you saw was what you got of her. She didn't bother to hide behind sensible social mannerisms; there was an express line between her thoughts and her mouth. One wouldn't dare to expect any warmth if faced with such reptilian eyes, and she could crush any healthy heart with one stare and pickle it with a breath of vinegar.

"But you have your own life now. You're certainly a very smart person who's received a top-notch education and looks that would make others envious. Surely you know you can be successful on your own," Dr. Min said to Sohee in one of their earlier sessions. He observed that her misery was all about socio-economic status. No matter how much she coated it with intellectualism, it was a sophisticated form of a temper tantrum.

His statement was met with instant hostility, as he had expected. She believed that her parents should pay, not in their afterlives in hell, but right now in cash. They damaged her, and they should pay in the sum of her likings.

What if her parents were poor? Has she ever thought about that, he wondered. He tried to make her see that she had all the tools to move on and free herself from old wounds for good, but he found himself facing a thick wall of childish excuses. She never admitted that perhaps she didn't have it in her or that she was too scared to try. Dr. Min noted that she believed she knew the prescription to her cure: she wanted her parents to kneel down in front of her and compensate for the hurt they caused, whatever the cost was. This was the wonder drug that would cure her. Nothing else would. But the cure that seemed so near and reachable was much too hard to get, and she began to taste yet another defeat, and the thought of closing the curtains for good became more and more comforting. Too many people suffered because other people didn't please them, he thought.

"She's odd. She's…spacey, lots of the time. But she could be clever, even wise," Sohee described Miri to him one day when he asked her to.

"You like her, I gather."

"She's my favorite. She has a talent for describing the most mundane things in quite an extraordinary way but simple enough for anyone to see her point. Very comical. She makes me laugh."

Dr. Min thought Miri must be the clown of that gloomy family until he met her.

When he saw Miri for the first time, he was taken by the startling differences between the sisters. She looked like she had slept in a garbage dump. Her school uniform was grungy and stained, and her white, cotton socks looked like overused rags. There were marks of bruises and scratches both fresh and old on her legs. The only resemblance he could see in the sisters was their high cheekbones, which their mother also owned. She was as tall as her sister but had a stronger build. He was both surprised and intrigued at the sight of her. Something about her made him feel that he was face to face with a thousand-year-old creature that was recently unearthed and encased in a sixteen-year-old body. There was an old wisdom and reserved sorrow in those eyes. Strangely, he noticed that she didn't look troubled; instead, there was a calm aura about her in spite of her disorderly appearance.

The first interview with her was brief. It ended with a prescription for mild sedatives that would help her sleep at night and weekly sessions with the doctor. He thought that she seemed very different from other teenagers brought to him by their parents. He sensed that the girl's problems were not originated in hormonal fluctuations.

- 3 -

Miri attended a Presbyterian school that was one of the most privileged institutes. Therefore, the doctor assumed that she couldn't be stupid or undisciplined. To be accepted into such a school, a youngster had to be academically outstanding. Children prepared themselves for years for the slim possibility of earning a place in the school. Long school hours were followed by tutoring until late at night. They ate, studied, and did not get enough sleep; in fact, parents became nervous when their kids slept a little longer than they should. Doctor Min saw many unnecessary tragedies due to this country's cruel educational system. A child was graded and labeled according to her or his academic score, and children were expected to read and write before they learned how to tie their shoelaces. The pitiful thing was that no one questioned this system. A mother might let out a sigh while tying her six-year-old son's shoelaces, thinking, this is so fucked up. But no, she was more likely to think how she would make him go over multiplication charts. You were your report card. Your family's happiness depended on it. It was statistically inevitable that only a tiny speck of this unfortunate population of youngsters could bring home satisfying grades. As a result, most of these youngsters had to endure harsh words from their parents as a daily routine. These children should have demanded to see their parents' own report cards from their school years to see if they were qualified to judge them. Dr. Min had seen kids brought in to him suffering from anxiety, violence, or attempted suicide thanks to the horror designed by this thing called a "report card." Their individual thinking was almost completely incapacitated. At such a tender age, when their lives should seem invincible, they had to carry the baggage of being underachievers.

Dr. Min asked Miri his first question. "How's your school life?"

She looked up and answered, "Good and bad," adding, "just like everything."

"What is it that you like?"

"I like learning, real learning. I like sharpening pencils, the smell of books, underlining agreeable stuff with colored pencils using a ruler." While he was making a mental shape of the presence of her mind, she continued. "Only, when I am on page ten, the school is on page fifty and running. That takes a lot of enjoyment away."

"So you feel left behind?" he said with a smile in his eyes.

"It's more like while you're enjoying a meal and someone takes it away." They both laughed.

He asked a few more "get-to-know-you" questions, adding friendly smiles and chuckles here and there. Then he asked decisively, taking a more authoritative posture, "I assume that you know why you're here, right? Shall we talk about it?" She straightened her torso, tucking in her chin. "We're going to run some tests on you regarding your fainting, but now let's talk about the night walks. I promise that what you and I talk about here will remain here. So, why?"

She looked up then down at the floor and fell silent. He waited. Her silence became deeper, and a very long couple of minutes went by. She remained looking down at the floor as she began to speak. "Our house is located at the bottom of this mountain. She—the mountain—calls me. Some time ago I could no longer resist her, so I started to visit her at night when no one knows."

"Do you actually hear her?" he asked.

"Not in the flesh, but loud and clear in my spirit," she answered slowly, raising her head with a faint but unmistakable mocking in her thousand-year-old eyes.

"So, it's not just random walking at night," he said, looking at the cuts and bruises on her legs. "Do you talk to the mountain? I mean, is there a conversation?" he asked, leaning forward on his desk, stretching his neck.

"Yes, there is. When we moved to that house, the room facing the mountain became mine because none of my sisters wanted it. They thought the mountain view was creepy, so they chose the rooms with a city view. But I loved it; it was a cocoon of my own. It's like living in a forest all by myself. I started to tell her everything from the very beginning."

"Did it respond to you from the beginning?"

"Not until recently. But when it happened, it was like God Himself was talking to me."

"But you describe it as 'she.' Any particular reason?"

"I said it was like God. I didn't say 'she' was God. She is just, just... Anyway, it's definitely female. Its contours, smell, and stillness, with all its emotions tucked inside. It's definitely a woman with a large womb," she said, narrowing her eyes with a tiny smile on her lips.

"Does she represent any religious figure, a deity perhaps?" he asked, unsure of himself, noticing her eyes dimming a bit.

She tilted her head, scratching it rather vigorously, and said, "Um...I'm not sure what you mean."

"Is she your protector, guardian, or someone who looks after you?" he asked again.

A small frown appeared between her brows. She turned to the sunlight seeping through the opening of the curtain, squinting her eyes. She whispered, "Spring is leaving..."

- 4 -

She couldn't remember what was on her mind when she climbed out the window the first night to go up the mountain. She just did; it just happened. She could remember the sweet fragrance of wisteria blossoms, the smell of the earth, the lonely song of a solitary bird of the night, and the sensuous breeze passing through the young leaves on the trees, gently rustling in velvety darkness as if they were breathing in unison, a symphony of intoxication. No desire, no passion, no heated emotion, no fear and no judgment, just a graceful acceptance of letting it be, the gratefulness of being. She was all spirit in that moment. New senses unknown to her before awakened in her, seducing her with possibility, a blank possibility whose presence was too powerful to doubt. Understanding and forgiveness were there, making sorrow a willing warrior. She could not articulate her feeling if she tried. The only way she could describe it was "rapture," a rapture that was depersonalizing. The life below the mountain that she would go back to when morning came seemed unreal, a dimension unknown, perhaps supernatural.

She yawned and yawned through the school hours, dozing off when the sunlight touched her forehead, like a sick, old mouse. But at night when the time arrived, she bolted out of her slumber state, climbed out the window and went up the hill.

Then the fainting started. The first time was during physical exercise class and the second time during science class. Both times she woke up at the nurse's station unhurt and rather refreshed. The old nurse, who was usually bored out of her skull, was excited by the incidents and diagnosed her with narcolepsy. She was sent home both times, but no medical attention was given to her.

One night, as she was climbing back into her room after her walk, she found herself face to face with her sister Zona, with her left leg still hanging outside the window. Zona had come to her room looking for an English dictionary that was on Miri's desk. She was composing a letter to her new love interest, using English words here and there to intellectualize the letter to impress the guy, and she needed to check her spelling. After the heart-stopping moment of fright at each other's sight, Zona ran her eyes up and down Miri a couple of times and left the room with the dictionary, without a word. Miri had come back earlier than usual because the light drizzle had become heavier. She was soaked and muddy. She threw herself on her bed, making a mental note to lock the door at night.

That afternoon when she came home from school, she found an interrogation waiting for her. "Who is he?!" her mother screamed, simultaneously landing her large hand across her face. The slap was a speedy and burning kind. Her brain rattled, and she lost her balance momentarily. If the blow were a little harder, she could have been decapitated. It kicked the memory box in her head out of place, causing her to wonder where she was for a second or so. Before she began to understand what was happening on that otherwise beautiful spring afternoon, full of new greens and budding flowers and baby birds chirping in honor of their lives, a second blow landed on her head with a hissing profanity that a good Christian woman should never possess in her vocabulary, successfully bringing her knees to the floor. Miri realized that a little mouse who took her dictionary told her mother what she saw the previous night, and they had concluded that Miri was having a romantic rendezvous with someone no good, a cardinal offense in the family. As she was getting up, holding onto a chair while listening to a potpourri of obscene words coming out of her mother's foaming mouth, her hair was yanked by the infamously huge hand inducing hot liquid from a pure pain that began to pump out of her eyes like desperate refugees. But the tears of pain brought out a persona of courage or rage. The persona, previously unknown to her, looked up with a murderous grin on her wet face, embedding her fingernails in her mother's hand that was engaged in hair pulling and spat out, "I'll tell you; do you want to know? It's Jesus, your boyfriend; I've been seeing him every night. Do you know what he said? You shame him, ha, ha, ha!" She let the laughter escape her mouth in the creepiest way possible, like the laugh of Vincent Price in horror films, with ominous organ music in the background.

Her mother let go of her hair, plopped down on the parquet floor and started to wail, pounding the floor with her palm. "Oh God, this evil blood! How come, how come this evil bitch had to come out of me?" Miri stood up and walked to her room, leaving her mother screaming and pounding, swaying and jerking her upper body as if to get free of a straitjacket. The household staff, who had been standing by, gathered around her in an attempt to let her know they were on her side.

She was left alone for the rest of the day. Later at night she sneaked into her grandmother's room and ate the food she had left on the tray for Miri. Grandma always did that for her when Miri missed dinner due to household conflict and become persona non grata at the dinner table. She was sleeping, and Miri devoured the food squatting in the dark, chewing and slurping like a dog who was stealing its master's meal.

The next morning when she was about to leave for school, two members of the household staff, the cook and the gardener, quickly grabbed her arms. They pushed her into the front passenger seat of the car. Sohee and her mother got in the backseat. Not a word was exchanged. After twenty long minutes of silence, they arrived at Dr. Min's office. This explained why Sohee looked like she just came out of a beauty shop. Her linen dress was so brilliantly white and crisp, Miri had to squint her eyes to look at her. When Sohee put on a pair of round sunglasses, Miri thought she resembled some-one like Jackie Kennedy or Audrey Hepburn. For some time Miri suspected something other than a strictly professional relationship going on between Sohee and Dr. Min. But more importantly, how relieved she was when they took her to the doctor instead of an exorcist. During the silent car ride, all she thought about was an impending exorcism in her immediate future and the image of herself after the exorcism, an empty vessel without a soul.

- 5 -

Ever since the first interview with Dr. Min, Miri saw him once a week. She knew that her mother wanted, even demanded her to be hospitalized right on that day. Frankly, she hoped he would agree with her mother, but he didn't.

She did not mind him. He was a man in his mid-forties, she thought, with a pair of round eyes in a round face. In fact, everything about him was round, down to his fingertips. This roundness made him approachable, harmless.

"Have you been going out at night?" he asked at their second meeting.

"No."

"Do you think the medicine helps you?"

"It makes me sleepy, dizzy at times."

"You'll adjust to it soon. So I gather that you are somewhat less obsessive about going out at night."

"Obsessive"? "Going out at night"? She did not care for those descriptions. "I don't think it has anything to do with the medication. I don't go out at night because the windows in my room are nailed shut."

He looked up at her, laughing with obvious confusion. Before he found anything proper to say, she said, "Dr. Min, it's okay, I can put up with it, and forgive me for saying this, but it offends me when you describe it as some kind of obsession."

His mind was surfing to find the right framework for the situation. He rubbed his left temple with his fingers then rested his elbows on his desk, relocating the rubbing to the chin. His eyes were looking at a notepad on his desk, empty of focus, and his right hand started to scribble something on it. Miri could see he was doodling, drawing something childish. Finally, he spoke slowly without stopping the doodling. "Miri, my job here is to make you well. My first and last obligation is to you, no one else. I want you to believe that. I barely know you, and in order to help you, I need to know and possibly understand who you are as much as possible." He said this with gentleness in his voice, tilting his head to one side. The fact that they nailed her windows shut disturbed him. He could not help feeling sorry for her.

"First of all, I don't think I need any help. My mind is sound, I promise you. But at the same time," she let out a sigh, "at the same time, I wonder how long I can hold on to it."

"Hold on to what?"

"My sound mind."

"So you do need help, don't you think?"

"I don't see how you could help me. To tell you the truth, I think my mother wants me to disappear for good," she said with no noticeable emotion. It came out as dry as a bone.

"You don't get along with her?" he asked, knowing the answer.

"It's a lot deeper and complicated than just not getting along."

"How about your father and sisters?"

"My sisters and I are indifferent to each other in times of peace. Sometimes we do have a good time together, mostly laughing at something. But it ends there. Such fun times together never created a bond among us, such a thing wasn't even on the horizon. My father...I think he's a very unhappy man, an angry man, perhaps. So the general idea is to avoid him as much as possible. My family should not have been."

She told him a few examples of how they acted with each other. He sensed that she didn't want to talk about her family at length, unlike Sohee. The content of Miri and Sohee's story was more or less the same, he noticed, but how they presented it was a difference of day and night. The picture Sohee drew was bleak, bitter, and lonely, but Miri's picture was theatrical, even humorous. They watched the same show, but one saw it as tragic, the other as comic.

He changed the line of questioning. "Tell me about the mountain trips."

There was a hesitation. She looked out the window tugging on her braided hair. He waited, then thrust his face toward her, blinking his round eyes, letting her know he was waiting for her reply. She started to speak slowly but decisively. "What do you want to know?"

He was surprised by the sudden change in her voice. It was low and thick, a voice of a heavy smoker, a man's voice. "Anything, everything," he said, trying to find any other change in her demeanor. He couldn't.

She started slowly, stretching the tail of each word in a deep voice. "When I'm up there, I'm free of fear and anxiety. It really feels wonderful. Have you experienced such a feeling?" She continued without waiting for his answer, "I feel like I own absolute knowledge of myself. Oh, I should correct that. I am not a self when I'm up there. I am not a self."

"What do you mean you are not a 'self'?"

"I am just a being."

"Are 'self' and 'being' separate entities to you?"

"Yes, like husband and wife. They are together but are also far from each other, as if serving different masters."

He had to laugh.

"So in your case, they don't have a good marriage," he said, still smiling, wondering which one was the wife or husband.

"Only when I'm up there they are separated. But the self takes over in the world down below."

"Separation of self and being..." He repeated those words inwardly and wrote them down on his notepad, next to his little drawing of a rabbit and a turtle. Sohee had told him that Miri said she sneaks out at night to meet with Jesus.

He tried the question she'd ignored in their previous interview again: "In your mind, do these night walks have any religious or spiritual bearing?"

She burst into loud laughter, folding her body in half, slapping her knees. Then her normal voice returned. "Oh, I get it now, the Jesus thing!" she said, still laughing. "I said that to my mother to stop her from half killing me. She's an avid believer of kinetic education. My mentioning the name 'Jesus' scared her and stopped her from going too far with the beating." Although she was laughing hard as if that incident was exceptionally funny, he sensed that there was a wall, thick and tall, behind the laugh. He asked nonchalantly if she could tell the Jesus incident in her own account. She did. She even played out the scene animatedly as if telling a story from a funny movie, giggling here and there. He didn't quite know how to receive that, wondering if he should keep a solemn expression or go along with her animated account of the tragic comedy. He chose to go along with the comical version partly because his experience in the profession told him that it was the wise thing to do, but partly because he couldn't hold his laughter. Truthfully, he could not deny that he was entertained.

When he sensed the show was winding down, he asked, "How did you come to think of Jesus being her boyfriend?"

"That's who he is to her."

"What do you mean?"

"He just is. When you see her or listen to her praying to Him, you'd come to same conclusion, easily." Then she added, "She flirts with him."

Their weekly sessions went on for about a month, and Dr. Min gained some knowledge about her past years. She rambled away, narrating for a while without being prompted, then ended it abruptly as if the show were over for the day and the audience had to wait until next time. When she was in such a mood, she spoke as if she were telling someone else's story or reciting a long poem.

But the fainting spells persisted, and one day she was brought in again by Sohee and their mother. She had fainted at the top of the stairs at her school and rolled down some twenty steps.

"Doesn't look like you broke anything," he said, applying antiseptic on some small cuts. He went back to his desk after giving her a tetanus shot. The blood work done on her at her first visit didn't show any sign of anemia. In fact, everything was quite normal. He thought that the fainting could be intentional but eliminated the doubt quickly. Something in him wanted to respect her more.

She sat across from him quietly. There was an air of defeat or abandonment in her eyes that bore no trace of hope, not even hope for tiny sympathy from a total stranger. The only sign of life he could detect was sadness. He waited for her to say something, making sure he wouldn't let out a sigh accidentally. He wanted the stillness in the room do its work. A long while had passed, it seemed, when he saw tears rolling down on her grimy face, making its way down to the chin, curving around a few pimples, leaving noodle-like marks along the way. He stayed silent while she wept. She wiped her face with her skirt and looked up not at him but at the window. A moment or two later, she sighed deeply and set her eyes on him as if saying, "Now what?" Meeting her eyes made him a little emotional. Such pain, an old, old pain... It was like she was sad for him, sad for everybody. And it was contagious. It made him think how tired he was with everything sometimes, many times. It moved him.

He made up his mind. As her mother wished, he decided to admit her to the hospital. "Just a week or so," he said to the woman with reptilian eyes. He wanted to give the girl a break.

- 6 -

The hospital was on an island about twenty minutes away by ferry boat from the city. He stayed three to four days a week on there and the rest in the city. He preferred the island to the city. When his boys got old enough to leave home, he would've liked to move to the island, although his wife wasn't yet sure of the idea.

The hospital building was once a luxurious hotel during the Japanese regime. The unique beauty of the landscape, which had a volcanic mountain that no longer breath life with hot springs and the ocean with plentiful sunlight and fresh seafood, offered a taste of small paradise. The mountain bore luscious vegetation and birds and other small furry creatures inhabited it, as well as the charms of old ruins which kings and their noble goons of times gone by had frequented to let it all hang out. It was said that poets could not pass the island without reciting a few lines about its beauty. In the year 1910, the Japanese came, removed the drunken king and his noble goons along with the poets, and built the magnificent hotel on the hilltop for their rich and powerful to come and relax and fill their bellies with delicacies from the ocean that were rare in Japan. The town below thrived by providing and satisfying the hedonistic desires of the hotel visitors. There were geisha houses and casinos with restaurants that served both food and sex. People still talked about many dark stories from that time on the island. After the Japanese left in the year 1945 with white flags in their hands, the place was abandoned. People in the village down below took the liberty of taking anything useful or totally useless from the abandoned hotel. Eventually they got bored with it, and natural inhabitants moved into the defaced building. The grand presence it once owned had to follow the rise and fall of fate just like anything else. Subject to defacement and animal feces, this once arrogant architecture had to suffer humiliations for about ten years. People didn't want to associate with anything Japanese, especially a place like the island that symbolized the Japanese ruling class once.

Then a second chance came for the long-neglected island. A fabulously rich man restored the hotel as a resort/spa for the well-to-do but not so healthy. But when this man's only son became ill with schizophrenia and met his death at a young age, he had an epiphany. He made a will to donate the facility to the mental health institution with all the necessary equipment. Soon after that he was killed by a freak accident; he fell off a horse, broke his neck, and died without much delay. It became a nationally renowned mental institute but available only for those who could afford the price tag. For pure business reasons, they offered services for elderly people as a retirement home, which became very successful with a long waiting list.

- 7 -

When she woke up in the morning, the white sunlight filled the tiny room, bleaching every corner. She pulled the cover up over her face, remembering those Sunday mornings when her mother came into her room and violently opened the curtains, letting the cruel sunlight fill the room. She yanked the cover off her and poked her forehead with her finger hissing that she wouldn't have her miss Sunday Mass.

Buried under the cover, she sighed thinking how she would befriend boredom that day. Reluctantly, she got up and went to the bathroom. Shuffling her way back from the bathroom, she saw her new neighbor's door was left open. She poked her head into the room, taking a step or two in. The room was huge and decorated in a manner worthy of a magazine spread. "The room is reserved for a gentleman who comes when he needs to," an orderly once mentioned.

He was asleep on a bed in the far corner of the room. The brilliant August sunlight that occupied half of the room made the shaded half where the occupant was asleep darker. She took a few more steps into the room, canvassing it with her eyes. There was an oriental rug under a large sofa, two wing chairs wrapped in gaudy-looking fabric, mahogany tables large and small with curvy legs as if they were dancing, a wardrobe carved like a Gothic church with a gold tassel dangling in its keyhole, and a writing table with a reddish-brown leather top embossed with gold trim in front of a chair that demanded obedience. There were tapestries and oil paintings on the wall and a few ceramic and glass objects sitting on the coffee table. The only thing that looked out of place was the hospital bed he was sleeping in and a large TV set. She decided she didn't care for those antiques very much. But the French door and the veranda led to one thing she wished to have in her room. She sat on the kingly chair at the writing table and followed the gold-trim embossment around the edge of the table with her fingertips for a while, deep with nameless thoughts and feelings, forgetting where she was. When she came to, realizing that she was daydreaming in a stranger's room, she got up to leave, feeling her heart beat starting to run. Then she saw an open pack of cigarettes behind a desk lamp with a bronze statue of a naked man holding up the shade. She took a couple cigarettes, putting one behind each ear, and turned toward the door.

"Aren't you too young to smoke?" A voice jilted her. She stopped, frozen solid. Regardless of her age, for a female to smoke cigarettes was considered a big no-no. If a young girl was caught smoking, it was treated almost as badly as losing her virginity. Her head couldn't suggest any immediate solution to help her out. There was no known precept written anywhere for such an occasion. The voice started to laugh and said, "What are you doing in my room, who are you?"

She stood still, fully exposed by the harsh sunlight. Acute shame stung her, wishing the sunlight would spontaneously combust her body right then and there.

"Come, come over here," he said with an exaggerated gentleness in his voice that didn't help her shame at all. She stood there looking down at the oriental rug as if she would eventually become invisible if she stayed there long enough. "How about this? I saw nothing. Come on over here, I just want to introduce myself."

She turned and walked slowly toward him, putting the cigarettes down on his bed and biting her lower lip with her eyes lowered.

"I don't want them back," he said, sitting up. "You can keep them. It never happened." He held out his hand and said, "My name is Sam, and you are?"

She didn't know how to take this gesture. Sam? Isn't that an American name? She blinked rapidly, still biting her lips but seeing her hand reach out to his without her full consent. "Miri, I live next door." She freed her hand from his.

Then he said, "Now, put those cigarettes behind your ears before anyone shows up."

She said, "No thanks," by shaking her head with her hands clasped behind her, her eyes still away from his. She bowed at him while stepping backward; she then turned and bolted out. She thought she heard him saying, "Come again soon."

She went back to her room and lay down on the bed in a fetal position, blinking at the sun-washed wall. "What just happened?" She shuddered with monstrous shame, wondering if she should have taken the cigarettes. She decided to hide in her room at least on that day, but she was too hungry to honor that decision.

- 8 -

Days went by after the cigarette incident. The merciless sunlight beating down from the August sky could at any moment switch into a furious thunderstorm as if it would crack the mountain into pieces. Sam liked the capricious weather, even though he rarely stepped out of the room. His meals were delivered to him, and his doctor and nurses checked in on him routinely. Staying in his room was what he did whenever he checked in a few times a year.

Lying on the sofa, he thought about the young girl next door. She amused him. Being single and without children, kids were like Martians to him. But that little encounter with her was fun, especially when he was watching her every move unnoticed lying in the bed. He wanted to know her, which was a foreign feeling for him. He lit a cigarette and stepped out onto the veranda. Heat and humidity hugged his body instantly. The afternoon sun was lighting up the mountain. "How green," he thought. Light green, dark green, how many different greens there were on the planet. He never knew he could actually distinguish one shade of green from another. He was momentarily happy about this discovery. He was not a nature enthusiast, but he always felt something special for the mountain that stood in front of him.

He looked down and saw a group of people coming down the hill. "It must be the afternoon group walk," he thought, putting out his cigarette. An orderly in front of the group and another at the end were like shepherds herding sheep. He leaned on the railing as he watched them come closer toward the building, fanning themselves with hats or visors. Mindlessly, he started to count the heads. Then he saw her.

That morning when she sneaked into his room, he was awake with his eyes closed. He opened his eyes sensing that someone was in his room. This figure walked into his room like an amateur criminal, placing her steps so carefully but comically, with her shoulders hunched up and her forearms fanned out, heels first then toes, looking around and touching things in that Frankenstein-like posture. She bent over to touch the rug, ran her finger along the carvings of the wardrobe, feeling its golden tassel on her face. Her shoulders were hunched, taking caution. She looked like a teenage Neanderthal, unkempt with a seeming lack of faculties that belonged to modern people. He watched her every move, feeling safe in the dark corner of the room. When she sat at the writing table pensively looking out the window, he could see her profile reflecting the sunlight along her forehead down to her nose and parted lips then to her chin and long neckline. She seemed to have forgotten where she was. She just sat there, and as he watched her, he was strangely moved. It was a picture of solemn serenity, mysterious yet meaningful. The quiet peacefulness of her reminded him of someone so close to his heart.

- 9 -

She missed her night walks to the mountain, but she couldn't complain about being away from home even for a short while. A week or so became a few months since she left home. What was even better was that no one called or visited her, only a small amount of pocket money and a change of clothes came by mail a couple of times. Being there was a good thing, if not wonderful for her. It felt like, finally, life gave her a little break.

She remembered the day she came to the island. She had packed a few things in a bag and looked for her mother to say good-bye. She was scrubbing the parquet floor in the living room on her knees. She had three maids, but she liked to do housework, especially cleaning. The house and the furniture were spotless, but they looked rather abused and hurt from excessive cleaning and polishing. Her days consisted of two repositories: house cleaning and praying. The peculiar thing was that she was always in her angriest mode when she was engaged in the things she loved doing the most. Her cleaning attire consisted of a nylon scarf, an old cotton shirt that once belonged to her husband, and a black muslin skirt. A broom and dirty rags were her security blanket. Miri knew to avoid her at any cost when she was engaged in this holy labor. To interfere with her at such a moment could potentially be quite lethal.

Miri stood there, waiting for her mother to acknowledge her. But she quickly turned away. Miri stood there for a moment longer then left without saying anything.

Mr. Yang, the family chauffeur, was waiting outside to take her to the ferry. Miri liked him. He was a tiny man in his thirties who squeezed his eyes tightly when he blinked, which he did a lot. He always looked happy just being alive. Occasionally, Miri found herself being envious of that quality in him. One time he told her about the lilies he grew in the country when he was a young boy. Every day when he came home from school, the first thing he did was check the little lily patch. "They bloomed in brilliant white with a fragrance that God would envy," he said, beaming with the memory that was both sweet and sad. One day he came home and found the lily patch destroyed, and he wept, broken-hearted. "To this day, I think about the lilies lying on the dirt, so helplessly," he said. He was always kind to Miri. A little hello he said to her whenever she ran into him always felt warm and sincere.

It was a warm and muggy day in the city, with the grey sky hanging low, a kind of day when people got irritated with each other for no reason. They drove in silence. Miri looked out the window, feeling strangely relieved and excited. When they arrived at the port, he insisted on carrying her small bag for her to the boat. Before she got on the ferry, he gently squeezed her hand and told her, "Look after yourself." It was as warm and sincere as his hello.

The ferry was nothing more than an upgraded fishing boat. It was her first time seeing the ocean, and unlike what she had seen in movies and magazines, the water here was dark and uninviting. It smelled of fish, and the thick, salty air stung her nostrils. But the sensation of relief was still there, lifting her spirit and ballooning her chest with portentous hope. A few men were talking across from her, throwing indifferent glances at her now and then. The boat was otherwise quite empty. She looked down at the water, holding onto the railing. She felt a little nauseous. Trusting one's life to a small vessel floating on an endless body of water suddenly felt absurd.

Three quarters of the earth is water, she thought. You will engulf us all one day, won't you?

A taxi driver was waiting for her, holding a sign with her name on it. They drove up the tortuous hill, whose narrow road was draped thickly with vegetation on both sides. She rolled down the window, and the smell of the earth and the trees in the air filled her lungs. She was overwhelmed with delight at the sight of a mountain standing handsomely across from the hospital building. She took it as a good omen. It felt like something was looking after her.

- 10 -

"Oh! Mighty sun, you give life then you murder. God and beast together in your forever burning flame." Sam was scribbling on a piece of paper, thinking about the greatest poet who ever lived, the Chinese poet, Li Bai. What a great drunk he was, he thought, drawing a sun next to the scribble that he would never call a poem. He felt silly but happy at the same time, having a glass of brandy sitting at the writing desk. He looked at the phone and then at the clock. After a couple of moments of hesitation, he picked up the receiver.

"How are you doing?" Mrs. Lim's voice from the other end of the phone was a bit distant.

"Are you pissed off at me?" he asked sheepishly.

"No, no. I'm in the middle of something. Is everything okay?" she asked in a more friendly tone.

"I'm sorry," he said.

"Wow, Sam, is it really you? You know how to say sorry?"

"I am sorry," he said it again, enjoying her girlish laughter on the phone.

"Well, Sam, you know I gave up on being pissed off at you a million moons ago. But it is touching to hear you apologizing."

"I'm sorry I left you with mounds of work, again," he said, hearing her still giggling.

"Okay, okay, enough. What do you want?"

"Can you come and spend the weekend here?"

"I was going to anyway. Do you want me to bring you anything?"

"Just the usual stuff."

When he met her the first time, nearly thirty years ago, she was a cashier at a coffee shop he frequented as a young man. He was a lawyer full of airs, rubbing elbows with the Japanese elite. Whenever he visited the coffee shop, he sat near the cashier who had introduced herself as Mrs. Lim. A friendly exchange of greetings and opinions over the weather or the rising price of grain gradually became more personal. Fragments of life were shared comfortably, with ease. Her large face, framed by a thick pair of glasses and a badly permed hairdo, made her look older than her age. She always had a book in front of her because she liked to read whenever possible. The drunken old man she was forced to marry when she was eighteen had died when their son just turned two. Even though he drank himself to death, her husband was actually a kind man, she said. He was the one who taught her how to read and write.

Sam liked being with her. She was calm but energetic, and Sam liked such a quality in her. Occasionally, he brought books and sweets for her. There was a friendship growing, but it only stayed in the coffee shop.

When Sam left the Japanese firm to set up his own company, he hired Mrs. Lim as his secretary. His father, who was concerned about the impending demise of the Japanese on the horizon, advised him to slowly and carefully detach himself from anything Japanese. During this time he told Sam, "Japan will lose the game, and America will be the dominating force. It will happen soon."

Mrs. Lim knew she had to learn a lot to be a proper secretary, but she was quick and natural. She was only too happy to have the opportunity given to her. They had been together as friends and business partners for over a quarter of a century.

Sam's father, a Korean-American, was a liaison working for the Japanese government. Some Koreans called him a traitor, but he truly believed that he was a simple man who did his best making a living. He believed in neither country nor social idealism and called those who called him a traitor cowards. "They use blame to defend their cowardly nature of dependency," he used to say. "When one believes he has to be in charge of his own life, he knows that blaming others is not only a waste of time but also as foolish as blaming the force of gravity." He also said, "The very brutality Koreans endured without resistance through their own kings and noblemen became unacceptable evil when the perpetrator happened to be Japanese, a foreign tribe," adding, "a sword is a sword no matter who holds it."

Although labeled as a traitor by some, he was a kind and generous man. His employees knew that they could count on him to help them out in times of need. He was quite aware of the brutality of the Japanese, but he believed that if it wasn't the Japanese it'd be someone else. His firm belief that every individual was responsible for his life stood before anything else.

When Sam's father was a little boy living in an orphanage run by an American missionary, a couple adopted him and took him to America. Although their Calvinistic religious devotion was stifling at times, he always believed that they were good people, his saviors. He knew they had given him the chance of a lifetime, and he thoroughly obeyed them without feeling guilt that he hadn't been able to bond with them on any level.

He never complained through the years of being teased and bullied by kids in school for looking different. He always believed that his time would come to prove that he was a productive citizen, that he'd be accepted with respect and received on equal footing with non-colored people. But the reality turned out to be different. When he was unable to find a job after graduating from a university with proper qualifications, he began to see that he had been naive. "He'll always be a yellow turd," the bullies used to say. His value would not be recognized. "The more qualified you are, the harder it is to be accepted," he realized. "How bizarre," he used to think, "that it's just because of the color of my skin." It didn't take too long for him to decide to go back to his native country. In his heart he knew he had a far better chance in his homeland. His adopted parents protested his decision, and for the first time, he disobeyed them.

He never complained through the years of being teased and bullied by kids in school for looking different. He always believed that his time would come to prove that he was a productive citizen, that he'd be accepted with respect and received on equal footing with non-colored people. But the reality turned out to be different. When he was unable to find a job after graduating from a university with proper qualifications, he began to see that he had been naive. "He'll always be a yellow turd," the bullies used to say. His value would not be recognized. "The more qualified you are, the harder it is to be accepted," he realized. How bizarre, he used to think, that it's just because of the color of my skin. It didn't take too long for him to decide to go back to his native country. In his heart he knew he had a far better chance in his homeland. His adopted parents protested his decision, and for the first time, he disobeyed them.

He was right. A western education and fluency in English opened the door wide for him in Korea. He held on to his American citizenship, which strangely brought out more respect from the Japanese. It didn't matter to him who ruled whom. They, whoever they were, took turns as it always had been in human history. "Survive and survive well" was what this quiet but shrewd man believed.

When Sam turned fifteen, his father sent him to his adoptive relatives in America. For seven years, he stayed in America to receive his education. He had a big smile on his face when he left for America and had the same smile when he came back. This concerned his father a bit, but he was happy to have him back all the same. A position at a Japanese law firm arranged by his father was waiting for him. Here, Sam's belief that every individual is responsible for his life, the belief inherited from his father, was somewhat modified.

His father's prediction of the Japanese downfall began to manifest. They acted like a cornered beast. More and more young Korean men, actually boys, were dragged out of their homes to be sent to the front to fight the losing war and die under the Japanese flag. Sam watched this atrocity around him, but somehow it felt like watching moving pictures. It was sad, upsetting, and even made him want to see justice. It seeped into his sleep as nightmares, but at the end of the day, it was someone else's pain, like in the moving pictures. "There's no nation, no country, when it comes to survival instincts in humans, like in beasts. Just like in the animal world, we have herbivores, omnivores, and carnivores. We make a kill, gather food to eat, and call it a day," his father used to say.

Sam wondered what kind of animal he would be. Dad would have made a smashing samurai, he often thought, whenever his father shared his philosophy of life with him. You kill for surviving, not for hatred!

One day, Sam, as a young boy, saw how his father conducted himself in front of high-ranking Japanese officials. He was all smiles and exaggerated politeness, repeatedly bowing at them with his hands rubbing up and down on his front thighs. Sam noticed shine on the upper front part of his pants. When he was alone, he laughed hard, remembering his father's behavior. But he didn't judge him as being a hypocrite. He only wished he could be more like him.

Sam knew nothing about his mother. He never asked, and no one uttered a word about her to him. He was raised by wet nurses and a caretaker, his dear *amah*, so there was no lack of female nurturing in his childhood. His amah, who let him suck his thumb to his heart's content behind his father's back, was a sufficient mother to him.

One rainy day he was sick in bed with a fever. He asked his amah, who was sitting next to his bed sewing, if she knew his mother. Kids in the neighborhood occasionally teased him that he was bought. His amah held him up to her chest, gently rocking him and said, "I don't know who she was, Botchang (little master)."

"Is it true that my father bought me from my mother?" he had to ask.

"Who said such an evil thing! No, no. This much I know for sure: your sweet mom died bringing you into this world. Don't listen to anyone who says otherwise. Promise me," she said, embracing him tightly. The feeling of her heartbeat, the comfort of her bosom on his cheek, and the sound of gentle rain remained in his memory for a long time.

-11-

It was the year 1943 when he opened up his own law firm. It was very slow. Mrs. Lim and Sam spent days in the small office having next to nothing to do, sipping many cups of tea and playing cards. His father told him to take non-Japanese clients: "Take Korean clients, even though they can't pay the fees. Build your reputation among them. This is an important transition you have to make."

It was Mrs. Lim who started to bring in Korean clients. In about several months, a steady stream of people walked into the office. Some could pay, some couldn't at all, and some paid him with whatever means—chickens, grains, or homemade straw baskets and so on—to show gratitude.

It was a very different practice to him, but strangely satisfying. Mrs. Lim, who herself came from the same background as most of his clients, knew exactly what to do with these people and helped Sam to gain a better understanding of their ethos, which he was not always good at. Even though it didn't bring in money, and some months he had to pay Mrs. Lim's salary out of his father's pocket, he truly appreciated this experience. But he knew this was a transitional state, and he would move on when the time came.

A year or so had gone by since he set up the firm, when his father announced his retirement. The times were very unsettling, to put it mildly. By the year 1944 the rations given by the Japanese were decreasing, which suggested that they might be on their way out, despite the daily announcements of their invincible force. There also was an increase in violence everywhere. Sam understood his father's intention to retire, but what he said next blew his mind. He and his buddy, who was actually his servant, Mr. Yu, decided to go to Manchuria to be Taoists. The news was too absurd for Sam to take seriously. He concluded that his father's bizarre notion of becoming a Taoist monk was another shrewd scheme of his to dodge a likely bullet when hell broke loose. If there had been such a scheme, his father never let him in on it. Even then he was not sure if his father's plan would unfold as reality. His father had always seemed indifferent to any form of spirituality. "My father, on a journey to spiritual enlightenment?" Sam couldn't get over it, scheme or not.

One day he was having dinner with Mrs. Lim and said, "I bet it's some kind of scheme, a cunning strategy to wash the Japanese flavor off of him to be ready for a new era." Mrs. Lim neither agreed nor disagreed. After the hearty meal, Mrs. Lim wiped her mouth and asked, "Do you think he'll ever come back?"

"Oh yeah, I know my father, he'll be back when this social unrest settles down."

His father never set foot on Korean soil again.

-12-

Miri could not remember how it started even if she tried. There was no thought, no hesitation. She climbed out the window and walked up the hill, being led by her feet. There was an old stone wall, now a ruin, that had been built during the Chosun Dynasty that snaked up along the north side of the hill like the Great Wall in China, only done on a small scale. She followed the stone steps along the wall for about fifteen to twenty minutes then turned right onto a narrow path leading to a rock formation arranged at an angle like a huge nose. Miri was not a stranger to the place. When she was younger and more agile, she used to come there often, but never at night. In spring the entire mountain fired up with many red and pink wild azaleas. When it rained she loved to watch the rocks being washed by the thin sheet of rainwater. In winter she sat on the warm radiator by the window, looking out at the snow-covered mountain glistening underneath the moonlight.

A small cave underneath the large slanted rock was where she visited at nights. She just sat there, at the mouth of the cave. A small breeze swayed the tree branches gently, rustling the leaves. The lonely songs of a solitary bird echoing through the rustling leaves stirred her mind with both beauty and sadness. It was ethereal. Her senses were in perfect harmony with her spirit.

In the small hours of the morning, she came down. She caught a few hours of sleep until it was time to go to school, where she spent her time gaping at empty space, which annoyed the teachers more than usual.

She was a mediocre student whom the teachers loved to hate, some more than others. The common denominator of their hatred was the way she looked at them. What they thought that they saw in her eyes was despisement and arrogance. What they actually saw was pity, which they read as despise and arrogance. She pitied them. So far, in her many years of school life, she had not met anyone who became a teacher for the love of teaching. To her these people were an angry bunch. They seemed to pursue her just to let her know how little they thought of her. During all those years of schooling, she could not come up with a single strategy to keep the army of teachers off her. She was a creature *non grata* to a species called *teacher* in a cage called *school*. It took hardly anything to make them explode. She knew her appearance wasn't as neat or tidy as the school demanded, was tardy sometimes, forgot things to bring to school, dozed off during classes specially after lunch but there were a whole bunch of girls who committed such offenses other than her. But it was always her who got the worst of the criticisms. She wondered once that her being taller than most of the teachers irritated them. Receiving extreme negative attention became so much a part of her daily routine that she felt something was wrong when a day passed without such attention from them. Early on she developed a habit of observing them in the hopes of trying to find a trick or two to get along, however superficially, with them. Nothing worked, as far as she remembered. She liked learning, but sadly, the teachers were in her way, exhausting her nerves and consuming all the concentration she could have used to learn.

One afternoon she walked home by way of a crowded street. She recognized a face coming toward her direction, zigzagging through the crowd. It was her math teacher, who had once called her something like a "hollow brain." She prepared to offer him a bow in case he noticed her. He passed by without noticing her. He was drunk, very drunk, which explained his unsteady steps. "What do you know!" she said inwardly, turning around to further witness his pathetic state on a bright, sunny afternoon. She could tell that it was not a happy drunkenness; it was a misery-driven intoxication. That day she learned to see her teachers the same as anyone who was let down by life. However, the emotion that went through her mind was not of compassion or kindness. It was a sense of revenge, in a vicarious way, although the dark pleasure she momentarily felt wasn't all that sweet.

It was always puzzling to her to notice the level of anger they displayed when they were displeased with her. It seemed out of proportion and personal. At some point Miri concluded that something about her reminded them of their unhappiness. Their insults were nothing other than an attempt to crush someone when feeling helpless with self-loathing. Miri didn't get crushed but stayed firm. And so did their torment directed at her.

The disappointment in their own lives, she analyzed, was the fuel for the simmering anger. "Life cheated me. I'm trapped in someone else's life" was what she read in them. One day her loathing of them matured and turned to pity. The teachers in her school held degrees from reputable institutions, and every one of them had high academic credentials. Miri doubted that any of them had a dream of becoming a high school teacher, but that's what they became. They must have felt exceptional during their school years and quite naturally believed that they would stay as the cream of the crop all the way through their lives.

By the time they learned that the map they had been following didn't lead them to the top of the world and that the reign of superiority they enjoyed during innocent school years was just an illusion, they found themselves in the land of bitter confusion called reality, with bills to pay, holes in socks, and egos that would not leave them in peace. Once Miri came up with her theory of "the demise of eggheads and the aftershock," it became not as hard to receive their tyranny. One by one, they fell into the collection of her subjects confirming her theory. The smell of alcohol on their morning breath made her shiver, feeling their pain migrating to her heart.

- 13 -

When she arrived at the front of the hospital building, she found a young nurse waiting for her. After introducing themselves, the nurse took her to a room on the third floor. It was a tiny room furnished with a single bed pushed against the wall, a small desk underneath a large window with a view of the mountain, two chairs, and a washbasin with a mirror on the wall. She put her bag down on the floor and walked to the window. "This will be fine," she thought, gazing at the mountain in front of the window, which stood before her looking trustworthy, exclusively welcoming her.

The nurse came back with a gown for her to change into and gave succinct information about the place. The dining room was on the ground floor next to the common lounge; on this floor there was also a library, a music room, and a gift shop that also provided service for hair management. She did not need any permission to go to these places, but she had to be on her floor after nine at night. "And the nurses' station is in the middle of the hallway. The dining room stays open all day for snacks and drinks. Meals are served on a regular schedule. Dinner will be served in an hour," the nurse said, looking at her watch. "Anything else?"

Miri answered by turning her head from left to right twice. After the nurse left the room, she lay down. She dozed off, her body melting as if she finally came home from a long journey.

She woke up feeling a sting on her arm. A man, a young doctor, was putting a needle into a vein in her arm. The needle was connected to an IV bottle. She saw the same nurse standing behind the doctor, along with an orderly. This scene was clear one moment and blurry the next. She was too tired to even ask what was going on. She looked up at the overhead light and fell back to sleep. This scene repeated itself a few times more, like a recurring dream. She could hear soft music and a dreamy voice. She turned her head and saw a nurse sitting on the chair, reading by the small lamp with the radio on, casting a large crooked shadow on the wall behind her. She was listening to a Christian program where a familiar classical tune accompanied a soothing female voice reciting something religious. Bach, she thought, *Air on the G String*. The dreamy voice from the radio whispered, "A good servant, bad servant, and reward and punishment given by the master..." It was a parable from the Bible that she was familiar with. Unsure whether or not it was a dream, she remembered wondering why this Christianity thing followed her around, even to a mental hospital. At that moment Christianity wasn't a friend she wanted to be with. She squeezed her eyes a couple of times in an attempt to wake herself and saw that the nurse sitting on the chair was real. Bach was real too. Whoever this woman was, she also searched for comfort just like everyone else. She thought, such a tune stirs the suffering within, sweetens it with ethereal superiority, and seduces the welted soul that it is a good thing to be forsaken.

Miri learned that she stayed in bed for three days and nights. The first day she came to the island she had fallen ill and became delirious with a high fever. She walked around the hallway knocking on other patients' doors, saying things like, "Let me out, there's no air here." Dr. Min ordered Nurse Yun to watch her at night.

She didn't care for teenagers, especially the ones who were brought to the place. They were mostly spoiled and lazy kids from wealthy families.

Behavioral problems were the most common reason for their occupancy in the hospital. They brought in a nice income for the hospital and offered some break to the parents. They were loud, disrespectful, and clueless, treating the staff as their servants. "Dumb kids!" she used to say under her breath. They mocked her as a fat virgin and imitated her lisp behind her back, which she knew. The stream of family and friends who visited these clueless youngsters made it quite unbearable for the more legitimate patients. Nurse Yun was so happy when the hospital board decided to move them to the west wing a year ago.

She was curious why Miri came to her ward and not the west wing. She learned from the chart that Miri had no visitors, not even a phone call, which she thought was unusual. She might as well have fallen out of the sky, she thought. One night she was watching Miri sleeping, curled up like a boiled shrimp, and she felt sorry for her but also curious. The thought of being kinder to her briefly passed her mind. She could not tell what it was, but her initial suspicion of her being one more unruly teenager faded away. It was about a week or so after Miri's arrival when they had a chance to meet properly. Nurse Yun found herself liking her a little, but she also made a note in her head that she was different. She could not put her finger on it.

One night they were listening to the transistor radio, to the Christian program with the background music that made a holy soup out of your emotions. Nurse Yun asked Miri if she believed in God. To her surprise Miri promptly said yes. She asked, "Do you go to church then?"

Miri answered, looking at her with a side glance, "I was born and raised in a Catholic family, a serious one. And my school is run by the Protestant church. So, yes, I am familiar with the church-going lifestyle."

"You believe in God, but am I right to assume that you don't like to go to church?" Nurse Yun asked with an uncertain smile on her lips.

Miri didn't care for religious talk with strangers but decided to be polite. It was her lisp that she kind of liked.

"I doubt if God likes to go to church."

Nurse Yun was taken back a little by this statement. "What makes you think that?" She pushed her eyeglasses upwardly with her finger.

"My idea of God is far from that of churches."

"How so?" the lisping voice asked.

"Oh, I don't know. The Church provokes judgment and bias in the name of peace and love. I like to imagine God as gentle and kind through and through. Nothing we do would be beyond God's understanding. We are to imitate and obtain this quality of God. But the Church teaches you 'sin' and promotes struggling through life in a whirlpool of guilt, or rather, in spiritual sewage. It also condones or even encourages judgment and punishment. It seems wrong. It seems too man made. They make God a psychotic being."

"You don't believe in heaven and hell, I gather?"

"I don't really think about the concept of heaven and hell. I can only tell you this way: I ran into some people that I wanted to be dead, maybe murdered brutally, but the idea of condemning them in burning fire eternally is way beyond me. The idea of 'hell' is evil itself. I can't accept God has anything to do with punishment, any punishment."

-14-

On August 15, 1945, the Japanese surrendered. As if it was nature's way, the Americans moved in. Chaotic confusion and uncertainty replaced thirty-six years of Japanese occupation. "It's a good thing, a very good thing freedom is, but what do I do with it? Will the freedom feed me and my family?" Nevertheless, people rushed out to the street waving Korean flags, shouting independence and freedom in a frenzy. Most of the Japanese left for their island, but some unfortunate remainders had to receive heinous acts of retaliation from angry Koreans, even though many of those who had stayed behind were harmless merchants. It was true that some of them were nasty, but some were gentle and kind and some indifferent, and some became good friends just like any society where human species congregate together, regardless of race or ideology. Thirty-six years of the humiliation of being slaves in your own land caused national amnesia. They forgot who they used to be, and many Koreans adopted the lifestyle and even ethos of the Japanese. Having knowledge of high-quality sake or Japanese delicacies or reciting haiku still belonged to the qualification of being refined, the elites. In fact, Japanese mannerisms became their own. During the occupation it was a fashionable thing for young Korean women to have their photos taken wearing a kimono.

When people got bored with flag waving and shouting freedom in the street, their excitement found something else to enhance the celebration. They looted the shops and homes of the Japanese and Japanese sympathizers, not without bloody violence.

Sam shuddered at this sight. His father's foresight prepared him to avoid such horror. Setting up his own business and serving Korean clients for the past couple of years saved him from being a target of the mob. He could not help trembling to see such evil nature in human beings, ordinary human beings turned so brutal and destructive in a seeming state of ecstasy. And yet, at the end of the day, when the dust of the feverish excitement settled down, they had to return to their dwellings to face the endless search for grains to feed their empty bellies, praying for someone to guide their lives, ready to hand over their trust to an unknown beast once again. And the new beast, only hungrier, stepped in, showing its teeth through beguiling smiles saying, "We promise you a new and better world." And the cycle repeats. Planted in the minds of the hungry people were promises of prosperity in the near future, and the weakness of human nature, wanting to hang on to the hope machine, took a ride with the vicious cycle. A certain kind of fish at the bottom of the sea finds food using what looks like a morsel of food attached to the tip of its long thread-like tongue, which can float out of the mouth to lure its prey. Perhaps this went on for millions of years, but those creatures of prey never learned the nature of their predator with the tricky tongue.

Sam lay low during the unrest, forming his own rudimentary theory of human psychology and waiting for the world outside to calm down. Mrs. Lim got annoyed by his attitude sometimes and said, "What's happening out there is monumental. How can you be so unmoved?"

"I am where I should be. I don't like what I see out there. It is what it is. I'm not indifferent; how could I be? After all, this will affect my life. But I'm not moved," he answered, irritated. But once or twice, he felt fear in his heart, tightening his throat. He missed his father.

He knew his servants participated in the looting, but he ignored it. It became a nightly event in the courtyard for them to entertain each other with "show and tell" with what they looted. It was like a marketplace; they were selling and buying, negotiating, arguing, and laughing. Sam let them be. He knew that it was not a smart thing to interfere with their business in such unsettling times. One evening he joined them, sitting on a large rock under a maple tree smoking and drinking with them, which delighted the servants. He found himself blushing from embarrassment over being genuinely entertained by the madness. "Nothing like observing the raw nature of humans," he had to admit. It was a carnival, it was atrocious, and it was underground, but there was a spirit of powerful oneness, moral or immoral. When this madness would come to an end, they would be called to resume their places of rule and order and pick up their worn-out hope.

The massive unrest lasted a little over a month. The weather was still warm and humid. He sat in the garden looking at a dark cloud gathering in the sky suggesting a storm, when one of his servants showed up with a puppy, a three–month-old German shepherd. The little guy was all smiles. Sam hugged him as if he saved one precious thing out of the whirlpool of chaos.

-15-

Seungman Lee was the name. He spoke Korean, his mother tongue, with a foreign accent. He was a freedom fighter against Japan, but how he fought was unclear. This middle-aged man, standing next to his bewildered and frightened-looking Caucasian wife in an awkward traditional Korean dress, became the first president of the Republic of Korea. He was handpicked by the Americans, and he had lived abroad long enough to speak his mother tongue with a funny accent. Even though he had supposedly been somewhere on the globe fighting for the liberation of his mother land, he seemed rather aloof and dispassionate. He was tall and thin with salt-and-pepper hair. He and his wife looked so ordinary, even timid. The Korean people's national pride being "one blooded nation" had to accept a Caucasian woman as its very first, first lady. It seemed as if the first couple were beamed out from their ordinary day while doing household chores; he was cutting the grass in his small backyard, wiping the sweat off his forehead as he waited for his wife to bring out something cold to drink, and she was doing the laundry, humming Christian hymns, unaware of the thirst her husband was enduring. The next moment they were standing in front of thousands of people who were chanting "*Manse* (long live) our president!" and waving flags that resembled a frowning face drawn by a child with no artistic gift. It was so bizarre; the only thing that told him that he was still himself was his 9:00 p.m., on-the-dot fart.

Sam imagined this last scene of new president's 9:00 p.m. fart, exchanging kisses with his puppy. "What should I name you?" he asked, gently holding the puppy's face, nuzzling their foreheads together. "How about *Jayu* (freedom)? Yeah, that's a perfect name. You guys must know what that means. Perhaps you will be good enough to teach me what freedom is."

-16-

A new year came, and it was bitterly cold. There were no more Japanese signs in the street, no more sounds of Japanese wooden clogs echoing through the alleys. Nothing Japanese was allowed, although they didn't go so far as to reject Japanese food and drink. Not only did food and drink survive the punishment, they remained as high-class treats. Other than that, nothing changed much. The misery of hunger still reigned as a cruel god to the people, and many of them began to forget they were free men with their own president.

Sam went back to his business too. There was nothing going on. He and Mrs. Lim took turns walking Jayu and spent most of the day at the office playing cards. One morning in the late spring, one of his father's old acquaintances visited him. The man informed him that the American authorities were looking for someone like Sam to work for them. Although he didn't need to worry about money, thanks to his father's wealth, he was more than glad to find work. Initially, it was nothing but translating documents in three languages, but before long he became their consultant, and slowly Koreans returned to his office for advice regarding new and old laws. By the end of the year, he had a full staff and had to turn down some clients due to the overload.

He was able to communicate with his father by post. The letters said he and Mr. Yu were doing well and that he was no longer in Mongolia. "Taoism was too complicated. At my age I don't care to work that hard to gain spirituality. And frankly, it was a yawn inducer. So we decided to try Lama Buddhism up in Tibet, and this is it, my son. We found our heaven!"

Sam didn't know what to think about his father's strange behavior. "In my wildest dreams, I could not imagine my father uttering the word 'heaven,'" he said to his amah.

One thing that concerned him very much was his amah's illness. In the last few years, she had been experiencing pain. It came and went, moving around to different parts of the body. She dismissed his concern, saying that it was just a part of growing old. Sam brought in doctors, but they could not tell what seemed to be the source of the pain. But lately, more and more, she stayed in bed. One evening when he visited her, she asked him if she could see a Chinese doctor. Although Sam was skeptical about traditional medicine, he obliged. The doctors practicing Western medicine he brought in weren't much help. "Amah, I will bring him tomorrow. Maybe that's just the thing you need. I'm sorry that I didn't follow your wish from the start."

"*Botchang*, don't be silly. I know you did what you thought best for me. If anything, it is I who should be ashamed lying down like this, being useless," she said, wetting her parched lips.

"Now who's being silly!" he said, exaggerating cheerfulness.

"How are things with you?" she asked.

"Everything is going well, very well." He was about to tell her what went on that day like he always did when he came home every evening, sometimes quite late at night, but when he saw her eyelid tremor a little, he said, "You need to rest. We can talk tomorrow when you're less tired."

"Yes, Botchang, I guess I am a bit tired now," she said in a voice that sounded more like a sigh. It alarmed him. She had always wanted to hear about his day no matter how tired she was. He saw her closing her eyes and left the room. He immediately called a servant and ordered him to have a maid stay with her at all times. He also told him to make her whatever she had an appetite for whenever she wanted.

The next day he found a Chinese doctor through Mrs. Lim. She said he was the very best in town, and Sam had no choice but to trust her. She said, "I don't know if he's available. I heard that there's always a long waiting list."

He urged her, "Do whatever you have to do to make him come today. Offer him money that he can't resist. Anything."

After she went to get the doctor, he went out and bought a record player that he had been intending to buy for his amah on her birthday, which was a few months away. He used to go out to dinner with her, once a week or so till she became bed ridden. After dinner they always went to the same teahouse to listen to music. Billie Holiday was her favorite.

It was midday when he came home with the record player. There was no sign of the doctor or Mrs. Lim.

He played the music on the machine, looking at her pale face rippling with a wide smile, telling her how popular the songs he picked for her were. Actually, he had no idea, as he had purchased albums recommended by the salesman. He asked for Billie Holiday and anything slow and easy; he noticed his amah enjoyed this kind of music. He got emotional seeing her swaying her upper body while listening to the tune; her palm rested on her chest with her eyes closed. He felt guilty for not buying her the machine sooner.

She asked with her eyes closed, "What is she singing about, Botchang?"

He explained that they were listening to "Stormy Weather" by Billie Holiday.

She replied, "I love the way she sings. It sounds like she sings to herself, only for herself, like singing to her pain…"

They had lunch together listening to the music. She barely took a few spoonfuls of porridge. Sam wanted her to eat more and insisted that she take more from the spoon he held out to her lips. She took more bites, laughing a little. "It used to be the other way around."

"Yes, indeed. It's my turn to force you to eat. Now open wide."

"I won't knock down the spoon like you used to, ha, ha."

After lunch he made her lie down listening to the music, laughing about the recent letter he received from his father. "I just can't imagine what it is he has up his sleeve this time. It seems rather too extreme, even for him," he said, hearing Jayu scratching the door, wanting to come in. He opened it and immediately was attacked by slurpy kisses like they hadn't seen each other for ages. He went to Amah and licked her face, which was screwed up from the tickling. After the exuberant canine greeting ritual, he plopped down next to her futon, making sure that there was no gap between his body and hers. He didn't seem to notice the music being played.

"He certainly has grown," she said, stroking him while he began to lick her hand.

It was about three in the afternoon when the doctor and Mrs. Lim showed up. He was a thin, old man who did not look that healthy himself. His grey beard reached down to the middle of his chest, and his upper body curved forward, giving the impression that his upper half was in a hurry and dragging the reluctant lower half. But when they shook hands, the grip of his hand felt strong, and his eyes were young and clear. He sat down next to Amah, cleared his throat, and checked her pulse from the wrist, with his eyes firmly shut as his other hand was stroking his long wiry beard, swaying his body as if in deep meditation. After that he poked her with numerous thin needles, none of which drew any blood. He let the needles stay in her body and occasionally flicked them with his fingers, all in deadly silence.

About half an hour later, he was done. He told her that he would come back the next day with medicine to ease her pain. Sam followed the old doctor to the courtyard as he was leaving. Before Sam asked him anything, the doctor turned to him and said that she had irregularities in the uterus. Sam held his tongue and refrained from asking how he knew. He needed to see some evidence; it seemed too unscientific. But the last thing he wanted to do was offend the old man. Sam gave in to the monumental confidence the doctor exuded from his eyes.

Sam asked politely, "Can she recover from it?"

The doctor shook his head, adding, "The only thing I can do at this point is to reduce her pain as much as possible. I'll treat her with a series of acupuncture. Hopefully, it will relax her organs enough to receive the medicine for her pain more efficiently. Tomorrow around the same time then."

He looked up at the sky, putting on his hat and said, "Oh! It looks like rain. We need that, don't we?"

Sam stepped into the courtyard. He lit a cigarette as he looked up at the sky. It was muggy, and the dark clouds hanging above the roof seemed impatient to relieve themselves into a thunderstorm. He wished it would come down hard with deafening thunder and blinding sparks of lightning across the sky. He stood next to the flowerbed and touched the hydrangeas, which were as big as a baby's head, and dabbed the tears trickling down his face. He sat on the rock smoking one cigarette after another. Mrs. Lim came out. He waved at her to go back to Amah, wanting to be alone. The thunder started. Large raindrops began to fall, releasing the smell of soil into the air. He heard music coming out of her room. "Amah is dying," he screamed inwardly but louder than a roar of thunder. He opened his palm to the raindrops, watching them become a pool in the cup of his palm. He poured it out and repeated it again, with the cigarette dangling in his mouth, wet and breaking apart. He washed the tears on his face with the raindrops. He could still hear the music through the thunder.

After he dried himself and changed, he went to her room. Mrs. Lim was drying sweat off Amah's forehead. Jayu was curled up at the bottom of her futon, and when he saw Sam, he dashed toward him and started to lick his face. He sat down, returning kisses to the dog. Mrs. Lim turned to him and said, "I think the acupuncture helped her a bit." He went over to her bedside and held her hand. She opened her eyes and told him that the acupuncture dulled her pain. He squeezed her hand gently and told her that the doctor would bring her medicine that would ease her pain.

She said with a faint smile, "I want both of you to know how happy I feel. Happy and guilty at the same time for being loved so much." She then added, raising her trembling body, "I'd like to see the storm." They turned the futon bed to face the large window overlooking the garden and propped her up with pillows. She was very weak but happy and peaceful. Sam opened the window. The sky was breaking up with thunder and lightning, frightening the dog who now scratched the door wanting someone to open it, as if he would escape the thunderstorm once he left the room. Sam hugged Jayu, whose eyes were full circles with fear. Sam could hear a tiny whimper trying to escape from his throat. They laughed at him, telling him how silly he was. Sweet Amah lifted her cover with a trembling hand, and as soon as he saw the invitation, he flew under it for safety. Soon he began to snore, fully tucked in beneath the cover. She mused, "It is beautiful, isn't it? Somehow the music makes it so much more beautiful. Why is that? I wonder." She sounded more like she was talking to herself.

Mrs. Lim asked, "How about we have some tea?"

Amah replied, "What a perfect idea," as if a cup of tea would complete her happiness. Right after Mrs. Lim went to get the tea, she held Sam's hand and said, "Don't lose that woman. She's the right one for you."

Sam burst into loud laughter, startling Jayu under the cover.

The thunder and lightning kept giving a show that delighted Amah's spirit. Sam tried to pull Jayu out from under the cover, but he would not budge. "Let him be," she said, without moving her eyes from the sky.

"Aren't you too warm with him in there?"

"I like it. There's something about an animal leaning against your body. It's like they possess healing powers or something, don't you think?" she said, stroking Jayu, who threw an arrogant side glance at Sam and resumed his previous position in triumph.

"I have something to ask you. Actually a promise."

"Anything but marrying her," he said and laughed a bit.

She didn't seem to hear him. "If possible, I would like my funeral done in a certain way," she said, reaching for his hand, sensing him tense up.

After a silent moment or two, he said, "Tell me."

She gave him her instructions, brief but precise. They heard steps outside coming toward the door, strong and quick; Mrs. Lim was back with the tea tray.

The storm moved away, and the sound of thunder receded to a distance. The three of them drank tea, watching the rain filter the view of the garden. The fragrance of the tea threading through the slow tune of the soft music and the sound of steady rain soaked through Sam's helpless heart. Jayu crawled out, smelling the tea cakes. Suddenly, the room felt crowded.

He devoured a cake Sam gave him and slurped the tea he poured out on a saucer.

The memory of that rainy afternoon stayed in him like embroidery on his heart. It was a humbling sadness participating in each other's pain, exchanging glances of both love and pride, of shared affection, but not without guilt. The sorrow cozily wrapped in a blanket of warm human hearts stopped all suspicion that being human was perhaps a mistake. And how thoroughly glad he was to be a human on that afternoon.

-17-

She was barely eighteen when she was hired as Sam's amah. Her long hair was braided behind her oval face with rosy cheeks. She was like his own shadow, always there with him and for him. She had been a mother, a sister, and a true companion. He remembered his father modernized her appearance when he was a schoolboy, making her cut and perm her hair, powder her face, and wear lipstick. She no longer wore traditional dresses but Western outfits of his father's choosing, stylish and pricey. Her delight over this new appearance seemed stupid and even annoying to him, but soon he joined in her happiness and occasionally uttered a word of encouragement to her. His father's intention was to make her look like a sophisticated governess now that she was to be seen in public with his son. When she was first hired, she was illiterate. She had a neat, even pretty appearance, but her language required some serious cleaning up. When his father decided to keep her, he made her promise to learn reading, writing, and basic arithmetic and provided her with a tutor. A Japanese woman came to teach her the etiquette of a sophisticated modern woman. She was eager to learn and was naturally gifted in assuming an artificial appearance when needed. The only thing she had trouble with was walking gracefully in high heels. He remembered holding her hand tightly, fearing that she would trip when they walked in the street together.

He remembered her on one spring day waiting outside of the classroom to take him home after school, wearing a pale green two-piece suit. How brilliant she looked! Sometimes she walked in front of him and asked, "Botchang, how do I look?" "Oh, not again," he would answer, annoyed. But she looked beautiful against the blue sky with a puff of cloud above her. In spite of the change in appearance, she remained the same as the first day she took Sam in her arms.

It was Amah who introduced life to him. The various fragrances of flowers, wonderful prints on a butterfly's wings, pebbles in his pocket, smooth and cool in his hand…folk stories, some funny and some scary, which he loved to listen to sitting on her lap. His home garden, which ran over a couple acres, was their playground. With large trees, wildflowers, rocks, and a pond, it was kept as natural as could be.

One day, they were lying down on a patch of grass, when out of the blue, she said, "Those leaves on the tree wouldn't look as beautiful without the spaces between them." He didn't know why, but he often thought about what she said when looking at a tree, and there was a new respect for her in his heart ever since that day. What she said rang as important wisdom in his young mind.

When he was about eight, his father hired a young chap with smelly feet to tutor him three times a week to advance his learning with the abacus and Chinese calligraphy. Sam particularly did not like the way he looked at his amah when she brought in refreshments. After she left the room, he always lit a cigarette, blowing the smoke to the ceiling, and lost himself in thought for a while. Sam loathed him. One day Sam noticed him looking at the door frequently when Amah was delayed. When she finally showed up with tea and cake, the chap was looking at her as if asking or complaining, "Where have you been?" while his eyes moved up and down her body. Sam shouted at her not to come during his lesson. Before he noticed Amah's face turning crimson with embarrassment, the tutor's hand landed on his face, which was promptly reciprocated with a shower of hot tea by none other than sweet Sam. He screamed, and Sam laughed. She ran out and brought a towel at the speed of light and wiped the tutor's face, now red with burns. She was profusely apologizing over his moaning. Sam ran out in half anger and half fear.

He was sitting by the pond for about half an hour throwing rocks at koi fish when she found him. She sat next to him without any words. Then she reached to him and stroked his hair gently. "It's okay, Botchang. He'll be fine."

He buried his head in her chest and started to cry. "Has he left?"

"Not yet. The doctor will be here to see him. I could tell he was faking a bit."

"He's really not hurt?"

"His face is a little red but not too bad. He'll recover fully, I promise you," she assured him, wiping his face with her apron.

Then she started to giggle. "I had to hold my breath when I was drying him. I was afraid I'd throw up on him. What a foul smell he carries with him!"

By the time the doctor arrived, the redness on the tutor's face had diminished by a shade or two. He said to Amah, "He's fine. I put some ointment on him. If he causes any trouble, let me know. I can tell he is determined to make you pay for it." Amah let out a sigh of relief with her palm on her chest. She thanked him and saw him off. The tutor was lying down in the room with white ointment on his face whimpering. Sam wanted to apologize, but when he peeked through the door, he looked like a corpse with blinking eyes. The sight of him discouraged Sam with a second set of fear; it scared him, and he could not utter a word.

The tutor stayed put, giving no sign or intention of leaving soon. They served him dinner, which he ate alone in the room. He smoked and had tea then resumed his position of lying down and blinking at the ceiling. Amah sent Mr. Hang, the head servant, to ask if they should fetch a cab for him. Mr. Hang came out shaking his head. "You know this kind. He's determined to wait for Master to come home. He won't leave before he's compensated. That kind of person will not let go of an opportunity like this." They could hear that loud snoring replaced the moaning.

When his father came home late at night, Amah rushed to him and told him what happened, making sure that his father understood that the tutor slapped Sam first, really hard. Without saying a word, his father went into the room where the tutor was sleeping. Sam, Amah, and Mr. Yu stayed close to the door and listened to them talking inside. It was mostly the tutor who did the talking, talking as if he had become disfigured. Then he talked about his miserable life, sobbing here and there. He never mentioned how he slapped Sam. His father listened to him quietly.

Mr. Yu was getting agitated as he held Sam's father's briefcase. He whispered rather sharply in a voice that sounded like whistling, "Master had a long day. He's not had supper yet, and he was sneezing on the way coming home. This urchin has to be stopped." His devotion to Sam's father was his meaning in life. Sam noticed that his father never treated him as hired help. They did everything together and truly appreciated each other's existence. He was pacing around, impatiently holding the briefcase against his chest while mumbling and looking up at the ceiling. Finally, he decided to interrupt and was about to open the door when they heard movements inside. "Would this help?" his father said. It seemed his father offered him money. A few moments later, they both came out of the room followed by a gush of noxious odor, as if the room had been holding its breath until the door opened. The tutor finally left. Sam's heart was beating so hard at the sight of his father, he felt dizzy. But his father just laid his hand on his head and said, "Hope you've learned something today." He checked the bruise on his face and told him, "Go to bed. It's late." Prompted by the gentleness of his father, Sam summoned up the courage to ask him if the tutor would come back. His father answered, "No, he won't," motioning him to go to bed. He walked down the hallway to his quarter followed by Mr. Yu, who quickly ordered the servant to bring in their supper. Sam heard them laughing.

The next day the entire household was talking about the incident. They were laughing about how the tutor exaggerated the pain, moaning, whimpering, and howling, with his face covered in the white ointment. Sam was proud of being the author of the humorous event. But as time went on, he began to feel sorry for the tutor.

One day he asked Amah, who was peeling a tangerine for him, "Amah, why did he demand money?"

"He was a poor man and in need of money," she answered, putting a segment of the fruit into his mouth.

"Why didn't he make his own money if he needs money?" he asked, chewing the tangy fruit.

"Well, Botchang, it's not that simple. You'll understand when you grow up," she said with a small sigh.

Sam thought about this over and over. Money and pride. When he became a little older, a few questions regarding money and pride occasionally popped up in his mind, realizing that dignity and pride do not bring food. At the end of the day, would he suffer because his hunger won over pride? Or vice versa? Are we born with a sense of dignity and pride, or are they totally artificial, and the real master is actually hunger? Those people who enjoyed the tutor's drama, they might've behaved the same way if they were in his place, wouldn't they? Wouldn't he? Wouldn't his father? Another thing he wondered about was why human beings find such humor in other people's falls. He knew he'd laugh again, perhaps harder, should he witness such a thing again. The event became some sort of a reference point in his life as one of his unfading memories.

-18-

It was about two months since the Chinese doctor's first visit. He came by every afternoon to check on her. She wasn't getting better, but Sam was grateful that she was still with him. Whatever the old doctor had been doing, she didn't seem to be suffering, even if extremely weak, and her pale face gained some color. At times he had to fight the hope bobbing in his heart. Sam stayed with her every evening with Jayu when he came home from work. She barely uttered a word, but when she could, she asked him if he still remembered what he promised. He assured her every time.

Every single memory of his childhood had her presence. A young girl of eighteen came into his life to be his virgin mother. Now at age fifty-two, she was leaving him. Even when he was abroad for seven years, he always felt her presence right next to him. When he was a child, he fancied the idea of giving her the very best of everything when he grew up. Oh, how much it pained him to see her leaving! After he came back from America, his father kept him busy establishing a firm footing in the business world, and he learned to indulge himself with the new experiences of adult life, like drinking and chasing women.

One Saturday evening in November, he was sitting next to her futon reading the newspaper, occasionally looking at her as she slept. The whistling wind rattled the window. She woke up and stretched out her hand, searching for his. He grabbed her hand and asked if she needed anything. She moved her head on the pillow sideways. Sam spooned some water into her mouth, seeing that her lips were parched. She looked at him for a moment or two then asked him to open the window. He did and asked her if she would like some music, which she had been enjoying every day since he got her the record player. She said that she'd like to listen to the wind without the music but wanted some candlelight. He promptly lit the candles, and when he returned to her side, she had her eyes closed. He knelt down next to her and held her lifeless hand. He could see a tiny bit of foam at the corner of her parted lips. There was a sigh, thin but long, exiting her mouth—once, twice, and the last. He buried his head into her chest and sobbed. Unbearable pain knocked the air out of him. No matter how long and how well he prepared himself for this moment, the abruptness was merciless. It felt like he was no longer Sam. He did not know how long he was crying. The November wind rushing through the open window blew out the candle. Jayu came to him and licked his tears. He hugged him and wept.

-19-

It was late afternoon when Miri woke up from a nap. She got out of bed, feeling that her legs were wobbly. She splashed cold water on her face from the basin and looked in the mirror. The girl in the mirror looked back at her as if she were a wrong image. What she saw disagreed with what she thought she would see. She did not like the image of herself, and the girl in the mirror loathed her likewise. She said to her reflection, "You are not me. Why don't you find your own mirror that shows your true self instead of following me?" The hostile relationship between Miri and her image was nothing new. Looking at her reflection was emotionally taxing business. She dried her face and briefly felt sleep coming on again. She thought about going back to bed but decided to walk it off. She walked down the long hallway to the nurse's station, hearing a familiar pop song from a radio. She smelled coffee when she poked her head through the counter." Oh, look who's here." It was the same nurse who received her the first day she came to the hospital.

Miri smiled at her and asked for a cup of coffee. "I don't want to fall asleep for another week."

"Wait here, I'll get you some." The nurse went inside. The pop song from the radio was reaching its dramatic notes, which were too high for the singer, making Miri anxious, even though she tapped her foot to the tune all the same. She saw another young nurse behind the partition, standing against a desk and talking to a young male doctor. She wore heavy makeup, and her uniform was rather tight and short, revealing her legs that resembled bowling pins. Together with an excessively starched white cap on her head, Miri was reminded of a horny but clueless hen: "ko, ko, kodaak!" The hen-nurse and the young doctor, whose balding head reflected the overhead light, were exchanging invisible hormonal secretions.

The nurse came back with half a cup of black coffee. "You drink it here," she ordered. While Miri was sipping the hot coffee and leaning against the counter and watching the doctor and hen-nurse, she had a thought. How odd it is that they were occupying the same space and time with her, yet the other side seemed an illusion from another dimension. It was a strangely comforting thought that they were not sharing the same dimension.

After she finished her coffee, she went up to the nurse-illusion and handed over the empty cup, asking her, "Do you have any reading material and some writing tools?"

"Writing tools?" the nurse asked, laughing a little.

"Yes, pen and papers," Miri translated.

"We have a library on the ground floor if you want something to read. You'll find all sorts of things to read there. And next door to the library is a gift store that sells writing tools."

As the nurse was speaking, Miri spotted a comic book on the far corner of the desk against which the hen-nurse was leaning. "Can I borrow that?" she asked, pointing at it with her forefinger. She detected a frown on the illusionary nurse's forehead, but she fetched the comic book and some blank papers and a pen and successfully passed them through the junction between dimensions.

"I don't know who this belongs to. Be sure to bring the book back."

She walked back to her room. Coffee made her less sleepy, but her eyelids still felt heavy. Walking down the hallway, she decided to write a letter to a friend, her one and only friend who was quickly becoming an ex-friend, who had moved to Tokyo not long ago. But when she stepped into her room, something else possessed her mind. The mountain, a green pyramid, was waiting for her. She pulled the chair out to the middle of the room and sat down facing the mountain. The luscious green of the sea pines looked iridescent under the blanket of low, grey clouds.

"It will rain, a storm possibly. I say yes to a storm, a fierce storm, the mother of storms, a storm that roars at you that you are nothing."

"Shut up."

She heard a voice, she thought. She waited a little and resumed her mindless chase after the derivatives of storm choo choo train. "Storm of karma, sexy storm, storm of pimps and his working women, storm of Jesus and Pontius Pilate, oh, how about storm with full moon…"

"That's sufficient." This time the voice was louder and clear. It was a male voice, a voice that tried to assert authority. She looked around and saw no one. She said, "Who are you?"

"Not so loud, girl. Just think. I hear better that way. I'm a messenger sent by the one you love."

Who could that be, she thought.

"The womb."

"I don't know any womb other than the unused one in my belly. Is an unused womb still a womb? And I don't want any message from the womb I came out from…" While she was searching for the owner of this womb in her head, she remembered. She asked, "How is she?"

"She's just fine, she misses you and worries about you."

Miri felt a pinch on her nose, and tears started to fill her eyes.

"Now, now, we don't want that. We have a lot of work to do. Earlier I introduced myself as a messenger, but my role is a little more than that. I'm the guide for your journey to yourself. Stop crying, will you? You can't hear me well with that crying, and I don't like to repeat myself."

"I'm listening. I'm just so touched and frankly a bit scared," she said through her thoughts. "Why don't you show yourself?" she asked, looking around.

"I couldn't if I wanted to, perhaps next time but not now. Think of it as a telephone call, only my phone has a lens to see you and yours doesn't. Anyway, let's skip this 'how' and 'why' stuff. As I said, we have a lot of work to do. Let's see, your name is Miri, which means 'Beautiful Reason.'" He started to laugh, his voice changing to a high pitch like that of a boy before puberty.

"What's so funny?" she asked.

"I'm laughing at your name. Think about it. Beauty and reason, the two worst enemies tied up together and that's your name. Ha, ha, ha…"

"How so?" she asked.

"Beauty can never be beautiful when there is a reason attached to it, got it?"

"It doesn't matter. I never think of myself as either beauty or reason. It means nothing to me. What's your name?"

"I don't have one. We don't need names to identify ourselves. We are transparent," he said, taking a mature man's voice but not as deep as the first one.

"Why do you keep changing voices? Are there more than one of you?"

"I'm alone. This is my real voice. In the beginning I used a deeper voice to fish out serious respect from you."

This time she laughed.

"No, no, don't ever let out a sound from your throat when you are with me. The last thing we need is to attract others. It will harm the string of energy that connects us."

"How do you expect me to laugh without making a sound?"

"Easy. Just don't."

Miri laughed again, which made him sigh.

"Listen, I have to go. I'll see you tomorrow."

"Here, in this room? When?" she asked, not wanting him to go.

"Meet me at the afternoon hike tomorrow; you might be able to see me in the flesh although I seriously doubt."

"Wait, am I really going to see you? In person?"

"You will see my full figure if everything is in sync. I'll try my best. No one else can see me, but you should never use your voice to talk to me."

"How do I know it's you? You don't even have a name."

He sighed again, annoyed.

"You will see a handsome goat walking erect in a blue satin outfit. Would that be easy enough for you to spot me?" Then he left, or rather, hung up.

Miri's eyes returned to the pyramid of the mountain whose green seemed greener, the clouds darker and heavier. She checked if she was still breathing. She was, but she felt like she came out of a trance. One drop, two drops, more drops on the windowpane. "The storm is here," she said to herself, feeling a surge of energy, untrustworthy energy. She was hungry.

The dining hall was busy with the dinner crowd. She picked out a few items of food on her tray and sat at a large round table with six chairs. Miri was the occupant of the fourth chair. Across from her, an elderly woman sat sandwiched between two men of a similar age. They sat so closely, as if their sides were joined together. All three of them wore rather sour expressions in silence, indicating some disagreeable matter had happened. They threw glances over Miri's head as if she was invisible. After a few moments one of the men got up, pushing the chair back with his legs, a motion that was copied by the remaining two. The three of them walked together to the exit. She looked around, chewing mouthfuls of food. People were sitting together, eating and chatting as normal people did. She thought, each one of them must have a sack of stories to tell about why they were there, noticing that there were more women than men. It wasn't a very interesting scene to observe. She looked out the glass doors to the patio, thinking what she would do next. It was pouring, and the glass doors looked like they were draped with liquid fabric. She thought about what happened that afternoon in her room. "Nothing happened. It was just one of those moments when my imagination took a bite out of reality or vice versa," she thought. But she could not dismiss the doubt about her doubt.

She finished her meal and got up to explore, remembering the library the nurse had mentioned. It had been nearly a month since she came to the hospital, but she hadn't had a proper tour of the place yet. It had been only a week or so since she started to eat in the dining room. Since she got ill from the first day she had arrived, she wasn't allowed to eat in the dining room for fear of spreading the virus. She left and walked to the lounge where people, some in hospital pajamas and some in regular clothing, were sitting around smoking, talking, reading papers, watching TV, or playing cards. It was another scene from another dimension. She remembered passing through the lounge the first day she had arrived, but this time it looked a little different. It looked rather fancy for a hospital lounge. A high ceiling with chandelier, carpeted floor with leather sofas and armchairs, and even flower arrangements, made the place inviting in a somewhat disturbing way. Everything looked ordinary, too ordinary, until she saw a man in striped pajamas shuffling around in a daze with a bowl of rice tucked in his underarm. He was about thirty with a dark complexion. His excessively elongated chin rested on his chest, and his widely opened eyes were dull underneath his bushy eyebrows. His nostrils were flared, and his mouth was open with a meaty lower lip dangling, glistening with saliva. No one paid attention to him. They stepped aside or moved their legs so as not to interfere with this man's shuffling, and they continued the matters that occupied them. Her eyes followed his shuffling until he reached the far corner of the room. "What made him do that?" she thought then she corrected herself. "What makes anybody do anything?"

She stared at him until the figure disappeared into the corridor behind the reception desk, which led to the bathroom. She later learned that he visited the bathroom with a bowl of rice and stayed standing in the corner after every meal. The doctors let him out of the fifth floor, which was for hardcore patients, having considered his behavior to be totally harmless.

She resumed her own shuffling to the direction of the library. When she reached the corridor leading to the library, her eyes caught a sign on a wooden door that said "music room." She pushed the door open and walked into the room, which was dimly lit and empty. There was an old grand piano, sofas, chairs scattered around a fireplace, and a record player with a large glass case filled with albums. She took out an album and saw Frank Sinatra smiling at her in a fashionably tilted fedora. "Why do they call them white?" she wondered, looking at the creepy smile on Frank's face. To her the Caucasian tribe seemed closer in shade to pink, an unsettling kind of pink—definitely not white. She put the album back and sat on the sofa facing the dark fireplace. She hummed one of Frank's songs, "over and over and keep going over...blah, blah, blah..." Another dishonest song, she thought and stopped humming. She felt a frequency of emptiness passing through her, taking its time. She thought, if it's emptiness, it shouldn't be felt. Maybe even emptiness isn't empty after all. It might be a substance with atoms, a molecular weight. Why not? It certainly has a presence that takes all the air in your lungs at times. It's definitely a substance, an organic matter, a living thing.

Her mind started to ramble again, but it was the only art form with which she was gifted. This gift enabled her to travel to the end of the universe and back in no time. It required no ticket, no luggage, no spending money, and no rush back home to dinnertime. She was able to take a ride with her rambling thoughts for hours. They made impossibilities seem possible to her, treated her to the taste of true freedom, gave her courage, and never failed to make her feel like an artist in the art of spacing out in her own right. She had revealed this gift of hers with her soon-to-be ex-friend who had moved to Tokyo not long ago.

"It sounds like ill wiring in your head. A signal received by a defective receptor. But philosophically speaking, I must say it is something, a little cuckoo but something," he said once. Miri couldn't tell if he was mocking her. She liked to listen to him. He was a bag full of theories and logic based on opinions, and she liked being with him.

-20-

Miri was a dreamer, literally. She could not remember a night without a dream. Her dreams were mythical and adventurous, and because of her dream life, she was always tired in the morning. Night after night, for months at a time, she would land in the same place, unknown to her real life. Then her dreams would take her to a new place where she had to study the new geography. And she was taken to the same place night after night. After several months the stage changed again. But the dreams became increasingly disturbing. "Please, don't take me there tonight," she prayed before she fell asleep. But she was there again. The dreams became more and more physical and darker.

A few years back, a certain dream started and repeated in the same sequence every single night. In this dream, she was a young child, four or five years old, in a red summer dress and bare feet. The setting was always in a dark woods at night. She was chased by a creature that looked like a large dog, but it wasn't a dog. It had six legs, nine tails with eyeballs on the tips, and a head that was nothing but gooey, saliva-dripping teeth. This creature chased after her in her dream every night. Her run through the woods in the pitch black night, being chased by this creature, was so real. The dream followed her into the waking hours. She even tried to come up with strategies to defeat the creature in next night's dream. The pot full of strong coffee and caffeine pills she took was useless when that time arrived at night. She got really fed up. Still scared and dreading to go to sleep, she developed a "take it or leave it" kind of courage or hopelessness. Sleep overwhelmed her, sucking her into the dark hole of the tunnel. Her heart sank, knowing for sure the creature was lurching at the entrance to her sleep. She prayed hard before she fell asleep, prayed to Jesus, Mary, and her guardian angels, with rosary beads in her hand.

Then one night, she was running through the woods in the same red dress and bare feet, and the creature came so close, much closer than any of the previous nights. She climbed a tree, but the creature with its six legs crawled up after her with its head of teeth dripping thick, goo-like saliva. The terrific terror in her suddenly turned to a horrendous anger when the teeth of the creature tore the bottom of her red dress. She reached down and grabbed the creature's head with her hands, staring at the nine eyeballs on the tails blinking in shock. The woods echoed with the growling of two beasts, hers and the creature's. She tore up the entire length of the creature at one go. It died without much resistance. It was easy. She threw the body to the ground and felt very, very close to God. After a while she came down from the tree and examined the creature, now in two pieces with all nine eyes peacefully closed. The next moment, she thought the dead body moved. She stepped back. It was going through a metamorphosis, turning into a person vertically torn into two pieces. It was her mother. She looked down at the torn body of her mother's without any notable emotion. The only thing she remembered was feeling that it had to be done. It was her mother, but it still had to be done for her and her mother's sake.

But the chase dreams continued. The setting of the dark woods was the same, but this time the pursuer was a man, a thousand-year-old man, bony and disheveled with long hair in a shabby white robe. The robe was open, revealing his torso in the middle of which was a large cavity. His face was covered by his long and stringy hair, and he followed her without a sound.

She was running without gaining an inch. He was right behind her with his arms stretched out but keeping the same distance as if they were frozen in a frame while the surrounding woods were quickly passing by. She remembered that she wasn't terribly scared of this man but still didn't want to be caught. This dream repeated every night like the previous one did, until one night when the man spoke. He asked her to return a lock of his hair that she had stolen from him. She saw a few strands of golden hair in her hand. She stopped running and turned to him to return the hair. He grabbed her, ignoring the hair, and started to eat her like an ear of corn. She felt nothing, no fear, no pain, just the eerie sound of crunching bones. Again the inner voice said, "It had to be done." After he consumed her body, she found herself sitting inside his torso where there was previously an empty cavity. It felt neither good nor bad. It was more like a feeling of "as is." And there were no more of such dreams. The dreams she dreaded stopped, but she felt abandoned, even useless. She really wanted to talk to someone, someone who didn't know her.

-21-

One day Miri paid a visit to a young priest at the church to which her family belonged. He was popular among the young members of the congregation. Miri overheard her sisters talking about him.

"The line for his confession booth is always long," one of her sisters mentioned.

"That's because he never gives a long penance. One cycle of the Lord's prayer and a Hail Mary, no matter what," Sohee said and laughed.

They also talked about a rumor that he'd received stigmata.

"His hands bleed every Friday night."

"No wonder he's so pale."

"Did you know he has a psychology degree?"

"Indeed he does. You can tell he's an intellectual from his sermons," Sohee said.

Listening to them talking about the young priest stirred Miri's curiosity, even though she couldn't help thinking that a Catholic priest/psychologist was rather an oxymoron.

-22-

It was during winter break when she visited him. It was bitterly cold with icy snow piles all around. He welcomed her into his tiny office with a burning stove in the middle. He pulled a chair near the stove for her to sit on. The room was dark but cozy and friendly. She looked around, fanning her frozen hands over the warmth coming from the stove. One desk, a couple of chairs and a book shelf—the simple belongings of a monk, she thought and felt at home with the minimalistic surroundings.

"Would you like something warm to drink? Coffee?" he asked. She said "yes," nodding her head. He brought her a cup of coffee and sat across from her, hugging his own cup with his hands. She noticed how meticulously groomed he was, down to his cuticles. He was of medium build, on the thin side with a plain boyish face.

"How's your family?" he started.

"They're fine." A phony answer to a phony question, she thought, beginning to think that coming to see him was a mistake. She took a sip of coffee and moved her glance to a small window behind him. A single crow was sitting on top of a bare tree. A black-robed priest and a crow together on the same page of her vision seemed ominous yet rather moving.

"Let's see, you are Sohee? Zona?"

She corrected him politely.

"Oh yes, Miri. I must say that your mom is a fabulous cook. We all get so excited when she cooks for us," he said, taking a sip from his cup.

Her mother entertained them once a month, usually the last Sunday of the month. She cooked up a storm and made a fuss about everything days before for the preparation of the dinner. When Miri saw them eating, drinking, and smoking large, sausage-like cigars in the dining room laughing at some Christian jokes, she thought the scene was sinister, malicious. It was not a pretty sight to her. The priest was now going on about her grandmother's steamed buns filled with sweet bean paste, which she brought to him occasionally. He went on and on about how her grandmother's buns tasted just like his mother's. He never thought anyone could make it as good as his mom, so what a delight it was when he took the first bite into her grandmother's version and found how perfectly the sweet bean paste was prepared, not too sweet but just perfect. "And your teeth find some whole beans still soft and juicy, yet they pop between the teeth…"

She was getting bored and annoyed at herself for having talked herself into seeing him. She had a simple question about her dreams and wondered how he would interpret them as a psychologist. She dropped that idea altogether and was busily thinking about how to get out of there as soon as possible. But a component in her, normally very lazy, that was in charge of bluntness woke up and caused her to say, "Where's the crucifix? How come I don't see one in this room?"

This abrupt question startled him. "Isn't there one?" he said, looking around, scratching the top of his head.

His demeanor stiffened a bit, Miri noticed.

The naughty component in her that unleashed the bluntness got a little more aggressive. "Father Mark, who is Jesus to you? Was he a real person? The Son of God? Savior?"

He rounded his eyes and said, "He was and is all of those. Are you troubled with the doctrine?"

"Yes, I am, Father Mark, and it scares me," she lied, half knowing what he was going to say next: "Pray, pray, and pray." She thought, let's see what he will say and waited for his response with a sarcastic grin inside her unlike the look of despair on the outside.

She was preparing for the next round when he said, "God reaches out to you in mysterious ways." She didn't like that she kind of liked his answer. It bore too much the essence of honesty.

"Is that from your own experience?" she asked, feigning innocence.

"More than once. Actually, many times. Be patient and don't let it go," he answered, nodding his head slowly, his narrowed eyes looking at hers with a touch of condescension.

What the fuck do you mean, "don't let it go"? How does one do that? She obviously didn't say that out loud, but the sly pleasure she was feeling asked her to keep going for a while longer.

"I confess, Father Mark, that I like Jesus. I always have, but as a human being. I like him plenty just as a person. But this idea of him being the Son of God and so on puts distance between us. For example, when I think of Jesus, a truly good human being who set the example for all of us to love one another, I really feel it in my heart. And I also share his sorrow and agony of being used and misunderstood by people. I feel so sorry for him, and when such a moment hits me, I feel so much love for him. And I can't help thinking his death on the crucifix was a form of suicide. I think after three years of trying with people, he was worn out, disappointed, and terribly depressed. When this opportunity of being crucified came, he took it. That is the Jesus Christ I could love and even weep for. But the idea of him dying for our sins, his resurrection three days after death, his ascension to heaven to sit at the right hand of the Father and so on… Well, I don't care for that part. That's how I feel. If he had died for our sins, judging by the world around us, his plan failed, didn't it? He died because he was fed up with us. He couldn't take it anymore. He gave up and went back to his Father, whomever that was…That makes far better sense to me, Father." She questioned herself, "What the heck?" as these words streamed out of her mouth, virgin thoughts to her own ears, not to mention still wanting to get out of there as soon as possible. True, she intended to annoy him a bit because she was annoyed at herself for making the mistake of coming. But all she did was let the beast out of the cage, the beast she had no knowledge was residing in her. She didn't feel all that clever after all. She invited unintended conversation and ended up trapping herself into a situation.

He listened to her intensely, pressing his lips with two fingers, which suggested that he was thinking carefully of what he was about to say. He stared up in the air with a faint smile on his lips. She looked over his shoulder to the window. The crow was gone. He took a sip of coffee and crossed his legs, indicating his readiness, and said, "Miri, Jesus is not a hero in a novel. It seems that you have this romantic notion of him like one feels for a hero in a tragic story. You're very right that we should follow his teaching and try to live by it, but he has to be much more than that. Religion is something more than moral guidance; it requires mysticism. The human psyche craves it. Without mysticism, there can't be faith. Faith exists only in the absence of proof. What I'm saying might not reach you at all, but please don't turn away just because you're frustrated that your understanding won't expand. I assure you it will, and that's how prayer works. People come to this church, attend Mass, read the same Bible, and recite the rosary together, but no two persons will have the same shape and shade of faith. They all interpret faith in their own individual way, albeit they worship the same God. That's how it should be."

She was pleasantly surprised and liked what she was hearing once again. It wasn't what she expected to hear. She decided to continue talking, this time, with a tinge more of sincere innocence. "Father Mark, I must say what you're saying is different than what I learned from Catholic teaching."

"Maybe so. The Church is an organic being. It changes, it grows, and it learns along the way, mostly from people. It has to. Therefore, Church dogma, in my opinion, isn't a dogma at all. When I was a young lad, I used to have many questions about God and the stories involving Him. I did not know what to make of Him. He seemed too angry, unfair, not likable. Frankly, He seemed too monstrous to be called 'Father.' Then I met Jesus, and he helped me to be courageous in faith. A blind man cannot see, but that doesn't mean what he can't see doesn't exist. I chose this path mostly because of the undying curiosity in me, if you will."

"Has your opinion of God, the Father of Jesus changed?" she asked, anticipating his answer.

"I decided to believe that the God I feared and disliked was created in such a way in order to control people, like many parents use fear tactics to keep their children out of harm's way. A mysticism created, like the boogeyman but in this case to set up the social orders. Rules and laws were created to confine a wild, unruly mass under one roof. Control through fear of God is the same idea."

"You mean the God in the Bible isn't the Father of Jesus but a myth?"

"A metaphor as a myth," he said thoughtfully, but the uncertainty in his voice was unmistakable. He wasn't uncertain in his belief that God was a metaphor but rather felt a speck of fear about saying too much to a young girl. But he continued, "When you compare God in the Old Testament with that of the New Testament, the difference is obvious. Like I said, the Church being organic, the notion of God moved on and changed and is changing. Have you read the Bible?"

"Not from top to bottom. I go to a high school run by the Presbyterian church, and Bible study is mandatory. I believe I have a good amount of knowledge of it," she answered with a knowing look. By then the sarcastic grin in her had gone to sleep.

"What is your opinion of the Bible? What stands out to you?"

She tilted her head, took a sip of lukewarm coffee, and said, "First of all, I must confess that it isn't fun reading. Other than being unexciting reading material, what stood out to me is its omission of nature, the most magnificent creation of God, his art. It almost gave me the feeling that nature is despised. There's nothing I found that indicates appreciation for nature. So far I haven't found a line that thanks God for creating such magnificent nature, the most obvious gift given to us by Him. It seems wrong, very wrong. Christianity teaches that we are above nature, and I think that's a mistake, a mistake of Jesus too."

"But don't you agree it's part of human nature that we innately believe we're above nature; therefore, it's possibly also God's intention?"

"I have to disagree. If you look into human history regarding the primordial habits of religious practice, you will find that nature played an important part of worship. I know it's dismissed as heresy by this particular religion, which is a relatively young religion. Tens of thousands of years of worshipping God through nature, nature being His temple, or God itself became a sin in this religion. I wonder why. As you know, those older practices, however heretical or non scientific they are, still go on in various forms. And I think, I believe, they are closer to our innate quality. I think the idea of being above or better than nature itself is a manifestation of inferiority. We feel inadequate and inferior to nature. As you know, nature can be horrific, deadly, and terrifying. We declared war against the power of nature, to eventually be able to tame it, to make it work for us. Going to war with nature is like going to war with God himself. I don't believe that we're better than and above nature, for we're not supposed to be. This religion kills the crucial part in us that runs in our veins."

"I must admit that you brought up very interesting points, something for me to think about, although I don't recall any condemnation of nature in the Scriptures. But it is true that nature's ignored. I don't think it's despised or challenged, but perhaps it's taken for granted."

"When you read the Bible, what kind of picture do you get surrounding the story? The picture I get is of a dusty desert, harsh and abandoned. No lovely green, songs of birds, a breeze that dries the sweat on your forehead… It's like having to listen to a righteous grandfather who has no idea how closed and one-sided his mind is. I think nature is the ultimate gift from God. Ignoring it is ignoring God's gift. If I were God, I would be hurt."

He laughed.

Briefly she thought about sharing her dream adventures with him since she was now more relaxed, but before she finished her thought, he spoke. "You know, this conversation we're having made me think about myself. I realize I've never been inspired by nature myself, sadly. Come to think of it, I've been indifferent to it. I thank you for this realization. I've only noticed it when the weather changes. I totally agree that nature is God's gift, and I've mistreated it," he said in all seriousness. She made a mental note that the young priest wasn't half bad. "I'm glad that we're having this talk. But you must have something you want to talk about with me, isn't that why you came to see me?" he asked.

Before her mind decided what to say, "nothing in particular" slipped out of her mouth. "I like to have a religious talk with someone sometimes. That's all," she said sheepishly.

"Oh, bless you. I welcome it anytime."

Again she thought about talking about her dreams. Instead she stood up and thanked him for his time with a slight bow.

"Do you have to go?" he asked.

"I don't want to take up any more of your time."

"If you can stay, I'd like to ask you a few things," he said, pointing to the chair, suggesting that she come back to sit. She obeyed.

"This is a random question I occasionally ask young people like yourself," he said, pulling his chair closer to hers. A whiff of aftershave reached her nose. He asked, "I assume you believe in God, right?" She nodded automatically. "Who is God to you?" he asked, leaning toward her with his eyes fixed on hers.

"I have no idea. It's impossible for me to form any idea of God. It's true, very true that I believe there's a God. This belief I own is not through the teaching of the Church. In fact, I try to unlearn what the Church taught me. But it's hard and at times even scary. And the confusion is here with me to stay. I need God. I need my God to be kind and gentle, and I must feel His presence from time to time. I need my God to be much better than me, so that I have no choice but to want to learn from Him," she spoke softly, looking down at the wooden floor.

Father Mark noticed the change in her. As a matter of fact, he was taken aback by her, not because of what she said, but the sudden heaviness the voice carried. She was no longer the same girl he was talking with a few minutes ago. There was suffering.

Silence fell between them. They were both gazing at the floor quietly as if they just shared sad news. Finally, he spoke. He was going to ask if he could be of any help in sorting out her confusion, but he asked instead, "Why do you think people search for God?"

She slowly raised her head and looked at him. There was a singleness, an agelessness in her eyes. Not young, not old, no age. She said in a much deeper voice, "We fear. We crave something powerful, perfect, and eternal that sides with you to protect and save you from the fear."

"So you agree that having faith in God is beneficial, right?" Before she answered, he continued, "I truly believe we, from the moment we are born, know God."

"Then what's the use of religious teaching, if everyone knows God already? Doesn't that make the function of religion only to confuse people?"

"Not at all. People need security. Worshipping God through the same agreed rituals together gives them security, reinforces their belief. We want to be close to God but don't know how. Religion and the Church put a face on God, give Him a physical form, so to speak. And worshipping, performing rituals in a group, makes them feel that they're not alone."

She nodded with her blank, ageless stare.

"If that's how it started, I appreciate its intention being noble and friendly. But..." she said as if talking to herself.

"But?" he asked, trying to find her in her blank stare.

"But...That's not how it is. That's not how it has been for a long, long time. It became an enforcer, a dictator, and mind-warping factory. It forbids individual thinking, which I happen to believe to be our duty to God. It became a poison that kills the will in people's minds, including mine. Animals know exactly what they are, and they live by the blueprint they've received. I envy them sometimes. We are at best tamed animals, livestock of these institutions called religion. We give them power to judge our lives, but the truth is that they are as blind as any one of us. I'm not criticizing but hurting, if you know what I mean. Our instincts, which I'd like to call our nature, is just the way God created us to be. Our instincts stay underground, alive but troubled and exhausted for having to battle with the inorganic aliens of man-made morality that are artificial and sometimes even cruel. This particular religion you and I belong to teaches us to go to war with ourselves. Everything about us is sin! Aren't you, therefore, condemning and murdering the very thing that God created, the God you worship and die for? Every individual has to struggle with the underground forces in them, mostly unknowingly. They try to bury them in fear of facing a personal evil which never goes away and doesn't always stay buried. I said 'personal evil,' but only according to the cruel and unreasonable morality we live by, not because I think of it as actually evil. We, perhaps, started out innocently in an attempt to promote a better society, creating a list of 'do this, don't do that' in the name of God, but we ended up chaining ourselves down in an unnatural, unbearable dungeon. We march on in uniform behavior with a uniform exchange of words and attitudes, empty of meaning, day in and day out. And the God we are chasing after moves farther and farther away."

Something, someone inside of Father Mark was blushing and trembling as if his inner secret was being read aloud by a total stranger, a very young stranger. That someone in him wanted to hold the hands of this stranger and scream together. But the more emotional he got, the harder he tried to maintain his dignified composure. He leaned back, folding his arms, and finally said, "So you think religion created a hypocritical world."

"It might've started with good intentions, but it ended up hurting people, hurting God."

"Are you talking about all religions, not just Christianity?"

"More or less. Any organized group, small or large, in the name of God, steals the very entity in one's heart that recognizes his God."

"But you agree that we have an innate desire to worship?" he asked.

"I tend to think so, but a part of me argues at times."

"Would you share that with me?"

"I think I answered you already. We fear, and we want a protector and to please the protector so as to receive more and better protection. I can't accept that as a behavior of pure worship."

"But is fear also the source of your belief?"

"When I was a young child, yes. As you know, Father Mark, my family has been Catholic for three generations. The whole package was there when I was born."

"How do you feel about that?"

"At that time, as a young child, non-believers seemed happier. I remember the secret pain of fear, punishment, and guilt that all my senses had to endure before the age of the proper formation of logic, reason, and even common sense. The worst of it was that you had to live in awful fear of the punishment of burning in hell. Okay, maybe just for a while, but eternity? Can you hate anyone that much, ever? This was the point when I began to doubt. Fear stayed, but doubt gained muscle of its own. My practice of faith slowly turned mechanical, hardly with any meaning. Come to think of it, what was quite disturbing to me, and frankly didn't make any sense to me as a young child, was people begging for help, for miracles more likely, from the saddest man hung on a tree, crucified, and dead after being put through unimaginable pain."

Father Mark could not contain his laughter. He let it loose.

"Forgive me for laughing, but that was funny." He cleared his throat, reset his posture, and asked, "How do you feel about the idea of punishment of burning in hell now that you're older?"

"Part of me says it's wrong, very wrong. It makes me angry. But the other part still shudders with fear. I resent it, and I'd like to be courageous to pursue my own image of God, but it's not easy."

"God loves us in mysterious ways, and we should trust His love. That is what faith means," he said almost in whisper, feeling inadequate and stupid.

"Mysterious or strange, I don't know. I can't fathom punishing anyone in such a horrendous way, can you? Maybe I don't get what love really means." This time she laughed. "Jesus said to love your enemy, Jesus said to forgive. But God doesn't forgive. Not only does He not forgive, He already built a prison of burning flames to throw in those He can't forgive! But what makes Him the worst psycho is that He keeps them alive in that fire. If He is really such a merciless God, then He needs to expand his prison massively because personally, I don't know anyone who would pass His astronomical categories of sin. So tell me, Father Mark, what are we supposed to do with this psychotic God the Almighty?" She continued laughing.

He felt embarrassed and trapped, but at the same time, strangely charged. Then there was a sudden change of direction in him. It was like being punched in the chest from inside out. The words crawled through his throat, which were then purged before he could control them. "I believe we, the Church, could be cunning. At some point it became to be a pure mechanism of surviving like anything and everything. And it grew bigger and more powerful as if God, after all, gave His blessing. As you see, it still stands after all these years. I'm not saying that makes it right. A person like me suffers every day because of it. What amazes me is how people are attracted to this symbol of hypocrisy. Hypocrisy is a form of self-deception. If one sees it works, it stays and becomes truth, like if one repeats the same lie over and over, he forgets that it's a lie. It even offers the reward of self-righteousness, which is a powerful feeling for the ego. It pumps endorphins into our brains, causing a pseudo-transcendental state. For example, right now I have no idea where this statement is coming from, but I feel quite clever, and I like it. It literally expands my chest. Once you have a taste of that, you automatically want more. The bottom line is that I haven't got the faintest idea." He buried his face in his hands, laughing.

She felt like reaching for him, stroking his hair, and saying, "There, there, I'm proud of you."

He raised his head and continued with his demeanor rather welted and said, "Whatever it is, I'm having a delightful time with you. You've certainly introduced me to a place where I've never been, and I thank you for that. This tug-of-war we have inside of us actually has a referee."

This last remark of Father Mark pricked her ears.

"Referee? Who could that be?"

"Sometimes you're torn between what you want to do and what you're supposed to do or what you're expected to do, with multiple voices deciding the matter, so to speak. And there's someone or something that observes this. I call this observer a 'referee,' like in a boxing match. It monitors the game, determining what's right, what's wrong, and what's fair. But this observer doesn't decide which voice to follow. It only informs. The decision is made by different entities. Self and Being—they go to war sometimes to be the deciding power."

"I think I know what 'Self' is, but who is this 'Being'?"

"It could be my soul, if you will," he said, humbling his heart.

"Your soul likes to fight?" she asked, which threw Father Mark into a roar of laugh.

"More like 'tug-of-war' instead of 'fight,'" he said, lightly squeezing the inner corners of his eyes with fingers. "Now tell me, what does your soul fancy?" he asked, continuing to laugh, feeling tremendous delight despite the uneasiness stirring inside. Oh, when was the last time I laughed like this, he thought.

"My soul is indifferent of what I do or don't do. She is moody, laconic, and likes to be left alone. When I picture her in my mind, she's a dark cloud on a hot and humid summer afternoon, patiently waiting for that one strand of energy to strike her, making her erupt into a humongous storm." She drew a large sphere in the air using her arms, rounding her eyes when saying the word 'humongous.' "I adore her. I adore her solitude, patience, and fearlessness. Only, I am hardly her."

"That is quite a summation. I like that."

"Forgive me for saying this, Father Mark, but what you described as a tug-of-war between Self and Being seems to me to be a drama that we can't have enough of. I think we are too serious about ourselves. We tend to place too much importance on everything we are about. At this point, I'd like to be just a spectator in a theater watching the show called my life, no referee, no power struggle between Self and Being. It makes me get out of bed in the morning. These dramas, both in me and in others I observe, are beyond entertaining. They're fascinating. There's no harm in it when it's just a drama. You not only watch it, but you also get to play in it. And obviously, sometimes you don't like the role you have to play, especially when it happens to be the daily show that's lasted for long years. But the idea of living in a drama has its benefit. There's no 'Self' in it but only roles that the Self plays. And 'Being,' which according to you is the soul, which I'm inclined to agree with, couldn't care less about the drama. It's occupied with other things. Well, so far that's how I like to see it."

"If you separate you, the person called Miri, from your own 'Self' and 'Being' then who are you when you refer to you as 'I'? It's very intriguing, but…" He could not finish the sentence, because he could not fully understand his own mind.

"Can it be that my 'I' happens to be your 'referee,' the observer? Perhaps unlike your referee, my observer has a different career. It became someone I call 'me.' Oh, what do I know, Father! Only, it's fun talking to you."

He saw a shadow of emptiness passing by her in his mind's eye. "Did you not say that the drama of life makes you get out of bed?"

"Something has to get me out of bed, right?" she said, stretching her torso.

"Are you happy with your life?" he asked, half knowing her reply, but then again, maybe not.

"There might be a thing or two in my life that could be called happiness. It's just that I detest the word 'happiness.' It belongs to the world of deception; it's manipulative. The word itself is too unreal."

"How would you describe the absence of unhappiness?" he asked.

"Contentment, wholesomeness."

He looked up and rolled his eyes from side to side as if searching for a spider on the ceiling, rubbing his chin until it turned pink. "Contentment, wholesomeness…Those words carry more weight. They're more substantial, grounded…"

"Trustworthy but not without patience," she finished his sentence.

"But they're just words. To some, or many, those words would be interpreted as happiness."

"I understand, but to me they have an obvious difference; it would be like calling sugar 'salt.'"

"Yes, yes. I can relate to that. But indulge me once again, why such detestation for the word 'happiness'? Why do you think it belongs to the world of deception?"

"It can't exist without being faced against sadness or darkness. To me, it's a seductive monster. It's greedy and thoughtless. It's like opium; you have to keep increasing the dosage to get the same effect. That's why I detest it. I know that feeling. But whenever I get that feeling, I get suspicious; I feel invaded. I know it's just a word, but I cringe when I hear it. I know contentment and wholesomeness are more trustworthy, more sturdy, but they can be boring and too mature. But I choose to be bored over being excited by deception. I don't know. My mind might be too lazy, weak, or lacking in courage to further investigate what happiness means…Oh, once again, I don't know what I'm saying. I'm just posing as a spiritual hedonist, a kind of wholesome one though."

"Meaning?"

"I'm not sure. I don't know why I said that. My rambling—unruly but free thoughts lift my spirit, they're intoxicating…" She left it at that, to which he gave a knowing nod even though in reality he had no clue. He wished he could have written down some of the things she said to think about them later.

"What is spirit to you?"

"Oh no. No more of the terminology stuff, Father. As you said, they're just words."

"Right, right. I thought I would hear your interesting description again. That's why I asked."

"I appreciate your frank talk with me. Honestly, when I came to see you I didn't plan on talking to you about this subject; this is by far better than what I expected from—"

"From a man of the cloth?" She smiled as an answer and received a smile back from him. "You're an intelligent girl, and I hope what we talked about here together will be beneficial to both of us. You certainly gave me a lot to think about, and I know I'll enjoy every minute of revisiting our conversation." He raised his hands and pressed his palms together in prayer.

"I have one more question. Why do you think I dread coming to Church, but I still do, and at times I resent the fact that I feel guilty when I skip Sunday Mass?" The deep voice she had been speaking with changed back to that of a teenage girl, and he was inwardly startled once again.

"Isn't that strange? You just told me you're a wholesome spiritual hedonist," he said jokingly.

"Posing as one, a rather confused spiritual hedonist, at the moment," she corrected him.

"Right," he said. "To answer your question, I can only compare what you say to my own habit of putting on this black robe every day."

"Father Mark," she said, "if I've been too obnoxious…I know I've been. Forgive me if I made you uncomfortable and perhaps caused you to sin on my behalf."

Her air of seriousness made him laugh.

"I'm more in a state of being somewhat taken aback than being uncomfortable. However, to be honest, I don't know the root of this feeling of being taken aback. I have yet to think about it. But I know I'll have fun with it. Going back to your question of why you feel guilty when you miss Sunday Mass and so on, I think you already have your answer. You just want to compare yours with mine. Isn't that right?"

"Yes and no. Yes, I have my own answer, sort of, but I'm not in sync with it. I've never liked being in church during service. Mass is always so long and boring. I feel like a stewed vegetable during Mass, but I feel better after an hour of enduring the torment, well actually, I could jump in the air and click my heels with joy that it's over one more time, which makes me feel silly, dishonest to myself, like I completed my duty by hating every second of its duration."

"Once our mind is trained to do certain things, it stays in you like the beams that support your house. One can't destroy it just because you dislike it. It's like taking strange satisfaction from completing things that you dread doing, a sense of having it done, getting it out of the way.

"But I think there's something else at work. Worshipping is all emotion. The tough world out there does not appreciate emotion, but the Church does allow it. I'm not talking about social activities provided by churches. The Church offers diversity, distraction, if you will. It's a place one goes to exercise his belief that he's in good hands, in spite of the daily harshness out there. There's a spot in our heart that all the reasoning and logic in the world cannot touch. This belief that something powerful is looking over you brings out a hope and strength that refreshes you with the energy to tackle another day out there. Even though you dread attending Sunday Mass, you know you feel better equipped and perhaps even shielded. It's also about the ritual. It offers a sense of completion, as you mentioned. It adds power to the will. However you look at it, it's powerful stuff, and you shouldn't feel silly about it. I do think Mass needs to improve. I understand how painfully boring it can be, for young people especially. Your disliking it is quite justified to me."

"We are superstitious creatures," she said.

"Why not?" he said, shrugging. "The word 'superstition' has gotten a bad rap throughout history from the Church and scientists, but this need of ours to worship stems from our nature of being superstitious."

"But we see people—intelligent, good people who deny that," Miri said.

"Oh, that's just self-importance that got carried away. I'd say they 'choose to deny' it to describe those people more accurately. Those people who put down others for believing in supernatural forces are simply in denial in an attempt to assert to themselves that they are not weak. Yes, they tend to discount superstition as a weakness. They scream that it's not scientific, not provable. But can they prove their truth? It's just a pointless argument. You know what I'm getting at. It's their belief, or rather, they claim it to be their belief, which makes it their form of religion, a religion that denies the existence of God. Think about it. What is science to us, to human beings? Scientists discovered things that were there to begin with. They invented things only by using things that were there to begin with. Granted, I am grateful for that. But why bash God or even witches?"

"Father Mark, you can't generalize all scientists as being non-believers. I do know some people with scientific minds who believe in God or are very superstitious. Some go to fortune-tellers religiously."

"Of course, but you know who I'm talking about. I'm talking about people who take pride in denying the human need to worship whatever it is. I think it began perhaps with the hatred for the Church, because sadly it caused a great deal of tragedy to humankind. People saw and experienced the unimaginable suffering that was committed in the name of God, which the Church enforced throughout history. Anyone who raises a weapon, either by words or actions, does so because they are insecure with their belief in being a non-believer, just like believers do with their opponents. They want more people to join their side in order to secure their belief of non-belief, the same way our Church has behaved."

"The Church, all Christian churches, condemn anything other than Christianity as heretical, don't they?" she asked.

"The same psychology as I've explained. And it's determined to stay as the most legitimate."

"It sounds like a bloody fight over the idea if there is a man on the moon."

"Well put," he said, looking at her with humor in his eyes. Then he said, "You asked me who Jesus is in the beginning of our conversation. I'd like to ask you the same question."

"Didn't I tell you already?"

"Yes, you did. Let me rephrase the question. You said he was a man, a good man, but how…"

He was struggling to form the question properly when she said, "Yeah, I think—no, I believe he was a man, a man with esoteric knowledge. Is that what you wanted to ask?"

Actually, he was not sure if that was his exact question, but strangely her statement covered more than what he was wondering. This quick and unhesitant answer from her before his question hit the air made his skin crawl. Why? He had no clue. But he knew he had to stop before more damage was done, damage to himself. "Well, overall, I like to think the Church is a barn to keep the cattle in. Ha, ha," he said, looking at the watch on his wrist. "Speaking of barns, it's been delightful, but I need to tend to my cattle."

She sensed an abrupt change in him as if he were retreating back. She got up and thanked him for indulging her. "It was most enlightening," she said sincerely, feeling a little awkward. They shook hands, and she left the office. She didn't forget about her disturbing dreams, but strangely, they didn't seem to matter anymore, at least not then. But Father Mark's abrupt dismissal of her was puzzling, and she wondered if, after all, he must have a pathology of his own. At that abrupt moment, he had looked rather imbalanced.

She felt sorry for him for no reason known to her. But that sorry feeling made her cheerful, like she did something nice for herself.

The sky was heavy with dark clouds. After being near a stove, the biting chill on her reddened cheeks felt refreshing. She was glad she went to see him, although the initial reason of the visit wasn't addressed. She couldn't tell if she liked him, but there was certainly a feeling of gain by meeting with him. She walked home the same route she had taken coming to the church. It looked foreign; it was the same road, yet it looked different. She could hear the noise of cars and people, which she didn't notice before. A vendor selling roasted chestnuts seemed like he just appeared out of nowhere. She walked slowly but lightly. About halfway to her house, she heard a piano playing. She looked around, following the sound. A beautiful, melancholy piece was flowing out of a cracked open window of the second floor of a small house with a sign that said "piano lessons." She stood next to a skeleton of a poplar tree and listened until the piece was over. She couldn't peel herself away even after the piece was over. She had to find out the name of the piece.

She walked up the stairs of the apartment and knocked. An old man who looked familiar opened the door. "Can I help you?"

She quickly bowed and apologized for intruding. "Can you tell me the name of the piece you've just played?"

"Oh, I know who you are," he said, stepping aside while motioning for her to come in. She hesitated, unable to remember who he was although the sense of familiarity was real. "Don't you remember me? I used to give your sister Sohee lessons at your house."

She couldn't remember. It must have been some years ago. The tiny old man invited her to sit on a chair and asked how her family was. She gave him an empty answer but politely sat on the edge of the chair.

"So, you liked the piece I played."

"It made me stop walking, and I listened to your playing right outside. What's the title?"

"It's 'Piano Concerto Number Two' by Rachmaninoff. Quite moody, wouldn't you say?"

"Quite."

"Do you play any instruments?"

"No, sir. I'm tone deaf," she said, smiling sheepishly, repeating the title of the piece in her head, hoping that he would play it one more time.

"Nonsense. Anyone who gets captured by a piece like this must have music in them. Rachmaninoff is my favorite. Have you heard of him before?"

She answered no by shaking her head.

"The piece you heard was a big comeback for him. He suffered from depression and writer's block for years after a disastrous concert, rumor has it, intentionally sabotaged by the conductor. His depression was treated through hypnosis by a doctor whose name escapes me now. This was the piece he wrote in dedication to the doctor who successfully treated him."

She stood up thanking him when he said, "Would you like to hear it again? I have about ten minutes until the next pupil arrives."

"I can't ask you to play on my behalf..." But she was sitting back on the chair. The tiny man started, and she listened with utter respect in her body and soul. It moved her again, sending her down to the bottom of the well where her orphaned sorrows were caged, scooping them in its arms and releasing them as doves. It was the ascension of sorrow.

Before the piece was over, his pupil arrived. Miri got up and gave him a deep bow, pursing her lips hard to prevent her eyes from welling up, and left. She ran down the stairs, freeing her tears. "Oh what a joy to cry over the emancipation of such nameless sorrow!" Snow began to fall, a puff here and a puff there, like the feathers of white birds.

She walked home briskly and went straight to her grandma's room, where she was doing her rosary. When she saw Miri, she put down the rosary and smiled.

"Grandma, Father Mark said that he loved your steamed buns, the kind with sweet bean paste," she said, getting a comb and hair oil from a drawer.

Her grandmother looked up with a wide smile, the wrinkles on her face rippling. "When did he say that?" she asked, delighted.

"I ran into him in the street".

"Oh, I do like him. I wished he could be my grandson-in-law".

"That's not possible, Grandma."

"Isn't that a shame."

Miri sat behind her grandma, undid her hairpins, and started to comb her long grey hair. She let out a long pleasure-soaked sigh, closing her eyes. "Grandma, could you bake the buns for me soon?"

"Why? For Father Mark?"

"No, I have someone else I'd like to bring them to. There's this piano man, you might know him too…"

- 23 -

Father Mark left his office right after Miri's departure. He didn't have cattle to attend to, as he had mentioned to Miri. Actually, he needed to see his mentor, Father Gregory. While he was talking with Miri, he realized that he was getting carried away. When she asked, "Who is Jesus to you?" he became excited, too excited. And when he saw the teenage girl taking such interest in what he had to say, he let his guard down. He felt that he finally met a youngster who reminded him of why he became a priest. When he was first assigned to this church, he was glad that there was an active youth group. He wanted to be a spiritual gardener for young people, to help them blossom with a healthy spiritual life.

Seven years later, his initial ambition had to be moved to the back burner. He enjoyed popularity among the youth, but not a single one of them was interested in their spirituality. He became a chaperone for their social activities, which made their parents happy. He had no choice but to carry on with an aching spot in his heart caused by disappointment. When he met his confessor Father Gregory, now partially retired, he poured out his disappointment. Father Gregory was a godsend to him in many ways. He not only made him perfectly comfortable but also was a man who possessed the gift of endless understanding and unconventional wisdom. Father Gregory became his spiritual gardener. Ever since he came to know him and learned to trust him, his days were never complete without seeing him.

When he arrived at Father Gregory's room in the rectory, which was located at the top of the hill looking over the church, he found him reading the sports section of the newspaper, sitting in front of a wood-burning fireplace. Father Gregory explained, "Now that I have so much time on my hands, I thought I'd get to know things I had no interest in all my life."

"Found anything interesting?" Father Mark asked, chuckling and sitting himself in a chair across from him.

"Well, not so far. I'll try again tomorrow," Father Gregory said, putting away the paper. "Cold out?"

"Biting."

"You look a little drained, what's the matter?" Father Gregory asked, signaling his desire for a cigarette. He used to be a heavy smoker. He claimed he quit, but he always wanted one whenever Father Mark showed up. "You know, son, smoking less requires more discipline than quitting," he used to say. Father Mark fetched a cigarette and lit it for him. He took a drag as if nothing pleased him more and said, "Let's have some tea. Sister Marina just brought a freshly brewed pot." Father Mark got up and poured tea into cups from thermos. "Lace mine with some brandy."

"I know, I know." He sat down, watching Father Gregory smoking and sipping tea with brandy.

"So, what's the reason behind this ashen face?" he asked, putting the teacup down on the table.

Father Mark told him about Miri's visit, their conversation, and his regrets. "I was overly excited to meet a young person that I had given up finding. But I got scared. I heard myself talking to this young girl like the way you talk to me. I wanted to stop, but I couldn't, until I managed to stop rather abruptly."

"It was a sensible thing that you stopped. You found your audience and couldn't let go of the opportunity. But it seems that you're more shocked at how much your understanding of faith has changed when you listened to yourself talking to this little lamb."

"But Greg, while I was talking to her, I forgot that my audience was a little lamb. When she asked, 'Who is Jesus to you,' I sensed that she asked the question just to confirm her suspicion. She was mocking me, I'm sure of it."

"So you unleashed your defense."

"Perhaps so. But I clearly saw her attitude changing. She liked what she heard, I'm sure of it. And we even laughed together. The conversation could've lasted longer if I hadn't cut it short. As I said, it scared me suddenly, and now I'm confused and full of regrets."

"How did it scare you?" Father Gregory asked.

"First, how easily she understood me. It excited me, but at the same time, she made me see how unstably rooted I was with my own assertions. Second, I enjoyed too much behaving like you, especially with a minor. I used your rhetoric as if it were mine without shame. Lastly, here I was imitating you, but she was not like me with you. Several times during the conversation, I was so taken aback, I had to rearrange my posture to disguise my inner gaping."

Father Gregory burst into loud laughter, jerking back his head. "She surely doesn't sound like how you used to be. You were such an ass. You argued about every single word I mentioned. Back then, blasphemy used to be your favorite word when you became uncomfortable with what I said. But you kept coming back, and honestly, there were times I dreaded seeing you at my door. You simply wouldn't let go until you were satisfied. And here you are, wondering how come this innocent lamb understood things you had to struggle so hard to achieve," he said, wiping his tears from laughing so hard. "But seriously, in all fairness, there are loads of people like her you haven't encountered. Those people don't need religion. It's in their blood. They know before they know that they know. You and I aren't one of them. Their ankles are chained to the tree of knowing. Being is all that matters to them. You and I still swim in solipsism. These people are surreal to us but natural. We are wannabes. Let's say I am at best a fetus and you, you are thinking about becoming an embryo. We are ordained yet shivering heathens. So there's no need for you to feel inadequate. It's one of those mysteries we frequently talk about. You and I are at least fortunate to have the seed in us."

Father Mark trembled and said, "Frankly, there was a moment when her demeanor changed as if someone other than herself took over. Her eyes became ageless, and her voice got deeper and raspy. Then, in a blink of an eye, she returned to her teenage self. I felt my skin crawl."

Father Gregory laughed again, handing him his empty cup for a refill. Father Mark got up and fetched him a fresh cup of tea laced again with brandy. He lit a second cigarette for him with a scold in his eyes. "Why? Did you feel you were chatting with the devil?" Father Gregory asked, still laughing, blowing the smoke to the ceiling.

"Oh, you should've seen her at that moment," Father Mark said, suggesting that he should stop laughing at him by hardening his eyes.

"She's what, fifteen, sixteen?"

"Somewhere around there."

"It's her youth that's bothering you. And…Perhaps you were resisting learning a thing or two from one who is so green."

"Is that what you think?"

"Such a quality has nothing to do with maturity. We might know of this kind more if we, our know-it-all ancestors and people like you and me, didn't burn them to death. Look, I'm not saying she's this or that. What do I know, she might be a poet in the making, an artist of the thinking kind. Mozart composed a symphony at age of five, and we know such a unique gift is possible. But if a certain five-year-old could fly and speak in tongues, what would you do? All the same, the five-year-old had as extraordinary a gift as Mozart. But we shouldn't try to categorize. They all belong to God's realm. We shouldn't try to decipher because we can't. Every single experience deserves its own shelf. This is just another sort. You wait and see what you come up with, with this experience. People like you and I who chose this journey have to welcome every experience. Our initial reaction to something out of the ordinary is useful only as a reference. You might say it's white, while I see it as blue, but it could be totally something else and continuously changing. Does it really matter who she is or what she is? What matters is that you've encountered something in you. A simple afternoon chat with a young person gave you a chance to peek at yourself." He continued, "Undoubtedly, it was an experience for you. That should be a precious enough thing."

"When you said 'chatting with the devil,' I felt that idea clicked or joined with the bewildered particle in me looking for a clue that explains this girl. I guess I still have devil phobia. But I know you're right. It's about me, not her."

"Well then, the mystery is solved for the time being."

"One more thing, Greg," he said, raising his forefinger in the air to keep Father Gregory's attention a while longer. He arched his brows and waited. "Don't laugh at what I'm about to say…Well, laugh if you want, I don't care…"

"I'll do what I want. Get to the point."

"I had a distinct feeling that she might be a shaman, a real young one."

Father Gregory laughed, not at what Father Mark said, but at his body language. He said the above statement in a metallic whisper, leaning his body toward him as if passing along unsavory gossip.

"Oh, that's what disturbed you. Your shaman complex was at work again. You still think they're the devil's disciples."

"Of course not. I happen to have met a few in my life, and I certainly don't think of them as such. They always emit a strange energy, timid and fearless at the same time. They seem lost and lugubrious but have no qualms about it. And that's the energy I received from her. And I felt sorry for her. I felt she was cursed. The emotion that passed through me was very foreign, intriguing, and unsettling. I liked it and repelled it simultaneously."

"Congratulations! You found fellowship with this young encounter."

"What do you mean?"

"Why do you think you're wearing that black robe with a thousand buttons, making the sign of the cross in the air sententiously? Are we not one of them, shamans, or aspiring shamans, to be more accurate, only without the blessing of such a gift but still existing on the same plane?" He giggled as he looked at the bewilderment spreading on the face of the young priest. "I was just amusing you. Yet I believe that there's a certain something in us. Perhaps our gift is being curious, and our curiosity receives some of these shamans' esoteric or sorcerer's signals, like inquisitive bystanders without the ability to interpret. I don't think we are shamans. Gravity behaves in a different manner toward these people. This world doesn't matter to them as much. They've been existing from the beginning of time. Without them religion could not have happened. You and I have talked about all religions being rooted in superstition, which comes from our desire to manipulate our fate. It's heresy to the Church, but Jesus walking on water is a holy miracle."

"Witchcraft," Father Mark said, narrowing his eyes humorously.

"Would you stop using that word 'witch'?" Father Gregory barked at him.

"Why? What's it to you?" Father Mark teased him, having a little fun doing it.

"It annoys me, that's all. It cheapens the moment. I prefer the word 'esoteric.'"

"I'm sorry. I didn't realize you were in a picky mood."

"Yes, I am quite in that mood. Please allow me that pleasure for a moment or two. Now, where was I?"

"We were discussing 'witchcraft.'" At this they exchanged side glances like two little boys.

"Holy water is a good example," Father Gregory continued, "But as you know, I don't denounce such a practice. It gives a sense of protection that brings out some courage in us, like a lucky charm. It also made us lazy and dependent, though. Anyway, holy water and the Cross were not good enough powers to satisfy people. The Church had to compete with the power esotericism still had over people, so it began to condemn these people as devil worshippers and burned them on the stake accordingly. Esotericism went underground, and the Church succeeded in stopping the individual practice of spirituality, although of course, not completely. And here we are representing the very Church that might have killed many answers to the mystery of the universe…a real charm of God…" Father Gregory's eyelids turned pinkish from the brandy.

They were silent for a while, looking at the burning wood in the fireplace. He started again, still looking at the fire, "Remember I told you about the time I was hiding in a Buddhist temple during the Korean War? That quiet monk who sheltered me told me once that a true shaman didn't engage in the teaching of others. 'It's impossible for them to do so,' he said."

"Did he tell you why?" Father Mark asked.

"No, but he mentioned that they were solitary beings. Their one and only goal is to find their home, whatever that means. They travel in and out of different dimensions, but with many difficulties and hardships, unlike the folklore that tells of their ability to turn on and off at a snap of the fingers."

"Then who are these people we see around us like fortune-tellers and séances, you know, people we usually describe as shamans in a nutshell."

"I asked this monk same question. He said those were failures. Gravity won them over too. And one interesting thing he said that I still think about from time to time was that true shamans—to describe in terms of Christian doctrine—were the ones who didn't take a bite out of the apple in the Garden of Eden. Isn't that marvelous! I strongly believe we, you and I, aren't the type who would pass up a free bite of an apple."

Father Mark felt a little inferior to these esoteric sorts. "But we're still blessed with this torment of wanting to know, right? There must be something in it for us. By no means should we discount that role," he said, rubbing his eyes.

"Have supper with me here. I'll call Sister Marina and tell her that you'll eat with me," Father Gregory said, picking up the phone.

"What are you having tonight?" Father Mark asked.

"Don't worry. It's chicken night." Father Gregory was Irish. He often enjoyed organ meat. Father Mark hated it. Father Gregory started to giggle, hanging up the phone and bobbing his head and shoulders.

"Did Sister Marina say something funny?" Father Mark asked, wanting to giggle like him.

"No, no. I just remembered what your young girl described, how she felt like a stewed vegetable during Mass."

That night Father Mark wrote in his journal:

Today I've learned something. Something about nothing. Nothing is what I left behind. But when am I going to catch up with this nothing, a nothing that is saturated with chaos? It's discouragingly dark, but there's a promise, like a mother's voice coming from the darkness.

-24-

Seven years ago when Father Mark was assigned to the church, he found it gloomy and depressing like a tomb. He organized a youth group, social gatherings for elderly, and a counseling program. The youth group and the social program for the elderly gave life and a human touch to the church. The congregation grew, which made the head priest happy in spite of his initial reluctance to approve Father Mark's idea of opening up the church to others. The head priest had thought the idea was rather vulgar. "Those activities belong to the Protestant church," he said, with the corners of his mouth turned down. But being a terribly indecisive person, the head priest always ultimately let others decide. After he saw that the congregation was growing, he pretty much let Father Mark do whatever he wanted.

There were four residing priests in the church, and Father Gregory was one of them. Father Mark was drawn to him from the beginning. He came to this remote place from Ireland as a Catholic priest some thirty years ago. Mark was curious and admired the faith of the man who made a journey to a land that was barely on the world map at the time to serve God. He wanted to find out the story of this man who drank and smoked too much and was criticized by other priests for his unorthodox ways. When Mark heard his homilies during Mass, he felt that Father Gregory possessed something beyond the knowledge of catechism. He chose him as his confessor. Through the years of their relationship, Father Gregory destroyed and rebuilt Mark's spiritual world many times. There were times, numerous times, when Mark swore never to see him again. But he found himself at his door again and again. Finally, Mark realized that Father Gregory was the only one with whom he could be absolutely honest about his doubts and bewilderment. Besides the arguments they had, being so raw and right in the face, made him forget that he was a grown man of thirty-something. Father Gregory made him revisit his youth and taught him to retrieve a long-forgotten innocence. When they were together, they became two young boys. There was no posturing, no gauging and weighing, or second-guessing. Father Gregory was a man of knowledge with a unique, or at times even frighteningly blasphemous, and also a good storyteller. He constantly read books that came from England or America. His first language being English, he had privileged access to these publications, for most of them were not available in Korean translation. He introduced the works of Western philosophers, writers, and artists to Mark, which he soaked up like a bone-dry sponge but not without heated arguments at times. Father Gregory never posed as a teacher; he always presented himself as a storyteller. But in Mark's heart, he became a mentor and a Godsend friend.

"You know the mistakes of these clever fellows?" Father Gregory said one day, criticizing the historical moguls of thought, who more or less shaped the intellectualism of the modern era. "They believed their own shit and shut their doors to disagreement. Their view of life became the ultimate truth to them, instead of seeing it as an angle, just one angle of the view. An object sitting on a table looks different from different angles, not to mention the object itself goes through endless changes like everything else. They mistook their version of truth as the Universal anatomy of truth. It's undeniable that they offered a person like me a thing or two to chew on. But to my mind, they are too conclusive. This is a tragedy. The same goes for the Church and any organized religions. But ironically, without them, I am not who I am, and my hat is off to them for that. Thanks to them, I was able to unlock many doors within me. Only, if they had said 'I was wrong,' or 'I don't know,' once in a while, they would be more beautiful. They crowned the brilliant thoughts they unleashed, thoughts which had received much applause, and became slaves to them."

Father Mark listened to him and said, "But you like them, whether or not you agree with them."

"Beyond liking. It's envy."

"How so?"

"Because I'd like to have a taste of that conclusive moment of 'this is it!'"

One evening years ago, Mark lay down on his bed, stuffing his face with nuts that his mother sent from the farm she lived, half dreaming nostalgically of his childhood on the farm. Suddenly, he realized that this was the first time he wasn't thinking about sharing what his mother sent with his fellow priests and nuns. He got up, his mouth full of nuts, and thought, "What's happening to me?" He quickly packed up the nuts and went to Father Gregory's room. Father Gregory looked at the nuts on the coffee table and laughed. "You couldn't wait until tomorrow? It's already after nine o'clock."

Father Mark said with a touch of embarrassment, "I had an attack. It felt like the nuts I swallowed refused to go down below my chest area. I couldn't breathe when I realized that the alien behavior of gluttony resided in me. It's like I was violated by my own self."

When their eyes locked in the air, they burst into laughter. "You're a miserable sod. Why do you have this need to dissect every behavior of yours? Which is it? Was it your psychology degree or priesthood that gave you the boo-boo on your tender chest?"

"To answer your question of having to dissect myself," Father Mark started, already feeling better. "Let's see. We both agreed that priesthood is a war with sins and that psychology upgrades sins to pathology."

"We also agreed that none of that mattered," Father Gregory interjected. "Wait a minute. I still need to picture which side I was on when I had that attack. Was I a priest or a psychologist?"

"Neither. You were in your mother's arms, suckling her breast." Father Gregory lit a cigarette and continued, "These beautiful nuts were picked by the loving hand of your mother. And you could not honor it just the way it should be honored. You have to bring morality into a situation where you were simply being like a child to your loving mother. Bringing guilt to such a holy moment is obscene. Mark, my dear son, do you see that bottle of brandy?" he said, pointing at the bottle on the bookshelf. "Have you ever seen me offering it to others? Well, I offered it to you, but thank God you don't like it. Ha, ha. My sister in Ireland sends them to me. Every time I drink it, I think about my sister, her red cheeks, her large-knuckled hands, and even the smell of her. 'No one but me,' she must have felt in her heart when she sent it to me, and I want to honor her special love for me by not sharing it with others. The love I feel, the love that's just for me. I can't let others who do not know her red cheeks, large knuckles, or the smell of her take a sip of it. I can't dishonor her love that's just for me."

"That's beautiful. You never told me about your sister," Father Mark said, picking one of the nuts on the table, giving it a look of love.

"Oh, she's my imaginary sister I didn't know of until now," Father Gregory said.

One early spring day during a period when they tended to argue more than agree with each other, Father Mark found himself agitated by people who surrounded him with their problems. He went to see Father Gregory, and he found him outside of the rectory looking at a large willow tree that was budding with pale green leaves. They took a long stroll around the hills. The sun was bright against the cloudless sky, but the early spring breeze still carried a chill.

"These people make me someone I don't want to be," Father Mark confessed in a face that was elongated from a bad mood.

"You believe you're better than them, that's why," Father Gregory said.

"Aren't we *supposed* to be better than them?"

"Listen to yourself. You're agitated by yourself because you think you should be better than them. It's not they who frustrate you. You saw yourself not measuring up to your erroneous idea of who you should be. Don't blame them," he said, looking down the hill against the breeze that was playfully making a tent out of his robe. "And God forbid, don't blame yourself for being agitated. Jesus cursed a fig tree and condemned it to hell when he was so hungry but couldn't find any fruit on the tree. These people are gifts to you. They're your opportunity to expand your limited experience of life, however vicarious it is."

"Then what am I for? I chose to be a shepherd to guide them."

"I'll tell you who you are. You're the blind leading the blind. You said you chose to be a shepherd, but the truth is that you believe you are chosen. Well, my son, it's high time you come down from that self-built pedestal and face who you really are."

"So I think too much of myself. Is that what you're implying?" Father Mark was getting angry. "You know, I can also tell you that you need to come down from your phantom pedestal!" he spat out, with his face turning the color of a carrot.

Father Gregory turned to him and said calmly, "I know that. But I don't have any conflict with it."

"Only a pervert thinks that way." Father Mark quickly regretted what he just said, but his anger prevented him from apologizing.

"That's a serious demotion you just gave me, my son. Didn't you once call me a mole planted by the devil in your sacred world?"

At this, Father Mark laughed in spite of himself. He loved the man. He was the only one with whom he could totally be himself.

"I'm sorry, Father," he said, bowing his head.

"No need. I kind of like that new description of me, Dr. Freud. Pervert..."

"I should've said 'idiosyncratic' instead. He, he, he," Mark laughed sheepishly, scratching the back of his head to emphasize how sorry he was.

"Oh no, don't dress it up with a fancy term. I like 'pervert' better, raw and vulgar as it should be. It feels more human and less clinical. Mark, let me tell you a story." Father Gregory, his hands folded behind his back, slowly turned to Mark, who was standing behind him. A small breeze combing through the strands of Father Gregory's grey hair and blowing his robe reminded Mark of a nineteenth-century oil painting he saw somewhere.

"A long time ago, I was an eager, self-appointed shepherd like you but empty headed. I was like an empty can that makes a louder noise than a full one. On top of that, I was a hot-headed young man, Irish blood, you know. I volunteered my life to help human suffering, in total ignorance of what human suffering consisted of. It didn't take very long for me to be hateful of these people up to the point that I called them names behind their backs. Trust me, you are a lot more patient and compassionate than I was. Their suffering seemed so stupid, selfish, and ridiculous. They listened to my guidance but kept coming back with the same problems. It was like pouring water into a bottomless pot. One time, a young woman in the village came with a bruise on her face. She said her husband did it, that he drank and beat her. He was a good member of the church. That evening I paid a visit to their home. I rode there on a bike, my heart inflated with joy at being a healer of human suffering. The woman wasn't at home. I was received by the husband, who was a big guy but had a kind face. But I have to confess that at that time I had a habit of reading a kind face as stupid or harmless at best. I confronted him about beating his wife, and he denied it in slow speech. He said that the bruise she got was from the goat. She was milking it and slipped, which startled the goat who then kicked her in the face.

"'Father Gregory, my wife has this weird notion of love. She likes to see me jealous. In the beginning I thought it was cute, even sweet. But it became tiresome, and I stopped showing or pretending to be jealous.'

"'That doesn't make much sense. Why would she accuse you of beating her, if all she wanted is to make you jealous?'

"'She gets crazy when I ignore her. This time she tried to tell me how you looked at her, complimented her, and so on. I knew where she was going, and as I said, I got sick of her game and ignored her crazy scheme. Believe me, it isn't the first time.'

"I didn't know who to believe. Maybe there was nothing to believe, but I ended up leaving him with some harsh words. At the time I thought I was being clever. I told him that if I saw any more bruises on her...blah, blah... stupid."

Father Gregory abruptly stopped the story and turned to Father Mark, his thin hair disheveled from the breeze. His large strawberry nose turned purplish from the chilly air, and what seemed to be regret in his eyes made him look older.

"So what happened after that?" Father Mark urged him to continue.

"Nothing. I got on my bike and rode through the country road lit by the beautiful moonlight, whistling."

Father Mark suspected that there was more to the story. He pressed him.

Father Gregory said, "I'd like to keep that part of the story to myself. People like you and I have to discipline our minds. Too often, our agitation comes from helplessness. You get agitated, angry, and even hateful all because you're helpless. Helplessness becomes disappointment at the very people you dedicated your life to help, and you find yourself being angry because they don't please you by getting better, by becoming more like you. You expect to see the fruits of your work. It takes discipline to give up that expectation. When they come with the same problems time after time, treat it as if it were the first time. Sometimes 'let it be' is the best wisdom. These people want sympathetic ears, not your mouth. Unless you have the magical power to fix their problems, no advice you give can reach them. People in general don't or refuse to see they are part of the problem that pains them. Offer them your presence, your ears by all means, but no 'how-to' lists. Your frustration comes from the zeal and belief that you should be a solution provider, which is a noble quality. Your attempt to help might be interference. You really don't know what they're talking about unless you experience their lives, unless you are them inside out. The 'interference' I mentioned can cause irreversible disaster. Listen to them, offer them a nice cup of tea, nod your head kindly, and tell them that your door is always open for them. Stepping beyond that is pseudo compassion produced by the ego. You're looking for a self-compliment to feel 'I'm a special boy,' nothing more. One day you'll realize that you learned more about yourself from these frustrating people and their stupid problems. Therefore, become a receiver rather than a giver. The wall of disappointment has to come down first. If you don't remove this wall, it will get thicker and you'll find yourself stale and trapped, missing opportunities to gain knowledge of yourself."

"I think I understand, but how does one break down this wall?" Father Mark asked.

"You can't ever completely demolish it, and you shouldn't. It's a tricky matter. You need the wall to protect yourself; it also acts like an emotional barometer. Without emotional fluctuations, one loses vitality, the taste of one's life. Perhaps 'breaking down' or 'demolishing' aren't the right way to put it. Actually, I sincerely apologize to my good friend 'disappointment' for misrepresenting it. Balance is the answer. Nothing gets too strong or too weak. Let everything in your mind and brain have an equal voice."

"Wouldn't one go insane by giving an equal voice to everything in your head? Just imagining such a state caves my head in."

"Not necessarily," he said, patting Father Mark's shoulder.

"Not necessarily means there's a possibility."

"Have you ever thought that people we call insane might be the ones who know something we don't? Maybe they have an ability to access the unknown, which is in abundance in this world. And the knowledge they acquired made them unable to function in this artificial world we live in." Father Gregory added, "We experience such states in our dreams. Something deeply tucked inside of us, whose existence we absolutely deny in waking hours, comes out in our least guarded state. Try to bring them out, examine them without prejudice. You'll find the essence of so-called 'insanity' in all of us. The possibility of being human is infinite whatever label—sane, insane, smart, or stupid—you use. All I'm saying is that you should first study yourself diligently in order to expand your understanding of others, especially if you're in the business of meddling with other people's lives. Otherwise, this noble business would become a crime. I call *that* crazy!"

That evening, Father Mark didn't see Father Gregory at supper time. Sister Marina was away, and he was to take his meal in the dining room. After eating he went to Father Gregory with a dinner tray and found him sitting near the fireplace wrapped in a blanket. "Are you not well?" Father

Mark asked, putting the food tray down on the table. The room was dark except for the light from the fireplace. When he was about to turn on the lamp, Father Gregory asked him not to. "What's the matter?" he asked again, placing himself on a chair.

"I've got a bit of a chill. An early spring treat," he said without moving his eyes from the wood-burning fire.

Father Mark felt unwelcome and said, "I brought you some food. I'll leave you alone. If you need me for anything, you know I'm right down the hall." Getting up, he said, "I have a bowl of broth that Sister Marina put in a thermos."

Motioning to Father Mark to sit down with his hand, Father Gregory said, "Your company is my one joy being here. Don't ever hesitate to bother me."

"You seem unusually aloof," Father Mark said, sitting back with a concerned look.

"I'm just enjoying being lazy. It feels so good."

"You look sad, though."

"I've been thinking about the story I told you earlier today, about the young couple," he said with his eyes still fixed on the fire.

"Don't tell me that was a lie again," Father Mark said, shaking his head sideways. Father Gregory occasionally told him stories of his life which he later revealed to be fictions.

"That wasn't a lie. And I'll tell you the remaining part of the story if you'd indulge me," he said, looking serious.

"Okay, you have my indulgence," Father Mark said not totally convinced that what he was about to hear wouldn't be another fiction. It didn't matter. Fiction or not, those stories were always entertaining and left him with a grain of thought to nibble on.

Father Gregory started slowly, very slowly. "When I was coming back on my bike whistling in the moonlight after visiting the husband, my heart was filled with happiness. I was flattered that the young woman had a crush on me, which was not remotely true, but I chose to feel that way. I was not the sort that girls paid attention to. Imagine what it did to me to be included in a love triangle. I forgot the reason why I went to see them. My heart was full of sanctimonious ambition when I rode to their home, feeling that I was an instrument of God. Had I thought about my ability to help them to live happily ever after? No, I hadn't. Had I noticed the reason for my inflated heart going there and coming back so absurdly different? No, I hadn't until much after.

"The next day, I was summoned to the police station for inquiry. The wife's body was found in the barn hung upside down with her throat slashed. The neighbor next door heard that the animals in their barn were being unusually noisy and kept him awake. He came out thinking a fox might've been around. He found her body instead. The husband confessed right then and there. During the police inquiry, I learned that her dead body was already hanging in the barn while I was visiting the husband. Every particle in me was awake and voiced in my head during the inquiry. 'I could've been killed by the husband. What if they think I'm involved? What am I to do with a scandal that's only inevitable in a small village? Am I to be ruined?' Not a single particle in me voiced compassion for the tragedy of this couple. I never forgot the smirk on that inspector's face when I was released. The husband was convicted, and death by hanging was the punishment. I received the sentence of having to live with a vicious scandal that grew like a snowball. I was hit by stones in the street, threatening letters came daily, and my bicycle was mangled more than once. My fellow priests offered no comfort but gave clear signs of avoiding me. I was eventually suspended from giving Mass or any priestly duties. The faded painting of Jesus showing his wounded heart and the cold floor of the dark church were my only solace. I prayed, prayed, and prayed. The loneliness was so abrupt and unreal, and the shame I had to endure that was not mine and the hatred growing inside of me was unbearable. One day it dawned on me that I was not alone in this nightmare; the husband who was waiting to be hanged was in it too. When I realized that, I summoned all my courage and went to see him. He was very grateful. When we shook hands he held onto mine with both of his hands for a while. I remember how this murderer's hands were so warm and human. Large teardrops fell on our hands when he said how glad he was I came to see him. All I could utter was how sorry I was. The obvious signs of suffering in his eyes were too much for me to look at. There was no evil in those eyes. There was only the unspeakable sorrow of a human being that gave up on all possibilities of being understood, however remote it could be. He started to tell me what really happened that day. Frankly, I didn't want to know, but I didn't or couldn't stop him.

"That day, a few hours before I had visited him, he and his wife were having tea together. Out of the blue, she had told him about her visit to me earlier. She started to tease him, saying how sympathetic I was upon seeing the bruise on her face. She told him how she had lied to me that he had beaten her often and that she feared for her life. 'She went too far this time,' he said. 'Here I was having a nice cup of tea, trying to enjoy a peaceful day in spite of her bad-mouthing people, which was her pastime...When she started her evil way of tormenting me again, someone else in me came out, and I struck her with my clenched fist. I had never hit her before, God as my witness. But it happened that day. She grabbed a kitchen knife and swung at me, laughing. She exposed her breasts, saying how men would like to have their hands on them. Part of me knew she must've been crazy, but I became crazy too at that instant. It was like her craziness jumped into me. I grabbed the knife from her hand and punched her out cold. By then the monster in me was in full charge, and I took her body to the barn and hung her upside down for those animals she had abused so much to see, and I cut her throat. I suffered so much from seeing her torturing those animals. It felt so good, God forgive me. And I came back to the kitchen and finished my tea.'

"I managed to ask him what went through his mind when I showed up that evening. He said, 'As I recall, you seemed to be at ease when I saw you that day. I wasn't quite thinking about what would happen to me. When I told you about her constant insane attempts to make me jealous, I almost told you what I had done, but I couldn't because I wanted to be left alone as long as possible. I'd forgotten how good life used to be before her. I wanted to sit with that old feeling alone for a while.'

"I asked, 'Don't you have any regret?'

"'No, she was poisoning me, and that day the poison worked. No regrets. How can you regret what was meant to be?' He added, 'It isn't bad—death, I mean.'

"I asked him, 'Have you thought about what will become of your soul?'

"He said, 'I don't know if I have a soul. I don't know if anyone has one, but I believe in God.'

"'Isn't it the soul in us that believes in God, heaven and hell?' I asked again, not knowing where I was going.

"He said, 'I don't know, and I don't think you can make me understand what the soul is. Maybe I'm too thick, but I'm being honest with you. God is God. I believe He created this world. I believe He created me too, just the way He wanted me to be. What comes next after this life is beyond my imagination.' More tears rolled down his cheeks. This simple man's heart was broken no matter what he said, and I, God's servant, could not help ease his pain. I felt ashamed trying to paint the picture of what becomes of him after his death, as if I had been there myself. How ridiculous my position was! Before I left, I asked him if he needed anything. He said, 'Roasted mutton leg.' I saw him a few more times and would bring roasted mutton leg.

"He was executed not long after. Something in me was executed too. This incident changed me. I learned to question everything, and my view of life, which was once basic black and white, was replaced by a murky whirlpool of chaos. The strange thing was that as I lived through the dark forest of confusion, I became more courageous. The loneliness and isolation forced upon me by the tragic incident became my best friends. Solitude, books—many of them forbidden by the Church—and my confusion were my obsessions.

"There was no sense of life in me during that period, but now I remember that time with the utmost respect. I was giving birth to myself. One day I got on the boat with the Jesuit missionary group heading east. And here I am, my boy." Father Gregory finished his story and sighed deeply.

"That's a tremendous story." Father Mark broke the silence, hoping for more. He decided otherwise when he saw that Father Gregory looked exhausted. "You look tired."

Father Gregory nodded without looking at him. "See you tomorrow, son."

After Father Mark came back to his room, he said a short prayer and went to bed. He woke up a few times from unsettling dreams. In his dream he was running in a pitch dark maze of alleys. He heard dogs barking somewhere, and he was running away from an object. The object that chased after him was two huge eyes. Once he made his way safely out of the maze, he immediately turned his heels and went back again into it. Now he had become the chaser. He was chasing the eyes, missing them terribly.

-25-

Miri stayed in the music room for a while, thinking about the winter day she first met with Father Mark. She came back out to the lounge and saw a group of young boys and girls about her age watching TV. The rice bowl man wasn't there anymore. She turned into the hallway to find the library. The long, narrow corridor was lined with glass walls beaded with raindrops, and the lightning flashed patterns on the carpet here and there. She stopped, leaned against the wall, and watched the lightning zigzagging across the sky. It flashed like an old-fashioned magnesium camera, blinding and surprising you every time. It tore through the sky, bruising it purple and pink. Then the thunder rolled as if it were angry at the lightning for taking off ahead of it. The needles of rain got stronger as they landed on the glass panes, rolling down hurriedly as if they were late for something important.

An orderly was reading a magazine in the corner when she entered the library. He looked up at her and went back to the magazine. It was a small room. A few people were reading in scattered chairs under obnoxious florescent light. The books on the shelves were mostly mystery novels: Sherlock Holmes, Agatha Christie, Sidney Sheldon. There was also a section devoted to Chinese historical novels with martial arts, and a selection of classics like Tolstoy, Jane Austen, and so on. Nothing interested her. They looked too grungy. She didn't like to borrow books from the library, actually. It made her imagine the previous readers turning the pages with their fingers wet with saliva or smearing boogers on the pages. She decided not to bother and left the room.

She walked down the corridor, slowly drawing a line on the wall with her fingertip. She felt like a little mouse walking close to the wall through the long hallway. This time the lightning and thunder didn't mean anything. She just felt like a mouse in a human house. Suddenly, uneasiness suffused through her. It felt like she forgot something important. The constant anticipation of drama both at home and school the tension that hardened her shoulders, drawing them close to her ears; having to wear the mask of one in permanent penitence; the anxiety of having to confront a pejorative bunch daily; and a thumping heart that erected every nerve ending in her body, these were the few items that were missing. This was a good thing, a very good thing indeed, but there was a shadow of concern that she might have lost something valuable, as if the absence of the enemy was the absence of the very breath of life.

Her tormentors' obsequious reminders that her life should not have been went silent. She didn't miss it, but she didn't feel whole either. Her tormentors taxed the air she breathed. Once in a while, they complimented her by calling her a monster; she secretly liked this title for a reason unknown to her. She endured them without altering the core of her nature. She used to think that God made a mistake and sent her to the wrong place. By the age of five, she learned that she had no value to them, and she didn't hesitate to reciprocate their feelings with pure dislike through subtle means. She refused to please them, permitting their loathing of her to be more righteous. She would absolutely lose her balance and harmony if any one of them declared love for her. They weren't attractive to her. This feeling of dislike saved her from lonely suffering, from the longing to be loved by them. She stayed the same no matter how much they pounded on her. One thing changed, though: when she was about twelve, they stopped calling her "stupid" or "idiot" when she began to surpass her sisters academically. She had no hidden motives; it was an unexpected by-product from the love of learning. But it changed her too. She became more outspoken and even somewhat arrogant. Occasionally, she had fun with her family, making them laugh at her clever jokes. Such fun times passed, however, without any suggestion of bonding. They quickly resumed their hostilities toward each other. Miri didn't want them to have a change of heart and suddenly decide to like her. That icy river between them and her was a good thing to her. It gave her a certain freedom, a space where she could keep her nature intact. It would've been a most scary thing to her if any one of them made a dent on her true nature. But living with them day in and day out had not been easy, for they tried to chisel the rock inside of her. So many times she said to herself that she would fly away from this hole but found herself without any plan. "Fly away where, to be what?" Life seemed too short and insignificant to have any plans. She began to feel sorry for anyone who had dreams. That included, to her amazement, her parents, sisters, teachers, and even strangers on the bus.

Her dislike of those people never changed, but it hurt her when she saw them sad and troubled, however ludicrous the reasons might be. A small patch of compassion was growing inside of her. It could've been some pathological coping mechanism. This did not make her life in that household any easier. If anything, it was harder. The pathological compassion got her involved with them. Feeling sorry for someone you dislike was a terrible burden. She saw her sisters sobbing bitterly sometimes. They weren't excluded from the hurt of being less than valuable in the family. No one loved anyone, but they all ached for love. For her sisters, Miri was the reflection of their own insignificance. Their meanness to her was after all hostility to themselves. They fought to gain an inch up the ladder of significance that would lead to their parents' imaginary loving bosom. They did their duties, and they were obedient. Different to Miri's experience, though, people praised them for their artificial pleasantness and plying prettiness. But that never earned them a solid plateau in their parents' hearts. Their parents gave them rewards for their good behavior, making them mistakenly hopeful once again that they would recognize their true value.

As time went by, they lost their grip on the ladder leading to the grand step of significance without gaining the insight that there was really no ladder to begin with. Miri used to question what sort of sickness her parents were suffering in their hearts to be the way they were. Their germs were contagious and infecting their offspring, killing their essential instinct to love and be loved. They wouldn't know what love was if they saw it. For them it was a gym where its members could exercise their neuroses. The family functioned as a small business. Who was the favorite of the day, who would occupy the seat of executive the next day? Father was the sitting despot, and Mother was the presiding enforcer. The girls chucked the hope for love and went for the scraps that their father might share. "Forget the love, I'll go for the wealth and power that the man has plenty of to dress me." Material satisfaction replaced the emptiness inside them, only, complete satisfaction was always a bit out of their reach. But still, it was more possible. Their father's wealth was his oxygen, and the money he gave them was like a treat to a dog. As a matter of fact, he called them dogs sometimes: "Bitch this, bitch that." He spat out the word while sitting on a futon seat, picking his nose until it turned red and lifting his butt to shoot out loud, multiple farts, all without changing his stern expression of a tyrant. When they needed money, they had to kneel down in front of him and show him written items of things they needed the money for. Her mother wasn't exempt from these obsequies. Everyone had a diary of daily expenditures and had to present them to the paymaster for review when required. There was no fixed allowance, and every penny had to be counted by the man. Receipts and exact change also had to be produced to him after any purchase. If he let you keep the change, you were having an exceptionally good day. Miri's mother, who was nearly illiterate, had the toughest time. Once in a while, she called one of her daughters to fill in her expense diary for her. A bunch of green onions for two cents, a few heads of cabbages for twenty cents, and so on. Then, using an abacus, the precise amount spent and left over had to be calculated and entered. They also had to note the rise or fall in price of every item from the previous purchase.

And yet, this was a man whose suits and shoes were made in Italy at a time when one had to go to the black market for any foreign products. His meticulously groomed and styled appearance made him look like a mannequin in a men's store. The most unfair thing here was that he was a good-looking man and clever like a fox.

- 2 6 -

When Miri was a sophomore in high school, she concentrated on her schoolwork, which unfortunately didn't deter the negative attention from her teachers. This was the time to think about college, and schoolwork became massive labor. Eight hours of school were followed by several hours of tutoring, and after coming home at around ten at night carrying a heavy book bag, she would have supper and hit the books again. This routine suited her. Home was a good boardinghouse. Food and shelter. She liked the quiet hours at night studying, listening to pop songs on the radio. She knew that what she was studying was all trivial information with no depth or bearing any consequences for her future. That didn't deter her from liking it. It relaxed her; it was an escape. There was also a shrewdness working in her. She was moving away from her former thought that "life is too short, why bother to make a plan." Her vague plan, which was barely an embryonic idea, started when she began to see the necessity of "food and shelter" while she resided on planet Earth. She had to give some credit to Sohee's unhappiness for this awareness. Although she had no inkling of what she would do to earn a living at that time, she warned herself not to make any hasty decisions. She wanted to have all possible options to choose from. When she was in such a state, something in her escalated, telling her to play the game to conquer, conquer everything. But at the same time, she laughed at herself, inflating her chest, flaring her nostrils, getting all worked up over an idea that she believed to be of the lamest kind. But recognizing such a state in her, however momentary, was disturbing, like she was being contaminated. But such indulgence in the grandiose was seductive and enjoyable. But she knew very well that these seductive, heart-warming, sweet thoughts didn't have a chance against her love of laziness.

Sohee's misstep in her marriage gave Miri a sense of how useful practical shrewdness was. Sohee's marriage was rather a shock to her. This ice queen, who tied the knot with a man who smelled like breast milk, seemed terribly wrong. Miri was nonplussed when her parents gave their consent to such an obvious ill match.

After the honeymoon Sohee came back to take her stuff to her new home, which was dinky, old fashioned, and located in a not-so-desirable area. Miri found her sitting in the living room looking out at the garden pensively. She was not looking at anything. Her eyes were filled with regret. Miri sat next to her and whispered in her ear, "Don't go. It's not too late. Just say you've made a mistake." Sohee laughed at this, but her eyes told her "it's not that simple." She left for her new dwelling only to frequently rush back with swollen red eyes.

By observing Sohee, Miri learned that Sohee's biggest enemy was herself. She had such a gift in blaming, blaming everything but herself. Someone had to pay for her misery. This intense habit of blaming blinded her to the immense potential within her. God forbid if anyone advised her how she could still repair her life! It only hardened her ego, the headmaster of her 'school of blame.' One thing she truly loved was her helplessness, which didn't understand small steps of effort. It only understood the picture of her bejeweled with a crown at the top of the world. Her misery turned ugly as time went by. When her expectations of the moon on a silver platter would require hard work, she started to take valium. And the drama began. She regularly attempted suicide, showing true resilience at this activity. She was resilient in trying to make others feel guilty for her misery. At times, to transfer guilt to others seemed to be the one and only goal in her life. But she underestimated those she tried so hard to squeeze out any juice of remorse; they were more resilient with their lack of caring. Sohee would wake up in the hospital, be sent home, and the cycle would repeat itself again. Miri was often puzzled. Why hurt herself to such an extreme? It must take so much pain and energy to attempt to kill oneself, so then why not use that energy for living? How can anyone treat you kindly when you treat yourself so badly? Perhaps Sohee believed kindness should be purchased. Perhaps she needed loads of money to buy the kindness of which her life was so empty. Sohee's method did not add up. Miri doubted if Sohee really meant to end her life and wondered if she would ever succeed, which couldn't be a success, a fruit she worked so resiliently to get. Miri also suspected, albeit feeling coldhearted, that this drama was aimed at one person and one thing: her dad and his money. But Miri understood her sister wholeheartedly, although she disagreed with her strategy. And frankly, Sohee was more ugly than pitiful to Miri during that period.

Sohee's husband's family had some aristocratic status but no money, a lot less than their lifestyle required. Her husband had no ambition but knew about the good stuff to enjoy life. Money became the source of all Sohee's misery. She expected her father to rescue her. This was the first time Miri saw the pathetic stupidity of her sister for having such an expectation from their father. But her expectation was supported by a new attitude. Instead of begging her father, which was the only method allowed in the family to gain access to some change in his pocket, she demanded and bullied for money as if she was collecting what was owed to her. She claimed she married the guy because he was tender and sweet unlike their father. If she didn't have a tyrant as a father, she wouldn't have made such a mistake as marrying the guy who turned out to be an imbecile in the practical world. She would justify to herself: "Yeah, it was Father's sin that drove her to such a marriage! He could have prevented it, he should have forbidden it, but no, he didn't!" The sins of her father and mother ruined her life. They owed her big time. She wanted, *demanded* the atonement. Her father started to give her money, never much, but with plenty of humiliation.

The money her father gave her went straight to her movie star-like outfits and large tips for the girls in the hair salon or people who waited on her
table at restaurants—you know, purchasing kindness. What she was after
was sharing his wealth. She wanted to be set for life by means of her father's
wealth. When this determination turned out to be fruitless, she began to
take barbiturates, which led her to an occasional overdose. That didn't move
her father, not at all.

-27-

Their father was generous, very generous to outsiders. Although he had stopped going to church since he was a young man, he built several churches around the country and helped modernize the lives of the farmers in the province in which he grew up. He brought electricity, built a water system, modernized their housing, and built a boy's high school for them. He bought them tractors and trucks, cows and pigs, and new roofs made of slate, replacing the old-fashioned roofs of thatched straw that needed constant repairing. The farmers erected a statue of him in their town, and for a while, much national attention was given to him as a philanthropist. Major newspapers wrote about his life story of being a self-made man and a pioneer industrialist. He, of course, wanted to welcome the attention with his chest fully inflated, but a small horror he carried with him lessened the glory: his education ended in the sixth grade. He shuddered; this was in danger of becoming national knowledge. His lack in schooling haunted him throughout his life up to the point that he would sometimes wake at night, sweating. He was extremely careful about using big words in public but always made sure he squeezed in a couple of them. Every occasion he had to speak in public, he doubted himself, thinking he sounded like a simpleton. Miri knew that his anger and hostility was rooted in this shame, and she felt sorry for him when she saw him shrinking in its shadow. He had everything that a man could want, but he chose to suffer with the shame of lacking in one thing rather than being proud of what he had achieved in spite of this lack, which wasn't a puny success in anyone's eyes. It was true in this society that one could never climb up to the status of an honorable man without having higher learning. His accumulation of wealth and reputation of being an industrial pioneer weren't enough to be where he wanted to be. A well-educated man received better seats than a rich man who was short of higher learning. A success story of a man like him always had an unflattering tail attached to it: "He's illiterate, a simpleton who got lucky." Omitted was the fact that he was a clever and hardworking man; this hurt him, shamed him, and angered him. It was like erosion through the nerve endings, like toothache that doesn't kill you yet makes you want to kill. People he had to wine and dine with often—politicians, lawyers, and other elite men—ignored his opinion of the price of rice and sugar or the prediction of the future economy of the country, knowledge which he took pride in. The conversation of their gatherings always fell to the subjects of the classic arts, literature, world history, and so on. They admired each other's depth of knowledge and intellectualism, ignoring him as he sat among them like a sack of potatoes in an Italian suit. He felt, actually believed, that they were conspiring against him to demoralize him. His wealth did not agree with them, however much they wanted to dip their finger in it, he thought. Sometimes after such an evening, he would think that they unanimously tried to crush him, out of their spitefulness of the fact that he, an ignorant simpleton, possessed much more than them by using orgulous means. He figured that out, but that didn't diminish the shame. At the end of such an evening of libations and "just good to be together" bullshit, he would pick up the tab that had been pushed toward his direction as if it were a kind thing to have him pay the bill, to put his heart at ease for experiencing the honor of sitting among them. He paid with gratitude on his face, making them believe that paying the bill for the honorable evening was the least he could do. He received patronizing pats on his shoulder as they said, "What a stimulating night we've had! We should do this more often." He despised them. His envy of them turned into loathing. Envy felt more like a devil. He concluded, "These men are nothing but parasites." They made his admiration of money seem more noble, but it did not take care of his shame. Such evenings left him simmering in anger and typically ended in spending the night with one of the hostesses at the bar.

"I'd rather give a pearl necklace to a pig than leave my money to you" was what he used to say to his daughters. This insult didn't mean much until Miri witnessed the ugly yet powerful dynamic that money played between him and Sohee. It made a human shed dignity like a piece of clothing, but it was a lesson that taught her that she might not be any different from them. It wasn't a sweet lesson. She felt matured by it, but no, it wasn't sweet. She began to pay attention to the meaning of what it was to have or have not mostly in terms of food and shelter. But the newly gained respect for food and shelter hammered a nail in her heart with indescribable discomfort. Her laziness wept inside at the thought of having to earn a living someday. All she wanted was to sail along in life, amusing herself with experiences until it was done. "Suffering or pleasure, life is a good thing," she used to think. Life owed her nothing, but she owed it.

- 2 8 -

By the time she came back to her floor from the library, she wasn't as bothered by the absence of her tormentors. She accepted the sense of emptiness as the presence of freedom. Freedom felt like nothing, she thought. It
was rather bland.

It was in the spring when she received a letter from Mun, who had
moved to Tokyo. By then her nocturnal activity of mountain climbing had
started. How she wished to talk with him! If there was anyone she could
share this with, it would have been him. He would be very interested. But
she could not bring it up in her reply to his letter, in which he had talked
about cherry blossoms, spring festivals for youth, and the many new friends
he made. He didn't say anything about missing her. It didn't particularly
hurt her; she knew that people come and go, that no one stayed. She knew
she'd cherish the memories with him and was deeply grateful that their lives
crossed once, weaving a chapter of their histories together. The melancholy
of missing him suggested a taste of new feelings, feelings of brand new sadness and forced maturity. She wasn't sure if she liked those feelings. She
found herself sometimes listening to corny songs that she detested before,

letting herself be moved by them. She thought her behavior was remarkable in a "who is this stranger in me?" kind of way. When she was released by the hand of the stranger, she resumed her disliking of corny stuff but preserved the knowledge that she would be touched by it again. She realized that the most mysterious thing wasn't the universe, or God, it was herself. When she reached this conclusion she got both excited and frightened. "Who the hell am I then? Why do I keep finding things in me that resemble the rest of the population?"

She met Mun at an English language class that she signed up for in the long winter break a couple of years ago. He and his buddy, Ahn, approached her from the start. Mun was a tall handsome boy with dark eyes, an olive complexion, and fuzzy facial hair. He reminded her of a young James Stewart. Ahn was taller and had a physique like a grown man, but his pudgy Buddha like face with rosy cheeks and cherry lips did not agree with the rest of his person. She used to think that his face didn't mature at the same rate as his body. "A lazy face on an impatient body," she used to say secretly. Those boys sat next to her whenever they could and waited for her to join them at a teahouse after class. She enjoyed their company, and the visit to the teahouse after class became a routine. There was an intelligent innocence about the boys that she liked. The mischievous grin in their eyes was contagious. Mun talked. A lot. He walked and talked in crowded streets without losing his flow and rhythm, as if there was no one but him in the street. Whatever he did seemed deliciously easy. Although there was no indication of surging teenage hormones between them, she wondered what was in her that made them approach her.

One day both boys teased her about how she managed to be not there when she was there. Mun continued laughing in a silly way and said, "You're like one of those stone sculptures in front of a Buddhist temple."

Ahn added, "You look like one too."

Miri laughed with them, even though she did not like Ahn's comment.

Mun quickly amended Ahn's anti-diplomatic comment by saying, "When I saw you first, I said to myself, 'She's right here but miles and miles away at the same time. How does she do that?' Your aloofness is powerfully magnetic." It wasn't much of an amendment, but Mun, in a way, answered her question. She wasn't a bad-looking girl. Her large-boned frame made her stand out among girls like a big fish swimming among anchovies. She looked masculine to eyes that were accustomed to the small delicate features of average girls. "I can't imagine her wearing an apron let alone a wedding dress. A pair of rain boots and a shovel might suit her better." Or, "You poor, unfortunate creature. You should have been born with a thingy between your legs." Such comments showered her when relatives came to visit her house. As a matter of fact, Ahn's unflattering comment, which hurt her a little, gave her a new thing to think about herself. She had thought about improving her looks; she tried, but she had no model to copy from and soon realized that it was too much work. She reconciled herself to her looks and told herself, "You are your own masterpiece. You are an abstraction." And that settled it.

The three of them signed up for the same classes, one session after another, but it was the teahouse gathering that brought them together. It was always Mun who opened up the topic of conversation. He knew a lot. Thanks to his vast knowledge, Miri learned about many "isms." Taoism, for example, which he was big on at that time, or Sufism, Confucianism, many different sectors of Buddhism, and Miri's favorite, Shamanism. This fascinated her. His stories about the "isms" nourished the part in her that had been unidentified until then. They took her to places of unknown time and beyond the horizon of the universe, delightfully expanding the territory of her inner world.

One day she asked Mun how did he accumulate such knowledge. He answered, "If you live in my home, you can't avoid it. This stuff is in the air we breathe. My brother and I grew up listening to this stuff as our bedtime stories."

"But living with music from birth on doesn't necessarily make one a musician," Miri said, shuddering at the image of her parents crawling into her bed to tell her a bedtime story.

"Well, you might say we clicked," he said. "My family is a group of thinkers. At the dinner table, we don't exchange tales of what happened on that day. I mean, we start from telling each other of how our days went, but that is just an introduction. Where we really jump into in the conversation is by talking about the thought process that we experienced from whatever happened or did not happen on that day. In the end our talk becomes such that the incidents that triggered the initial thought shrinks to a minimum. I can tell you are a thinker too, Miri. A thinker smells a fellow thinker. You must have smelled me also, didn't you, ha, ha?" Miri didn't show any expression at that, and the chatty boy continued. "I noticed that you observe rather intensely. I bet there must be an over-accumulation of stuff underneath your massive hair. I can see a budding philosopher in that head. I know I talk a lot, but I like to listen to others too," he continued, stealing a glance at his buddy who was smirking at his last comment. "You need to empty your head once in a while, otherwise there's no room for new thoughts. Am I not right?" he asked, giving a look of "so what?" to Ahn in response to the smirk.

Frankly, Miri could not figure out if what he just said was a compliment or criticism. The title of "thinker" was a brand new concept to her. She believed thinking belonged to the natural bodily functions, like eating and sleeping. She could not fathom that "thinking" was an extra quality. Without resolving her confusion, she made an attempt to reply to Mun on a neutral platform.

"Until I met you, I never paid attention to my inner world. What I think or what I feel or even what I do just passed me by like the air I breathe. True, I tend to remember them on cue, but they pass me by again as memories of memories. What I mean is that I never thought thinking could have any meaningful presence. It's just there. But because of you, I began to notice my observations, thoughts, and feelings, and what they are to me more intently. There's a certain activity that tries to organize my thoughts going on in me. It's like watching your own self for the first time. You're right, I am an observer. I observe to a fault. For example, when I observe something intensely, I wouldn't know if I had caught on fire from hell. I do that even in the midst of being criticized or punished. In such a situation, I become one of the characters, and a part of me participates in what I observe. Thinking comes later, when the memory of the observation revisits me, usually in the form of an analysis. That's when I find out a thing or two about myself, which is good fun. I shouldn't say I analyze my thoughts and feelings only; I tend to analyze the whole situation, trying to give equal weight to all that was presented, which helps me to understand others, even my enemies. One thing is puzzling, though. Whenever I try to write down these things, it takes on different characteristics and becomes a little bit dishonest. I'm rambling here. I learned the value of thinking from you, Mun."

"For a while I was afraid you'd never stop," Mun said gently, elbowing Ahn, winking.

"As Confucius said, 'A decent human being is a man of few words,' which makes you two vulgar," Ahn said, nodding his head like an old man in agreement with himself.

Ahn's family lived by the words according to Confucius.

"He wasn't a man of sound mind. He was a bitter man, a borderline psycho who believed in controlling people, down to how to shit, how to wipe your ass to avoid sin…" Mun said, showing an expression of disgust.

Miri agreed with Mun's disgust. "I would love to throw a rock at him. He believed in the holiness of the hard life. I don't understand why our country adopted his teachings to define what is moral and immoral?"

"I often wonder about that too," Ahn said. "Speaking of bedtime stories, my grandfather read books that ancient psycho wrote over and over. They are his Bible. He reads them aloud, swaying his body. I share a room with him and have to endure this chanting. Sometimes I laugh under my breath because it sounds so stupid and hypocritical, but mostly, I dislike the harshness it preaches. Think about it, you know about the 'seven unforgivable sins of woman' this guy said. What kind of decent human being says that you have a right to abandon or kick your wife out if she could not produce a son, which is one of the seven sins? How about this? You should obey. Obey your king, your government, and your elderly. No question should be asked because they are always right. Obey even your older brother. I bet he didn't have an older brother. Uttering an opinion to your elderly is immoral and should be punished by severe means of shame."

Mun shared his opinion. "He's extreme. Such extremeness only can be produced by mental illness. He said that it's a son's duty to live in a hut next to the grave of his parents for three years after the burial. He should cry day and night in front of the grave, shouldn't take baths, change clothes, or cut his hair for three years. When I heard that the first time, I laughed so hard. But I also realized how the core of our society is still run by his teaching. It's rather scary to see how one sick man's idea became the wisdom, if not truth, that controlled the masses for many generations."

Ahn took over. "This guy dictated how one should eat. He even once said, 'The amount of food an honorable man puts in his mouth should never bulge out his cheeks.' He was a jerk who had issues. We don't really practice the specific details of his teachings in our family, but the core of it is still there, more or less like this society we live in."

"Like what?" Miri asked.

"Ancestor worship, sub-humanizing females, and so on. But we put as much food as we'd like into our mouths, including my grandpa."

She thought about the three girls in her family, treated as subhuman, and how her half-brothers, even though born illegitimately to her father's mistresses, had more privileges than them. "You know, Ahn, sub-humanizing females is not confined to Confucianism. It's a universal male conspiracy to control the fairer sex with the threat of their bigger and stronger fists. But I have to admit that it is females who perpetuated the system and handed it down to generations of younger females as the feminine virtue. You might deny vociferously that you are one of those men who consider a woman as a sub-human. Think again. I assure you that you feel superior or glad when you see the wangbangdoodle hanging between your legs. Veracity isn't always what it seems to be." The boys giggled but cut it short, realizing that Miri wasn't one of the gigglers.

In the fourteenth century, the Yi Chosun Dynasty imported Confucianism to be the new national religion, eliminating the traces of Buddhism from the previous regime. Dead ancestors replaced Buddha, and the series of prescriptive lists, according to the words of Confucius, became like orders from the god of godless religion. You worship the spirits of your ancestors; you sacrifice yourself for your dead ancestors. This morbid philosophy of anachronism taught the people to walk backwards, dominating their lives for several hundred years. Even people who converted to Christianity centuries afterward could not totally abandon the practice. Christianity was for the afterlife, and Confucianism was for the here and now, offering a "how-to-do" list. It was woven into the people's psyche.

Mun said thoughtfully, "We can sit here and criticize leisurely, but none of us here is totally free from it, as Miri pointed out. Our ill-gotten notion of being superior for possessing a penis and testicles remains."

He continued, "I loathe them, those so-called enlightened thinkers. What they did to fellow human beings was irresponsible. They should have kept their thoughts to themselves or politely admitted, 'I'm only speaking for myself.' But no, they had to assert that what they knew was celestial knowledge. Narcissists! I think Confucius belongs to that category, but others such as Lao Tzou or Chang Tzou don't. To me, they were artists, unlike Confucius; I don't get the feeling that they had a special agenda. They happened to express their art, which touches people to this day. I'm grateful for that." Mun spoke with the air of a defensive yet patronizing professor.

Ahn said, "I appreciate your obsequiousness to that bunch, but you are being purblind.

Wasn't it Sun Tzou who declared that humans are born evil? What do you call that, an art? Didn't you tell me that they went into the woods with jugs of wine to spend their days? What would they know about life consuming their lives in woods, in stupor, avoiding life itself? I would gladly accept that it was their form of practicing art or choice of lifestyle. But when they came out and tried to spread their alcohol-based theory to common folks with blank pages, it became narcissistic and irresponsible."

"Art is art, narcissistic or not. Remember when I told you how Chang Tzou woke up from a dream in which he turned into a butterfly, and then he wondered if his waking moment was a dream of a butterfly turning into him? Remember that? And remember you said how beautifully touching that was? What do you call that, an assertion of a drunken man?"

"Wait a minute, I think we have derailed," Miri stepped in. "The main thing is that these guys aren't the blame—narcissistic, psychotic, whatever they were. It was the people who chose to follow them and gave them their power. We don't know how it started, but we know human nature craves for things that give meaning to their lives, things that explain their existence. These guys who we've been putting on trial only happened to be signs on the road. People had the choice to follow those signs or not. Isn't that the base of the argument?"

"One should be quite vigilant not to lose himself in them," Ahn commented.

"That's impossible. One always believes in something," Mun murmured.

"Like how you put all your beliefs under the umbrella of art."

"What do you have against art?"

"It's a vague definition. It seems to be a foggy spray. When people don't understand something but don't want to admit it, they say 'Ah! I don't get it. Therefore, it has to be art!' as if art wasn't supposed to be understood."

"Art is free, and it frees you too. If you and I looked at the same painting or listened to the same music at the same exact moment, would we feel and imagine the same thing? I don't think so. You're right. People tend to abuse the free spirit of art to cover their own insecurity. But art is for your heart only. True art had nothing to do with general opinions."

The conversation derailed once again, but this time Miri retired and let the boys continue, vaguely digesting what the boys were debating.

"I have a feeling we're arguing about different subjects. Is that what you see?" Ahn asked Miri, waking her up from her silent debate, frowning deeply.

"Are we?" he asked again.

"You boys always do that. You start with birds and end up with the tail of a snake."

"What did we start with?"

"We were on the subject of Confucianism in our land…"

"Right. And then?"

"It moved to the hedonistic philosophers or artists…"

They both looked down at the table searching through their memory.

"Actually, Confucius could not mingle with them although history says that they were friendly with each other. His rank was a notch or two lower than the wine-jug-carrying sort. Perhaps that's why he was so angry.

Wouldn't you say he was a bitter man? They say he was super ugly, that a hungry stray dog was more handsome than him. Anyway, he found his destination here, in our country, and unfortunately, his ill thoughts blossomed poisonous flowers that grew like weeds."

"Poisonous flowers, indeed. They're designed to kill human spirits," Mun agreed with Ahn, with an expression of universal concern.

"Why here, in our soil? Could it be possible that our tribe thrives on anger? We all know our people loved to inflict fear in others by methods of quick anger and punishment in the name of 'for your own good.'"

"So true. But I don't think such a practice is uniquely limited to our society alone. One can see that throughout history such a method of maintaining society is global. It's the energy produced by fear that keeps the order in society. Orders and the enforcement of order kills humans by denying the spirits within."

"Confucianism was used cleverly here in this country," Miri spoke, rubbing her eyes and half yawning. "It was introduced as a moral code defining how a decent human being should conduct his life, not as enforced law. It was your neighbors, relatives, family, and anyone you ran into that you had to be careful of. People love to police others, you know. Therefore, the social order expands autonomously at some point. Because it can be a more frightening thing to go against a law than to break it."

The boys nodded with their arms folded on their chests, thoughts rolling by in their eyes. No one talked for a while.

"It kills creativity, the freedom to desire, and injures the human spirit, eventually driving society to depression."

"Maybe for a person like you, but the larger body of the population doesn't, can't, and even won't engage in thinking. They hate thinking. After all—"

"Are you talking about yourself?" Mun interrupted Ahn.

"Don't mind me if I agree with your insult-laced rhetorical question. I don't think much because it simply doesn't happen. I enjoy our conversations about thinking, but that's about it. It never charges me up or leaves me with a grain of salt to taste for later days."

"After all, what?" Miri ignored this particular exchange, wanting to hear what Ahn was about to say before the interruption.

"Where was I...oh yeah. After all, private thoughts are free of danger, but in general, people don't pay attention to their private thoughts. Their attention is too much concentrated on something else."

"And what is this something else?"

"The desire for an easier life for the here and now, which is very hard to do, right? Don't tell me you don't desire an easy life of being well fed, well sheltered, and well clothed. As long as we are flesh and blood, we can't escape from those needs that everyday people have that impels them to use everything within them to get any closer to some security. They don't want to wrestle with the bewilderment of life any more than they need to. So society shouldn't be built by the production of metaphysical thinking, otherwise we would starve, right?"

Miri said, "To tell you the truth, I'm so sick of our country being so economically poor. Will it change, ever?"

"It will when the bourgeoisie hopefuls grow big enough to overthrow the present ruling class."

"Speaking of the ruling class, Confucianism is a godsend to them. We have to wait until it goes out of fashion. Ruling class or not, people would rather die than be unfashionable," Mun said.

"Wow, buddy, that's what I wanted to say before. Art and fashion. Get it?" Ahn shouted, shaking and nodding his head.

"The metamorphosis of morality by the power of fashion," Miri said, smiling widely.

Mun beamed with satisfaction, seeing that the conversation was being pulled toward his alley once again.

Miri asked, "Before I forget, I want to know why you are so attracted to Taoism, Mun?"

"I'm glad you asked. I want my buddy here to listen to what I'm going to say about that. It's true that they were supposedly hedonistic, but that doesn't diminish my interest in them. Unlike Confucius, their thoughts were not rooted in 'how and what to do.' They had more to do with abstract wisdom, allegorical thinking. If they needed to be drunk to come up with what they said, so be it. They spat out spiritual thoughts of beauty like auto-writing, in psychological terms. I'm glad they were drunk to leave those words for a person like me. I suspect that they suffered from the boredom of life, like I suspect of Socrates and Plato, deadly bored. But however you look at it, it's captivating, like strange dreams. I must say, their pain of boredom gave birth to art." He gave a solitary laugh and continued, "But I heard that Taoism became a serious religious practice with temples and monks. Now that is a whole different matter to me. My affection for Taoism has nothing to do with this religious practice".

"Do you know anything about Taoist religious practice?"

"Not much. All I know is that one has to be over forty to be eligible to be a monk. One should sit staring at a blank wall until the third eye emerges, preferably on the forehead..."

"Like the monsters in a comic book, an extra eye in the middle of forehead, ha, ha, ha," Ahn said and laughed.

"Of course you don't grow an eye physically; it means you gain insight into the metaphysical world."

"I know, I know. But imagine one of them gaining an extra eye on his chin," Ahn laughed, taking out a piece of paper and pencil. He started to draw a bald man with a third eye on his forehead, then a man with a third eye on his chin, a man with one on his cheek, and a man with many eyes covering the face looking in all different directions with the exception of one that was sleeping.

They all laughed, looking at the funny drawings. "I like the sleeping eye," Miri said, pointing at the drawing.

One evening after class, they sat quietly munching on the cakes and slurping the hot tea. Miri started out of the blue as if thinking out loud. "Mun, sometimes I wonder if the expression of your thoughts is genuinely yours. Sometimes I notice that you try to match your thoughts to the philosophers. These are people who lived in a different culture and time. There's no doubt that they were gifted with great minds. But after all, it's their minds, their individual minds from their individual experiences. And I'm not sure if I want my experience explained by others," she said.

"You mean you want to disagree when you agree?" Mun said, stuffing his mouth with a cake with a mischievous grin in his eyes.

"I'm saying that I can't be comfortable with the idea that someone else's opinion influenced my life." She continued, "As you guys know, I hardly knew what those great minds had to say. Because of you, I had a chance to be exposed to their knowledge, which undoubtedly fascinates me. But I found something in me challenges some of their assertions. Unlike you, I can't accept their thoughts as the truth of the highest kind. To me, it still remains as someone else's point of view. It's delightful when I find some of their views agree with mine, and I appreciate that someone articulated the floating stuff in my mind. But I reserve the suspicion that our agreements have totally different contexts. I don't know why, but I find myself resisting, too. Whenever their words touch me, I also feel that I'm betraying myself. I agree, but it's not mine. Does that make sense to you?" she said, checking their faces.

Ahn had his eyes closed, leaning on the wall with his arms crossed. Mun was listening to her intently, urging her to continue with blinking eyes. She took a sip of tea, losing interest in continuing.

Still leaning on the wall with his arms crossed and eyes firmly shut, Ahn opened his mouth: "When I was a young boy, I wondered why we have only a handful of descriptions of the color green—the greens of trees, plants, and what not. Because I could see there were hundreds and hundreds of different shades of green among them. But we tend to throw them into a pile of wholesale marked as 'green.' I think you'd refuse to be marked in such a way. What you're saying is that one shouldn't borrow the shade of others just because there's a similarity."

"So what you guys are saying is that I'm a borrower of other's opinions, who lacks any of his own," Mun said, in all seriousness.

"Oh, you do have opinions, loads of them," Miri said. "Only you tend to yield to the opinions of philosophers, dismissing your own. Just because you like what they say, or just because they touch you, it doesn't become yours. All I'm saying is that you should treat your original opinions as well as theirs, if not better. You know a lot, really a lot, and I envy that for sure. But someday I'd like to see that your opinion matters the most to you."

She was stopped by Ahn's interjection.

"I grant that too. You amaze me with how much you know of this particular field. But honestly, sometimes I get the feeling that you're representing them. Somehow it's a waste; it's too aristocratic."

"Really?" Mun said, rounding his eyes. "Am I a show-off?" he said, leaving his mouth open.

"I didn't say that. If anyone has a right to show off, you have that right, I assure you. And I don't think there's anything wrong in showing off, nothing at all. But I never thought that you're a show-off. You like to share what you know, and as you know, I love to listen to you. It is, how should I put it? Help me out here, Miri." Ahn looked at her, searching for a right word. There was an urgent SOS in his eyes when he asked for Miri's help, with a desperate need to be saved from making the mistake of hurting his best buddy's feelings by being misunderstood.

"I think what Ahn is trying to say is that your individual voice, your own argument that is uniquely yours, should be heard along with the thoughts of these great minds. You should hold onto yours. You are a keeper of your own truth. I don't think one should replace it with someone else's. As Ahn said, there are many more shades of green than we bother to describe and unconsciously ignore the unique varieties of the rest."

Miri heard Ahn's voice immediately tailing her own.

"Buddy, that's it. When you asked, 'Am I a show-off?' that says it all. You're not a swank, no, no, no. I know it, and you know it. You don't obsessively accumulate this knowledge to intimidate others, but you do it purely out of love. It's just that we have to inform you of a danger that this knowledge might cause you to abandon your own unique perceptions of shade. Are you consciously aware that your own thoughts are marks of erudition? You can be soaked in, for example, that poetic narration of Chang Tzou, the butterfly thingy. But be sure to come out of it to your own spot. Honestly, my grandpa says things like that all the time, especially when he's tipsy. Would you give my grandpa the same attention? If not, then you have to ask yourself, why not?"

Mun asked, "You don't see the profoundness in the philosophers' thoughts? In their genius?"

"Not really," Miri and Ahn both said at the same time.

"Let me adjust that response a little." Miri explained, "I don't know about Ahn, but I hesitate to call anyone a genius just because they earned fame. I have to talk about my mother here. It's not easy for me to talk about her, especially in a favorable way. One day a small boy, my mother's grand-nephew, stayed with us. His tiny white underpants were being air-dried in the garden, all alone, on the clothesline, moving slightly in the breeze. My mother, who has a heart of stone, said something so beautiful about the tiny underpants hanging on the clothesline and playing with the breeze. If I didn't know her, I would've admired her at that moment. She was a poet, a true one at that moment. At that moment she was absolutely in tune with something perfect. All of us, including my mother and other people of the thickest emotions, experience such moments. No, I don't think these phi-losophers were extraordinary. The reason behind my saying this is not to degrade their teaching or art, but because I'm worried that you think they're way above you, and you are lowering yourself. Meet them on the same plane where you stand. That's what Ahn and I mean."

Mun leaned back and looked up the ceiling, plowing his hair with his fingers. Miri got concerned that they might have upset him again after all. After a few moments he opened his mouth and said, "This is good stuff! You guys put me on a pedestal that I don't deserve. But more importantly, you've helped me to have a glimpse of my future." He looked genuinely touched.

"I'd like to ask you something, Ahn," Miri said with obvious teasing in her eyes.

"Let's have it," Ahn answered.

"When you brought out the 'green' analogy, is it true you wondered about that as a young boy? Or is it someone else's idea. Somehow I can't imagine you…"

"It's mine alright, although the source of it isn't as pleasant as you guys might be imagining."

"Well?" Mun asked.

"Tell us all the same. I smell something funny behind it," Mun urged him, already smiling.

"It is a smelly tale, alright," Ahn said, bending over, motioning for them to put their heads closer together because the content of the tale should be spilled out in the form of a whisper. They nearly joined their heads in the center of the table.

"My grandpa…"

"Your grandpa again?" Mun interrupted, receiving a jab from Miri's elbow at his side.

"My grandpa," Ahn continued, "had some chronic problem in his GI tract at that time. Every greeting exchanged between him and the family during that time was about his bowel movement. Doctors were mostly concerned about its unusual green color. Before anyone asked him if he slept well or how he felt, they would ask him 'what color was it?' My grandpa would answer them trying his best to describe the accurate shade of the persistent greenness of his stool. He thought it was utterly important to describe it as precisely as possible, and as a young boy, I saw him struggling with a lack of words to accurately describe the shade. He couldn't say simply that it was still green or greenish. He had to describe the shade as close as possible, to his satisfaction. Sometimes he looked around for the shade that would match, finding it in the wallpaper or a little speck of green in someone's socks…cabbage-worm green, green as so-and-so's new roof, egg-yolk green, green when you boil chopped parsley and fennel together, seaweed green up against the sunlight…" Ahn stopped a moment, waiting for his two friends who were struggling to keep their laughter as quiet as possible, which eventually caused Miri to hiccup. Ahn resumed. "That's the source of my green analogy. But his accuracy was like a weather forecast. My parents judged his condition that day according to this communication. That was when I realized that there are a million different entities contained within a word."

-29-

Miri found herself speaking freely with them from the beginning. This was very unusual behavior for her. As her natural demeanor tended to be interpreted as rude and inconsiderate, she was generally left alone. She talked to the boys without thinking about being judged, as a welcome participant, and they actually listened to her. Until she met them, she could not remember anyone who paid attention to what she had to say. She was surprised at herself for talking about her life without filtering out the potentially embarrassing or shameful bits. She realized the verbal exercise of describing her life story unlocked a certain gate in her that had been guarded in fear of being judged. The boys' interest in what she had to say encouraged her; she had found an audience for her stories.

One day she told them about the incessant drama in her family. What could have been a sob story was delivered with humor and comical animations. When she noticed that she had the serious attention of her audience, she got all charged up. They laughed, holding their bellies. "It's better than TV drama," Ahn said.

After a while Mun took a polite posture of the exaggerated kindness and asked, "How can you tell us such painful, personal stories in the way you did, I mean, making it sound so funny?"

"Does it bother you?" she asked.

"A little," he answered.

"But you laughed with us," Ahn said, shaking his head in disbelief.

"Would it have sat with you better if I had said it with tears and sighs?" she asked, a bit irritated.

He looked up, his face devoid of his usual mischievous grin, and said, "Oh, no. Not at all. I guess I was asking myself why I'm laughing when I had to feel sorry. I guess I feel guilty for laughing. Isn't it strange, though?"

"I think you're put off by the crude and coarse way I presented the misery of my life. Maybe you are surprised at seeing an unexpected side of me. You think you are a person who'd never laugh at another's misery, but you caught yourself doing otherwise, and it bugs you. Isn't that the case? I tell you, being able to see humor in that situation is a blessing. It's not a distortion, it's a consolation, at least to me. There's nothing strange or immoral about it to me," she said, slightly unsure of her defense. She felt she was being judged.

There was a heavy silence for a moment or two, which was broken by Ahn. "I kind of know what she's saying. As you know, my grandpa and I share a room. One night while he was asleep, he fell out of his futon bed, which was only about five inches in height. I was studying, lying on my futon. I saw him jerking around, out of breath. He was having a heart attack. I ran across the courtyard to my brother, who was in the last year of medical school, and while I was explaining to him the reason why I had to wake him up, I could not stop laughing. The image of my grandpa having a heart attack by falling off a five-inch-tall futon was just too funny. Initially, obvious fright appeared on my brother's face, but soon it was replaced with a painful distortion from trying to control his laughter. I woke up the rest of the family by shouting.

"My grandpa was conscious but moaning with great pain when my brother carried him on his back to the local doctor's. We were running through the dark alleys with the rest of the family following us, including John, our dog. My grandpa was loudly moaning, for the bad teeth in his mouth were rattling from my brother's running, adding to his pain. My mom was crying behind us, my father shouting at her to stop, and the dog was barking, passing us as if it were a family marathon in the moonlight. Then the dog who was running in front of us suddenly stopped, making my brother trip and throwing my grandpa to the bumpy ground. I put him on my back, and we made it to the doctor's, my brother and I unable to control our devilish giggling. Turns out, it wasn't a heart attack. It was gas trapped in his throat. He had buttoned his pajama shirt all the way to the top, which squeezed his neck, trapping a bubble of gas that pressed down on his windpipe."

"Now, that's a funny story. But it doesn't have the same tone as Miri's. Hers is dark and even a little creepy," Mun analyzed.

"My opinion here is that one can see and feel and react to an incident in more than one way. My grandpa is the one important person in my entire life, but my brother and I laughed in the moment of a dire situation that could have been a matter of life and death to our beloved grandpa. Being able to see humor, no matter how gloomy the situation is, is a blessing as Miri said, not a sin. If it's so hard to understand, call it an art; you understand art, right?" Ahn used sarcasm knowing that Mun liked to call anything he couldn't understand "art."

Miri said, "I think the difference is that my humor comes from hostility and Ahn's comes from affection. Mun is right to say that our stories don't ring the same bell, but humor is humor. It's one useful and kind mechanism God planted in us, and it shouldn't be put on trial."

"Come to think of it, I haven't met anyone who doesn't laugh at bathroom humor. That's universal humor, but it's treated as offensive, as low class and insulting. One of the very few things we all share is treated as dirty. We're trained to behave as if we don't subscribe to such bodily functions, but everybody laughs at bathroom humor. One might choose an underground bunker or closet to enjoy bathroom humor, but it's seriously pleasurable stuff. Anyone who says 'no' to it is not only a liar but also has no business hanging around in the human world," Ahn said, beaming. The three of them giggled together for a while, exchanging a few poo jokes.

Miri was the first to stop the giggling and said, "Before I forget, I'd like to tell you something. I'd like to know what you think. Not long ago, a farmer at my father's farm came to see him, bringing with him a fat chicken as a present, a live one. The next morning I woke up from the sound of the screaming chicken. I went out to the balcony and saw my father squatting in the middle of the garden lawn, trying to twist the chicken's neck. He was in his pajamas with a burning cigarette dangling from his mouth. When he realized twisting the neck was not as easy as he thought, he grabbed the hunting knife next to him and stabbed the snow-white bird. But it got away and ran across the lawn, with blood on its white feathers and its neck hung sideways. My father chased after it, shrieking like a sadistic animal with his hunting knife. The dogs tied to their house barked, pulling their chains with excitement. Finally, he got hold of the chicken, stomped on its head with his foot, and ran the knife through its chest. He took off his bloody pajamas and underpants and threw them next to the dead chicken. He stood there naked, his shoulders hunched over, his hair messed up and covering his forehead, the bloody hunting knife still in his hand, with a heart-freezing grin. He stood there like that for a while before he walked back to his room.

"Later I overheard the house staff whispering that his underpants were soiled. They were exchanging not–so–pleasant smiles. Of course the chicken was for dinner that day, nicely browned. My family laughed and laughed, reenacting the clumsy attempt of my father to butcher the chicken. They imitated the chicken running for its life with its neck dangling sideways, and they imitated my father chasing after it with the hunting knife raised in one hand while holding onto the loose drawstring of his pajama pants, which slipped down to his ankles when he had to use both hands to finish the job. And his soiled pants were not forgotten."

She saw the boys stifling laughter with their shoulders waving. "Go ahead, laugh, I don't mind," she said, noticing that the boys didn't want to be callous since she had delivered the story in a somber tone. "I told you guys the story, especially to you, Mun. I couldn't laugh along with my family over the death of the chicken. Yet I fully understood their laughing, like I do yours now. I relived the incident in my head over and over. It really disturbed me. It still does.

"Are you telling me this because I questioned how you could deliver the troubling story of your life so humorously?" Mun asked.

"My point is that I understand that you were disturbed by my humorous attitude toward heart-wrenching stuff. But I, in turn, can be totally disturbed and sad at a matter at which the entire world would laugh."

"Oh, I get it. You felt I was judging you. I'm sorry that it came out that way. I wasn't judging you," Mun explained.

"Yes you were, buddy," Ahn said.

Mun turned his head to him, blinked his dark eyes a few times in silence then said, "You're right. I was judging her."

Innocent laughter broke out again. Miri felt warm affection being with them, like being with two sweet puppies. When they were recovering from their laughter, Miri started to describe the disturbing feeling she had over the chicken incident. "It's true I hated my father's inhumane way of butchering the creature. But apart from that, while I was watching that scene, for a nanosecond it was like *I* was the chicken, it was *me* who was running in a frenzy with a half-broken neck."

"You must've experienced at that moment a metaphor of your life," Mun said sympathetically.

"That could be. But it was definitely my choosing. I decided to feel what the chicken would feel. I remember my heart pounding, making me tremble uncontrollably. I heard people cheering and laughing, saying 'it went there, no, no, over there!' I even felt a part of my neck hurting, like it was going sideways and that I was seeing the world sideways, making me nauseous. The most disturbing part was when the chicken was caught, there was a relief, a peaceful relief, and there was a strange rapture when it ended, something transcendental. Like the triumph was mine, not his. Unintentionally, he freed me."

"That's very Ingmar Bergman," Mun said, almost to himself.

"Who? Ingrid Bergman?" both of them asked.

"No, Ingmar Bergman."

"No buddy, her name is Ingrid Bergman," Ahn corrected him, stretching his mouth to emphasize the 'rid' in the word Ingrid.

"I know who the actress is. Ingmar Bergman is a Scandinavian filmmaker." Mun's father was also a filmmaker, and Mun had the privilege of viewing unusual films.

"Anyway, didn't the chicken kick and scream until its last breath, or did it give up the fight at that last moment?" Ahn asked, ignoring Mun.

"Of course it fought, fought its way to the kingdom of death. But that was a show to end the game perfectly. It was definitely smiling when my father's big foot was about to smash its head."

"Hum…A human being identifying herself with a chicken. It surely is disturbing but deep in weird way. But I like the last part, a smiling chicken under the foot of a slayer. I don't know why. It's kind of beautiful," Ahn spoke with a theatrical expression of soliloquy. Miri couldn't tell if he was joking.

"Did you eat the chicken?" Ahn asked with some suspicion.

"Yeah, I did," she answered, lifting her chin toward him.

"That means, metaphorically speaking, you ate yourself. What did you taste like?" Ahn asked again, exchanging grins with Mun.

Miri leaned forward to the middle of the table, stretching her neck toward the boys, which made the boys do the same. She whispered, "I was disappointed that I tasted just like chicken!" They laughed throwing back their heads.

"But honestly, didn't it bother you, just a little, eating it?" Ahn asked, with his voice in staccato from laughing.

"Not at all. I remembered what Jesus said to his disciples, which came to me via roasted chicken: 'Take this, all of you. This is my body, which is given up for you. Do this in memory of me…' Watching them eating the chicken felt like part of me conquered something in them."

- 30 -

Miri didn't tell them the whole story. There was a sequel to the incident of the chicken from which the boys' ears were excluded. It was impossible to carry on with full concentration on any subject with them. Their conversation always took a detour in the middle and ended up as shapeless as an amoeba. But when she thought about it later, she wasn't sure if she would have told them the whole story anyway. After that day, a new chicken was brought in pretty much every day. Her father was obsessed in perfecting his skill of butchering the animal. It always ended up in a bloody mess. The screeching screams of the desperate bird, the barking dogs, and her father's high-pitched, evil-sounding laugh echoed through the sky. He used a hunting knife, bare hands, and even a rifle, or sometimes let the dogs chase after the bird and tear it apart. He peeled off all his clothes on the lawn when it was over and went straight to his bathroom where he would take a shower listening to his favorite old Japanese pop song, sweet and mellow, called "An Apple Tree." This went on for a while, about three weeks, but then one day, he stopped. He lost interest. It was a dreadful three weeks. People in the house who had cheered and laughed hard in the beginning started to shake their heads in disbelief. They got sick of having chicken for dinner, and no one would say anything about the particular death of the chicken on the dinner table. It usually ended in the dogs' bowls.

Miri missed the time when her father almost never came home. It had been about three years that he started to come home regularly, then it became every day, although late at night, right before curfew, then it became earlier and earlier in the evening. It seemed that he stopped going to his mistresses, each of whom lived in a different house.

He started arriving home at curfew, which was sometimes before the sun went down. Unless you were out doing something legitimate like tutoring, coming home after him called for a long lecture, which usually involved his vulgar view of the world. He always assumed that if you came home late you must have been making out with a boy in some dark sleazy place. "Man looks at woman as a meal. Once he fills his belly, that's it" was his typical line.

"Why can't he disappear like before?" Her sisters sighed.

"I wonder what made him decide to come home so religiously, as if he suddenly realized that he had to restore his fatherhood. Well, no thanks to that," Sohee said one summer night when the three girls sat together eating concord grapes that turned their mouths purple.

"Why doesn't he find some new whores?" Zona complained.

Miri tilted her head and said with a dark purplish mouth, "It's because he's all dried out. He overused his thingy and it doesn't work anymore. It has nothing to do with his conscience over redeeming his place as a father. He has nowhere else to go with his limp noodle. Can't you see he's angrier and cheaper? The most pleasurable thing in his life is no more. Haven't you noticed that he describes and analyzes things or matters more and more in terms of sex, fornication, and urology? The man's obsessed with it. He must be suffering dreadfully, being unable to satisfy his obsession."

The girls laughed with their blackish-purple mouths. Zona said, "You know what he said to me the other day? 'Where are you going, you forgot to wear pants!' I was wearing a dress that was barely an inch above my knees. He shouted at me, accusing me of dressing like a whore and inviting all the goons in town to my groin. Can you believe that?"

Sohee said, "Oh yeah, the other day he was sitting on the living room sofa thumbing through a book on the coffee table. It was a book on Renaissance art with pictures of paintings and sculptures of nudes. He looked at the pictures shaking his head and mumbled something like, 'Is this a dirty book or what?'"

"Did he want to find out who that book belongs to?" Miri asked.

"I hid myself in the kitchen waiting for him to shout. Thank God he didn't."

"Perhaps he secretly liked it. You know his type of woman, and those naked Renaissance women are his type," Miri said.

"How do you know, have you seen any of his mistresses?" Zona asked.

"No, no such discovery. But one time he was watching TV and I happened to be there. A woman on the screen had a small head with a roundish body, like the nude figures of Renaissance art. I happened to say under my breath that she was fat. He heard me and said that I have no idea what a beautiful woman should look like. Then he pointed to the woman on the screen and said in her defense, 'That is a woman of beauty to which you are not even remotely close. Your face is too big; your bone structure is too masculine. I'm telling you that you might as well give up the idea of being picked up as somebody's bride looking as you do. You are done as a woman,'" Miri imitated him perfectly, making her sisters roll around with breathless laughter.

There were numerous episodes concerning their father. Most of them were laughable to Miri except for the "art of killing a chicken." Whenever she remembered, it immediately chilled her heart. It was like she had witnessed something she should never have. It could not find a voice, but it was screaming painfully inside of her. It was a mixture of disgust and compassion churning in her stomach, which were unable to agree on forming a voice so that they could escape through the throat as one. What will he do next, she wondered with dread. It's an act of self-loathing. He must hate himself, she thought another time. It took many moons for her to come to that opinion. Another set of many moons passed by when she, against her will, began to feel pity for her father. Pity, not understanding or sympathy, but a long-distance pity. "What made you turn so ugly, what caused you to be so distorted?" She would never find out.

One day when her nurse was away visiting relatives, she washed her grandma's hair. She then combed her long grey hair in her room filled with afternoon sunlight. In the mirror she saw her grandma's eyes contentedly closed as she let out deep sighs of pleasure. "What kind of a boy was he?" Miri asked.

"Who?" her grandma asked, turning her head slightly.

"Your son, my father."

"Oh, your father. He's hardly my son these days. I almost never see him living in the same house. What is it that you want to know?" she asked, handing Miri a bottle of oil.

"Anything, anything you remember," she said, pouring the oil in her palm. She worked the oil between her palms and started to rub it on her grandma's hair.

"Oh, let's see." She closed her eyes again and started to speak slowly. "He was born premature. When he was born his head was wobbly like that of an octopus. No one thought he would survive, but he did. He wasn't a happy boy, rather cranky most of the time. I mean, I'd never seen him laughing like other kids. He liked running; he was fast. I can't say he was athletic, but he surely liked speed. In the winter he made skies out of bamboo sticks and skied down the snow-covered hills as if he were flying. He didn't like farm life. He learned to read and write in a school run by our church, which was free. He wasn't a particularly good pupil, though. He daydreamed in his permanent crankiness. When he wanted to go to a middle school that was not free, I paid for the school by selling vegetables at the market, but that wasn't enough. Your grandfather made me stop altogether one day because your father did not seem to take the learning to his heart. He was less than average. I had to agree with your grandfather, and your father had to stop his education. I remember seeing him standing in the middle of the rice field we were working in, leaning on his shovel and watching schoolboys pass by in their uniforms with shiny golden buttons, with his eyes following them until they vanished from his sight. Your grandfather and I talked about it, thinking maybe we should try to send him back to school. But in the end, your grandfather said, 'We can't break our backs so that he can wear that fancy uniform.' At that time men and boys wore their hair long and braided, but those high school boys were allowed to have it short and greased. People thought it was disrespectful. As Confucius said, 'one should not harm what one received from his parents.' We were Catholics, but his teaching became the tradition we had to live by. Even then I thought it was stupid. You cut your nails but not your hair? Hair comes from the parents but not nails, is that what he was saying? Anyway, one day your father, fifteen or so at that time, came home with his hair cut and greased like a drowning rat. This made your grandfather go crazy. He beat your father to a pulp and threw a bucketful of water on him when he was losing consciousness, revived him, and repeated his beating until he couldn't continue anymore. The next day your father disappeared. Five years later he showed up in a suit and tie. I remember how shiny his leather shoes were. They reconciled. We were just glad that he came home alive."

"What was he doing during those five years?" Miri asked, drawn to the history of her father.

"I really don't know. All I know is that he had worked as an errand boy for a Japanese man who owned a small factory of some kind. Somehow he made his way up to be an office clerk. How he became the owner of the factory after the Japanese lost the war, or how he made the company so successful is a mystery to me, if not to everybody."

"How did my mother and father get together? Wasn't it an arranged marriage?" Miri asked, a little afraid that her grandma would fall asleep and stop telling her the juicy story.

"Yes, it was. Your mom was introduced to us through a church member. She looked sturdy and pleasant, and most important, she was from a family of Catholic faith. But I must confess that it surprised me a bit when your father agreed to marry her. They got married, and three days after the wedding he left for Seoul, leaving your mom with us. To this day your mom blames me for holding onto her to use her as an extra laborer on the farm. But it was your father who refused to take her, making excuses like he didn't have a proper place to settle with her. I didn't insist because she was a hardworking girl. We needed the extra help, and she certainly was useful. She was really good at everything she did. At that time your uncle was still a young boy, and your late aunt was ill with an infection in her lungs. I came to rely on your mother. Your father visited us now and then but not often. Several years went by, and then he finally came to take her with him. He said he bought a small house and asked us to move in with him. Your mom went with him, but we stayed behind. By then, the first thing I would do when I woke up in the morning was to visit my daughter's grave, the one who died of a lung infection. I couldn't bear the thought of leaving her in the grave alone at that time. Some years later when your grandfather became ill, we came to Seoul to see a Western doctor. Sohee was just a toddler. Your father was a good son then. He fully supported us. Your mother was cold as usual, but we knew that's how she was with anybody. It was always puzzling to me that her family-her parents, brothers, and a sister-were very warm folk, kind and gentle. All the church people and the villagers agreed. In the beginning we thought her coldness was just her way of being shy. As time went by, we realized that was all her, always angry at something, at someone mostly. It seemed she was cold to her own child. Then we noticed that your father didn't come home quite so often and found out that he had a mistress who gave birth to a son before Sohee was born. It seemed that he preferred to stay at her house. Your grandfather got better although not fully. He still had to stay in bed most of the time but he hung in there until when you were three or four, a long, long time.

Miri wanted to hear more but noticed her grandmother, who suffered from a pulmonary illness, was fatigued from talking. She regretfully left her to rest, full of new things in her chest to analyze.

She revisited her grandmother's tale in her head over and over, making a motion picture in her head. It was a black-and-white film. The people on the dusty farm looked sallow and undernourished, as disturbing as hungry ghosts in a dream. The bleak appearance of the farm seemed cursed and empty of spirit, as if God forgot to put some color in it. Life in exile, its prisoners long forgotten.

-31-

M iri's indifference toward others began to share its space with feelings of compassion, but she found no enjoyment in it. If anything, it was burdensome. The suffering of others, even that of her enemies, affected her. She became sensitive to their moods, and slight changes in their expression concerned her. She wanted to reach out to them, thinking some miraculous power in her would heal them, but any small attempt she made to reach out for them was thrown back at her with hostility. She had no idea where it came from, and it made her feel like giving up, like she was emptying herself out but also that she was above life, without joy but still with a sense of duty. During such moments of floating above everything called Life, she was in a murky place between the physical and spiritual worlds. Fear and anxiety were covered by a fog of ancient sadness that was wise, gentle, and comforting. It made her believe she knew something that others didn't, that she was the answer. She felt solid when such sadness sat with her.

"Catharsis!" Mun exclaimed when she shared her newly experienced feelings.

"What?" she asked, squinting her eyes at him.

"Catharsis. People feel relieved after an episode of violence," he explained.

"I don't recall any violent act. And what does violence have to do with sadness?"

It wasn't really a question, but he answered.

"First of all, you might not have been violent physically. But violent thoughts, creative imaginings of revenge, cursing, or making voodoo dolls out of pincushions, they're all violent energies. Let's face it, the environment you live in has been a hostile one, to put it mildly, a very hostile one. Who wouldn't get angry and feel violent emotions in such circumstances? I know I would. In your case, the form of anger and violence manifested as stone-like indifference. Somehow, something shifted your energy, possibly causing a breakthrough, and now you're stationed in a spot of catharsis. What do you think of my theory?" He was proud of the speech he gave. Miri thought he was cute. He continued. "I think sorrow and violent emotions come from the same root, brothers like Cain and Abel. I'm getting so good at this, ha, ha." Miri and Ahn rolled their eyes but let him continue. "I see catharsis as a temporary break. During catharsis, people get quiet, gentle, and even euphoric. These feelings can be interpreted as sorrow. It's a lethargic state of not having to fight for a moment, a time out, so to speak." He was beaming, satisfied with his statement.

"So what you're saying is that the sadness I feel is a cathartic state, a temporary break," Miri said, feeling there was more to it than that. She understood what he said, but it didn't quite explain everything to her. Her new experience was grand, and she didn't want it to be compromised by human psychology. "No," she said inwardly, "I feel the fingertips of someone or something that is close to God."

As usual the conversation took a route of its own, having not much to do with its origin. Mun said, "It's like, Cain and Abel are sitting on opposite ends of a seesaw. Catharsis is when the seesaw is in perfect balance. Before you know it, it will tilt again."

"Cain is rage and Abel is sorrow; when the seesaw is in perfect balance, it's called catharsis. Am I explaining your theory correctly?" Ahn asked, with a hint of an argument emerging.

"Something like that," Mun replied.

"According to you, the sensation of sadness that gives her solidness is actually catharsis. It doesn't seem fitting; it's an extensive stretch, to put it kindly."

"Oh yeah? Then enlighten me, Mr. Judeo-Buddhist," Mun teased him.

Ahn thought Buddhism would be the religion for him if he could choose one, but he liked, even if he didn't admire, the stories from the Old Testament. He also saw a resemblance between the Old Testament and the teaching of Confucianism. "I can't imagine Cain and Abel seesawing together. Cain is a much more threatening character, and he hated Abel. Anyway, Cain kills Abel and runs away, which means he killed your metaphor of sorrow, which means only rage survived. And from the groin of this rage, we, the human race emerged."

"I see your point, whatever your point may be. And I tell you that I have no problem picturing them seesawing," Mun's teasing continued.

"Suppose you erase the Cain and Abel analogy, can you imagine 'rage' and 'sorrow' seesawing together?" Mun asked Ahn.

Ahn lifted his eyes to the ceiling, shifting his eyes from one direction to the other. Then he said, "Kind of. I can picture it better if it were 'rage' versus 'self-pity.' Yeah, I can definitely imagine the two on a seesaw."

"What do you think, Miri?" Mun asked her opinion.

She wasn't paying attention to the subject. After she made them repeat their argument, she answered, "Sorrow and self-pity aren't the same thing."

"Oh yes they are. Sorrow is simply glorified self-pity," Mun said, turning to Ahn, who returned the sharp glance back at him and said, "Don't look at me. I haven't come to terms with it yet."

She imagined, actually had a vision, of a thorny bush with white, delicate puffs of flowers. Gentle and delicate flowers of sorrow with thorny branches of self-pity. She sat with this vision for a while.

By the time her attention came back to the boys, they were still talking about Cain. Mun was saying, "God made Adam and Eve, they had two sons, Cain and Abel, and Cain killed Abel. Cain ran away to a village, met a woman, and had a family with her. Who is this woman; who are the people in the village? Doesn't the Bible say Adam and Eve were the first humans God created?"

"I wondered about that too," Ahn said. "Perhaps the author made a faux pas in continuity?" Ahn continued, "Then I thought of something that explains both the Bible and Darwin's theory. Suppose these people in the village were actually apes." Abrupt laughter from Miri and Mun stopped him. "Hear me out, guys." Ahn waved his hand at them to pay attention to what he was about to say. "I don't think Darwin's theory is much of a theory. It's more like a personal point of view, an attempt of sedition against the Church, perhaps? It doesn't matter. But I have to wonder where did he get that idea? He could've arrived at the idea the same way I have, by hypothesizing that Cain fell in love with an ape. There's no data, no concrete proof of God or Darwin's evolution. Yet people turn against each other over the issue. Battle of imagination! But clearly doesn't that say something extraordinarily stupid about us?"

"Facing your own stupidity can be rewarding," finally Miri spoke. "Speaking of evolution versus creation, why do we always insist on one being right and the other wrong, and therefore, evil? How do you fight over matters that have no solid answer? And why do people think God never changes His mind? If anyone has a right to change his mind, it's Him. In the very beginning, He could have decided to create everything with His own hands. But in the midst of His project, He changed his mind and planted a device for His unfinished project to evolve on its own, like an auto-creation. Darwin happened to notice that but in the name of science. In my mind God is still working on the world. He never stopped. The universe is His pet project. He might like what he worked on one day and went to sleep satisfied but found the same thing abominable the next day and destroy it."

"Very human," Mun said, pursing his lips.

"Why not?" Miri said, more to herself.

"So your idea of God is that he is uncertain of Himself."

"Just like us humans, could be like you and me, even like my father." Miri answered, maintaining her "why not" attitude.

"Could what you've just said be spur of the moment…I don't know why, but what you've said makes me shiver," Ahn said, embracing his arms.

"I chose to believe Him to be that way. I can like Him, and I have to like Him. And no, it's not spur of the moment."

"You sound like life has no meaning. Kind of, like an atheist who believes in God," Ahn said, looking concerned, which made her smile.

"I don't think there's any meaning in life. We create religion in pursuit of meaning, but I can't think God works through meaning. We are pursuing phantom. God is, in my opinion for now, what you make of Him. He could be an alien, and we are His machine."

"You know, Miri, I can't help liking your idea of God, but at the same time, I feel fooled," Mun said in all seriousness.

"Because we, you and I and anyone who wants God in his life, are conditioned to perceive God in a certain way. Our minds are corrupted. We are conditioned to believe we mean something precious to God, but are we?"

"But you believe in God, don't you?"

"Yes," she said without hesitation.

"Even if He is an alien?"

"What choice do I have? I have to have something, someone however imaginary. I have to believe that I am not alone. As I said God is custom made for individual need."

"He is who he is. I can't change that. I might as well imagine Him to be someone better than me, alien or not", she quickly added seeing Mun's bewildered face,

"Oh, I'm sorry if I unintentionally burdened your heart. But my idea of God isn't for sale. It's for me, it's mine only, and I happened to share it with you, nothing more. You shouldn't let anyone influence what's between you and your God, ever."

She felt strange about Mun's mood. He looked like he was about to cry.

Her inner eye was reading words passing by, "We believe in one God, the Father, the Almighty Maker of Heaven and Earth, of all that is seen and unseen…"

- 3 2 -

February was a month of sleet. It came down hissing and splattering on the ground like an army of men continually discharging loogies from the sky in full force. People stayed inside as much as possible. Miri and the boys continued attending the same tutoring classes. One evening on their way to the teahouse, by a small alley lined with cheap restaurants, they heard the loud and primitive sounds of instruments banging in discord. There was the sound of bamboo flutes, metallic drumming, and an ass-ripping voice singing. There was no harmony, as if the sound consisted of tangled threads. They were walking down the dark alley trying to avoid puddles here and there when Mun stopped and suggested that they investigate the noise. Ahn was reluctant and said, "They're performing a shamanic ritual. It creeps me out." Mun ignored him and walked ahead, waving at them to follow, which they did. They saw him disappear into a narrow space separating some houses. He was looking in a window with his forehead pressed against it and both hands covering the sides of his head like parentheses for better peeping. They reluctantly but automatically followed him as if tied in a rope together.

The room was lower than ground level and brightly lit in contrast to the dark in which they were standing. People were sitting on the floor against the walls. A shaman, whether a man or woman, they couldn't tell, was standing in the middle of the room with two flute players, a drummer, and a brass cymbal-clapper sitting in one corner. The shaman was dressed in the primary colors of red, yellow, and blue and held two large swords, one in each hand. He or she danced, jumping up and down like on a trampoline, swinging the swords. Then the shaman walked around the room in a circle, singing with a screeching voice and pointing the swords at the other people. They put their palms together in prayer, bowing repeatedly at the shaman. It looked like some of them were crying. At the far end of the room was a large table with various foods neatly piled up without being mixed: apples, pears, tangerines, chestnuts, walnuts, and rice cakes in pink, white, and green, were stacked up in a cylindrical shape about a foot and a half tall. In the middle of it was the head of a boiled pig, smiling with its eyes closed. Hideous-looking statues were lined up at the back of the table, and between them were brass pots of burning incense and candles. The shaman was shouting something, but they could not understand.

"What is he saying?" Mun turned his head to Ahn, who was standing behind them blowing on his cold hands.

"I'm cold and hungry," Ahn complained.

"That's not what he's saying," Mun said. "Hang on, buddy. This is too fascinating. I've never seen it before. Have you, Miri?" he asked, half whispering.

Miri shook her head, knowing that he wasn't looking at her. She couldn't share his fascination. She felt she was much too close to something she was not ready for.

Suddenly, the music stopped, and the shaman approached the table with his two swords and then put them vertically upside down in front of the table. The next thing they saw were the swords standing on the bare floor on their own. The shaman gave a stick to one of the present women. She cautiously walked up toward the table in a bowing posture and then hit the standing swords with the stick three or four times. The swords vibrated a little but stood firmly. Then two men brought out what seemed to be a whole rib cage of a large cow. They lay it on top of the standing swords as if on a big table. The swords and the cow ribs stood there firmly, looking like Stonehenge, defying Newton's theory. The shaman beamed and started to twirl around in ecstasy. People started to bow repeatedly with expressions of gratefulness. "Something must be going right for them," Miri guessed. The music picked up speed and volume, and a man put a bottle of rice wine, three cups, and a candle on a medium-sized wooden tray, which he then placed on the head of the shaman. The music became faster and faster, and the shaman started to twirl around with his arms stretched out away from his sides. The tray on his head stayed as if it were joined to his head, without anything spilling or moving. At this sight people were bowing, shouting, and crying in frenzy. "Things must really be going in their favor," Miri guessed again.

Since the room was beneath where they stood, they had a good view from where they could observe this phenomenon. Suddenly, the shaman stopped twirling and looked up to the window where they were standing. For a split second, Miri felt that this feminine-looking man looked at her as if he knew who she was. It sent a chill through her spine; it felt like thousands of ants were crawling on her. They quickly moved away from the window and walked back out to the main alley without exchanging a word. They didn't talk until they sat down in the teahouse.

Mun opened his mouth first holding the tea cup between hands. "There must be a trick; it can't be real."

"There are many fake shamans, I've heard," Ahn said.

"You mean what we saw can be real?" Mun raised his eyebrows in disbelief.

"Real or not, it has been here for thousands of years," Ahn said, munching on a cake. "What do you think, Miri?" he turned to her. She looked drained and pale. "Are you okay? You look like you're about to throw up."

"Yeah, I feel a little disoriented," she said, reaching for the tea. "It was too loud, and I was freezing." Her hand holding the tea cup was trembling.

"Perhaps the Catholic gene in you disagreed with what you saw," Ahn said, smiling. There was some truth in his statement, but she didn't want to go there.

She said, "The head of the pig scared me. It seemed like it was smiling at me. I don't want to see it in my dreams."

Ahn shook his head, looking straight at Miri and said, "I thought I smelled shit in my pants when the pig winked at me."

Miri was annoyed but laughed with them. She leaned back, crossing her arms. Mun detected her defensiveness and said, "This guy always cracks a joke when he has to ease his pain of being frightened. Please forgive him, madam."

Ahn said that he was sorry by holding his palms in prayer. Miri rolled her eyes, showing that she didn't believe him. Ahn made pleading eyes like a dog who did a bad thing. "Part of it was true. The pig didn't wink at me, we know that, but the shit part deserves partial credit. It's true that I was frightened when the guy was twirling around and swinging the swords. At one moment I thought one of the swords would fly through the window to where we were standing, and that was when I heard a 'quack' popping out of my ass. Honest!"

They giggled.

Mun buried his head in his hands giggling and said, "Did it materialize?"

"It was one of those uncontrollable, unpredictable mishaps of nature," he answered, laughing aloud.

Nothing like bathroom humor for successful diplomacy, Miri thought. They saw people coming into the teahouse dripping with wet snow. The sleet started again.

- 3 3 -

Shamanism, astrology, fortune-telling, and superstitions of the everyday kind were the main topics they talked about after that evening. Mun's fascination turned into an obsession, and he wanted to meet a shaman in person. He was an example of how the most skeptical person can become the most zealous. He was reading a book called *Shaman's Door* during tutoring and making notes from it. Since that evening Miri had been having disturbing dreams that were both beautiful and frightening. During the waking hours, she found herself thinking about the dreams, and at times, missing the mysterious places in the dreams. She went to bed wondering if she'd see the place again. Her dreams repeated faithfully. The place her dreams took her was dark and foggy, but it was but pleasant and gave her a sense of relief like she was among friends. She sat on the same rock in the middle of the street, observing creatures passing by who were oblivious of her and each other. She remembered wanting to have a cup of hot coffee. A large Siberian tiger who was walking upright on his hind legs and munching on chips from a bag smiled at her. He disappeared before she asked him where she could get some coffee. In these dreams she always came to the same place, the same rock. She became obsessively curious about her dreams, believing that there was a message she couldn't decipher. She missed the Siberian tiger. She wanted to grab him and ask if he was her friend.

One day when Mun expressed his desire to visit a shaman, she said, "I'd like to visit one too," to which Mun replied with sparks of joy in his eyes. They both looked at Ahn, knowing that he controlled the possibilities of getting the information they needed, for his family regularly contacted one of those people.

"Even if I found one, they're expensive. How are we going to pay?" Ahn said without sharing enthusiasm.

"How much, do you know?" Miri asked.

"Good ones probably charge about a hundred dollars," he answered.

Miri said, "I'll get the money. You work on finding a good shaman. This will be my parting gift to Mun." In the coming April, he was to move back to Tokyo where he was born and raised as a child.

The constant sleet in February turned March into mostly sunny weather with the occasional soft spring rain. Small buds of green began their cycle of nature after the long winter months of rest. The three of them met one Sunday in mid-March to visit a shaman that Ahn had found from a magazine article. It said that she was a direct descendent of the Tungus tribe of Mongolia. The Tungus were supposedly a shaman clan who specialized in healing. The article said that this particular shaman was discovered by a university professor as his research subject. The three of them were filled with the excitement of heading for a new adventure.

"Are you sure you have enough money?" Ahn asked Miri. They were walking up the hill, checking the addresses on both sides of the unpaved dirt road.

"Not to worry, I have more than enough. As a matter of fact, I have enough to feed you guys at the Tang Dynasty for dim sum later," Miri told him proudly.

"Really? For real?" Mun jumped, throwing his fists in the air with the joy of an unexpected pleasure approaching from the very near future. "Where did you get the money?" he asked, not all that interested in her answer due to his excitement.

"I had some savings," she answered.

"Oh, that's the last thing I'd believe," Ahn said. "Many times you don't even have enough money to pay for tea cakes," he added. It was true that the boys paid for her many times.

Miri gave him a side glance of annoyance and said, "I don't save. You're so right about that. I wouldn't know how if I tried. Let's just say the savings belong to someone else, and I took a temporary loan."

"Don't tell me you stole it," Ahn said.

"Leave her alone. She doesn't even pick up money lying on the ground. Remember that time at the marketplace?" Mun said and laughed, shaking his head.

Ahn looked at him and said, "I was just teasing. I know she wouldn't steal even from herself." He patted her shoulder, assuring her that he was just teasing.

She smiled remembering the scene Mun just mentioned. They had gone to a marketplace together one day before going to the teahouse. Ahn wanted to buy a couple of red mullets for his grandpa's birthday. Red mullet was in season. "You'll smell up the teahouse," Mun warned him.

"But the fishmonger will be closed soon," Ahn said, adding that he couldn't disappoint his grandpa.

It was already dark but still crowded. They were standing in the line at the fishmonger's when they saw a bill lying on the ground, wet with mud and glistening under the bare lightbulbs hanging along the awning. "Look, there's money," Mun whispered in Miri's ear, which Ahn overheard.

"I know," Miri said indifferently, looking at it.

Ahn reached for it and rubbed it clean on his pants with a wide, silent smile. "This will pay for our tea twice!" he said, pocketing the bill in his pants.

Later on they teased her for being a weirdo. "You saw the money and didn't reach for it? That's sick."

Little did they know that the money she had in her pocket to pay for the shaman was not so innocent. She had stolen the money by a series of well-planned executions. Her mother had several hiding places Miri knew about. The money was saved and hidden carefully for the priest at church. She saw her mother sitting in the dark corner of her room, counting the bills, then ironing them with her palm and putting them in an envelope. Miri knew where the envelopes would go. Whenever her mother received money from her father to pay for household expenses, money which was barely sufficient, she would take some and hide it, forging the budget book she had to produce to her husband, stashing some inside of her winter footwear stored deep in a wardrobe drawer, some in a wooden panel behind the dresser, and some in the hollow space inside of a large statue of the Madonna. It was through pure chance that Miri acquired the secret information. When her father gave her mother money to give to the house staff as their holiday bonus, she kept it to herself and gave them some cheap fabrics and such instead. Miri justified her actions in her head: "It was stolen money to begin with, and its destination would have been the pockets of lazy priests." The mission was successfully completed. The act of stealing was intoxicating. It warmed her blood, making her almost feverish, heating up cold fear into a distorted pleasure. It was an art. It might be a crime, but it was not a sin. Still, it pinched the core of her dignity. She also felt it was the act of a coward, that it definitely was not something to announce to the world. Self-preservation was at work, which turned on and off much faster and more accurately than conscience. She was skillful, shrewd, and thorough, which surprised her. It felt vulgar, but at the same time, it testified to her ability to survive. She discovered that she had a gift in stealing.

They were received by a borderline middle-aged man in grey traditional robes. He didn't look happy to see the three youngsters at his door, giving them a once-over disapprovingly while holding the door. Miri was ready to show him the money in case he asked if they had enough. Without a word, he motioned them to come in and led them into a dark hallway smelling of incense. The room was also dark and filled with clouds from the burning incense.

The shaman was tiny, almost like a child. She was sitting on the floor in front of an altar decorated with paper flowers, where bowls of fruit were placed around a Buddha statue sitting on a lotus. The dancing flames of the candles changed the expression on his golden face. She told them to sit. They obeyed and sat on the floor cushions facing her. She looked to be in her thirties. She wore a traditional gown, and her long dark hair was piled up on top of her small head. When Miri's eyes were better adjusted to the dark room, she saw a much younger face underneath the massive hair. The face was sad and seemed without hope. A living corpse, a talking corpse, a corpse with colossal black hair with its loose bun wobbling at the slightest movement, reflecting the lights from the candles. There's something awfully sad about this picture, Miri thought.

"Is it cold out?" the shaman spoke with a southern accent, which sounded naturally gentle and soothing. Her voice was more mature than her appearance. Mun answered that the weather was still chilly. "I don't usually receive people on Sundays. But here you are. Who wants to be the first?" she asked, moving a small wooden table towards the middle of the room.

Mun volunteered and told her, "We are not here to have our fortunes read. We just wanted to meet with you, to ask a few questions. Hope you don't mind."

She looked up with a wide smile across her tiny face, showing uneven teeth. It was a relief; Miri was worried that she would kick them out. "You want to know how I became who I am, right?" she said, adjusting the front of her robes, her tiny hands popping out of the long sleeves like two weasels that quickly went back inside.

"Precisely. If you can only indulge us," Mun said, politely bowing his head. One of the weasels came out and rang a bell. The man came in. "Bring me the pipe and tea," she ordered him. She then turned to the three.

"I was born this way. There isn't much to say. Where I grew up, there was a graveyard on a hill behind our house. As a child I often went up there to play. People left food or coins in the grave site where their loved ones were buried. They carried on the rituals when their own bellies were empty. It was a good place for me to get extra food. Touching those foods was taboo and was supposed to bring a curse upon your life. I was only five or six, and hunger had more power over me than any fear. But I began to see things, spirits hovering like patches of shredded fabric. It scared me, and I stopped going there. Ever since the day I saw ghosts, ordinary people I used to know look different, even my own family. They looked like they were encased in vapor, in various shades and lights. I was too young to make anything out of this change in me. I didn't tell anyone what was happening to me but lived with it, and I got used to it. When I turned sixteen, right after my first menstruation, I started to walk in my sleep and would climb up the hill. It was the greatest feeling, sleepwalking or not. When my family found out, I took a beating, but I couldn't stop. Eventually, they had to lock me up, and I became sick with fever. Fever made me delirious, and I began to say things like 'there will be a fire in so-and-so's house. So-and-so is pregnant. So-and-so will receive a knife attack for cheating in a card game.' When my father found out that I predicted such incidents correctly, he called for a shaman living in the next village who told my father that I would not survive if I didn't practice my calling. 'She is one of us. If you want her to live, you have to let her be,' he said to my father, who was pounding the floor with his fists in despair.

"'If I let her be, she'll run around like a crazy bitch, and no one in the village will take her to give them a grandson. She might as well die,' my father said.

"The shaman said, 'Or she can earn you some money. She can be a fortune-teller. If you want her to be a real one who performs rituals like me, I can teach her a thing or two.' He convinced my reluctant father, and that settled that. I was sent to the shaman and learned a few things. It was all about appearance: how to dress, how to set up the altar, how to dance, and how to shout. To tell you the truth, my heart was not in it, but I had no choice. I was allowed to go up the mountain at night, and gradually, I regained strength. Fortune-telling brought in some money, and that made my father less unhappy. The most unexpected thing happened when I performed rituals. In the beginning I was faking as if I knew what I was doing. It was easy to fool people. But it began to possess me. The greatest feeling I experienced in the mountain was also there when I performed. I felt I could fly when I jumped. I felt an incredible strength but without any weight. People at the rituals witnessed these magical, unnatural phenomena, and some sick people got well afterwards. My name became known, and people all over began to come to me to solve their problems. And here I am." She narrated the story almost in one breath.

The man brought in the pipe and tea. He left, giving her a disapproving look. She told them to pour the tea and drink while she lit the pipe. Miri poured the tea and handed the cups to her friends. The tea had a reddish tint like bloody water, and it tasted like sweetened dirt. The shaman gulped down her tea and passed the pipe to them. They looked at each other hesitantly. She laughed. "It won't hurt. You don't want your fortune read, which is peculiar, and I can't take your money for nothing. This will make your trip here worthwhile. Go on." Miri took the pipe and puffed, feeling the silent stare of the boys. "Hold the smoke, don't blow it out so quickly," she said to Miri. Miri looked like she was having fun. She gave it a second puff and passed the pipe to Mun, holding the smoke in with her face screwed up. Mun took the pipe and made a determined, strong face; he puffed once then twice before he passed it to Ahn. Unlike Mun, Ahn was eager. He smoked it with ease. No one coughed. Mungsil, the shaman, laughed and said, "You guys must sneak cigarette smoking." They looked at each other.

She laid down the pipe in an ashtray and started to hum a tune, moving her body side to side. It sounded like Miri's grandma's old song, no words, just sweet, soothing tunes. Miri was the first one who went down. The boys followed. They were lying on the floor as if there was nothing else to do but hear her humming, which became a narration in an unknown language. Their eyelids got heavier, their breathing deep and even, their bodies in total relaxation to the point that if anyone was about to cut their throats they wouldn't care. Miri thought she heard a drum. Mungsil instructed them to close their eyes with their eyeballs crossed. They giggled at the instructions. She hushed them and told them to be still. She continued humming. Miri still heard the drum. She crossed her eyes underneath her eyelids as much as was possible. She felt her body descending into a bottomless pit. It frightened her and made her body jerk. What the hell am I doing, she thought. Something inside of her resisted.

Before it became too uncomfortable, suddenly all her resistance evaporated. She was all alone. It was ethereal, like she was without a body or mind of her own. A certain rapture engulfed her entire being. Then the vision started. She was climbing a mountain unknown to her, moving so fast she didn't feel her feet touching the ground. It was a beautiful night with a full moon. She saw herself wearing a white gown of chiffon that revealed her naked body under the moonlight. A cool breeze carrying the scent of earth and vegetation blew her gown around playfully, making her feel beautiful and angelic. She wandered about effortlessly but with intention, searching for something. Finally, she arrived at a giant rock that was glowing under the night sky full of stars and moonlight. There was a cave under the rock. She walked through the narrow tunnel and reached an opening onto a large space lit brightly by hundreds of candles. Animals large and small were all standing upright as they greeted her. Each one of them was wearing some kind of garment; some were fully dressed with ornaments and trinkets, and others only with scarves and fancy footwear. She noticed odd creatures: a bear whose body was that of a tiger, a head of an owl on top of a coyote's body, a large albino snake with a monkey's head floating in the air, and so on. They were celebrating something. The food and drinks on a table in the middle of the room gave out a strong but appetizing smell. "You found us this time. Welcome," a creature with a deer head whose body was wrapped in layers of garments greeted her warmly. In this scene she behaved as if she knew who they were. They embraced each other. "Our long lost child finally came to visit us. We've been concerned that the hard training out there made you forget us," the bear head said, handing her an empty glass. "Let the celebration begin!" someone shouted, and small creatures came out of the wall with tiny glasses in their hands. They all raised empty glasses towards the far end of the cave, and what seemed to be a woman emerged, holding a large decanter with amber-colored liquid. She had on a white chiffon gown like Miri's. Chanting started low and soft, in perfect harmony. She walked down and poured the amber elixir into the glasses they were holding out. A creature next to the lady, which could've been a goat or an enormous rat in an ostentatious red-and-gold silk robe, was passing out cigars and lighting them. When she came near, Miri saw her face underneath the veil that was draped over her head. It seemed to be a large boiled egg with its shell peeled off. There were no eyes, nose, or lips. Her hands had no fingers, but they had thumbs, which also had the texture of a boiled egg. When she—Miri still believed that it was a female—stood in front of her, she saw a yolk inside of her head with the face of an infant, giving her a toothless smile. She gave the decanter to the giant rat next to her and raised her chiffon gown and invited Miri to step inside, making a tent over them. She whispered to Miri, "You have my permission." The tornado of chanting began to pick up higher notes, and it soon filled up the cave with high "C."

When the chanting was done, everybody raised their glasses and started to drink. Miri drank the elixir without hesitating, like the rest. She could not define the taste, but it was pleasant. She saw her glass refilled over and over. They drank and smoked something that was not a cigar; it was dried something wrapped in leaves that smelled like earth. A part of her was observing this in awe, but a larger part of her participated in the extraordinary happenings as naturally as it came. When the egg lady resumed her original place at the far end of the cave, they became silent. A sudden frenzy broke out, and everyone unscrewed their heads and threw them to the ground. Then the headless creatures crawled on the ground trying to find new heads, all of which were laughing. A few moments later, it was over. They got their new heads that had belonged to someone else a short while ago. Some were obviously disappointed at their new heads, and some didn't care, but some were ecstatic. A few of them found the right heads, which meant that they were going back home with the egg lady. A wolf, a ram, and a hawk found their matching heads and departed with the egg lady into thin air. Disappointed creatures comforted each other, but soon they merrily resumed the party. The endless refilling of the glasses got them drunk. A creature with a horse face who previously had a wolf head approached Miri and started to disrobe. "I need a head like yours," it said, revealing a woman's body. "Maybe next time," it said, covering its body again with the robe.

"Why did you bother to change heads then? There's no one with a human head among you," Miri said sympathetically.

"I can't deprive a chance for a guy who needs my head."

"I'm sorry, I couldn't unscrew my head even if I tried," Miri said.

"Oh, someday it will," it said, making googly eyes.

"Are you waiting for my head?" Miri asked.

"At the moment you seem to be my only chance. One can't rush this, though, or even plan."

"What can I do to help, meanwhile?" she asked anxiously.

"Send your experiences to us, any experience. That will refresh our minds, crank up our creativity and improve us so that we have a better chance the next time round. And it entertains us a great deal."

"How? Tell me how can I deliver it?" she started to shout. Everything was fading away.

"Well, you received permission from your soul, your queen, didn't you?"

Everything went dark. She began to hear the drum again. She was back in her flesh. It felt unnatural and claustrophobic. She slowly opened her eyes and remembered where she was. She tried to get up, but her body felt like it was trapped in heavy armor. "Take your time." She heard Mungsil's soft voice. She sat up slowly. Mun was already up, and Ahn was curled up like a shrimp, snoring. She looked at her watch.

"It's been only ten minutes," Mungsil said.

"It feels like I've been sleeping for hours," Miri said, seeing Ahn stretching and yawning while lying on the floor. He sat up, rubbing his eyes. "What a dream! You should have been there, Mun," Miri said to Mun, dying to talk about her dream.

"Please don't talk about it here. Not to me. You can tell each other as much as you want once you leave here," Mungsil warned. "Are you sure you don't want your fortune read?" she asked, relighting the pipe. She didn't pass the pipe to them this time. They shook their heads. She laughed and told them she was pretty good at it.

"We have no doubt," Mun said. "If you don't mind, I have some questions to ask."

"You can ask as many as you want. What is it that you want to know?" she said.

"I'm curious if your kind of people, I mean your job, your calling, is to guide and help others in this world, like priests," Mun asked.

"Oh, no, no, nothing like that. We have no business in saving people. It's fate or a calling, as you put it, but we are not so different from you. We're just exceptionally sensitive to energy, some more so than others. Our sensitivity to the energy around us enables us to reach what we call 'unreality.' We let our spirits be in charge of our lives, not our bodies. What I'm doing here is earning a living, not because I have a duty to serve people. I'm a body after all. It's cheating, though. I'm corrupted by the comfort of material things." She tilted her head thoughtfully, puffing the pipe.

"You aren't supposed to make a living this way, is that what you're saying?" Miri asked, feeling sad for her.

"I'm not pure in that sense. I try not to get too comfortable with the material world, but it's hard. It's exhausting business."

"But you still have to eat," Ahn participated.

"My attachment to the material world diminishes my sensitivity to energy. I still climb up the mountains some nights to renew myself. It's no longer like it used to be. The weakness of my body is winning."

"Is there a special meaning in that fated journey your kind of people pursue?" Mun asked.

Suddenly, she dropped her head forward, as if having a narcoleptic attack. They looked at each other alarmed. The woman slowly raised her head; her eyes closed tightly, and she began to speak without a southern accent. Miri detected the slight change in her voice; the gentleness seemed to be gone. "If you're born left handed, is there supposed be a special meaning? Life is given to you to live. It isn't given to you because you are special and supposed to complete a god's duty. Life is perfect as is, but human beings have to correct it, deface it, and deform it beyond recognition. This talk about meaning and personal duty is an attempt to deface it. Why? Because when you pursue meaning when there is none whatsoever to begin with, you only end up believing someone else's idea of 'meaning' as your own. In the process you get farther and farther away from knowledge of yourself. You must know that knowing who you are is not the same thing as the meaning of life. I know it's a scary thing to realize that there's no meaning, especially being so young and green as yourselves. But I recommend the vigorous exercise of learning about yourself. Live your life with the knowledge of yourself, accept it whole-heartedly, and take delight in it. Once you sit with the knowledge of yourself, you'll be so glad that there's no meaning in life. It's a good thing that life has no meaning, for emptiness of meaning gives you the right to freedom. Save yourself from being prisoners of this 'meaning of life.' It's an intellectualized game and entertainment for people in their desperate attempt to swim out of their drowning boredom. However, there's a side effect in the search of the meaning. It creates hierarchy, a pecking order. As we know, this side effect can be quite lethal. It's nothing but playing musical chairs with each other's heads, ha ha."

Miri's ears perked up at the mention of "musical chair with heads," wondering if Mungsil saw what she had seen. Mun seemed agitated. His idols, the great thinkers, the intellectuals, and his mentors were being dismantled by this woman who did not sit right with him.

"But the searchers of the meaning of life helped in leading so many of us and teaching us to be better human beings, for a better world and a better future," Mun said with an attitude of defiance.

"Oh really? If you want to believe that it's their calling, then so be it. When one tells others how to live, how to behave, what is the right thing and wrong, one is still questioning himself. It's an attempt to fill a void that isn't possible to fill. But I'm not having a debate with you. I have no desire to make you understand what I know. You asked and I answered, nothing more," she tossed her head in irritation, her eyes still firmly closed.

Mun made a quick apology, and in the same breath, asked another question which made her laugh. "Do you believe in God?"

"I must confess I rather enjoy this. You guys are fresh air to me." Then she said, "Of course I do. God is energy. Therefore, He's omnipresent, as Christianity says."

"That means we worship energy," Ahn murmured.

"Our kind manipulates energy. It's the ultimate manifestation of God," she said.

"Then who is this God? If God is energy, then He is everything, good or bad. Your idea of God being energy—I'm not making an argument here;

I rather like the idea of this new knowledge of God—tells me that there's no distinction between good and evil, and therefore, there are no rewards or punishment. I must say that's a rather comforting thing to hear about God. I can see myself liking such a God. I wonder which part of our nature drove us to a disastrous path in terms of understanding God?" Miri said, feeling strangely angry.

"It happened because human beings are basically lazy but clever, an unpleasant combination like stupidity and ambition. They see surviving as hardship and are constantly searching for devices and means to reduce the hardship, in the hope of granting their lives a full-blown laziness some day. And yet this goal actually creates more work, it's too much work in the process. Victims of their own cleverness, so to speak. Their cleverness would not accept that the life given to them is a mere surviving mechanism. They turned against nature, God's creation, and therefore, proof of God. They refuse to be just part of nature, a half-brother to nature, so to speak. They want to be more important to God, the most important among all His creations. They do not want the same fate as their half-brother's, that is, nature. They have to prove that they mean something far better than nature to God, but they only tore Him in half in the process, taking a half piece as their God but tossing out the other half. Half of God is not a half-god, it's a useless god. There you have it as the answer to your bewilderment. Either you get it or don't."

"Then, civilization is the error," Mun said thoughtfully. "If we human beings are so lazy, why did we put so much work into building civilization?"

"When laziness is joined with cleverness, it breeds fear. But fear is as powerful a catalyst as desire, and often they join forces. When they reach a certain point, they flip over and mix with the emotion of anger, which can also be an enormous force, making unimaginable things possible. The result of human action called 'civilization' also confirms their suspicion of being above the rest of God's creation."

"So, civilization was built because of anger?" Mun asked, checking Miri's expression.

"The accumulation of a fear that joins anger."

"I thought we built civilization because our nature strives to improve," Miri said.

"Wanting to improve or conquer is all based in fear. They come from the desire to remove the fear. We'd like to eliminate fear instead of taming it. As I said, fear is a powerful energy, a wild beast. We think we're capable of defeating it by witnessing the great civilization in front of us. Think about how many more complications it brought. Can you honestly say it made people happier? We lost our ability to survive as our ancestors did, one vertebrate after another. People will be or are already dying from an illness that has nothing to do with germs or known pathogens."

Mungsil's words came out as if she was reading Miri's mind. It impressed her and made her proud but frightened at the same time.

"But you said energy is God. If civilization is a manifestation of fear and desire in the form of energy, it should also mean God's doing, shouldn't it?" Miri said.

Mungsil chuckled. "I said God is energy; I didn't say energy comes from God. Do you see the difference? You have the notion that God is a protector. He is energy, and how you go about with this energy is up to you. Good or evil, useful or not, it all depends on your doing."

Miri was surprised at how intelligent the woman was, or the spirit that was possessing her at that time was.

"I get up in the morning, go to school, do my responsibilities as a participant of the civilization, all because I am motivated by fear? How sad!" Mun said, gaping as if someone snatched his meal away in the blink of an eye.

Miri was surprised at Mun because the statement he made sounded like something Ahn would have said. Mungsil chuckled again, and this time the two weasels of her hands came out of their sleeves clapping, her eyes still closed. "You're trapped, miserably trapped. Your dreams, hopes, even pride are illusions. In fact, they are the illusions of others. Think about it, can you honestly say your illusion is all yours? Ha, ha," she said and laughed, swaying her body. Her voice got deeper. It could've been a man's voice, but still there was no southern accent. The voice continued, "Borrowed illusions will only make your emptiness emptier until the end. Ask yourself if your life is truly yours. I'm sure your minds are bombarded with voices that tell you what to do, what you should be. Is that voice yours? Or do you sigh in despair when you hear the voice?" she said, snaking her head toward Mun, showing uneven pointed teeth, maliciously giggling. It was creepy.

Mun retreated his head back toward his shoulder. Miri felt hostility rising in her and said, "What's so funny?"

"Oh, aren't you the compassionate one, Miss Bodhisattva. You like to protect, huh?" she swung her snake-like head to her direction. She looked like a drunken puppet. This sudden change in the woman alarmed her. Her demeanor and the voice changed again. She opened her eyes wide, turned to her pipe, and the weasels popped out and re-lighted it. Miri looked at the boys and saw their obvious uneasiness. Miri quickly whispered in Mun's ear that they should leave, but he poked her knee with his finger, indicating that he wanted to stay.

Mungsil puffed on her pipe looking at the ceiling and started to speak in a calmer voice of what was clearly a man. This time she didn't close her eyes. "What is achievement in this world? What is success when we are mortal? Every moment of your life is dodging bullets of mortality. How well ahead can you plan against this force? We muddle through illusion after illusion against one definite truth, death, as if we can make it go away. Knowledge of yourself is food for your soul. You might not like what you find about yourself, and that's because you are tied to the knowledge of others, their desire, envy, and fear."

Mun restored his easy posture and asked, "Can you tell us how I can start that journey of following the path that is me, all me?"

"I'll give you a simple example. Suppose you like red or blue or yellow. Is your liking of the color true to yourself, or you choose it because it serves your ego better. Which is it? Simple enough to think about. What does ego have to do with it? What do you think ego is?" she answered with a question.

"Ego is pride. Isn't it?" Ahn answered.

"It's a strength, a drive but not pride. When your embryonic self-knowledge is tied to the ego, the ego takes the seat of pride, producing the ups and downs of emotions. You become a slave to it. Pride is self-respect. It's a loyal dog to you. No emotion can shake it or shame it. If you own it or not, that's another matter."

Something told Miri that Mungsil herself was fully back. Miri was still uneasy but tried to appear calm. The woman threw a sharp glance at her with a smile on her lips that was cold and unfriendly. She looked exhausted and troubled. "You don't have to guard them from me," she said to Miri in a full southern accent.

"What do you mean?" Miri asked, feeling somewhat antagonistic, which tempted her to cause friction. It was rather strange, like some force was urging her on.

"Don't you ever come back here again, you hear?" the woman spat out, throwing a forefinger in Miri's face. Something was not right between her and Miri. She was startled but stayed silent, fighting the foreign urge to tangle with this woman, feeling her eyes getting warm and hard.

Mungsil turned to the boys and continued, and what do you know, it was the man's voice again. "The ego is a freelancer that has an agenda. It doesn't conform with spirituality, but it can manipulate the spirit. The ego is a biological being that learns how to survive. It's resourceful, reserving information and generally keeping you from harm. It poses as a clever servant, but it has a tremendous drive, and we become dependent on it. The ego becomes you when you become addicted to its drive. Like any drug, the right dose helps, but an overdose becomes poison and kills. The ego does not know retrospection. It's with us only in this life of flesh and blood. When we leave this world, it dies along with our body. You end up choosing a favorite color according to the information supplied by the ego whose main function is judging what is useful in terms of self-preservation, the here and now. One good example is the desire to be in the mainstream of what's fashionable. You want to be accepted, even admired by the masses, which might enhance the chance to preserve yourself better. The ego has the drive to eliminate and conquer. Yes, it works with fear. Therefore, it also serves up feelings of shame and the desire for admiration. Strong stuff!" Her head dropped down, a second narcoleptic attack. She stayed that way longer than the first time.

Finally when she raised her head, she looked at Miri again, narrowing her eyes. Why is she giving me the attitude, Miri wondered, resisting the part in her still wanting to play nasty.

"You guys go to church?" Mungsil asked, facing the boys. Then the weasely forefinger popped out again pointing at Miri. Her eyes still on the boys, she said, "I know she does," twisting her lips. Then she closed her eyes again with a knowing attitude and started to speak in the man's voice without the accent. Miri wanted to leave, but Mun was seriously involved, and since this outing was part of Miri's going-away gift to him, she stayed put.

"Civilization brought war with nature. It stole human nature. The more we are separated from nature, the more we crave physical comfort and pleasure. The endless pursuit of comfort and pleasure comes with the heavy price of greed, envy, and suffering. People turn to God not for their wilted soul and spirits, but for the security of the here and now. Humongous churches were erected to help the void within the confused and troubled hearts of the people, a void created because of their own ignorance of themselves. This is a new kind of fear that won't be helped by physical and material comforts. Churches of various religions stand as a manifestation of collective fear, the new fear, and words of God were composed to confirm each other's faith that there's meaning, a good one, for suffering after all, however mysterious and unbelievable it might be. The already weakened spirits of the people gave up their strength, gave up trust in their own thoughts, and instead learned to judge, which seemed to raise the weakened spirit back to good health. We are the most judgmental creatures on earth. People rely on the Church to draw a map for them. This dependency lowers the self-esteem of society as a whole. People lost the ability to think for themselves and became mindless followers. If every person thrived and relied on their own thoughts, churches wouldn't have been so monstrously successful. People choose leaders and empower them to handle their lives without realizing that they have everything already." There was a hint of a tremor in her voice. It sounded like the volume was also being turned down. Abruptly, she raised her head, her eyes glassy, and her breathing was shallow. "I've had enough with you guys. Now pay and leave," she said, putting out her pipe on the ashtray. Miri gave her the money. She told her to give it to Mun and told him to rub the money on his head three times before handing it to her. Mun followed the order. She took it, put it on the altar behind her, and said, "This girl zaps my energy." She turned to the altar.

Miri got up first, her right leg asleep. She walked to the door, dragging her sleepy leg, feeling the weight of complete insult by the woman's last comment. She saw the boys thanking her, bowing at her deeply before getting up.

The whole thing took a little more than an hour. "It felt like hours, didn't it?" Ahn said, inhaling the cool, fresh air and flaring his nostrils. The boys ran down the hill pushing each other like kids released from school.

They were zigzagging down the road pulling and pushing each other into muddy puddles along the way. By the time Miri caught up with them, both of their shoes and pants bottoms were muddy and wet. They sat on a brick wall surrounding an empty flower bed, squeezing out the muddy water from their pants, blaming each other. Miri found torn newspapers in the road and took them to clean their shoes. They were cleaning their shoes, still giggling and calling each other names, acting like nothing unusual happened during the previous hour. The experience was disturbing to Miri. The woman's hostility towards the end troubled her. "This girl zaps my energy" sank deeply in her, to join her personal history with people. She didn't know how to describe the emotion that went through her, but she needed to find out what it was. She had never been so confused about her feelings, and that seemed to be what troubled her the most. One thing she could put her finger on was that it was insulting, and the boys' silence completed the insult. She couldn't decide if it was funny or sad.

They got on the bus headed to the town, which only had a few passengers. "I can't wait to sink my teeth into that fat, juicy dumpling," Ahn said, rubbing his palms together. Mun joined his delighted anticipation, reminiscing over the best Chinese cuisine he'd ever had. As she looked out the dirty window, Miri thought about the origin of the money in her pocket, blushing a little, not from the shame of stealing but from the memory of the intoxication from the pumped up adrenalin. No one talked about Mungsil.

A few stops later, a young woman in a miniskirt got on. When she walked down the aisle in the middle of the bus looking for a seat, a tiny old woman yanked on her miniskirt. The old woman hissed at her, "I can see half of your pussy hair. Your mother let you go out like that?" The startled young woman yanked back her skirt and said, "Crazy old bitch!" and walked to the back of the bus. The tiny old woman ran after her with amazing agility on the moving bus and started to swing an umbrella at her. The young one screamed and grabbed the umbrella and threw it on the floor. The old one reached for her hair, pulling it with such vehemence, calling her all the possible names available for describing a dirty girl. The young one fell to the floor, crying loudly. The boys got up to separate them. The driver stopped the bus, ran down the aisle, and ejected the old woman, umbrella, and her bag out of the bus. They saw the old woman swinging the umbrella at the departing bus shouting something, twisting her body in utter anger. Miri saw the young woman adjusting her clothes and hair, looking out the window. Miri, Mun, and Ahn looked at each other with a promise of laughter for the near future in their eyes.

It was at the teahouse, after lunch at Tang Dynasty, that they talked about the topic of the day. "I saw something in my dream after we took the tea and pipe," Mun said.

"I had a vision too. It was too real to call it a dream, but tell us what you saw first," Miri asked him.

Ahn was leaning on the wall sideways with his arms crossed, his eyes droopy and unfocused, moaning from overeating.

Mun said, "I saw a man who was me as a grown-up in a black robe rowing a boat down a narrow bank of a river. It was more like a canoe. There were many books in the boat. I rowed standing up, enjoying the beauty of the pleasant surroundings. Then I saw a group of large penguins as big as humans standing conspicuously on the right side of the bank. I thought 'how odd,' but waved at them. Suddenly, they made disgusting sounds and threw rocks at me. I lay down flat on the bottom of the boat until it was quiet. In the next scene, I was throwing books into the river one by one, saying good-bye to each one of them, sobbing, totally heartbroken. The boat was traveling alone. Then through the lens of my tears, I saw something white sitting on the bank. I ducked down, afraid of being ambushed again. But my curiosity got the better of me, and I raised my head to see who the white creature was. It was a woman in a white shroud, and next to her was a humongous black bird sitting down like a dog, like a Doberman. It was staring at me. I became nervous when the boat was heading to the bank near these creatures. I was too scared to expose myself by rowing it away from the bank. Then the woman lifted the veil and showed her face. It was an old woman, but I knew it was you, Miri. It comforted my grief having to depart with all my books. Then everything turned dark, and I found myself passing through a narrow tunnel or cave flying upwardly like a torpedo. Along the walls of the cave were windows, and I could see people inside displayed like dolls in dimly lit rooms. Then I heard the drum and woke up." He finished with both a question mark and exclamation mark on his face.

"Was it like your normal dreams?" Miri asked.

"Well, let's see. Sometimes I do dream something that seems to have meaning, but nothing so vivid and real as this. I only remember bits and pieces of my dreams, never the whole sequence. But in this dream, I felt the warm sun and the soft breeze, heard the water splashing, and even smelled that typical odor of country."

"What do you think? Did you like what you see? Did it suggest anything to you?" she asked.

"I can't tell if I liked it or not. Come to think of it, when I threw away my books I was crying with such heartache. But it—the aching heart, the uncontrollable sadness—was strangely enjoyable, if that's possible. Part of me didn't want it to stop." He looked up at the ceiling with a puzzled expression for a moment. Ahn had his hat lowered to cover his eyes and was breathing softly. Mun continued, returning his eyes to Miri, "I didn't like what I was wearing though, the black robe. I was fine with the outfit in my dream, but when I awoke, the mental picture of me wearing that thing was almost upsetting. And I don't have any clue why I should feel such strong emotions over mere clothing in a dream…"

"I think you were a Catholic priest and those large penguins were nuns," Ahn startled them. He lifted his hat, still leaning on the wall.

"I was, was I?" Mun said turning his head to him. He seemed disappointed.

"I can see you being a Catholic priest. Ha, ha," Ahn's teasing started.

"I think it's just a symbolic vision," Miri said, hardening her eyes toward Ahn.

Mun asked Miri to share her dream, ignoring Ahn, who was yawning and scratching his neck. Miri told them what she saw. They laughed as if watching an animal cartoon.

"That was great. You've got your money's worth," Mun said rather enviously. "But the scene you described had some elements of hedonism or decadence. Don't you agree?"

"I didn't feel that at all. It seemed chaotic, but there was an order, one which respected free spirits," Miri tried to explain.

"I think it's great! It's like a somber version of a Bugs Bunny cartoon," Ahn said with a big smile getting ready to, it seemed, to derail the train of conversation. Mun warned him to have more respect and show some sensitivity when other people are engaged in metaphysical conversation. Ahn gave him a salute, sticking out the tip of his tongue. Miri could never tell when they were serious or pulling each other's legs.

"Do you remember, Miri, that once you said your idea of heaven is a Bugs Bunny cartoon?" Ahn said. Mun turned to him blinking, with brows raised in exaggerated disbelief. "What? This is a deep question for me," Ahn said, shrugging.

Miri ignored them and answered, "Yeah, I remember. It was a bit like the cartoon, but there was a certain melancholy. These creatures were longing, waiting. They live with hopes. Hope shouldn't exist in heaven, should it? It's a state of imperfection…"

"I think you visited inside of your head. That's it. All those animals and creatures depict your inner world. They can't behave properly because they have the wrong heads. If a bear had a tiger's head, it must be confusing. Who am I supposed to mate with, a bear or a tiger?" Ahn started again. They laughed helplessly.

"We'll never know what it means, but I do like your interpretation. It's funny and clever," she said, wanting to own her vision unconditionally. She wanted it to stay in her as it was, no distortions should be applied for the time being. There was something sacred about it, and I won't meddle with it, she thought.

"It's your turn," she said, looking at Ahn, half anticipating that she was about to hear some silly stuff.

"Wait a minute, didn't Mungsil say something like playing 'musical chairs with heads'? Didn't she?" Mun interfered. "She knew what your vision was, then, right?"

Ahn turned to him and nodded in agreement, "I remember too. Wow, she was worth every penny."

Miri thought briefly about denying having heard it, for reasons she couldn't know. Instead she said, "Maybe I was talking in my sleep, and she overheard it. That's possible, isn't it?"

Mun sensed that she was reluctant in fully disclosing her experience. He thought about pressing her but decided against it. He said to Ahn instead, "Okay, buddy, it's your turn."

"Mine is just a usual doggy dream," Ahn started, uncrossing his arms, "it doesn't have any profound question mark like yours. I was about five or six wearing shorts, and my favorite bumblebee-striped shirt. It was a hot day. I felt the warmth from the sun and the breeze—no, there was no breeze. Did I smell something? I'm not sure, maybe my sweaty pants…" Mun's fist landed on his shoulder. Ahn giggled, rubbing his shoulder: "That was a more than necessary use of force, buddy. It hurts." Mun shook his head, pursing his lips. "Okay, okay, time to get serious. Here I go, where was I? Oh, yes…I got thirsty playing outside. I went into my grandpa's room knowing that he kept a thermos with cold water. The kitchen was too far for a busy boy pressured with time. My grandpa was napping. I gulped down the water from the thermos, only it was not water, it was an alcoholic beverage. He must've switched the water in it with cold sake, which he wasn't allowed to drink too much. Anyway, it was too late. My head started spinning immediately. I lay down next to him and fell asleep. I fell asleep in my sleep! When I woke up, that is, still in my sleep, I found that our bodies had been switched. I was him, and he was me in my bumblebee-striped shirt. My grandpa still had his old man's voice, but in a five-year-old boy's body, and he was laughing, clapping with my birth hands. I was devastated and called out for my mom. My mom showed up and saw me in my grandpa's body crying out for her. All she said was, 'Be patient, dinner will be soon.' Then she left." He finished his story with his palms raised as if he was still pissed off at his mom.

"You were right. It is a doggy dream. But I'm so sorry that you were so frightened. Nevertheless, I see question marks here and there in a doggy kind of way." Mun's teasing was interrupted by Ahn's elbow landing in his rib cage. They started nudging each other's shoulders, chests, and the sides of their heads with their fists. The annoyed stares of neighboring tea drinkers stopped the pushing, ducking, and giggling of the two boys. Mun looked at them apologetically, blushing a bit and urged his buddy to join him in resuming a civilized posture.

Mun turned down the volume of his voice, so low they had to gather their heads in the center of the table. He asked them if they had noticed how intelligent Mungsil sounded. "It was like someone else took her over. She almost sounded like a professor of something, a bit sententious, though."

"I noticed that too. One moment she was like a peasant, and the next a philosophy professor, a guru, even," Ahn agreed. "Did you learn anything from the lecture given by the bucolic professor?"

"Maybe. I can't say. I was more amazed by the abrupt change in her and her abilities in articulation. What she was saying was that the world is controlled by our egos; therefore, we are fucked up, right?"

"Is that what you believe?" Ahn asked.

"Do you?" Mun asked back.

"To a degree. But I sensed that she had an axe to grind with the ego. I disagree with her characterization of the ego being brainless and heartless. I know mine is tender and completely under my wings," Ahn answered. He stopped Mun who was about to open his mouth by raising his forefinger at him. Mun made a gesture of offering him the stage. "Her description of the ego belongs to a certain kind of person, one with an unhealthy mind.

Personally, I know no one who fits that description. Such an ego belongs to parasites. Her generalization is simply wrong. 'Civilization was built by the overly empowered ego who is a slave to fear; the ambition to succeed in life is the sign of neurosis.' She sounded like the world is a breeding ground for parasites. I refuse to believe our parents worked their asses off to support me to see me turn into a parasite."

"I didn't feel that she generalized that all egos had the same characteristics, although I appreciate your opinion. That was good," Mun said condescendingly but thoughtfully.

"I've learned something," Miri jumped in when she got the boys' attention. "I believe it's true that one should recognize the source of their thoughts, their ideas. I believe if one lifts his ego and notices what's underneath and is able to maintain a careful balance, one's life could be in harmony. Knowledge of oneself would help the ego to serve you better. I don't like to think that our ego is some kind of ugly pig we carry inside. It could be a good soldier. An egoless life is like food without salt. By the way," she continued, "Did you guys notice if I offended her in any way? She became unfriendly to me toward the end."

"Yeah, she said you were zapping her energy. She acted like you were about to steal her liver," Mun acknowledged, blank faced.

"I felt it to be the other way around," Miri said.

"She was definitely defensive not offensive," Ahn interjected. "It was funny, though, when Mun rubbed the money on his hair without his typical 'why should I?' response." They laughed, revisiting the scene.

"I wanted to get out of there, especially when I saw foam at the corner of her mouth. I felt an urgency that she was about to do something that we might regret. When you kept asking her questions, I wanted to kick you, Mun," Miri said, checking the emotions on the boys' faces. There was none.

"Yeah, why not ask something like if she could fly or if she could turn wine into water?" Ahn started. "Well, overall it was rather boring. I felt like I was enduring a lecture when I didn't do anything wrong, you know what I mean, not to mention having to pay for it. I expected to see some supernatural action," Ahn said, yawning.

"Didn't you say she was worth every penny a few minutes ago?" Mun said with an exaggerated expression of disgust on his face.

"Did I? Can't I own two opinions for one thing? Yes, I can." He narrowed his eyes, pushing out his cherry lips at Mun.

Miri said, "Speaking of supernatural stuff, haven't you guys noticed anything?" The boys looked at each other and shook their heads in the negative. "Didn't you notice she spoke without a southern accent, in a man's voice at times?" she asked.

"No, I might've not noticed if she did," Mun said, searching through his thoughts.

"Me neither, Ahn said.

"Did you?" they both asked.

"I did. I clearly experienced that she was occupied by foreign entities."

"More than one?"

She nodded in answer to their question.

"How did we miss that? I thought she was in a trance, that's all. No man's voice, no change in accent," Mun said, lowering his eyes, pouting as if he had missed dessert.

April came. Mun had gone, and Ahn disappeared, as if he no longer existed without his buddy. A cycle of her life was abruptly broken. Before she knew them, she was fine being alone, but it was not fine anymore. Their circle of three, tightly joined together, was now broken, and the ends of the broken circle wriggled in pain trying to find each other. Missing someone was a brand new feeling that she could not enjoy. It was like she came back from a trip and was saddened by the temporariness of good things. Everything that she was able to ignore at home or at school when the boys were in her life had returned. They were the same, oh so same, yet not that familiar. She wasn't the same. People looked ugly and smelly. Fuzzy hairs of hatred were growing in her.

At night she sat at her desk, looking at the mountain endlessly. When she tried to study, a task which became much more demanding, the letters on the book looked like tiny bugs lined up for a military drill. She often skipped going to her tutor after school and wandered around the park. The warm spring weather with budding flowers of cheerful colors and the young greens on the trees seemed childish and naive. The bright sunlight against the blue sky shone for everything else but her. It was like they did not want to do anything with her or vice versa. They turned as artificial as her book bag, her school uniform, and her cotton socks. Only the darkness at night restored her. She started to stroll around the neighborhood at night, letting her feet take her wherever they wanted to go.

One night she found her feet walking up steps built along an old stone wall leading up to the top of the mountain. The wall, now a ruin, was built during the Yi Dynasty in an attempt to keep the enemy out of the capitol. She walked up for about ten minutes then turned onto a small path leading to a large rock that was embedded in the middle of the mountain like a giant nose. The bottom part of the rock stuck out, making an awning for the space below it. She sat there looking down at the city lights, shivering from the night chill, holding her body tightly. The rustling leaves on the trees, a night bird singing a heart-wrenching tune that echoed through the dark air, and the sound of water from the brook nearby filled her mind with deep sorrow. The quiet wisdom of the sorrow nudged her, telling her that her life was a sham. Who the hell am I? Am I my desire? How would I know my desire is truly mine when I know nothing about myself? She curled up there like a fetus in its mother's womb, trying not to remember the inveigling world down below that infected her heart. Up there in the womb, she was allowed to pity herself. She knew she wasn't hardened. If she were lonely, she wouldn't know it. Solitude began to mean something, and that was the kindest place she could be in. Unkindness, either said or unsaid, showered upon her, trained her mind to believe that she was a thorn. She couldn't impress her world; she couldn't turn it around. The world needed her to be just the way she had been, a thorn; it was her duty. "The sun comes up, and the sun goes down, and here she is again another day to know that she doesn't belong." It had been a constant battle with herself just to endure, endure more, though never with fortitude, and she felt she was almost done for. She needed to hide, get patched up, and heal somehow. But this was new. She had no map, no instructions. She was a shivering neophyte with a fist in her mouth to stop the scream, the scream that wanted to call out, "Mom, Mom where are you?"

- 3 4 -

"The girl in the next room, how long has she been here?" Sam asked an orderly who came in to check up on him.

A heavyset guy with a red, sweaty face, the orderly spoke with a voice that sounded like it was coming through his nose. "A little over a month. Is she bothering you?"

"No, I thought she was awfully young to be here. I thought you have a section for youngsters. What's she in here for, do you know?"

"I think she walks in her sleep, something like that," he answered, tucking in the sheets on Sam's bed while breathing heavily. "The young ones normally stay in the west wing, but Dr. Min decided to keep her here." The west wing was for "problem kids" whose parents had deep pockets. "Anything else you need, Mr. Sam?" he asked, adjusting the sleeves of his jacket.

"I'll have my dinner in the dining room today. That's all."

The orderly bowed and left. Sam went out to the balcony. The warm air rising up from the ground was humid from the evaporated rain that had poured the night before like it was the end of the world. He could smell the soil. It filled his heart with nostalgia. He sat on the lounge chair and lit a cigarette. Still pictures of his past floated on the stream of his thought, filling up his heart with both yearning and regrets. He thought of his father, Jayu, and mostly his sweet amah.

A grown-up man who couldn't be one when faced with the death of his loved one was how he behaved when she became terminally ill. He avoided her, worked hard, played hard, and drank more than usual, as if he were trying to master the pain ahead of him, the pain of life without her. He even got angry with her and told her harsh things. "I guess we all have to go one day. I can't hold you here when you want to go." He said such things more than once, as if it were her desire to leave him. It was the stupid mouth selfishly purging pain, a pain from the anger over his powerlessness to help her. How he wished he could take those words back. How many times he woke up in the middle of the night and sobbed, wishing that he could ask for her forgiveness, holding her hands. How betrayed and lonely she must have felt with those words. It gouged out a chunk of his heart.

"Botchang, you'll keep that promise. Say 'yes' one more time." This was the last thing she murmured before she closed her eyes for the last time. It was a balmy night when she departed. He held her pale hands, small hands that fed him, cleaned him, ran through his hair, and pinched his cheek lovingly. He wept, holding her lifeless hand until dawn.

Amah was superstitious. She believed in reincarnation, karma, and evil spirits, and she had sets of ridiculous rules that she insisted that Sam keep. It amused him, but he obeyed, and even when he grew up, he found himself practicing those rules. "One shouldn't stand or sit in a doorway; it blocks the good energy." "Don't sleep with your head to the north, the spirit of death will get confused and take you." There were many dos and don'ts. It was serious business to her. When he was leaving for America, she gave him a small piece of red wood with an engraving on it. "Always keep this with you. This will protect you from harm. This isn't just a piece of wood; it's from a date tree that was hit by lightning, very hard to come by," she said. He remembered how he became frantic when he misplaced it and couldn't find it for days.

She used to say that she was water and he was a tree, and that was why they were good together. She warned him not to be with fire for it burned trees. She explained the five elements of fire, water, tree, metal, and soil. "You have the best one. None of those can kill water," he said to her as a young boy.

"Not really, Botchang, they can dry me up," she said.

She told him many folktales of heroes and villains involving this belief of hers. "Am I going to be a hero?" he once asked, sitting on a rock around the pond looking at the koi fish swimming lazily.

"Do you want to be?"

"I don't know. Those bad guys in your stories seem stronger."

"But in the end, they always lose," she said with concern.

"Then why do those heroes die and come back to life as a corn tree or a rice tree and not as a king? Why do some of them die to begin with?" he said, not liking how many of those stories ended with the deaths of heroes.

"They are just stories of a man sacrificing his life for many others. He comes back as food for people to nourish themselves," she said, combing his hair with her fingers.

"Well, then I don't want to be a hero for sure."

"Why is that?"

"Who wants to be reborn as vegetables? And I'll be eaten," he said shuddering, screwing up his face.

Sitting next to her lifeless body, a whirlpool of memory spun violently in his head, making him cry loudly, wanting to go back to that time and stay there forever.

Sam hired the very people amah wished to perform her funeral ceremony. They came and prepared the body. He followed her instructions carefully as he had promised her. Her body was placed at the north side of the room behind a silk screen with beautiful embroideries of the four seasons. In front of the screen was a long table with meticulously arranged fruits, rice cakes, origami flowers, burning candles, and incense. She didn't want her photo displayed nor for any animal meat on the table. She wanted those who came to pay their respects to have a cup of sake, which was left on a tray next to the table. The group of men who were to perform the ceremony was mostly middle aged and had somewhat feminine attitudes with delicate features, makeup, and colorful costumes. The ceremony was to be performed for three days and nights in the belief that the soul lingered around the body for that long, and the ceremony was supposed to guide the departing soul to the right path to the journey beyond. They believed that a departing soul did not necessarily know where to go, and if you took the wrong path, you could end up in the womb of a hideous creature. A man in the group started chanting with a low, silky voice to the tune of a stringed instrument. People walked in one by one, knelt down in front of the table, took a deep bow, and drank the sake. Sam was sitting in the corner of the room wearing a funeral costume made out of coarse burlap. It was a tradition designed to humble or even humiliate the family who didn't follow the dead. Since she had no blood family, Sam decided to wear the burlap as her son. The rest of the house staff also chose to wear the outfit in honor of her, including Jayu, who had a piece of burlap around his neck. Sighs of grief and suppressed sobbing mixed with the burning incense filled up the house. Sam had quite a bit of sake with Jayu. He leaned against the wall stroking Jayu, who slept with his head on his lap, feeling numb and surreal. He dozed off here and there. He then woke up startled at the scene being performed in front of him. A full-blown ceremony was being executed. Those feminine males were jumping to the primitive tune played by the instruments. It was happening right in front of him, and yet it felt like he was invisible, observing it from a different dimension.

A lamp hanging outside of the gate indicated the house in mourning, and the gate was left open for those who wished to come in to pay their respects. An enormous amount of food and drinks were served in the courtyard for anyone who came to say a good wish to the departing soul. Mrs. Lim oversaw the whole event and brought in meals for Sam and Jayu. Jayu only left Sam to go to bathroom. On the fourth day she was cremated, and Sam and Mrs. Lim took the ashes to the River Okchon from where she came. They sprinkled the ashes. She didn't want any of them kept.

- 3 5 -

A boy about Miri's age checked into her floor. He was initially placed in the west wing then transferred because there were complaints about him. He sang. He sang a lot. His incessant singing made the tenants of the west wing unhappy, especially because he sang opera, with arias as his specialty.

He was a scrawny, ugly boy who talked and talked in between songs. His ugliness was endearingly comical rather than monstrous. His small shaven head with scabs and scars resembled a potato thrown back to the field, unwanted. Half of his face was occupied with large pink lips, which were glistening with saliva and that from a distance looked like a piece of medium-rare steak. When he talked, these lips stretched out in all directions on his face. He hung around the nurse's station and amused them all day. Sometimes he tried to grab their breasts or pinch their bottoms, whether they were young or old, making them shriek and often laugh loudly. His name was Hakyu, and he was a year younger than Miri. He sang beautifully, and no one on the floor objected. He shuffled back and forth in the hallway singing. Sometimes he stopped abruptly then would repeat the same line over and over like a skipping record player, all the while standing in the same spot in the hallway. People began to make requests, which he obliged graciously. Sometimes people clapped in their rooms when he finished an aria in the hallway. He visited Miri from time to time and talked to her, which was his second best pastime. He called her "sis" and talked to her as if she were his real sister who had known him all his life. When he talked he gave no introduction, as if his audience had the full history of his life, even his thoughts. Miri grew to be fond of him. He made her laugh.

One morning Dr. Min came in during his rounds. He squeezed Miri's toes and asked how she was. She gave him a positive nod. She'd had no visitors, no calls since she came there. Dr. Min's initial plan to keep her for a short while turned into many weeks. Honestly, he didn't know what to do. She seemed perfectly normal. At the same time, he didn't feel right discharging her back to where she came from. Somehow he felt obligated to prepare the girl better before releasing her, but he had no idea what he should do.

Two to three times a week, they had sessions at his office. Sometimes she talked a lot and other times said nothing. Whether she talked or not, either way there was no emotion, narrating as if she were telling someone else's stories. Nothing seemed alive and moving in her even when she laughed. But there was someone behind her eyes looking out, seeing through him. The more he talked with her, the more he wanted to meet whoever this "someone" was.

He wondered if Miri knew about his affair with Sohee. He found himself blushing at the thought, feeling naked in front of those thousand-year-old eyes. He liked women. Sohee was just one of many; they were all married and were all his patients. His affair with Sohee was not any more special than the others. No romance, no particular attraction; if anything, it was maybe a bit of spice added to his life. They came to him looking for comfort, and his compassionate nature embraced them, making them forget the threats in their lives. This intoxicated him, making him lose his boundaries, and he let things take their natural course.

"I'll see you at one o'clock today, right?" he said to Miri, scribbling on the chart. He squeezed her toes one more time and left.

She showed up at one o'clock at his office with the comic book called *Madam Yumla* (Queen of Hell), the one she had borrowed from the nurse some time ago. His heart sank when he saw the book in her hand. This was the third time she brought the book, and he had not yet read it; he had been hoping she'd forgotten about it. He motioned her to sit down in the chair across from his desk without raising his head from the notes he was writing. He wasn't writing anything particular, just doodling. He wanted to make her feel that he was in power and also to see how she handled the indifference in silence. This went on a while. She did not move or say anything, not even a sigh of impatience. Eventually, her stare scorching his forehead won.

"So, Miss Miri, I see you brought the comic book again," he said, putting down the pen. The rabbit with eyeglasses that he drew on the notepad was staring at him. Why do I always draw rabbits, he thought, like he did many times, throwing one last look at the rabbit disapprovingly.

"Have you had a chance to read it?" she asked, half knowing the answer.

"No, I was hoping we'd move on." He spoke slowly, wondering how she would trap him with the issue of the comic book again. "We haven't had a good talk for the last few sessions. I'm concerned and frankly curious. It feels like you're intentionally trying to block your thoughts, refusing to step forward."

"Maybe so, doctor. Only it's not intentional; perhaps it's unconscious, I don't know. But I'm stuck with the thought of a character in the book, and I can't stop," she said, looking almost pained, which was a rare exhibition of emotion, however faint.

"Okay, let's talk about it," he said, putting his elbows on the desk, making a pyramid with his hands. He reluctantly admitted to himself that something about her last statement triggered his curiosity.

"Do you know the character I'm talking about?" she asked.

"I know the book is quite popular, but no, I can't say I'm familiar with the character." He paused then said, "I do know she is a mean person."

"Mean as the title indicates."

"So, she must be a hellish woman. What sort of things does she do to earn such a grand title?"

"She does what she wants, which causes misery to others around her. She has no conscience for the outcome of her actions. She behaves only according to her needs, which vary from one moment to another. Everybody is afraid of her. Her husband, her father-in-law, and neighbors tremble at her sight. They avoid her at any length but strangely never talk badly behind her back. The neighbors laugh at her shameless behavior but immediately freeze up at her sight." At this she stopped and showed the doctor the picture of the woman on the cover of the book.

"She's not a nice-looking woman, is she?" He smiled genuinely. It was a funny drawing, funnier than his rabbit.

"She reminds me of a bulldog."

He smiled at the comparison, nodding his head, wondering if he should get a copy after all. "What's your fascination about this awful woman?"

"Her will. She doesn't see any red lights in her way."

"Would you like to be like her? An antisocial person?"

"She doesn't suffer from it. The perceptions of others have little importance to her. I'm not sure if I'd like to be like her, but I envy or even admire her will. She lives her life all the way, being true to herself."

"Her will seems to be destructive. Is that also your will?"

"I don't know what mine is, constructive or destructive. Her will is who she is. Our will makes who we are, I think. Until I find my will, I will never know who I am."

"Aren't you giving too much value to a comic book character? It's entertainment, a fiction to sell."

"I know I'm intellectualizing a stupid comic book figure, but humor me for a little while, Dr. Min. Why do you think it's so popular? What is it in us that make us have such fun with it? You wouldn't want to know such a person in real life, and yet people love this awful woman."

"That's an interesting point. But let's go back to her will and yours for now, shall we?"

"As I mentioned, I found myself envying her blind will, fiction or not. Part of me wishes to taste how it feels to own such a force of will. True, the character's personality is unsavory, but let's forget about her being a good or bad person for a moment. She behaves like an uncontrollable toddler, I know that. I believe I have my will, which I brought with me to this world. Where is it? Where did it go? Who and what killed it? How am I going to retrieve it? I need to know very badly."

"Well, let me think. First of all, I do agree that we come to this world equipped with certain will, however various they are from one to another in quantity and quality. The common will we share is the will to survive. Then there's a will to survive well, a will to achieve or contribute. But that's not the kind of will you're talking about, I gather."

"I honestly don't know what kind of will I'm talking about. If I could remember who I was when I was an infant, perhaps I could answer you. Those kinds of will you've just mentioned could be more or less learned will, not genuine or original will, wouldn't you say?"

"What would you do if you found your original will, the one you came to this world with, right now?"

"I'll know who I'm meant to be…And I'd be very loyal to who I'm supposed to be."

Dr. Min looked at her intently, not knowing what to say for a while. He would've felt easier if she had asked, "Doctor, why can't I fly?" It was true that she had occasionally been challenging and sometimes made him think about his own self, which wasn't a happy moment for him. Somehow she always was able to tangle him with her mind. Once again, he tried to pull the conversation to a more clinical side and said rather bluntly, "You don't like your present self and you can't be loyal to this present self. But you would like to, am I right?"

"My character doesn't sit with me very well. But not liking myself doesn't feel right either. Yes, I'd like to serve something, preferably me."

"You know the issue we're talking about now is what most people think about one way or another in their lifetime. Some think more, some think less, and some, like you, like to dig into it intensely. But here we are talking about you, your young life. Let's say your infantile will had been long gone, never to return in its full form, what would you do to carry on as best as you can? This takes will, a sound will, a great deal of will that you can serve. If this is the best fit for you, then wouldn't you say it's your choice of will and yours only, not planted or learned or borrowed?"

"So what you're saying is that I can still be whole, my own master and servant. All I have to do is to find it…right?" she said, resigning. It felt like the doctor was selling the idea of the possibility of a full and rich life to a handicapped person. "It's all up to you!" She didn't want the conversation anymore. She wanted to talk like she had done with the boys, but she realized the doctor had a job to do. It didn't seem that he would dismiss her soon.

She changed the tone of the dialogue.

"Yes, doctor. It's mighty confusing. Everything is. I think too much, make too much out of things. Confusion is the penance for those who over think," she said, stretching her arms, her demeanor quite different from a moment ago.

He knew she was dismissing him slightly, but he actually welcomed it, at least for the time being. He took a lighter tone himself and asked, "I wonder if everyone kept a 'two-year-old will' what would the world be like?"

"Chaotic," she said and chuckled.

"You'd like to see such chaos?"

"Why not. It would be interesting. But if everyone is two years old, no one would see it as chaos." They laughed.

Then Miri's rambling started. The topic was something about cosmic force, how old folktales correctly explained the cosmic message and how someday all physicists will be shamans as well. She said these things as if talking to herself, for her ears only, but these were coherent, intelligent, and even careful, organized ramblings. Dr. Min called this rambling, because when she embarked on a certain word, she dressed it up with various nuances in an attempt to articulate her thoughts as closely and accurately as possible but also excessively. It could be almost funny, but it also wore him out thinly. By no means did he think of it as a mental problem, a somatic mental problem. It was hyperactivity in need of a release of tension. She feels easy with me, at least, he thought, liking the girl. He nodded here and there, listening to her. It took all his energy keeping his eyes on hers without revealing when his thoughts were straying. He tried to retrieve what his head might have recorded of her voice while he was blanking out. There was nothing, as if the tape were broken or finished.

Suddenly, he realized she had stopped talking. An awkward silence landed between them. She looked like she was expecting his response. He looked up at the ceiling, tilted his head this way and that, and squeezed his nose gently with his thumb and index finger as if searching for words. Then he saw a shadow of hurt passing on her face. She detected the truth behind his performance, which he always gave himself credit for being of a professional level. Not this time. A few moments of silence passed. She withdrew in the chair looking regretful, her eyes cast down with certain determination on her lips. He was sinking in quicksand of shame, fidgeting with the innocent pen in his hands. Finally, he took a chance and said, "I'm sorry, I wasn't listening. I was, I think, but I…I went blank at some point, I'm really sorry." He cleared his throat with his eyes darting all over in anticipation of the shower of self-imposed humiliation. He managed to meet her eyes and was relieved by what he saw. There was a smile, a tease, understanding, and even a touch of friendship in her eyes.

"Shall we continue?" she asked.

"We shall, we shall," he answered, fussing with things on the desk. He was glad she didn't require his excuses but was quite crushed inside like a scolded puppy. He confessed where he went blank. She basically repeated the part he had missed while drifting away.

Somehow the woman in the comic book made a comeback to their conversation. "I get the feeling you are annoyed when I bring up the subject of Madam Yumla."

He was going to say "Oh, not at all," but the shame still circling in his bloodstream got aggressive, and he said honestly, bluntly, and proudly, "Yes I am, can't help it. But it's my problem, not yours. And I see it has some merit. Where are we going with it? That's the source of annoyance, which is wrong of me and unprofessional. But professional or not, I'm in the business of dealing with human dynamics, and I have to have my humanness fully available, which also comes with the expression of my own emotion. So please don't think twice about what or how I seem to feel. It shouldn't mean anything to you." He felt good about what he just said. It somewhat restored him.

"I still have a few more things to say about her and I promise you that'll be it."

"Go on."

"She exercises her will without conflict like a two-year-old. She removes obstacles using whatever means available but without anger or hatred. She just does. She's assertive, aggressive, and stubborn, as if she sees no other choice available. Those adjectives I just listed mean nothing to her. There's no such thing as a backup plan in her life. True, she makes other people miserable, but I saw that these people brought the misery themselves by not exercising their own will against hers. She has no need to judge others."

"Do you find anything in her that you identify with?"

"No, I don't think so. That much I am sure of. She taught me to question what my will could be. What's the right direction for me to take? I feel like I'm on a raft floating in the wrong direction."

"Do you have any idea which direction you want to go?"

"Not a clue. Just a vague feeling that I'm heading for the wrong direction."

"Don't you have any desire to be anything or do anything in your life?"

"No, I don't. That's why it's peculiar that I feel like I'm heading for the wrong direction."

"Do you have a will to live?" He regretted the question. He asked himself, Where did the idiotic question come from? But he was tired.

She answered nonchalantly as if it were an everyday thing to throw a question like that at another person.

"I'm not sure. One thing I can say is that if such a will exists in me, I don't have full access to it." She looked down, suddenly looking old and shabby. He lit a cigarette carefully, thinking what to say next. She spoke before him. "I think everyone is born with a will, the master of our senses, but we're conditioned and distracted by the teachings of others, which are forced upon us. Our free will becomes a nuisance, to say the least. We either lose it or hide it because of so many nos and don'ts that rain down on us from birth. The moment we're born, our will gets snipped away like the umbilical cord and is constantly pruned, dwarfing and deforming our will like a bonsai tree. I know people dream, hope, and believe, but are those really theirs? Do those things constitute the will to live? If I have a dream, is it really mine, how do I know?"

He saw a godly sorrow in her eyes, making him feel inadequate. "Let's talk about your favorite thing to do. You must have something you like. Let's start from there, shall we?"

"I do have many favorite things. I get excited over changes of weather, the smell of books, sharpening pencils, candlelight, steamed rice. Quite pathetic!" She laughed, looking up the ceiling, covering her mouth with her hand as if she would cry at the same time.

"It sounds like you like things that relax you."

"They don't relax me. Liking those things makes me anxious, as if I'm betraying something important. My favorite things make me anxious! When I do schoolwork, I lose the anxiety, but I feel artificial. All the wheels, nuts, and bolts in my brain work smoothly and easily, and I even feel proud that I'm a good girl, a good student, and clever when I'm engaged in artificial stuff. But it never gives me a sense of life. I feel life much more when I stand in the pouring rain soaked to the bone or endlessly staring at candlelight despite the anxiety tugging at me."

"That's the mind of a poet, an artist perhaps, and a thinker. But it seems you don't feel free to be that. You might be quite right that most of us live not knowing the origin of our will. An individual like you who questions, who has a very different agenda than the rest of us, is bound to suffer more. You and I should work together for you to realize that such suffering is unnecessary. I truly think you have a great mind. I see your will there. You are very much involved with yourself, almost painfully," he said, feeling a pain in his heart that was strangely joyous at the same time. So much burden on such a tender young heart. "I have a request, though. From now on can we be totally candid, meaning say whatever comes to mind?" he asked.

"I'd like that," she answered.

He lit a second cigarette, blew the smoke to the ceiling, and swiveled the chair he occupied. "I've met your sister Sohee and your mom, as you know. My educated guess told me that none of you are fond of each other. You told me briefly about your upbringing, but you told me what you observed, not what you felt. I need to have a better picture of your life: at home, at school, and so on. So far, when you've talked about your life at home, you narrated as if you weren't in it, ignoring the wounds and scars you must've undoubtedly received. This is the place where you can let it all come out. With our joint effort, we might be able to put some stitches in your wounds and heal them. After the healing you can take your journey to find your will. Certainly, you should know you can't go far with open wounds," he said, looking at her straight in the eyes, which now reminded him of the eyes of fish that had been caught. He continued, "I want you to tell me in detail who and what they—your family, relatives, neighbors, or teachers, anybody—are to you, what's your opinion of them, how you see your relationships with them, and your emotional boundaries concerning the environment you live in, as honestly as possible." He said this while hardening his eyes at her.

She relaxed her fish eyes, smiled sheepishly, and said she did not know how to begin. He was quite aware of the fact that kids didn't like to talk about their family unless it was something worthy of bragging.

"Don't think of me as a grown-up with authority. Say whatever comes to your mind. No filtering. Try to remember any incidents and start from there." He tore up the page with the drawing of a rabbit with eyeglasses, getting ready to make notes on what she was about to say. The fatigue he felt a while ago disappeared, and he felt like a man on a mission.

"I was basically ignored from as far as I can remember." She started slowly as if dictating to him. "I remember walking around town alone at an age when I still had accidents in my pants. I got up alone and went to bed alone. When I think about that time I hardly remember anyone around me. There were no kids my age in the neighborhood, so I learned to play by myself with dirt in the street or watching ants. There was a small preschool open nearby, but my father refused to send me there when my grandmother begged him to. He said he wouldn't have money go rotten by sending a girl to preschool. Mind you, he had more than enough already at that time. I was dressed as a boy with a boy's haircut, in my parents' superstitious hope of having a son the next time. Every day I hung around the preschool playground watching them singing and dancing, and I hid away when anyone turned towards me. I was envious of them but never thought I could be one of them. I was nobody's nobody. It never made me sad or feel ashamed. I saw my sisters nagging my mother day and night for things they wanted. Sometimes they kicked and screamed until my mother gave in, but I never tried such a method. At that age I already knew that such a performance from me wouldn't move a single hair on them. I don't remember feeling suffering for what I couldn't have. Such right to suffering belonged to others. I don't remember ever thinking 'I wish I had this and that.'"

"When you visit your childhood memories of a remarkably young age, what kind of thoughts pass through your mind?"

"It's like I'm watching a girl who I want to hug and take home with me."

"You don't feel anger or hatred?"

"No, perhaps some sadness, but there's also pride and richness of emotions. I like the girl in my memory. Yeah, I like her alright."

"Were you abused physically?"

"No, not at that young age. That started to happen at an older age—slapping and pushing but never serious beating. The verbal abuse was constant, though. One thing I remember that still sinks my heart to this day was the time when my mother took us to a bathhouse. I was three or four. It was dark, steamy, and crowded. Naked people with dripping wet hair, washing their bodies and squatting all around seemed like a picture of hell to me. The water was too hot, and every time my mother poured the hot water on me, I almost screamed with burning pain. She washed my hair holding my head so that I was facing her. There I saw a chilling hatred in my mother's eyes and the hatred was all for me. Until then, I didn't know she hated me. But that look on her, how should I put it…It was like she would kill me if she could. Later when we came back home, I hid in a wardrobe and wept. I'm not sure if I wept because of hurt or fear. But after that day, I clearly put a distance between her and me. I began to dislike her. It wasn't hatred. It was a 'I'd rather not know her' kind of mindset."

Dr. Min wasn't taking any notes. He reached for another cigarette but decided against it. Instead he asked her, picking up the phone, "I'd like some coffee. Would you like something to drink?"

"Coffee sounds good, thanks."

He called the secretary for coffee, reached for a cigarette after all, and lit it. He blew out the smoke in a long stream, swiveled his chair a few times, and said, "Your father and sisters. I gather you aren't close to them either, but tell me who they are to you."

"Random encounters. My father, I don't know who he is. He's an angry subject whose door is locked with chains and bolts that are rusty. Sometimes I imagine his blood being green and oily. Whatever's behind that chained door, I have no interest in knowing. If possible, I want to have nothing to do with him. I do feel pity for him sometimes, though, like I feel sorry for my sisters."

"Is it possible that you feel sorry for them because you see yourself in them? Especially your sisters."

"Does it make any difference? Seeing them suffering over petty things brings out the pity in me. It's like watching a sad movie, something of that nature. It doesn't move me or stay with me. I don't know if I saw a mirror image of myself in them or not, but I do feel such pity for my mother too. Perfectly good lives are being wasted on them."

"Is your mother your main nemesis?"

She laughed at this question. The receptionist brought the coffee, put the tray on the desk, bowed, and left. Miri caught Dr. Min checking out her flat behind wrapped in a tight skirt. She took a sip of coffee and answered his question, still smiling. Something about the word "nemesis" was funny to her.

"She's not my nemesis, but I am to her. She and I have this primordial thing going on between us. My presence brings out a sour energy in her that must be painful."

He laughed this time. Her demeanor was quite different now, he noticed. She seemed to be more in charge and comfortable. It was as if she were enjoying talking about the painful stuff of her life. He noticed that she described these painful things as her research subjects. They were her annoying pets. "Obviously you are able to see humor in hurtful, even tragic, situations. Is that useful for you?"

"Tragic? You give too much credit. It's nothing more than a pile of dung. The interactions and dynamics in my family are so raw and pathetically primitive, one cannot witness it without humor. Any day you were able to dodge the bullets of this dung was a day of nirvana. Come to think of it, you almost feel as if something important was missing on such a heavenly day, that the day wasn't complete without some dung landing on you."

"Describe these bullets of…"

"Dung?"

"Yeah, tell me what consists of this matter."

"Demoralizing, humiliating, blunt remarks at each other. One evening I said 'hello, how are you' to my father when he came home. He hissed at my face saying, 'Cut that bullshit!' Another time he said my skull should be hammered down to powder after I gave him a bow of hello. Lately, I've noticed it's getting more and more creative, even poetic."

"He said that out of the blue?"

"Without any preexisting condition. It comes out of his mouth as if we were having a bad argument. But all of us are used to it," she said, remembering how oddly and consistently polite he was to the house staff.

"Is it mostly your father?"

"I think people tend to learn or mimic bad behaviors much quicker from the one who holds power. They seem to be engaged in competing with each other over who could come up with the more hurtful item. Everyone participates in the competition rather eagerly, in a sort of trickling-down way."

"Do you?"

"No. Not that I'm more civilized, but someone has to be a recipient, and that's my designated role."

Dr. Min thought this was an important part he needed to understand better.

"Seriously, why do you think you don't behave like them?"

She closed her eyes for a few seconds, pursed her lips, and said, "Because it's too ugly." She sipped her coffee, ran her forefinger along the rim of the cup, and said, "I can never be like them, even if I tried."

"You must feel proud that they couldn't corrupt you. That is a strength."

"I don't know about that. Frankly, I feel like a coward, a clown. And it's true at times I wish I could say something wonderfully smart and scary that makes the hair on the back of their necks stand up."

"So, you do get angry with them."

"Momentarily, but it dissipates as soon as it comes. All I can think about at such a moment is to remove myself from the scene, and the moment I get out of it, I feel too relieved to dwell in it. Besides, I don't like to keep anger in me. It's unpleasant and fruitless. I learned that indifference serves me better. It even empowers me."

"That's a great point. But you're so young, and you've gained such wisdom only through defense, a silent discipline of defense by molding yourself to fit the problems. What I'm saying is that one should gain such wisdom after giving an equal chance to one's anger. Your coping mechanism is lopsided; it's from hurt, not anger."

"Why promote anger when it's not there, doctor?"

"Because they're tightly connected, in a way, the same thing."

She frowned, tilting her head. "Are they the same thing?"

"Let's say that they are dual personalities of the same entity," he said, noticing that she was still in the dark. "Somehow you think anger is an ugly thing, but it's a form of hurt, an important emotion we own to keep us well. Anger has a right to exist and can be respected when expressed in fairness. You said you feel anger, and it dissipates. But trust me, it does not evaporate on its own. If you don't acknowledge it and guide it in a positive manner, it will eventually accumulate and thrust a dagger in you. Anger becomes angry, so to speak. Somehow you taught yourself to manage your anger with humor. It's a gift to be able to see humor, but in your case, you're poking fun at your anger. You're shaming your own righteous emotion. That's why you feel like a coward and a clown. Are you following me?" he asked, noticing a faint frown between her brows.

She gave him a hesitant nod and said, "I think so. I mean, I understand what you are saying mentally, but emotionally it's foreign to me. What you're telling me is like explaining how to fly to a fish. And you don't understand why I'd rather poke a beehive with a stick butt naked than tangle with my family. It is, after all, surviving, reserving myself the best way I know. If expressing anger served me better, I would do so. But I do understand what you said. Especially the part of my feeling like a coward."

He scratched his chin, poured more coffee into both cups from the pot, and decidedly said, "Can we revisit the day when you had a run-in with your mother, the day before you first came to see me?" He was referring to the day when her nocturnal outings were discovered. "According to your mom and your sister, you acted violently."

"Sohee wasn't there, and no, I just made a statement directed to my mother, which was the first time in my life. Come to think of it, I certainly behaved unusually forcefully, but in the mouth only. It was my mother who was violent. Maybe I was developing the art of anger a bit, after all." She laughed then apologized quickly, saying that she didn't mean to joke about it.

"What did you say to her? You told me a part of it once, but exactly what did you say?"

"I don't remember the exact words I used. I said something like Jesus was her boyfriend and I had been seeing him at night...And Jesus said that he couldn't stand her, my mother, but I didn't use any vulgar language. That much I remember clearly."

He put down the pen, crossed his arms, and started to laugh, more like giggle. He issued a multi-colored handkerchief and wiped his eyes, heaving his shoulders with left-over laughs. Finally, he said picking up the pen for no reason, "What do you call that, a peace offering? The remark you made to your mom was certainly an expression of anger, verbal violence. You used those words as a weapon. With your mom being super religious, that must've been the ultimate blasphemy. What happened next, what went through your mind after that?" he asked, writing on the pad with a pen that was bored being held hostage in his hand for a long time.

"She plopped down on the floor and was held back by the house staff. I went to my room, hearing her beastly screaming that I was no stranger to. I don't remember what I felt or thought afterwards; I was too tired."

"Did you apologize to her later?"

"No, we don't do that. We just move on to the next round. She didn't speak a word to me after that, and here I am."

"When you go out at night to the mountain, could it be an intentional exercise, for example, to get fresh air or clear your mind that got you carried away, or is it a random spiritual quest?"

A solemn silence fell between them abruptly but conclusively. Finally, she spoke in a low voice: "It called me. The cosmic mother sat with me, restored me. She gave me permission to see the insignificance of the world. No heaven and hell. The wisdom of blankness, of neither black nor white. I'm not a human but a complete life, a patch of breeze, or a grain of soil." Her demeanor was changing again. She narrowed her eyes, looking in the air as if she were seeing something for her eyes only. The faint crooked smile on her lips was ghostly. Then she stopped talking altogether.

-36-

D r. Min had been a textbook kind of man in the beginning of his career. He liked to think of himself as a man of science. When he chose psychiatry against his father's wish for him to be a surgeon, he had believed the human mind was not out of the realm of science. A nerve ending squirting neurotransmitters to the tip of another nerve delivers a message according to a meticulously designed map enabling a human to think, feel, and act by the massive highway systems of wiring in the body. He had believed that one day technology would be able to fix damaged wiring in the human anatomy and correct any irregularities. Several years into his practice, he began to doubt the possibility of this conviction. "What is a normal state of mind?" was the seed of his doubt. Now some twenty years later, he no longer thought psychiatry was all that scientific. It was a guessing game where your tool as a doctor was your own individual experience as a spectator. You treat them with medication to dull their minds and monitor any threatening side effects to keep them alive, and the rest is *que sera, sera* although with a very organized, intellectualized appearance. His intense study of personality theories by Freud, Jung, Horney, Adler, Maslow, and many more troubled him. They were more autobiographies than universal theory. Jung observed the spiritual phenomena of the human psyche unlike his contemporaries, which brought out criticism that he was psychotic himself. At least Jung's mind seemed to be reaching for the endless horizon of the human mind, whereas Freud, whose brilliant mind was sadly devoured by his ego, became a prisoner of his own dogma. Who are these people? How dare they assume that their dishonest experiences with their own selves would explain those of someone else. But people bought into them, applauded, and spread their words as the science of the human mind. The more he practiced, the more skeptical he became of what he learned, including his theory of the human mind being the product of its nerve and brain wiring. Now he became a believer of mysterious forces. But unlearning what he had learnt was not an easy thing to do. It required daily discipline.

Every single patient he treated existed in his or her own unique wonderland. The ocean of vagueness in one's brain, which reminded him of soft tofu, never ceased to amaze him. Normal or abnormal, hero or villain, proud or ashamed, everyone was owned by this wobbly mass of soft tofu. Jammed inside of the skull, the tofu creates drama, and we play the role it creates. It's God's entertainment center, and God is in love with tragedy.

He was making a few notes on his session with Miri when his phone rang. It was his wife wanting to know when he'd arrive home that day. "I've got a beautiful bass for you," she said.

"Plain or striped?" he asked.

"Of course, striped," she answered.

He exaggerated his excitement, told her when to expect him, and hung up. Every Friday he went home in the city for the weekend. His wife and two boys, ages seven and eight, welcomed him every time as if a long-lost husband and father finally came home. He enjoyed his wife fussing around him and his boys' eagerness to please him with their progress in school or karate lessons. When he was with them, he was all there, but when Sunday evening came, his mind was fully transferred to the island. The cozy comfort of his home life felt unreal sometimes, anxiously unreal in comparison with the lives he had to face on the island. Actually, this cozy life of his at home had a dilemma. One day he discovered that his wife, the last woman on earth anyone would suspect to have an affair, was having one with a young man, the son of a local fishmonger who worked with his father at the store. His wife gave piano lessons at home, and this young man was one of her students, which he thought odd. He had a reputation of being a lady's man. His boys complained about too much seafood and said their mom smelled like fish all the time. A tiny frequency of suspicion went through him from time to time, but he dismissed it as his own guilty conscience. One weekend when he was at home, a traveling vendor selling fried silkworms passed in front of the house. His boys asked him for money for the fried silkworms, but he couldn't find any on him. The boys pressured him in fear of missing the vendor, so he reached for his wife's purse and scooped out change at the bottom and also a folded piece of paper. He dropped the change into the boys' impatient palms and unfolded the paper without thinking anything. It was a receipt from a hotel that was newly opened in a developing area and took three bus transfers to get there from their house. To him, this proved that the tiny frequency of suspicion passing through him was telling the truth. His jaw dropped and stayed that way for a while. The first thing that came to his mind was to hide. He went inside a small closet filled with winter coats, heavily scented with mothballs. He tried to think. Nothing. His brain abandoned him, leaving control with the emotions that acted badly. He stood in the dark closet among the coats smelling mothballs when he heard the boys coming in. They called him, and he came out of the closet before they saw him. He managed to smile at the younger boy who offered him some of the fried silkworms. He shook his head, telling him that his tummy felt peculiar. He locked himself in the bathroom and smoked one cigarette after another, sitting on the pot. After two cigarettes his brain reluctantly resumed work. Strangely, he was not angry. It was more embarrassing, which felt wrong. He couldn't decide if he should confront her or not. "Perhaps she knew about my extra activity all along." He broke into a sweat, thinking about his own affairs with various women. "My impeccable wife who would do anything to make me feel loved. Is it some kind of phase? She seems so full of life, happy, proud. Not a patch of cloud on her, never. Maybe I should ask her. Maybe

it isn't what I think it is. What do I do? I can't think of my life without her."
It was the moment of awakening. He didn't realize she meant that much to
him. Sure, she was important to him but never had he thought that she took
possession of his life until then.

He had met her through a marriage broker hired by his parents. She was
over thirty, an old virgin who made a living teaching piano. She was rather
homely looking, a type that someone's parents would fall in love with. In
spite of her plain appearance, she was sensibly groomed and dressed. From
the beginning he felt easy with her. She had a certain quality of making him
feel good about himself. Whenever he felt less than he should about himself,
he wanted to be with her. Six months later they got married. Over the years
she put on quite a bit of weight, but when he looked at her, he could not help
but feel lucky. She made him a proud family man. His life went on, being
content with her existence, but he never asked himself if he loved her. Now
sitting on the toilet, sweating from the free radicals of unguided emotions
that were urging him violently to notice them, he began to see that she, his
fat, unfaithful wife, had managed to secure the seat in him that he reserved
for the very best. How? When? It didn't matter, it happened without his
knowledge. He had been kept in the dark for so long, but oh, how glad and
painful he felt simultaneously to have learned that his wife had been sitting
in the throne in his heart.

He heard the boys banging on the door. He told them that his tummy
was angry, adding grunts to his voice. "Are you doing stinky?" the younger
one said, making the older one giggle. His wife knocked on the door. "Are
you okay, honey?" Hearing her voice made his eyes well up. The only person he was truly comfortable with was not so solid; she was untruthful, im-
perfect. Did he ever think she was perfect for him? Hardly. But he always
believed that he was to her. His imperfection was above her idea of perfection. She was incapable of detecting such imperfection even if she'd tried.
His imperfection belonged to him, not to her. Well, that was an assump-
tion in disguise. He witnessed such self-deception among his patients, who
assumed their superiority over others. Realizing all this in an unbearable
state of embarrassment and emotional exhaustion, he wanted to hide from

himself. What if she is in love with him and runs away? No, she would never. We are too important to her. That much I am sure of. It must be just sex, an exercise, a sport, he thought. Before any rational mind took hold of him, he shouted at the door aloud, "I'll be okay, I think the crab stew I had last night was too spicy." A loud empty fart escaped his body simultaneously. A single laugh escaped his lips with moisture in his eyes. It must be God's hand cueing him to surrender to humbleness, the simplest but most powerful wisdom to which no logic in the world can hold a candle. "I'll make some honey tea. That will help settle your stomach." He heard her steps moving away from the door. He smoked one more cigarette, which caused him a real pain in his stomach, making him an honest man. He ended up doing his business, massaging his stomach to ease the pain, alternating empty laughs with sighs. The whole thing didn't take long, but it flipped him inside out. It was exhausting, but the spasmodic giggles persisted. His own ugliness and stupidity seemed wise and kind. He got up, washed his face, took a deep breath flaring his nostrils, and expelled the air through his wide open mouth, looking at the unbecoming reflection of himself in the mirror. He tried deep breathing a few more times. It was to gain the air of determination. He was determined to ignore the whole thing and let it take its course. He walked out the bathroom as a slightly more mature man, at least he thought.

-37-

Sam dozed off sitting on the balcony. He was woken up by a large fly buzzing around his face. It was as big as a honeybee and had a greenish golden back. He watched it aimlessly flying about, keeping him company. "Does your life have any meaning?" he asked the fly. "I know mine doesn't." His shirt was sticking to his body from the humidity in the air. He thought he saw emptiness passing by him. He went inside the air-conditioned room. After he took a shower, he remembered the dream he had napping on the balcony, a dream of watching himself sleeping. He quickly went back to the balcony to see if he was still sleeping. He realized he was no longer in his dream. "I'm boring even in my dream," he said to himself. He looked at the clock. It was half past six, and the sun was packing up for the day. He changed into fresh clothes and went down to the dining room, which was crowded with early diners since many people had their weekend visitors with them. He gathered a few items of food on his tray and looked for a seat. He spotted a shabby, pink blouse. It was the girl next door sitting with three elderly people at a table for six. He walked over to the table and sat next to her. "Hello neighbor," he said, wondering how she'd respond to his greeting.

She looked up and simply said, "Hi, Mr. Sam," and turned her eyes to the three sitting across from her. The dishes and bowls on her tray were empty, and judging by the number of empty dishes, he thought the girl must have a healthy appetite. He looked at her with a side glance, putting a morsel of food in his mouth. The shabby, pink blouse was a size or so too small on her, and her dark hair was bushy and dull. She looked like she just got out of bed and accidentally put on her younger sister's blouse. He wanted to know her. He didn't know why. He wanted her to like him, to tell him her story. An absurd idea that she'd make him happy went through his mind.

Suddenly, she pulled her chair close to him and whispered, "These people are always together and always argue."

Delighted with this friendly approach, he asked, even though he was not at all interested in the three, "What are they arguing about?"

"Today they are arguing about what was in the soup and what was not. They're quiet now because they're pissed off at each other. They're always together, inseparable. And most of the time they don't even look each other eye to eye."

Two men and a woman in their late sixties or early seventies sat together closely as if they were one large body with three heads. It was obvious that they weren't enjoying each other's company.

"Do you take enjoyment in watching people arguing?" he asked, spreading a generous smile on his face, fearing that she might take offense.

"Who doesn't?" she said with her eyes fixed on them. One of the men got up and the other two followed without saying a word, and they left in oneness. Miri's eyes followed them until they walked out the door.

"What's so fascinating about them?" he asked quickly, not wanting her to follow them.

"It's both amusing and sad. They argue over nothing. It turns to name calling, which then escalates into a new argument, and they forget the initial one. And yet they are inseparable, carrying their disgust for one another. I wonder what it is that binds them together."

"When you get to be old, you can benefit from stimulation. It might be their way of stimulating their minds, mental sport."

"Actually, they're not that different from the rest of us. People are so eager to agree when they really disagree underneath. Those three show me how unpainted human dynamics work. The interactions of human beings, no matter how sophisticated they are, no matter how civilized, are basically basic. What I learned to be proper social mannerisms, basic virtues if you will, are a disguise. The better you disguise yourself, the more approval comes your way. If you are really, really good at it, you fool everyone to the point that they believe you are all they see, which makes *you* believe you are who they say you are."

He smiled, feeling happy talking to her. "So what you're saying is that we believe our own lies."

"We have to. And why not. After all, truth is an illusion," she said, narrowing her eyes while lifting her eyebrows, making her expression rather comical.

"We're lying, but we're not really lying, is that right?" He was beginning to have fun, although he was not sure if she was playing a game with him. After all, there must be a good reason why she landed in a place like this. He added, "You said earlier that human interactions are basically basic. In your opinion, no matter how hard we polish ourselves, we can't escape it, am I correct?"

She gave him the look of "did I say that?" but just as quickly recovered and said, "Yeah, that's my opinion, and you're correct. I think people's main motivation for engaging with each other is for self-serving needs. Our behavior, high or low, comes from the need to gain and protect."

"I see nothing wrong with that."

"Neither do I. But we don't simply stay in fair 'gain and protect' mode. We like to be better than others. We created 'virtue,' which bears good intentions, but the virtue we created is rather distant and foreign from human nature. The bar was set too high, and no one yet has the courage to yell out to lower the bar. In the end, virtue became the garment we put on our bodies, an appearance, a mask. The truth of the matter is that we all know inside that our real dealings with each other happen underground. You wear the mask of a 'virtuous, law-abiding citizen,' hoping the mask helps you to increase your gains, but at the end of the day, you wonder if someone else's mask outdid yours and feel thoroughly cheated. Ha, ha, ha. We're all walking around in the emperor's clothes."

"You don't think it's because we're the most intelligent creatures; therefore, we're bound to desire better behavior from one another, unlike animals?" he asked for the sake of continuing the conversation.

She blinked her eyes as if asking him where the dumb question came from. She said, "Animals know who they are, but we don't. How intelligent does that make us! God cursed us with ambition. Frankly, I think animals laugh at our talent in making life more difficult than it already is. We don't know what freedom is like, but they do. They are the true law-abiding citizens in nature."

"Speaking of God, I think our keeping up with fake virtue has something to do with the tradition of religion," he said, feeling a bit phony, but at the same time, surprised at the unexpected statement coming out of his mouth. Religion meant next to nothing to him. He was neither for nor against it. It was just one more fabric people draped around them. He briefly wondered if there was any indentation made in him, unbeknownst to him, regarding religion.

"I think religion and God are two separate things. I'm sure God doesn't like the religions we have. They cheapen Him at best. They destroyed the divine being in us. It's a crime how religion stood between God and people. But what is it in us that makes so many of us cling to it?" She continued, "I grew up Catholic. My mother is super religious, and if we missed Sunday Mass, she would hang us upside down by the toenails. When I was young, during Mass I would look around and see no happy faces. They taught Mass is a celebration of the life of Christ, but the entire church seemed to be filled with the bad energy of misery pouring out from every orifice of these people, people who were begging for something from this man who looked so helpless."

Sam laughed, imagining the scene she described. "How old were you?" he asked.

"Young, very young. I used to break into a cold sweat at night at the thought of being thrown into a burning hell with no possibility of a second chance. Cruel, isn't it?"

"Cruel and stupid. Do you still go to church?" he asked, certain that her answer would be 'no.'

"I do. I guess I'm brainwashed too, ha, ha. There was a time I went to church because I was afraid, not of my mother's rage but of something else. I used to get seized by the terror of what if they were right. I believe there is a god or gods. I mean, I need to believe there is someone. As I grew older, I began to form my idea of God. He is all the goodness that I'd like to be and more. God should be felt, not understood. I like to sit in a quiet, empty church. It feels like I'm visiting my own soul."

Sam suspected that she might have an issue with her religious upbringing. He wasn't paying attention to the content of her talk, but it struck him in awe how she spoke to him as if they had known each other for a long time. He couldn't say if he liked that, but he also sensed that she was trying hard to prove that she was an intelligent person, not a common cigarette thief. The dining room was busy. Two women who looked alike joined their table. Miri stood up, gave him a little bow, and was ready to leave.

Even though the topic of their conversation wasn't his cup of tea, he wanted her to stay and talk to him some more. "I enjoyed talking with you," he said, waving his hand. His eyes followed her walking towards the door. Her blouse was too small, her pants were too big, and the rubber soles of her sneakers were loose. She walked as if she were late for something. He decided he liked her more as a cigarette thief.

He stepped outside to the patio. The warm and humid night air felt rather good. He walked to the darker area, passing by people talking and playing cards on the patio. Numerous moths were buzzing around the lamps. Is it the light or the heat that attracts them? Or are they at war with light, the invader of their night? He lit a cigarette and looked up at the sky studded with stars. The chorus of night creatures rang out the hollowness in his chest. Something different was happening to him. The many times he had stayed at the island before were to avoid and escape. This time he was looking for something, and that something was approaching him, he could sense that. There was caution in him as much as curiosity. "What could it be? Perhaps I am feeling God."

He stayed out for some time, thinking this and that. He felt nicely tired and decided to go up to his room. He walked through the lounge, where some teenagers were watching a game show on TV. Some sat alone deep in thought, and others in pairs or groups were talking together. He heard faint music when he passed by the music room. Someone was playing the piano. He opened the door carefully not to disturb the player and walked in. The dim light barely allowed him to make out the silhouettes of scattered furniture at first. It was Nurse Yun who was giving the concert. The classical piece she was playing sounded familiar to his musically unsophisticated ears. A small piano lamp showed her round body swaying, her stubby fingers gracefully moving up and down. Then he saw Miri sitting in a wing chair behind her in lotus position with her eyes closed. He took a couple of steps backwards into a darker spot and watched them communicating through the music. He stood in the shadows, watched the duo as if in a dream, then left silently before the piece was over.

After he came back to his room, he lay down on the bed and fell asleep. When he woke up, he thought, how long have I been sleeping? He didn't bother to see what time it was. He saw that his shoes were still on his feet. He couldn't remember when he fell asleep or if he was that tired. It took a little while for his dream to revive. He was looking at a foggy mirror in his dream. He wiped it with his hand, and instead of seeing his reflection, he saw his young amah in her light green suit standing in the bright sunlight with her arms wide open, saying something he could not hear. He banged on the mirror telling her to speak louder, anxious to find out what she was telling him. The scene repeated over and over, and the image of her became smaller until it turned dark, dark as the midnight ocean. He poured himself a drink, feeling tremors in his hand, and went out to the balcony. The mountain looked bigger and closer in the dark of night. Through the chorus of night creatures, he heard a faint music overlapping with a woman's voice. It was coming from Miri's room. He approached her window. It sounded like the radio. He sat down and coiled up with one hand holding onto the railing. The woman's soothing voice faded away, and he slipped into a state between knowing and unknowing, reality and unreality. He began to sob.

-38-

The goat didn't show up as he said he would. Ever since the day she first communicated with the goat, she never missed the morning hike unless it rained. On the desk in her room, she set up an altar for the goat to contact her again. She offered a couple of fruits she took from the dining room, origami flowers she made with colored papers she bought from the gift shop, and some pebbles she picked up from the hiking trail. She wanted to light a candle, but it was not allowed. She sat facing the mountain and sent the message every night until Nurse Yun, her night keeper, showed up.

She saw him finally. He was a large goat standing upright, leaning on a large rock on the edge of a landing where hikers would take a break before heading down. He was about her height and wearing a blue satin coat over creamy beige puffy trousers, the bottoms of which were tucked into a pair of reddish leather boots. He had two swimming green eyes, two negligible horns, and a handsome beard that reached down to the middle of his chest.

"You said tomorrow, but it's been more than a week," she said, overwhelmed with excitement, which drew attention from other hikers in the group.

"No, no, no. Talk to me in your thoughts. They can't see me or hear me. If they saw you talking to the air, you'd be shipped to the fifth floor where they'd gladly administer electric shocks through your head." He motioned for her to follow him to a pine tree looking down the other side of the hill. She could see the ocean far down below; it was blue, opaque, and still, like a single brushstroke in a painting. He continued, "You scold me for being tardy? I've been here every day, but you couldn't see me or hear me until today. I even visited your room, sat next to you, watched you reading that comic book. One night I tried to tap into your dream but that woman, 'Madam Yumla,' was sitting in the front of the gate and would not let me pass. I almost thought about moving on. But here we are, finally."

"Is Madam Yumla real?" she asked through her thoughts. If she were able to speak normally, she would have said something like, "I'm sorry that I wasn't able to see you sooner." But since there was no control over her thoughts, she could not help but be rude.

"As real as me," he said, draping his weightless arm around her shoulder.

"Why was I not able to see you before?"

"Your expectations were overly active. They blinded and deafened you. Everybody, including those people, your fellow patients, has the ability to see me. They're so charmed by the horror of this world that their minds have blocked or erased the ability to see beyond. Some of you still can, but as you know, it isn't exactly the thing one brags about."

"My encounter with you is an accident."

"Your desire to know or experience who you really are has opened the hardened earth within you, making the plants of extraordinary knowledge grow. When I saw those tiny plants in you, I couldn't resist. So here we are."

"Are you here to help me find who I am?"

"Sorry to disappoint you, but I'm here purely for selfish reasons. No need to be threatened, I assure you. It's funny, though; you people always judge a phenomenon like this as angelic or evil. You see my beard is moving by the same breeze that blows your hair, you hear my foot stepping on the soil like yours, I duck my head under a tree branch so as to not be hit by it, just like you'd do."

"What's your selfish reason?"

"You are my passage to the next phase to which I aspire. You're going to replace me one day. Trust me. It's a far better place than you are right now. Eventually, it will work out for you for the better. My selfish reason is beneficial to you if we work together."

"Am I to die? Are you going to take my soul?"

"I have no use of your soul. Chasing after souls is your game, not ours. Boy, the way you people go after each other's souls is chilling. You blame evil for possessing your soul. What I want is your ego. I will give you freedom in exchange."

"But without an ego, I'll perish. I wouldn't know how to survive. I might as well be dead."

"Nonsense. Why do you think freedom is some spineless fool? I guarantee you that freedom is much more powerful. Freedom has no consequences. It's courage after courage. It'll weave your life into a fabric big enough to cover the universe."

"How does one give up the ego? Do you vomit it out, do you wash it off? I wouldn't know how to give it to you if I tried."

"All you have to do is say yes to me. But no rush. You take your time and think about it. We will talk more in time. Meanwhile, don't forget to tend to the garden in you. Once the plants take root, they will grow like weeds, and you'll have many friends visiting you from my part of the universe."

"Are they going to want something from me?"

"No. Maybe a cup of tea in your garden of weeds."

She felt her heart doing jump rope and saw pitch black darkness moving in rapidly from all corners of her vision, sickening her as acidic juice welled up in her throat. She leaned on the tree, watching the goat give her a courteous theatrical bow, sweeping his arm across his body. "Until next time," he said, fading away. He first turned black and white then to sepia and was gone. She collapsed, seeing the sky turning inky black.

She woke up in her bed. An orderly and a nurse were eating a watermelon, talking and slurping. "Oh, there you are," the young nurse said. She came to her bedside after wiping her hands. "How do you feel?"

"I'm fine."

She put a thermometer in Miri's mouth and told the orderly to update Dr. Min. She quickly disposed of the traces of their watermelon party and came back to check the thermometer. "You still have a fever, not as high as earlier."

"Did I faint?" Miri asked, remembering everything turning dark.

"You collapsed, vomiting," she said, spreading her arms and throwing her head back with her eyes rolled up in impersonation of Miri's demise, making her already short uniform pull up showing her chubby thighs. She was trying to describe how Miri looked when she was brought in. "We thought you were having a seizure, but the doctor thought not. He said it might be a bug. That's good news, isn't it?"

Miri didn't care. She was achy and weak but feeling helpless always relaxed her mind, for nothing was expected of her, and her inner voice was quiet. "Being helpless is a blessing," she thought. She did not care what time or what day it was, or how long she'd been out.

Dr. Huang came instead of Dr. Min. He listened to her chest, drummed her stomach with his fingers and asked if she felt nauseous. "Not at all." He said something to the nurse and left. The nurse came back with a bottle of IV fluid. She searched Miri's arm here and there until she found the right spot, rubbed an alcohol-soaked cotton pad on it, and inserted the needle. Miri could see the drips escaping the bottle into the clear plastic tube on their way into her body. This enhanced her helplessness, therefore, relaxing her more. She went back to sleep, feeling pleasantly helpless. Death should be as sweet as this. No desire, no fear, and no more absurd role playing. Life is a puff, then no more you, and no more me…was the last sweet thought that passed through her mind before she drifted away.

The next morning a beautiful tenor singing "Sleepless Nights of the Princess" woke her. It was the new boy, Hakyu, with the forceps-delivery head. He was sitting on the chair singing with an amazingly beautiful voice. She peeked through the cover, both amazed and amused at the uninvited performance. He had an asymmetrical, small head, which was shaven down to his scalp, large ears that stuck out like pot holders, and large lips that looked like a medium-rare steak occupying half of his face, small eyes, and a skinny nose, the sum of which reminded Miri of a child's drawing. One more victim of social rejection, she thought. She clapped when he was done.

"How did I do, sis?"

"You did well, getting better and better, if that's possible." She found him strangely adorable. "You could be a professional singer," she said, praising him more.

"Did I tell you I sang at my sister's wedding reception? It was my first appearance in front of a crowd, in a tuxedo. There was a full band."

"I bet you received a standing ovation: *encore, bravo, bravissimo!*"

"No, it didn't go that way. My father stopped me before I finished my first song," he said, twisting his lips.

"Why did he do that, was he drunk?" Miri sat up to give him more attention.

"He didn't approve of the song. It was inappropriate, vulgar, he said."

"What was the song?"

"It was that song by Neil Diamond, 'Girl, You'll Be a Woman Soon.'" He started to giggle, and Miri joined him. The song was very popular among young people that year. Soon the song took on special connotations and was used to insinuate a girl losing her virginity. Hakyu said he didn't know that, being strictly an opera singer, but he had simply followed the selection of songs that friends of the groom had chosen for him. He said he noticed that when he was singing the song his sister dropped her head and a commotion of giggling spread.

"Did your father know about the song?"

"I don't know. If he didn't, someone must have told him."

"What did your father say when he stopped you? Obviously, he assumed wrongly that the song you sang was about your sister losing her virginity that night. Did you tell him that he misunderstood?"

"My father doesn't know how to misunderstand. Such a process is impossible to him. He switches on the high beams in his eyes, smoke comes out of his ears, nostrils, every orifice of his body, and it's all over like

Godzilla destroying the city. You don't know when it starts or when it's over. Only when you see cuts and bruises on your body do you know that Godzilla paid a visit. But this time, the wedding night, Godzilla outdid himself by breaking a couple of my ribs, dislocating a shoulder, and giving me a concussion," he said, pointing at the window with a smile that rippled up his face.

Miri looked at the window. A flock of birds was flying away in an upside down V. Geese or ducks migrating south for the winter, already? Summer was not quite over. She didn't know what to say. Frankly, she didn't want to hear any more of that. It evoked the memory of her mother, with her big, masculine hands, foaming at the corners of her mouth with half-smiling eyes that turned reddish brown before she struck. She was a random striker, so Miri could never be prepared. Her hand of brick would land on Miri's head wherever and whenever. She knew better than to ask, "What did I do wrong?" It was also better to sustain the blow of her hand and let her finish the job than trying to dodge or run. Such a challenge cued her mother to pick up a weapon, and you only ended up prolonging the session. Miri learned that humiliation was much more painful than physical pain at an early age. She also realized that humiliation left a larger, bigger, and longer-lasting bruise. It disoriented her head, mangled her mind, and disfigured her whole being, making her avoid her own reflection in the mirror for fear of the self-loathing looking back and hurting her one more time. Her mother was succeeding in grinding her down to nothing. Miri began to say Hail Mary incessantly. When it didn't help to shut down her mind, she talked to angels and demons. Her sisters were not exempt from the brick hand of their mother, but as long as they appeared to be within the boundary of her scale of good and evil, they were safe. That wasn't the case with Miri. Why not kill me and get it over with, she thought. But if I died, then she'd have no one to play with. As she grew older, her mother's physical violence subsided, and God took pity, making Miri grow bigger than her mother quickly, but the verbal assaults grew exponentially. Strangely, she never saw her mother as her enemy. The only emotion she felt for her mother was an immense dislike, maybe a shame that she used her body to be born. It was a cold, indifferent dislike but never hatred. But when Miri turned thirteen or fourteen, she began to feel pity for her mother just like she did for her father. It was the most peculiar feeling. She didn't welcome this new development in her, for that meant involvement; she would have to work on returning to cool indifference. She thought her pain was unhinged and losing its identity. It felt like she was appeasing herself in an attempt to make her life more bearable, that she was becoming a coward. She refused to go there, but she was already there. She could not help but see her mother as another human being trapped in a dark, lonely well, unable to climb up to see the opening, and whose only companion was misery, who never told her that she was a good girl. Miri let this new feeling of pity stay, but she didn't let it act out. When this new development started, she noticed life was less threatening, and her backbone was erect. Nothing had changed except that she became an observer rather than a participant.

"I'm sorry to hear that, Hakyu." Her attention went back to him. "Are you fully repaired now?"

"Partially. My ribs and shoulder are healed, but the head isn't quite recovered. There's still swelling. They gave me electric shock treatment at my father's request."

"Does it hurt?"

"Don't remember, but I do remember that I remembered nothing for a while, a week or so. I couldn't remember where the bathroom was."

"Did it make you better?"

"I have no idea. I thought electric shocks were used for crazy people. I'm not crazy. When I asked them 'why, why?' they said it would modify my behavior for the better. And that was that."

Miri shuddered. "But you still grab…you know what…" Miri was talking about Hakyu's breast squeezing.

"Ha, ha. That didn't get modified, you are so right."

They laughed together about the various treatments and tests they had to have. "How come you've never tried to squeeze mine?" she asked.

"Ha! I have standards, sis. Yours aren't boobs; they are mosquito bites with two raisins."

- 39 -

The fainting incident kept Miri in bed for a couple of days. When her fever went down, the doctor told her that she could go back to doing normal activities. After the conversation in the dining room, Miri and Sam saw each other regularly. Sam began to feel confident that Miri welcomed his company as well. He synchronized his daily schedule with hers; he ate with her, took strolls with her, smoked with her in his room when they could, and almost every evening after dinner, they sat together in the music room listening to Nurse Yun's piano concert. He was very happy with this young, unkempt companion. He found her odd and amusing. The things she said and did—things he wouldn't normally find funny—made him laugh hard. When he was with her, all of him was there for her with delight in his heart.

One weekend Mrs. Lim came with his two German shepherds that she had given him a few years back. After Jayu's passing Sam couldn't bring himself up to getting another one: 'nothing can replace Jayu. He was my brother.' But Sam couldn't resist them the moment he saw them. He named them Gongja and Maengja, names of ancient Chinese philosophers. "You look too well to my liking," she said to him.

"I'm only too happy to see you and my guys."

Mrs. Lim stepped back and gave him a once-over and said, "Nah, there must be something going on. A budding romance? Is that it? Or have you totally decided to be a full-blown loony?"

He unleashed the dogs. They weren't strangers to the place. "I think I'm developing maternal feelings," he said to her, beaming from ear to ear.

"Did you get knocked up by the Holy Spirit? You know, an Immaculate Conception of the twentieth-century kind."

Sam laughed, shaking his head, and she laughed with her eyes fixed on him in anticipation of his explanation of the mystery.

"Ever since you became a born-again Christian, your mouth has become more and more unchristian, do you realize that?" he managed to say through his laughter.

"Leave my religion alone for the last time. You benefited the most from my faith. But seriously, are you trying to tell me that you may be a she-man?"

"What?" He continued to laugh then said, "I don't even know what she-man means."

She chuckled along and said, "You know, a man who is a woman inside. You just said you were experiencing 'maternal feelings.'"

Sam shrugged and called the dogs. "Let's go up to my room. I'm too sweaty out here."

"I need a drink," she said.

"Some born-again Christian you are."

After a long drink of cold water, the dogs jumped on the bed and almost immediately fell asleep. Sam made a gin and tonic for Mrs. Lim and vodka on the rocks for himself. She took off her shoes and stretched her legs on the sofa across from him. She had a shoe fetish, and she always bought them a half size too small, saying that it made her feet look smaller and cuter. Her feet suffered swelling with red indentations on the top. This never discouraged her, and Sam had long stopped trying to persuade her to buy the right size shoes. "What's a little suffering for vanity!"

"Well, I'm glad you look so happy, whatever the reason is," she said, raising her glass.

"If I look happy, it's probably because I laugh a lot these days. Laughing therapy, you know, it works." He told her about Miri.

Mrs. Lim listened to him without interrupting. She understood what he meant by "maternal feelings." But was that what it really was? He had never liked kids, especially teenagers. All those years they had been together, he'd never, not once, expressed any desire to have kids. So what is this, a midlife crisis? Testosterone being invaded by estrogen? A red flag went up in her head when he said excitedly, "She reminds me of my amah." She hid her concern and said, "I'll be the judge of that. Certainly you will introduce her to me."

"This evening, at dinner," he said, lying down between the dogs.

- 40 -

"Are you feeling all better?" Dr. Min asked, thinking that Miri's complexion was pale even a week or so after the collapse. Although she said she was fine, something about her had changed after her illness. He thought maybe the virus was still lingering in her. He couldn't shake off the nagging feeling that something else, virus or not, must have happened up in the hills before she collapsed. She seemed aloof and wasn't very eager to talk to him. He had seen her being uncommunicative before, but it wasn't the same this time. He noticed that she spent much time with Sam, which concerned him a little. He had known Sam for years. Sam had a set of issues of his own, but he knew he was a decent man. Whenever Sam came to stay, he usually kept to himself. This was the first time he was out and about mingling with people. Dr. Min didn't know if he should take it as an improvement or a warning sign.

"Dr. Min, you look different," Miri started in a parched voice.

He raised his eyebrow and said, "How so?"

"You look mature."

"You mean I look older."

"No, no, I didn't mean physically older. You seem, well, how should I describe it, like you gave up something, sad and peaceful."

He smiled, not knowing how to take the greeting. He cleared his throat, pulled up a chair and changed the subject. "Let's talk about what's on your mind, not my youthfulness, shall we?" he said, jotting down something on his notepad. "Is being here helpful to you?" he asked without looking at her.

"I wish I could stay here for a long time," she said, crossing her arms.

"You know that's unrealistic. You're going to resume your life at some point."

"That's why I said 'I wish,' not 'I will.'"

"From my personal point of view, I'm glad you like being here. We have many elderly people who've made this place their home. This place serves them well, and I know they're better for being here. Kids are a different story. Most of them are anxious to get out of here," he said, tilting his head, suggesting that he didn't get how Miri felt.

"Dr. Min, I know I have to leave one day, but please don't rush me out, not for a while."

"I know your home is the last place you want to be. I know that. But I have my job to do. Somehow I have to make you come to terms with your situation so that you can make the best out of your life."

"Is my family pressuring you?"

"Not so far. Miri, suppose I sent you home now, what do you think would happen?"

She looked up directly into his eyes, looked down, and started to bite her fingernails.

"Well, what do you say?" he said, trying to remove the deep silence that was only getting deeper.

"You have to do what you have to do, sir."

"That's not what I have to do now. I want to know how you'd picture your life like if you were sent home at this moment."

She stopped biting her nails and tapped her teeth, still looking down. There was caution in her demeanor. "No picture comes to mind. Things will never be the same at home, though."

"What do you mean?"

"It would be a real letdown for my mom if I went back. I can't even imagine what it would be like. Honestly, I can't."

"Are you scared of going back home?"

"Right now, yes. I'm not scared of the usual stuff, but I am of the new, unknown kind. There will be a new kind after this. I am, I feel weak. I enjoy being here. I can breathe; I have a right to breathe here. That's good, very good, indeed. But it also makes me weak. The absence of daily friction makes me feel weak, isn't that awful? My guard is too weakened even for the kind of friction that I became so used to. I asked you not to rush me home because I need time to think. As long as home is the only place available for me, I have to be ready at least in my mind. I have to come up with something concrete even if it's delusional. Do I make any sense?"

"Miri—" He was about to answer her, but she continued.

"I want, I need, to make some sense of all this nonsense in my life. I need time to think. I have to decide which direction I want to go. This place allows me time, time to consider everything."

He saw her eyes welling up, and beads of tears soon rolled down her cheeks. He handed her tissues, pursing his lips that were faintly quivering. "So much pain at such a tender age." The naked innocence of being a human being heightened his emotion, sanitizing his soul. Being a participant in another fellow human's pain felt both heart aching and sacred. He wanted to know, he wanted to find some answers for him and for her. "Being here weakened you?" he asked when she seemed to be ready to continue.

She dabbed her eyes with a balled-up tissue and cleared her voice. "Yes, it changed me. After being here for a while I found that I don't observe like I used to. I mean, it isn't a game anymore. I observe with a touch of affection. You might say that I've become a better person. To a degree, I'm at ease with this change. It almost feels like I belong. Oh, Dr. Min, how I used to hate that word 'belong.' I've gained something and lost something here."

"So you like the new you, but it won't do. You have to find something else with which to arm yourself before you return. Because in your mind, it will be worse. Am I right?"

"Not in my mind. I know so." She lived in her inner world. Any environment that forced her to do otherwise could be unbearable. She had managed so far, but her inner world was growing out of her, moving ahead of her, making her unsteady.

She told him about her childhood. At an early age, she learned that solitude was the safest place for her. She made a life out of the relationship with her thoughts in solitude. She said once that the most unbearable pain was boredom. At that time he thought her life lacked stimulation. Now he knew what her painful boredom meant: it meant the interruption of her thoughts in solitude. Her solitude went everywhere she went. She was the solitude. She said she was only five years old when she decided life was a long stretch of boredom. Although she believed that nothing in her childhood altered her, she was already an altered self long before. She lost the notion of "I" or "my" long before she was able to write the words. And now she wanted to find the real her, her "I" and "my."

- 41 -

"Idlers!" Dr. Min's father used to say that "thinking" was the pastime of a man whose belly was full of idlers; therefore, it was not the activity of a decent man. Few people Dr. Min met in his life were troubled by the question of "who am I?" They went about their lives aspiring to be like machines. For them, being a human meant weakness, incompletion. These machines would break down because of the damaged humans within them, but instead of healing their humanity, they wanted their machine parts repaired. And thus the malignant cycle repeated. The noble profession he chose ended up doing just that, patching up the machine. "Tune them, oil them, and send them back out until next time," one of his colleagues used to say. Dr. Min had his share of torments. The more he practiced, the more bewildered he became. Earning a good living off the indescribable misery of fellow human beings irked him. He regretted not going in to cosmetic surgery as his father had recommended. The hypocrisy and lack of conscience found in his practice weighed heavily on him, injuring his own mental health. There was a shepherd within him, and it was hard for him to see his poor lambs not getting better.

Years ago he had received a brochure regarding a seminar in Tokyo on *The humanistic approach in psychotherapy*. Dr. Morita, who was his classmate back in medical school in Japan, was one of the leading speakers. He was an interesting guy, driving professors crazy with his wacko ideas. There was a period in their school years when they became quite close. They lost contact through the years, and the last thing Dr. Min heard about him was a rumor that he was an outcast in the field of psychiatry in Japan, which wasn't all that surprising. In need of change of air, Dr. Min went to the seminar. He was pleasantly surprised by the attendance. The theme of the seminar was about the essence of altruism, unmasking the individual, and breaking down the walls of normalcy. He found that Dr. Morita had ardent followers, mostly young professionals in mental health. It warmed his heart to see Dr. Morita standing firm on shaky and lonely, unconventional ground after all these years. He couldn't deny a certain envy welling up in him, envy of his courage perhaps. He remembered the teasing and mockery Morita had received from their classmates, but at the same time, he was well liked.

An enthusiastic young doctor talked about how from the day we are born our vessel of altruism is rattled by the logic of "I'll please you so that you'll…" It was taught to the child in hopes of making him a useful person at best: "Altruism is misguided toward an act of even exchange when it should be the act of our autonomy. When a baby is only babbling, you teach him to say 'thank you' and 'please.' You refuse to grant their desire if they don't follow your demand. Animals are trained in such a way, by giving them treats when they perform what you want them to perform. Although we see trained animals doing amazing stuff, can we really accept this as a universal truth that applies to human beings? Do we consider what is un-trainable to be abnormal?" His conclusion was that mental illness was not an illness. It was yet another type of human characteristic that could not be trained.

Dr. Min thought the assertion interesting but too vague. He had the most fun at Dr. Morita's lectures. He gave out masks to the audience and asked them to put them on. After the audience obliged him, filling the auditorium with chuckles, he asked them to notice if someone else in them was emerging. "Masks are wonderful means to meet with our unconsciousness.

People behave differently when they put on masks. Different masks bring out different behaviors, therefore, different personalities. Try wearing a mask sometime and observe the change. Let it take you to the savage land within you and help you gain better truth about who you really are. You will find it fun as well. We become closer to ourselves with the mask than without. We feel hidden and slightly freer. Take a moment, stay with the mask and give a good, solid moment or two to the raw emotions passing through your mind. Ask yourself if you are familiar with that emotion. Are you truly you? Are we our thoughts or actions? When you go to bed at night after a full day, you feel satisfied because you carried on another day according to the framework of rules and regulations of being a good boy or a good girl. This satisfaction that you enjoy and hope to have keep coming, is that really all yours or is it a learned, manufactured, artificial feeling? Can such artificial satisfaction sustain us? If your emotion is the one that was guided and molded, does that mean what you feel isn't yours? How many of you own personal vices? Who is this, our good friend vice? Something that's supposed to be wrong but pleasurable. Why are they wrong in the first place, why? Then why are they, our vices, so pleasurable? Civilization came with a heavy price for us to pay. There are too many 'shoulds' and 'should nots' in this proud achievement of ours called civilization. One thing that resiliently tagged along throughout history to join the modern world is morality from ancient religious teachings. No one I know escapes from this prison, not even atheists. It brings so much suffering to humankind, but we still uphold it as the only way to go by. We all wear it as an appearance like a proper dress code, nursing the wounded beast underneath. Some of us can't do well in such a structure. Virtue and vice are Siamese twins. They're forced to be separated, but you can never separate them completely. As proof, virtue survives with deception and vice with pleasure. If the separation is perfect, it should be the other way around. I suspect this attempt to sever the two causes mental torment. I'm not talking in terms of what is normal or not, rather, I'm raising the question of whether we really know what it is to be normal. Aren't we all a bit sick inside, trying to be the 'normal, thoroughly virtuous' individual? We forgot to be human in the true sense. People in our profession must vigorously question our original selves. We owe it to our patients. We should use ourselves as guinea pigs. Unlearn the learned. Un-condition the conditioned. Accept the truth of endless possibilities in the human mind. Then you will obtain the courage to un-label the labeled. Let's not treat our patients as abnormal but misunderstood. Let's try to restore their sense of altruism by reducing demands, because altruism is the key to autonomy. We have to help them to see they are full human beings. Their condition is a mystery, not a disease. It's a mystery to us self-proclaimed normal human beings but not to them. They might be just lost in this chaotic maze of the world we live in."

Dr. Min forgot many of the lectures except for what was described above, which remained with him to this day. He had a pleasant lunch with Dr. Morita. One thing Morita said to him made a crucial mark in him: "Through their torments and pain, I received healing. I'm much more courageous now, and it emancipates me. Emancipation into the pain, so to speak."

- 4 2 -

Mrs. Lim could be Nurse Yun's future twin. They looked alike: round, homely features from top to bottom and an immaculately organized yet relaxed appearance, which was the sign of someone who enjoyed waking up early to tackle a new day. Next to her, Sam looked rather like an under-nourished pet. It was apparent who took care of whom in that relationship. Unlike Nurse Yun's low voice and her slow way of talking due to her lisp, Mrs. Lim had a crisp, angular, staccato voice. When introduced to Mrs. Lim, Miri felt as if she were being examined like livestock at an auction.

They had dinner together in the dining room. Sam and Mrs. Lim talked about how little it rained in the city, but how it rained too much in the countryside, ruining the crops, the price of grains and so on—the typical things people conversed about when not comfortable with their company. Occasionally, Sam gave Miri a sheepish smile and said things like, "The soup is good today." Miri returned a number of nods and a number of also sheepish smiles at them. They moved to the music room after dinner. Nurse Yun was not there yet. The sofa in the dark corner was occupied by a couple of teens flirting with each other. Once they sat down, Mrs. Lim immediately sent Sam out for coffee. As soon as he left, she asked, "How old are you? Which school do you go to? Where do you live? What business is your father in? And why are you here?" Miri answered her as the inquisition came, brief and precise. Except about her father. She told her simply that he was a businessman. "Only God knows why I am here" was her response to the last question. Miri was a bit annoyed but understood that Mrs. Lim was very protective of Sam.

Sam brought the coffee, or rather, a woman servant in the dining room carried the tray behind him. Mrs. Lim said, "That man can't do anything by himself." Mundane topics came back, mostly initiated by Mrs. Lim. "How many girls are there in your school? What is your favorite subject?" and on and on. Miri answered her as much as she could then started to laugh loudly. Mrs. Lim sounded like a drill sergeant, and Miri heard herself answering her with the same intensity and even adding staccato tones here and there. Her answers overlapped the tail ends of the questions, and suddenly, it felt like a verbal ping-pong game.

Sam laughed along, telling Mrs. Lim to stop the interrogation.

"What's so funny?" she said, giving a side glance at Sam. "I'd like to know her better." She let out an empty laugh looking at Miri somewhat patronizingly.

Miri said, "It's like I'm being interviewed for a job in military fashion. I don't remember the last time I was so polite to anyone." She continued to laugh with Sam, shifting the oppressor to the place of the oppressed. Unfriendly sparks came from Mrs. Lim's headlights through her oversized glasses. Miri enjoyed the laugh but also could not ignore the smallness of it.

"I like your shoes. They're pretty," Miri said to Mrs. Lim as a peace offering.

What a perfect thing to say, Sam thought, delightfully surprised. Mrs. Lim quickly recovered her ego and started talking about her love of shoes. Miri was attentive and agreeable to her.

When her ego was fully restored, she began to criticize the kids in the dark corner who were consumed with making out. "They should monitor the kids more carefully before they have a mom and dad on their hands."

"Why do you always jump to the worst possible conclusion?" Sam criticized her.

"All I'm saying is that they have to watch these kids more carefully."

"I find it sweet. They're in love."

"Look at them. That's more like a sexual overture, not love."

"It starts from there. It's human nature. Either they are in love or comforting each other's surge of hormones, I don't know, but it is what it is. One of the few things we know for sure."

"They're too young and should be watched better before it's too late. I know I'm right."

"I know that you think things are either 'A' or 'Z.' There are no letters in between in your mind. One thing peculiar about you is that you could be very crude and even vulgar then you have this side of puritanical conviction."

"Interesting, isn't it?" Mrs. Lim said. They looked at each other with a grimace but not without affection. This last statement of Mrs. Lim triggered Miri's curiosity about her.

"I think Nurse Yun isn't coming." Sam had told Mrs. Lim about Nurse Yun's piano concert every evening. "How about we take a stroll with the dogs," he suggested, getting up. When he brought the dogs down to the lounge, people got excited by the unusual guests. The dogs made their rounds, being praised and petted, gently wagging their tails. Miri was happy to see people being happy with these furry creatures. Actually, she was happier seeing the dogs were welcomed and loved. She thought about her father's hunting dogs at home. At the sight of her mother or father, their tails disappeared between their legs.

It took a while before they made it outside. Miri ran with the dogs, playing with them, screaming and shrieking in delight. Her childlike shrieking and the barking of the beasts echoed through the night sky.

- 43 -

"So, you fainted," the goat said.

She wasn't allowed to hike for a week. The weather was getting more tolerable, and the sky seemed to have moved farther up, bluer than blue. Her heart pumped fast with excitement when she saw him. "He's real, he's so real" was what went through her mind, which the goat heard. "The doctor said it was a bug," she said, using her voice. He reminded her to speak with her thoughts.

The goat said, "I thought I scared you into thinking that I wanted your ego. It was careless of me, I apologize. I should've permitted more time for you to get to know me."

"I don't feel particularly threatened by you, although there was a vague sensation while I was losing consciousness that you took something from me, a part of my organs."

"I didn't take anything from you, not yet. As I said before, you have what I want, but what I'll give you in exchange is far more useful for you and probably, maybe exactly, what you're looking for. Now, there are no cons or tricks here. Such things don't exist in my world. Are you interested?"

"I'm struggling with the fact that I'm seeing you, hearing you. I'd like to think that you're from an unknown dimension, but at the same time I can't help wondering if I'm seeing my own imagination coming undone."

He laughed and said, "No matter how hard you try, you'll never arrive at the truth, not even a whiff of it, as long as you use confusion as a guard. Isn't it boring to be so serious? I'm only asking for a game. Give it a go, have fun."

Miri looked at him chewing a twig, unable to sort out the resistance and curiosity fluctuating in her mind. She didn't want him to leave, that much she was sure of. "How about you play my game first?"

"Fine," he answered, too quickly, suspiciously.

"You're going to answer my questions, all of them, with the promise of sincerity and honesty."

"Begin."

"I have to warn you that it might take time, beyond your patience."

"I'm not very patient, but I'm determined. I'm also not that polite. You have to understand it is against our rules of conduct to use human fashions of politeness. I go by my mood, and you shouldn't take it personally. Your first question?"

"You said 'our rules.' Are you part of a group, a world, or what?"

"There are many of us. No, it's not a group or a gang of spirits. We do have some rules, so to speak, although no one breaks them. Let me rephrase that. We don't know how to be un-free. Hypocrisy humans engage in is poison to us."

"You're not an angel or a devil or spirit or ghost or—"

"Enough. Stop wasting time. You can't understand who I am even if you tried for a million earthly years. You wouldn't know what it is if I showed you my identification card. Your limited idea of the world beyond is the first thing you ought to destroy, if you want to continue this. Those are ideas created by humans as storytelling, to keep your minds occupied. Otherwise, your world is an unbearably boring place. Humankind wouldn't have continued this far with such boredom."

"Tell me about your world. Make me understand."

"I'll give it a try, but I'm afraid you'll have to rely on your limited imagination." He paced back and forth with his hands on his back, his chin to his chest, and his eyes cast down. Faint green beams from his eyes landed on his blue coat as two yellowish moving circles. "Where you are standing now? There are seven different dimensions simultaneously existing," he started. "Can you fathom that? And no, I don't belong to any of the seven. I don't belong to any so-called dimension. I'm a freelancer. I'm very content where I am. However, there's one more leap I have to make. When I complete the leap successfully then I'm home free."

He hadn't quite answered her question, but she let it go. She wanted to hear the description of his world. Are there landscapes, houses, families? Do you eat and mate? Is there art, beauty, or magic? She asked, "If you're so content with where you are, why the trouble to make this leap?"

"Contentment isn't everything. It's always a notch or two short of bliss. One has to have conflicts; contentment is the tail end of it. No conflicts mean no satisfaction. We are free but not home free. Many of us stay here for eternity, but some of us want to take that leap. But if we fail, well, that's a disaster."

"Is it somewhere between heaven and hell?"

"Purgatory? No." He looked determined not to elaborate.

"Why do you need my ego?"

"I need to be a human to take the leap. It's a risk, but it's the fastest way if it works."

"Why do you need mine?" she asked, looking at the people around them, suggesting many other possibilities for the goat to fish for an ego.

"Once I choose to go back to your world I have no control over who I'm going to be. The stakes are too high. I can fail and be lost forever. The only thing I can rely on to guide me safely home is the ego, one as dumb as yours." He didn't apologize, and she didn't care. It was just a confirmation. He continued.

"Your ego is the one I can trust. If you offer it to me, I hope, it will be mine to carry."

"How many times have you been a human?"

"More than once. Then I went through a few of the dimensions I told you about until I reached where I am. What a spectacular journey I've had! But I still couldn't make it all the way home. I'm ready to go back, and this time I'll make it home."

He seemed sad and lonely, which made her feel likewise.

The goat saw the puzzled look on her face, read her mind, and said, "Your ego is a fetus, unborn, still connected to the soul by an umbilical cord. Therefore, it's perfect for me; it'll let me glide through life without being tainted. That's the best I can explain."

"You are after my soul too?" she asked, raising a red flag in her.

"No, I'm not. I couldn't have your soul if I tried. You see, your unborn ego can be hooked onto my future soul. It will keep my soul always maternal."

She smiled, taking a deep breath. "I feel strangely proud."

The goat laughed along and said, "Are we done yet?"

"Hardly," she replied, keeping her smile. She was enjoying the moment of recognition that she might own something precious.

"It's hard to believe that my ego is unborn. I have survived this far. Isn't ego the surviving mechanism? Funny though, I like the idea that my ego is a fetus, a sixteen-year-old fetus. It feels sweet."

"You've survived purely on the strength of your spirit. It's the gardener, the caretaker of your being."

"I don't know why, but that sounds beautiful, comforting..."

"What else?" he asked, putting the twig in his mouth, unable to hide his impatience.

"Why do you want to come back here? That doesn't seem wise. What if you don't make it, what if you end up being somewhere less than where you already are?"

"You mean like hell or purgatory? Ha, ha. First of all, I don't desire to go back to your world. It's the built-up energy in me that has to be recognized and processed. It urges me that it's time for me to try to go back home, and that requires visiting your world once again."

"Does everyone where you come from end up having this built-up energy at one point?"

"Not at all. But when it happens, there's no way of going around it."

"Can you tell me what the soul is? Doesn't everyone have a soul?"

"There's no definition regarding the soul. It's everything and anything. Therefore, every soul carries its own definition. Does everyone have a soul? I'm sure you've met quite a few beings without it."

"Who are they? I mean, why they don't have souls?"

"They are spontaneous formations by the remnant energy of the universe. They're all about drawing energy from others. One common factor they have is that they don't have the ups and downs of moods, which is produced by the soul. They are good at keeping rules and regulations because they are built like a clock. Naturally, they become good citizens."

"They are all egos?"

"They have none of those properties. They go by the source of energy. Parasites. One astounding property they have is the ability to mimic."

"So they must be an intelligent organism."

"Everything has intelligence, even your shoes. The soles of them are telling you to let them go already."

She looked down at her shoes who were blushing with shame at being exposed to the goat's fancy pair of red Corinthian leather boots. She had been meaning to get a new pair. Her mind returned to the goat and asked, "Are they amoral?"

"Your shoes?" At this, she laughed aloud, drawing the attention of fellow hikers.

"I meant the soulless human beings, are they amoral?"

"Morality is a fiction. And being moral in your world is a show, a performance so that you don't get stoned. Those people, natural mimickers, do very well with the performance. Speaking about this fictional morality, it has nothing to do with possession of a soul. Intelligence and ego give birth to morality; it's a pretty powerful and deadly force. It springs from taking advantage of each other's confusion and fear, which produces energy that could destroy soul. So there are people born without souls, and there are people who possess souls but let their ego and intelligence take leave from their souls. The latter suffer from the hurt they inflict on their souls, but the mimickers do not suffer. They have no one inside. 'The lights are on, but no one is home,' as some wise guy said. One thing, though, the mimickers don't and can't examine their lives as a whole. I tell you, the easiest way to recognize the mimickers is to see the quality and quantity of their compassion. They are good mimickers, but when it comes to sacrificing something, they become very weak, too weak to perform a perfect act of mimicking. They're all about preserving their lives and can't waste their energy for others. It's the most painful and unnatural act to them."

She listened to him as if listening to her own voice. What he said made perfect sense to her.

"I already know too many of them, I think. Scary but interesting. I know clergymen who are like that." She shook her head, her glance far and remote, remembering those who fit the goat's description.

"They come in all walks of life. Here comes your friend," he said, pointing at Sam who was approaching her saying, "We're about to go down."

Miri said good-bye, thanked the goat in the blue satin coat for all the useful information, and turned to Sam.

"I'll see you next time," the goat said, soaring into the sky like a large bird with fancy feathers.

- 44 -

M iri told Sam that she liked to meditate on the hill, so he didn't interfere with her meditation. Sam rather enjoyed chatting with the group, participating in conversations about the weather, hospital gossip, more weather, mosquito bites, and pharmaceutical information. They all seemed to have glassy eyes, probably from sedatives, but they were normal as anyone could be. Who was he kidding, was he really one of them? How well he would function one day, but the next moment his entire rhythm of thoughts and judgments would be turned upside down. How unbearable that was. How immobilized he became when he felt the dark murky waters of the bottomless lake rising up, drowning his soul. This mood was a strange but curious visitor at first. It was a seductive mood that sank him down slowly. He let it seduce him as he swam through the dark waters of an unknown sorrow that caressed his senses with the joy of teardrops. He was touched and moved by the pleasure of sadness. He was a lonely hero in a melodrama. Things looked more round than angular, more fluid than solid. The moonlight seemed brighter than the sunlight.

He used to sit in a room with all the curtains drawn for hours without moving until one day he no longer wanted to continue living. His attempt at suicide did not succeed. He got violently ill, which made him purge the pills he swallowed. The next day he woke up next to the toilet bowl in a puddle of vomit. He looked into a mirror and saw a hideous thing that vaguely resembled him. The episode had a short life span; it went away as if it had never happened. But it would come back at the same speed, taking him hostage once again. He did not hold onto the remnant, resilient part of reality. The sweet melancholy turned into a stalker, wilting him away. He saw a serpent's tongue in a sweet lover's mouth. He was already owned. Something else had taken its claim over him. It started out as a long rest, rest he deserved. It came with the whisper of permission, permission to see the cheapness of being. Saying no to life seemed to be the most courageous thing; in this way he justified to himself his falling. But a few loyal nerves in his brain put up a fight, agitating his long rest and fighting to reclaim their domain against the deadly virus of melancholy. And one day Dr. Min happened, and he became a resident at the island. He still couldn't make any sense out of what had become of him, and he barely recognized the few loyal nerves within him as his true friends.

Sam saw Miri walking towards him smiling, although noticeably pale. He wanted to pick her up and swing her around if he could. He couldn't, even if she let him. He was too small for her. "Did you have a successful meditation?" he asked.

"If it had been any more successful, I would've been vaporized." She added, "You know, it makes you feel lighter and lighter, like a breeze."

He noticed the difference in her. When they had walked up the hill earlier, she had been silent with her eyes full of thoughts and intention. Now she became chatty and had a bounce in her step that betrayed her pale complexion. He looked up at the sky and said, "Oh, I can smell autumn in the air." He felt his scrawny chest expanding. He felt so good he wanted to weep. The word "why" passed through his mind, but he dismissed it as quickly as it came.

"This mountain will soon be covered with trees with changing leaves. It's like a giant flower arrangement."

"The season of harvest is near, too." He didn't understand what made him say that. Sometimes people say things of a rootless nature when their emotion is heightened.

"Do you know anything about farming?" Miri asked, which was a polite way of saying "oh, yeah, as if you know anything about farming."

"Next to nothing. I once lived at a Buddhist temple a long time ago. There was an old monk and a young boy who he raised. I used to watch them farming the harsh land behind the temple. What endless work that seemed to be, not to mention the poor yield. I don't know about farming, but I think about farmers with great respect because of that experience."

"What were you doing at the temple?" she asked, and her interest made him happy.

He said, walking leisurely with a thoughtful posture, "During the war I had to hide. The communists were after me."

"Were you part of the underground resistance?"

"I wish it was romantic like that. I was labeled as an imperialistic pig, their ultimate enemy. You were born around that time, right?"

"Right after the war. As a matter of fact, my father had to hide for about two years too."

"How did your mother conceive you if they had been separated; are you your father's child?"

"There is no doubt that he is the author of me. I look just like him, regretfully so. What happened was that my father came by one day to give some money to my mother. She was staying in the countryside at her parents' home with my sisters, where she lived without much for nearly two years. My father stayed one night with her, and here I am. My mother resented having been pregnant again, especially during such a hard time. In my opinion, she never recovered from it." She laughed, but Sam didn't miss the faint frown between her brows.

They arrived at the main building. "I'm hungry. Would you join me for lunch?" Sam asked.

"I want to go to my room for a while, but I'll eat with you at dinner." She wanted to write down in her journal the conversation she had with the goat while it was still fresh in her head. Sam watched her walking away. He really wanted to buy her some clothes.

- 4 5 -

Mrs. Lim was a good soul. She was reliable, pathologically honest, and protected her close ones fiercely, and above all, she was a goddess of practicality. When she became a Christian, Sam was puzzled and wondered which part of her practicality was at work. He was sure that she would give up the Christian halo sooner or later. He was wrong. A few years had gone by, and she proudly announced that she had become a born-again Christian. He lost at his own bet and bought her a diamond necklace with a cross to congratulate her deepening faith. A kind of fate tied them as brother and sister. For so many years, they tugged and pulled at each other, trying to help the other to not step in quicksand. The loss of her son as a young mother left her heart bleeding for decades. There was a period when she frequented fortunetellers, hoping for a message from her son. Then it was Buddhist temples for some years and now Jesus. When Sam asked her why she made the change, she answered, "I still worship Buddha and his teachings, but he isn't a god. I can visualize my Chulsoo(her son) being with Jesus." And that was that.

After the Japanese were defeated, Americans filled their ruling positions; they ignored the fact that the country did not belong to them. Nothing much had changed for people. They were unprotected and malnourished as they always had been. "We are a democratic nation." The new president was nothing but a puppet of America, but he urged them to take pride in their newly obtained freedom. The only freedom these people dreamed of was the freedom from hunger, and democracy didn't come with food. Hungry bellies turned on the faucet of hatred, and the salty taste of blood and violence was filling the air. Communist allies came to their aid, and the oppressed found the chance to sink their fangs into the flesh of the oppressor. An already unsettling time turned into a whirlpool of chaos. Young men and women were recruited to spread the new idea of communism. People gathered up to listen to them, denouncing capitalism, shouting that communism was the only solution for a perfect democracy, waving their fists vehemently. "Join the movement, my friends. Together we'll defeat the hypocrisy of aristocracy and the 'haves' who've enslaved us and stole from us. The end of your suffering is near. Fight with us to claim the freedom that is rightfully yours!" People clapped and whistled in the frenzy of excitement. It wasn't a well-thought-out argument, but it was enough to stir up the pent-up anger in people. Their excitement was not about the possibility of utopia, it was about revenge. But revenge needed energy, and the constant challenge of having to look for a grain of rice diminished the excitement. Only the young and delinquent types, of which were plenty, joined them with the eagerness of a gang mentality. The situation got worse. These groups were more and more visible, and people began to notice they weren't that nice either. They walked around the town with red bands around their arms intimidating people, calling everyone "mate" regardless of age and gender, which was a capital offense according to the book of Confucianism. People shook their heads behind them and began to turn away from them. But as uncertain years went by, the movement grew with the support of the North, and Russia was breeding yet again another bloodbath. Life resumed the only path these people had ever known: living in fear and uncertainty.

One January evening in 1950, Sam went to a small pub near his office to have a light supper. A loud and obnoxious group of young hoodlum communists were drinking sake. When the owner of the pub with whom he was friendly for many years came to his table to take his order, Sam found his old face pale and cobwebbed with wrinkles, and his hands were trembling. "Are they harassing you?" Sam asked.

The old man quickly put his forefinger to his lips, urging Sam to be quiet. He said under his breath, "Every night they come and drink without paying."

"I'll inform the police for you," Sam whispered.

"No sir, no sir. They're all the same. You'll have me killed."

One of the guys shouted. "Hey, old mate, didn't I tell you to bring more sake? Didn't I tell you to keep it coming?" He was banging on the table with a cup. They were sitting a couple of tables away from Sam. The guy who was shouting sat facing Sam diagonally. He was hardly an adult. His face was the color of a beet from drunkenness. Sam stared at him briefly but long enough for the guy to notice. "You, you, what the fuck are you staring at?" The old man went to them at an amazing speed and told them the sake would be served shortly, trying to distract them, bowing profusely. Then another guy who sat across from the beet face turned to look at Sam, young and with a face only his mother could love. They recognized each other immediately. It was a boy who had worked at his office as an errand boy for a short period of time. Sam couldn't remember his name but remembered all the teasing he received by the employees for his unattractive face. "I saw an old rag prettier than you" and "your mom must have sat on your face with her big butt at your birth" were a couple of examples. One day he stopped coming and no one missed him. When Sam recognized who he was, the hair on his back stood up.

"I know him. He's the most capitalistic pig I've ever met," the youth said with a curled-up tongue, jerking his body. Sam looked around. There were people drinking and dining, but they acted like they heard or saw nothing. All five of them got up, and before he knew it, they dragged him out into the dark alley behind the pub and beat him. He took the beating lying in the puddle in a fetal position, fearing that he might be face to face with his end.

His father's recent letter was the last thing on his mind before the light in his head went out:

Dear Sam,

It's been quite a while since my last letter to you. Yu and I are fine as always. Although we're situated far away from the menacing touch of the Chinese, our fellow Buddhists in Tibet aren't so lucky. Not to worry. We're too isolated and remote, so it's not economical for the Chinese to bother us. Here we have small villages with various races and traditions, but people enjoy living in harmony. The people here are generally too lazy to go to war, it seems. I heard the situation in Korea is alarming. The rumor is that Chairman Mao will join Russia in his attempt to impress Stalin by aiding North Korean communists to invade the South. This letter might be my last one to you until, well, until whenever...

The letter urged Sam to hide as soon as possible. He wrote detailed instructions for Sam to follow.

He was in and out of consciousness for days. He had a concussion, a few broken ribs, a hairline fracture on his tailbone, and dislocated kneecaps. Mrs. Lim came to the hospital every afternoon after work, and she would tell him the news on the street. This will not pass without touching her, he thought and started to give her instructions about what to do with the office. The president had made an announcement on the radio telling people not to act in haste because the "red elements" are under control and would soon be removed completely; these words did not gain the people's trust. They could not trust their own family or friends. These people were familiar with wars and unrest, but this time they knew they were facing a very different beast.

Sam got out of the hospital bed before he was fully recovered and went to work. He followed his father's instructions step by step. First, he cleaned out his bank account and spent a large amount in buying gold nuggets. Mrs. Lim told him about an old temple where he could hide. "It's near the village where I grew up. It's a tiny village tucked in the valley with mountains as screens."

April came, and he was ready to leave but unsure of where he'd head. The night before his departure, he called his servants and distributed gold nuggets among them. "Soon, paper money will mean nothing. Hold onto this, and it will be useful. It's not wise to let others know or to sell it for the time being."

"Are you leaving us?" asked the oldest servant, who had been there before Sam's birth, wiping tears with a trembling hand. They all started to cry. Sam looked down, seeing his own teardrops landing on the floor. This was his family, and he theirs. Finally, he composed himself and said, "What I'm about to ask you to do is very important. It's important for all of us. I need you to have a funeral for me. I'm dead from the injuries I received. Mrs. Lim will instruct you on how to go about it. It has to be a cremation. As you all know, the situation is getting worse by the day, and it won't get better until it gets worse. It's very likely that one of these days they will look for me if they know I'm alive. They would harass you and hurt you to find out where I'm hiding, even though you wouldn't know where I'd be. Actually, this injury came in handy for all of us. It is of the utmost seriousness that you keep this secret for your own safety."

The next day before daybreak, as soon as the curfew was lifted, he left. He wept, rubbing his wet face on Jayu's neck, telling him "I'll be back. You have to stay well, look after yourself" over and over. He held Mrs. Lim's hands and didn't know what to say. Her eyeglasses were fogged up, and her shoulders were heaving. The driver, a young American who worked at the embassy, was getting impatient. An American acquaintance arranged for the driver to drive him to a small train station some thirty miles outside of Seoul. As soon as he got in the jeep, he sped away through the chilly air between darkness and the light of the April dawn. The driver, who knew nothing, was chatty. Through his tears and aching heart and body, Sam did his best to be a good listener. How far apart their worlds are, how envious Sam was of his lightheartedness!

He had to wait for the train for a few hours. A two-hour train ride took four. It was crowded and lively. He noticed many of the passengers spoke in the northern dialect and realized that they were early refugees from the north heading south. They talked about the increasing numbers of the Chinese and Russian armies in the north. Sam tried to stay awake in fear of missing his stop but dozed off here and there.

- 4 6 -

The station was deserted. It didn't have a platform, but there was a hut that looked like an outdoor house. Sam walked to the hut not expecting to see anyone in there, and there was no one, just an old three-legged stool and torn newspapers scattered around. He sat on the stool and lit a cigarette, blowing the smoke through the square opening that seemed to be the ticket window. It felt like a miracle that the train didn't forget to stop at the station. He was the only one who got off there. The train dropped him off like a turd in the wilderness. The railroad, under the midday sunlight framed by the square opening of the ticket window, looked more fortunate than him. He was too exhausted to feel anything more than that. If he felt anything, it was the presence of stillness. He drank some water from the bottle in his knapsack. He saw a pack of rice balls that Mrs. Lim had prepared for him. It made his eyes well up again but it also somewhat restored his spirit. He got up, put the knapsack on his back, and stepped out of the hut.

On one side of the railroad was a mountain with heavy vegetation, as if it alone had skipped the winter. Opposite of it was an abandoned field leading up to the horizon. He walked to the side with the mountain, looking for a path that would lead up to it, as Mrs. Lim had instructed. He had to go up and down along the side several times to find a particular path. It was as wide as Sam's hip. As he went up the narrow path, it became darker with tall, thick evergreens. The sunlight needled through the leaves and branches of the tall trees, and it jumped on the leaves of the shorter trees, drawing moving shadows of blue and purple. He began to notice the path getting wider, which relaxed his mind. "How did they survive the Japanese?" he said to himself, looking up at the thick screens of trees. The Japanese stole just about any natural resource in the land. They stripped the mountains and hills of their trees, causing landslides when it rained. He started to walk with intention. He drank water and ate the rice balls he had in his knapsack. He kept walking, following the path as if he knew where he was heading. Whenever dark thoughts tried to sink his heart, he whistled or counted numbers. A strange rush in him lightened his steps, and the sweat on his back made him feel that he was worthy of something; a new meaning, perhaps, was budding inside. He wanted his father to see him and be proud.

The road wound up then down endlessly, making him suspicious that he might have been going around in a circle. He took out a pocketknife and made marks on some trees. The sun was fading. The rush of energy he felt before was shaky at the thought that he would maybe have to spend the night in the woods. He could not help but worry that the temple or the village was long gone. He looked for any hint of human traces: footprints, the smell of cooking, the sound of domestic animals with bells around their necks. Nothing. For a moment he felt the rhythm in him start to beat in fear of the unknown. The injuries in his body that weren't completely healed protested and screamed at him. He was disappointed at his fear. He sat leaning against a tree trunk nearby and smoked. Not a single cell in him advised him to get up and move on. He kept seeing his father's manly face. "What would he have done if he was faced with the same situation? What would he tell me now?" He went through three cigarettes with his eyes closed.

A bird on the tree startled him. He opened his eyes, got up, grabbed the knapsack, and ran down. "Okay, down, I am going, down, down, not up." He shouted at himself, "Don't think, just keep going." He walked for about half an hour more. The sun was getting dim. He had to reconcile his fear. He was both afraid and embarrassed; fear and self-loathing were competing with each other inside him. Self-loathing won; it made him angry and worthless. But self-loathing's victory turned out to be useful because it made him angry, and anger charged him with energy, which he needed more than anything. Thirty-something-year-old man that he was, he was on the verge of throwing up with fear because he had to spend the night alone in the woods among creatures big and small. The possibility of being lost for many days and nights in the woods crossed his mind. He called himself all sorts of names. His mind stubbornly remained as a five-year-old.

He decided to take advantage of the energy provided by anger, a side effect of self-loathing, and started to prepare for the night in the woods. At this point the self-loathing was so great that he didn't think he cared. He gathered twigs and rocks to make a fire under a tree and found a tree branch about his height in case any animal tried to eat him. He imitated a scene from a Western movie. That was about all he could do. He sat down leaning against the tree. His feet were burning, his legs were wobbly, and the sudden chill made him shiver. He lit a cigarette and wished he had a hot cup of coffee, the last coffee before he became dinner for a beast. He looked up at the sky through the leaves and branches of the tree. Patches of clouds were turning pink and orange by the setting sun, and the rustling leaves on the trees turned up the volume, ominously dancing. He closed his eyes and imagined himself fighting with wolves or raccoons with the stick in his hand, feeling totally pathetic at the same time. He forced his mind to not remember what had happened to his life. He sat like that for some time, stick in hand, knees drawn up to his chest for what seemed to be eternity.

The wind picked up, and he was so cold his teeth wouldn't stop chattering. He took a jacket out from his knapsack when he thought he smelled smoke in the air, wood-burning smoke. He hadn't yet lit the twigs in the campfire he had made earlier. The smoke belonged to somewhere else. He bolted and climbed up to the highest place there, and he saw the smoke and what looked like the tip of chimney from where the smoke was escaping, like the smoke Indians used to send a message in a Western movie. It was quite a drop from where he was standing. He grabbed the knapsack, tossed away the stick that was his lifeguard a few moments ago, and ran headfirst towards the smoke, not hearing himself saying, "Oh God, oh God. Thank you, God, thank you, thank you." He even said, "Hallelujah," standing in front of an old dilapidated Buddhist temple. A mummified thousand- years old, beyond-rundown structure stood tilted to the eastside about 20 degree. It seemed a small wind could blow it down to dust. The roof was covered with weeds and debris. The wood beams that supported the ceiling seemed like their tears of fatigue became fossilized. Large and steep rock formations surrounding the sad creature could be its captor. But at that moment it was Versailles.

A young boy of five or six with a shaven head and grey monk's robe was washing vegetables when Sam approached him. The boy dropped the vegetables and ran inside. Sam stood there until the young boy came out with an old monk holding his hand. Sam quickly bowed to him. The old man came closer but with caution. "I'm very sorry for the intrusion." He introduced himself and briefly told his situation.

The old man cleared his throat and said, "You must have walked all day. Come inside first." Sam followed him, fighting the threat of being choked up with emotion.

The room was dark, and the young boy lit a kerosene lamp. The old monk listened to Sam's story nodding his head here and there with a deep sigh. When the boy went out, the old man introduced himself as Bongsan. "You can stay. For how long, I can't say. The way we live here might be a hardship for you," he said with a shy smile, making his small eyes disappear between the folds of deep wrinkles.

Sam quickly opened his knapsack and offered him the money he had. "Please take this. I can't thank you enough for your kindness," he said, bowing his head deeply.

"So much money," Bongsan mused. Then he bowed, thanking Sam with his hands in prayer and said, "Kwanseum bosal." He crawled to a wooden box sitting at the far corner of the room and crawled back to Sam with a monk uniform and said, "Put this on. Tomorrow we'll shave your hair. It's better that you act like one of us."

He called the boy and told him to show Sam the room where he'd stay. He followed the boy who darted in front of him, grey uniform in his hands. They passed the main floor, which squeaked, where a large statue of Buddha was sitting in lotus position, his face glistening by the candlelight below him. The bedroom was dark, and it was narrow but long. The boy lit a candle for him and showed him his bedding, which was neatly stacked up at the corner of the room. Sam nodded and thanked him, which produced a big smile with a couple of missing teeth on the boy's face. "My name is Sam, what's yours?"

"Kuju."

"How old are you?"

"Five or six, I don't know."

"What age would you like to be?"

"Seven."

Sam laughed. He was too tired to say anything more. He plopped down on the floor, feeling his eyelids fluttering like two dying moths. After the boy left, he lay down on the bare floor and fell asleep.

When he woke up, it was light outside. Someone had put a cover on him, and there was a small tray of food left near the door. He could hear Bongsan praying and smelled the incense. He closed his eyes, listening to the soothing sound of prayer with the occasional sound of a wooden ball being tapped. It was just a humming sound in monotone, in a language he did not understand. The abrupt change in his life and an unknown future made him coil under the cover. "What will be of my life?" He knew he had fallen into kind hands once again. Saved again. He thought about the day before when he walked through the woods. It was a person he did not know that existed in him. He was afraid and dreadfully sad, but he was ignited by the fear and self-loathing. "What would I have done if I had to spend the night in the woods or got lost? Could I have survived? How sheltered my entire life has been. Why do I feel so ashamed? Am I being confronted with a missing component of my life? Is it a blessing in disguise? Do I have what it takes to be a man, or is that a useless question?" It felt like he was holding a flower but couldn't tell its fragrance. It was as if torn pages from a book were blowing away in the wind, and he wouldn't move to catch them. Something was leaving him, but he didn't mind. He got up, changed into the monk's robe, and opened the rice-papered window. Pink puffs of peach flowers greeted him. The brilliant sunlight of April seemed so kind. He didn't have the power to say yes or no anymore. He wanted to ask for forgiveness from anyone, for everything.

The war broke out two months later in June. The North invaded the South. The president was still urging people to stay put. "We will defeat them by noon today, by three o'clock. By tomorrow…" People didn't listen. Soon the streets were filled with refugees heading south. Air raids began bombing the city, killing people who were already half dead with broken lives.

Sam heard the news from Bongsan, who came back from his routine visit to the village for supplies. "This will pass, just like anything else," Bongsan said, delivering the news, handing him a carton of cigarettes. Sam's heart was troubled and moved at the same time.

"Where did you get the cigarettes? Wouldn't they think it's strange for you to buy them?" he asked, with his hands tearing the box in a hurry. It had been a while since his last smoke. Kuju ran inside and brought a box of matches and insisted on lighting his cigarette, ignoring Bongsan's disapproving eyes.

He said he went further out to another town to find out what was going on. "The people in the village where I usually go are outsiders. They hardly know anything or care what is going on in the world. The town I went to is usually empty and quiet, but this time it was crowded with refugees from the city. It was like a marketplace. A man was selling cigarettes and a few other items from his bag. He was only too glad to find a buyer." Bongsan smiled and took out a roll of candy wrapped in rainbow-colored paper from his pocket. "Here." Kuju ran over to him and took the candy with his mouth.

"What is it?"

"It's hardened sugar like the one I make you, only it's prettier and fancier. Don't eat it all at once, and don't give it to the chickens."

"I won't," Kuju said, dropping it in his pocket and giving it a pat. Kuju had two pet chickens.

Sam thanked him for the cigarettes and the extra travel he made to get him the news. "Don't mention it. It's nothing compared to your generosity," Bongsan said gently and went inside with the boy.

It was approaching evening, but the sun was still strong. Sam sat on the stone steps smoking one cigarette after another. He got up and started to walk slowly at first with his hands behind him then he ran up the hill. When he was at the top, he stood on his toes, stretching his neck to see something, anything. Miles and miles of green all around, the same as the other day, the same as a month ago. He sank down and buried his face in his hands. He was worried sick about Mrs. Lim and his dog. In his head he could see and hear people screaming, fathers and sons dragged out of their homes to be beaten and killed, mothers and daughters raped and thrown into ditches half dead. Indescribable suffering for one side was a carnival for the other side. He had seen such atrocities done by the Japanese. That average men who must have once been innocent children could perform such monstrosities in a heartbeat filled him with nausea and horror. One day they were young men or boys, perfectly harmless creatures who blushed easily, and the next day they turned into unimaginable beasts. When he came down the hill, he went to the well behind the temple, got undressed, and poured the cold water over him, silently crying, missing his amah.

Later at night he sat with Bongsan in the courtyard looking at thousands and thousands of stars. He told him about his disturbing thoughts of human behavior and morality. He sighed and said, "Why do you think we have morality? It's to make others to behave, it's to rule our unruly nature. This instinctual unruliness in us is so suppressed that when the guard is lifted it explodes. Our unruly nature is much more instinctual than morality, because morality is an artificial design. It isn't necessarily created for the love of humankind. Our nature is not bad, it's just misunderstood. If our unruly nature is understood and acknowledged, it will serve the human world better than not. I keep saying 'unruly nature,' but what I mean by that, is that we

have an innate need to be free. Morality robbed human beings of their freedom. Isn't it funny, though, that it is mostly used to hurt others? Human beings created the most awkward world in an attempt to sustain their sanity."

"We'll never know what the world would be like if all of us were free."

"I thought about that, but honestly I can't even imagine it. That's how
far off we are from who we really are. When you look at animals, they don't
bother to change their ways."

"What is it do you think that made us be so different from animals?"

"Who knows?"

They sat there in silence for a while, listening to frogs and crickets. They
got up and said good night to each other. Bongsan turned around and said,
"Those men who committed such heinous atrocities probably have families
that they love dearly. Isn't that something?"

It was midsummer when a traveling monk came to visit. It was a hot
day, and Bongsan, Sam, and Kuju had decided to quit their work of tending
to vegetables and fruits. They were sitting under a tree hoping for a kind
breeze to pass by, when the traveling monk arrived. "I thought it was about
time you'd show up," Bongsan greeted him, beaming. After they exchanged
proper greetings with their palms in prayer and murmuring Sanskrit to each
other, the monk sat next to them. He took off his wide-brimmed straw hat
and fanned his sweat-beaded face with it. Bongsan told Kuju to get water,
and the boy ran to the well.

The monk rummaged through a sack he carried and handed Bongsan a
bag of rice, saying, "Bongie, when was the last time you've had pure white rice?"

"Zhangzhi, you don't have to bring me anything. This must have been
so heavy to carry up here. Are you here for good this time?" Bongsan said,
scooping the rice with his hand and letting it fall through his fingers back
into the bag.

"Someday, someday, my good friend. It's getting closer but not as long
as I can walk," he said, looking at Sam. Sam introduced himself and bowed.
Zhangzhi returned a bow to Sam, receiving a bowl of water from Kuju. He
drank the water, wiped his mouth with the back of his hand, and asked Sam,
"From Seoul?"

"Yes."

"I was there not long ago. If I were Christian, I would've believed that hell was happening right in front of me," he said, shaking his head. Zhangzhi looked to be in his sixties. He was a big man whose hands were covered with scars, old and new. His robe had more patches than the original fabric, and he gave out an odor of sulfur and ammonia, but his voice gave him presence and even youthfulness. Sam hoped to hear more about what the traveling monk saw in Seoul but decided to leave Bongsan and Zhangzhi alone to catch up with each other.

Sam hadn't had white rice ever since he came there. It was so scarce one could not find it anywhere. The only grain available was barley and some inferior stuff which bulked up in the intestines and produced noxious gas. The steamy white rice in his mouth was heavenly. He didn't realize how much he missed it.

After the memorable dinner, Sam and Zhangzhi strolled around the temple. They talked about the war. Zhangzhi told him the horror stories he had witnessed.

Sam uttered, "What kind of animal would do such things?" It was more like a thought that voiced itself. "The same animal as you and me," Zhangzhi said, asking for a cigarette, seeing Sam light one. Sam offered and lit it for him. He took a deep drag, blew out the smoke in a stream, narrowing his mouth, and said, "You've never seen a monk smoking, right?" He smiled and continued, "I, when possible, eat meat too."

"You don't have to explain it to me." Sam meant what he said. He could care less if he were a whoremonger. It became cooler in the evening, humid but cooler. "What I can't imagine is that ordinary people possess such venom," Sam said, going back to the subject of war.

"We have both lamb and wolf in us. It might be impossible for you to think you'd do the same if you were them, but you would. That is, if you had the same life as theirs, how would you escape from being them? I'm not by any means defending them. All I'm saying is that human beings are quite capable of such acts. We love like a lamb and hurt like a wolf."

"What about conscience, aren't we born with it?" Sam asked.

"I'd like to think so. All I know is that people throw away things that don't serve them well," he said, stepping on the cigarette butt he just threw on the ground.

"I know, I mean, I understand what you're saying, but I believe that we aspire to be good, all of us," Sam said, quite confused. "Have you ever seen people doing a so-called 'good thing' as powerfully as they do acts of destruction? Doing a good thing is work, but bad things are fun. However, there is someone inside who becomes unhappy when you're happy doing what you shouldn't do."

Zhangzhi laughed, rubbing his chin, and said, "I know exactly what you mean. That must be the conscience in us. "Well, whatever you call it or however you describe it is up to you, but I don't know if it's universal."

"I truly believe we are born with at least a desire to be good."

"Does it really matter?"

"I guess not. But please bear with me. Who is this someone who becomes unhappy when we are happy doing bad things? Does everyone own this someone?"

"First of all, we have a watcher who is aware of what you are doing. For example, when you are thinking of something there is someone in you who is aware of the fact that you are engaged in those exact thoughts. When this information reaches the judge within you, the judge disagrees, and you receive his ruling. What kind of power the judge has is another matter. I have to answer 'yes' to your second question. You can call it a conscience or whatever. Only I disagree that it's all that holy. One thing that is clear is that from the very beginning of our lives we are expected to do what is good, what's already decided as the right thing to do. And to ensure the so-called good and positive behavior, punishments were introduced. Your meaning of conscience, a tiny organism we'd like to believe that benevolent God blessed us with, to me, is another form of punishment, self-torture so to speak. The truth is that I'm in the dark as you are, as anybody is. And what would you do if you gained the answer? Take Jesus Christ or Buddha, for instance; people presume that they knew the truth, and people like the truth that they gave them. However, those owners of the truth made mistakes in assuming the equal ability and quality of human beings and skipped the crucial 'how-to' instructions in details. They left too much room for individuals to wander around in their heads. Thousands of years after, their truth is still upheld by millions of people. How well have those truths served us? Quite poorly, wouldn't you say? Because people don't like to live with such truths. It's too boring to them. They like conflict too much. Life is energy. The source of our energy is in conflict, not in the holiness of conscience. Nothing wrong with that. This noble truth landed in human hands only to be misused or abused in the name of eliminating and judging one's enemy, precisely the things Jesus and Buddha said not to do. It's a lot easier to suffer through life being a sinner than to follow in Jesus and Buddha's steps. Because it is, as I said, too boring to be like them."

"I can relate to that a bit. When I was in America, I stayed with my father's adopted family who were serious Christians. I noticed that they were very hard on others. What struck me the most was how unhappy they seemed. They always looked angry, even when praying. Then they went way out to make sure others live the way they do. Ever since my experience with them, whenever I encounter a Christian, a warning sign goes up in my head. I know that isn't fair, but I can't help it," Sam said, remembering the dislike he harbored for them.

"People demand others to behave according to the teachings of these great men so that they can trust and depend on them, and therefore, make their own lives easier. A stupid practice, isn't it? After all, one way or another, one would find out that everyone plays the exact same game. We are peculiar creatures, aren't we?" Zhangzhi continued, "I understand Christianity is all about life after death, isn't it? Life in preparation for life after death, the eternal one? They all sell that stuff—heaven, hell, nirvana, reincarnation. What do you think?"

"Frankly, I don't think I've ever given it thought. The very idea of eternal life isn't so attractive to me."

"Eternal life in paradise, as if we know what paradise is like, ha, ha," Zhangzhi said and laughed. "True, it's frightening that you're here one day, and poof, you're no more, not your spirit and not your soul, not even a déjà vu." He continued to laugh. Sam offered him another cigarette, and they both smoked in silence. They walked to the well, drank water, and poured some over their heads, unable to control the animal-like sound escaping from their mouths from the pleasure of feeling cold water running down their heads on a hot summer night.

"How long have you been traveling?" Sam asked when they resumed their walk, dripping.

"About seventeen years."

"Did you just get up one day and say 'this is it'?"

"More or less. While I was studying at university in Japan, I liked to visit Buddhist temples in my free time. It was a strange time for me. I could not stay away from the temple. I liked drinking, women, and things that any normal young man would. I was vain, greedier than ambitious, and a lazy student. To this day I can't explain why the temple appealed to me, but I began to visit it instead of those fun places more and more. I became a monk, persuading my devastated parents that it was a temporary detour. I felt what I should feel about my life when I stayed at the temple. It almost seemed as if the anger and despair in me due to my disagreement with the world turned into wisdom that was uniquely mine. The harsh discipline of physical labor that every rookie has to go through before they let you sit among them for meditation and prayer sent a shock to my tender hands and knees at first. You see, I grew up in an aristocratic family like a semi-prince, ha, ha. As time went by, I moved from one temple to another, quite a few of them in a period of twenty-some years. I wasn't much of a monk. I couldn't follow the teachings blindly. Many of the monks said one thing and did another, just like any other human being in the world. Once in a while, I would run into a monk whose devotion to enlightenment was everything to him, and these monks touched me deeply but not without melancholy. Something was sadly missing. I realized what the missing feature was. Reality, real experience. That was when I decided that I wanted my life to be abandoned to the randomness of it all. I started to walk, and here I am."

"Why did you stay when you learned that you weren't much of a monk?"

"There was something I learned that I couldn't give up. An addiction, if you will. The game of discipline; it possessed me. When you're a monk, discipline is what you do and what you become. It was a good place to practice that without interference."

"Game of discipline?"

"I grabbed onto something in me that I wished to change. My body and soul went to war to make the change happen. While I was consumed by the war with my own self, I began to notice that I was obsessed with practicing discipline. It wasn't a war at all. It was a game I played with myself and that I was hooked on. It was a never-ending game, and just like any other game, it came with the taste of victory and defeat. Suppose you love a certain food that makes your mouth water just thinking about it but find another kind abominable, have you ever tried to reverse that?"

"I can't say I have. But I don't see the value in trying that. It seems a waste of discipline."

"Not at all. Anything that got caught in my net, including any negligible habits, had their trial days. I must say it has been those insignificant habits that led me to the deepest part in me."

"It sounds like a journey to your personal psyche, gaining knowledge of yourself. Have there been many victories?"

"While I'm engaged in the game, I'm all about reaching my goal. Naturally, I go through ups and downs with it, which is the most fun. Once I claim a victory, something else always emerges. It used to annoy me, but I realized what it was. It's the mystery itself. You can do anything to break yourself apart to see what's in it, but trying to break the mystery is a sin against yourself. I still like to call it a game, but it's just an intentional attempt to reach the part that has been unknown to me. What sort of mystery am I?"

"I envy your drive, your passion." Sam didn't mean what he said. In truth, he wouldn't want to be like him at all. He was simply enjoying having company to talk to, to listen to.

"Ha, ha, ha. I haven't heard the word 'passion' for such a long time. I don't think passion is a friendly thing. A passionate state of mind is not a desirable thing to me. The word passion reminds me of a feverish hungry creature that is ready to devour you. I tend to believe that it's an outside force, not the one that arises inside of you. But the way you said it feels rather sweet, youthful, and innocent. Please don't take offense. None was intended."

"None taken. Well, you said it was an addiction or obsession. To me 'passion' involves those words. I'm sure you detected that I'm a blank page when it comes to discussions of the mind," he said in half-hearted humbleness.

"If I search for a meaning behind an addiction or obsession, I must say I find none. It turned out to be the best companion for me to pass time within this life. Yes, it passes time without noticing it passing. I can go in a muga state with the obsession and stay there for long time."

"What's a 'muga state'?"

"The state of no self. Everyone knows that state. Have you noticed whenever you're doing something you're deeply involved in that you forget to eat, you lose sense of time, and you don't even realize you are you? That's the muga state. As we grow older, the less we experience such a state."

What an interesting man, Sam thought, although he was a tad bored with this type of conversation. They joined Bongsan and Kuju, who had fallen asleep on his lap in the courtyard where he had a mosquito fire on. Sam lay down on the straw mat, and as the sound of two monks talking and Kuju's snoring slowly and steadily faded away, he fell asleep. The last thought on his mind before he fell asleep was, What kind of tree would I be if I were one? Would it have many leaves with strong branches, or just bare dry branches? Would it bloom with flowers and bear fruit?

In his dream that night, he saw an apple tree with red apples dangling, soaking up the autumn sunlight. He approached the tree with such delight in his heart, and as he touched one, he saw that all the apples bore the smiling face of Kuju.

He woke up from the sound of heavy breathing. He didn't remember how and when he came to the room the previous night. Kuju was breathing down on him to see if he was awake, which he did every morning. Sam looked up and pinched his cheek gently.

"Does Mr. Sam want sweet shrimp today?" the raspy, sweet voice asked. Ever since Sam came to the temple, he followed the boy like a puppy. The little boy taught him how to take care of daily chores, endlessly surprising him. The little man could handle things so skillfully, and he had great fun laughing at Sam's clumsiness. The first thing he did in the morning was to feed his pet chickens. He let them out of their cage, fed them, talked to them, and ran around with them, squealing. They were ordinary chickens who acted like dogs, if that's possible. Among the chores Sam and Kuju had was to gather wood, search for edible herbs and mushrooms, and to bring water from the well to the kitchen for daily use. After breakfast the three of them tended the vegetable garden.

Once a week Sam and Kuju went to the brook down below to wash clothes. Sam enthusiastically participated in everything that needed to be done. He was too grateful to them, and he discovered this abrupt change in his fate made him see someone in him that had formerly been in total darkness. He was intrigued by the new person emerging in him. The life of largely relying on nature was both backbreaking and a blessing. It was a blessing to have no time or energy to be sad or worried about the life he left behind. It was almost like he had to make an appointment with himself to remember the items that belonged to sadness and worry. From time to time, it hit him hard, especially when it rained and there wasn't much to do.

One day he and Kuju were washing clothes down in the brook. As usual Kuju finished his load before Sam. He was playing, balancing on the rocks in the shallow stream. He found two shrimps under a rock and showed them to Sam. He was balanced on the rocks, holding the wriggling shrimps by their tails between his fingers. He said, giggling, "Mr. Sam, would you like to eat them?" Sam hadn't had any meat since he came to the temple. Sweet-water shrimp was a delicacy in the sushi world.

He really wanted to say "YES!" but instead he said, "You're not supposed to kill."

"But you can," Kuju said. "Come, I'll boil water and you can put them in." Before Sam uttered any words, the boy was already running towards the kitchen. Sam hung the washed clothes on a tree branch next to the boy's and followed him with a watering mouth.

"Out of this world" was the phrase that repeated in his head when he sank his teeth into the flesh of the boiled shrimps. After he finished he asked Kuju how did he know people eat them. He simply said he learned from the villagers. Sam felt awkward devouring them without offering any to the boy, even though he knew he was a strict vegetarian. "Don't you want to eat meat sometimes?"

"I get sick when I eat meat, even eggs or milk."

"How do you know? Have you had it before?"

"Bongsan used to force me. I had a bad fever once, and even after the fever was gone, I was very weak. He got worried and the village people told him to feed me some meat as medicine. I took it with my nose pinched so that I couldn't smell it. I hate it," he said, screwing up his face as if he could still taste it in his mouth.

After that day they would go shrimp hunting regularly behind Bongsan's back. Although they had so much fun trying to catch the shrimp, sometimes Sam felt guilty corrupting a nice Buddhist boy. He said to Kuju, "I don't think Bongsan would approve, and I feel bad doing it behind his back, killing living things and so on…"

"It's okay."

"Did he tell you it's okay?"

"No, but I saw him peeing on ants."

Sam laughed so hard he lost his balance and slipped, which caused the boy to laugh hard, clapping. They laughed as if there was nothing else to do in the world, ever.

In this timeless place, Sam felt life pounding in his heart. His heart pumped with the simple rhythms of nature, but it skipped a beat or two now and then with a certain reluctance that wouldn't permit him to accept the perfect peace he was experiencing to be totally his. "This isn't your path." The small inner voice stirred in him, drawing a faint frown between his brows. What is this in him that says "no" to this agreeable stretch of life? Why couldn't he embrace this?

On their way down to the brook, he saw Zhangzhi exchanging bows with Bongsan in the courtyard. "Leaving us already?" Sam asked, bowing his head to him. Zhangzhi bowed at Sam with his palms in prayer, saying something in Sanskrit. They watched him until he disappeared from their sight. "Where is he heading now?" Sam murmured.

"I don't think he wants to know. Things have to be exceptionally tough for him to feel alive," Bongsan said with his eyes fixed on the road far down below, where his friend became invisible. He turned and told them, "We need to do some weeding today." Sam nodded obediently, but as soon as Bongsan disappeared behind the temple, they ran down to the brook. The sun was merciless already. He looked up at the cloudless sky. The dry heat was making jerky out of his face.

The winter was brutal, the kind where one couldn't bear to be separated from the wood-burning stove. In order to save wood, they shared a room together. The second room was occupied by the noisy chickens during the winter time. They still went out every morning to gather wood and fetch water from the brook by breaking the ice. The water in the well had become frozen solid. Sam's once buttery fingers became those of a real man, red and chafed. His hands looked at him with the air of superiority when he rubbed glycerin on them to soothe their soreness at night. Many days they sat together in the room weaving baskets and straw footwear. It snowed and snowed, three or four days in a row, day and night. Sam looked at the snow-covered hills and thought how such magnificent beauty could be so harsh and brutal. On some days Bongsan would give Kuju lessons in reading and writing calligraphy. Sometimes Sam joined them, but mostly he curled up and took a nap hearing the raspy, sweet voice of Kuju reading. When Bongsan corrected him, the boy sulked, refusing to continue, which brought a smile to Sam's lips. A little while later, he resumed his reading, persuaded by old monk's gentle begging.

At the end of February 1951, the weather began to show signs of spring approaching. Melting snow on the hills drizzled down for days and turned into ice sculptures by night; some looked suspended in midair. Sam and Kuju walked up the hill to gather branches and twigs, warning each other not to step on slippery ice or mud. The three layers of robes on their bodies made their movements unnatural and clumsy. During the severe winter months, Sam began to wonder if the winter would ever go away. He couldn't remember how sweaty summer days felt like. Although the sun was bright above yet couldn't send warmth through the chilly air, it reawakened a hope hibernating in him.

One such a day, he and the boy went up the hill to gather wood. As usual Kuju was ahead of him. About thirty feet ahead of Sam, Kuju suddenly turned and ran back to him. Sam laughed knowingly. The boy needed help to undo the drawstrings of three layers of pants to relieve himself. A couple of times the urge lost its patience, ending up soiling all three comrades of the pants' gang. Sam walked toward him, laughing, with his hands reaching out to undo the drawstrings of the boy's pants. But Kuju shook his head, pointing at the bush ahead. He saw what seemed to be a leg underneath a pile of bush. When he lifted the bush, he saw a man lying there, lifeless. Sam rushed to the body and touched it. The body didn't move, and there was a blood stain on his leg. His head and hands were caked with mud, and his eyes were shut, but his mouth was open. Sam put his ear to his mouth and detected a faint sign of air passing. He told Kuju to stop poking him with a stick and looked for large branches. They broke off branches, tied them with vines, and rolled him onto it. He was a large man. They both heard him moaning. By pulling the branches underneath him, they were able to slide him down the hill.

Bongsan took him in the chickens' room, which was unheated, saying that was a safer way to restore a frozen body. They undressed him and washed him. There was a deep cut on his right shin. When they washed the muddy cake from his head, fine red hair appeared, which made Kuju scream. He'd never seen a Western man. Even after they explained to him that he was a foreigner and a human being just like him, he would not come close to him. When they covered him with a blanket after cleaning, he briefly opened his eyes slightly, showing a sign that he might make it. "Oh my, Kuju will scream again," Bongsan said, seeing the man's emerald green eyes.

They nursed him through the day, taking turns. Late in the evening, although still incoherent, he opened his eyes. He was a middle-aged man with a large frame. Bongsan held his hand and patted him gently to assure him that he was in a safe place. "Where am I?" he managed to ask in English. Sam answered him in English. "Thank you, thank you," the man said and fell back to sleep. They heated the room before they turned in and moved the chickens to their room. Bongsan spent the night with the red-haired foreigner.

When Sam lay down that night next to Kuju with the chickens sleeping in the upper corner of the room, Sam explained to him about different races. Kuju had so many questions Sam used the examples of his pet chickens to explain how they are all chickens but had different feathers. "Those candies and chewing gum you like very much come from the West, where the man we saved today is from." Somehow, Sam sensed, that eased Kuju's suspicion. Sam drifted into a deep slumber, unable to answer any more questions of the boy whose eyes got wider and wider into the night.

The man stayed in bed for two days but was able to eat and talk on the second day. He spoke Korean well. He was a Roman Catholic priest residing in a small town some thirty miles away from Seoul. The small farm village was known as the Mecca of Korean Roman Catholics.

Christianity had spread like wildfire in Korea during the mid- to late-nineteenth century. "All men are created equal" was all these farmers and underlings needed to hear to embrace the religion wholeheartedly. Persecution of the new growing faith was started by Confucians, who represented the national order in terms of ethics and morality. "All men being equal" was a very wrong thing to them. They decided Christianity was a religion of savages, and they called Jesus a Western ghost. There were uprisings of farmers who demanded the freedom to practice the new faith. As a result, many of them were executed. Persecution died down after the Japanese occupation, and the foreign god was resurrected, however sporadically. Actually, the Yi dynasty initially did not have a problem with the new religion. The people treated foreigners politely as their strange-looking guests until some of them were caught digging up the graves of kings and queens for buried treasure. In fact, those foreign thieves changed the course of the country. War against anything Western had started while their immediate neighbor, Japan, was diligently educating itself about Western civilization, especially of its killing machines. It was too easy for them to move into Korea and claim to be the owner.

The priest introduced himself as Father Gregory. He had lived and served in the village church for nearly twenty years. When the village was raided by communists, people took turns hiding him. He couldn't bear to think of the danger innocent people had to go through because of him, so he left the village not knowing where to go. He headed out to a temple he had known, which was some miles away. The communists, who were out to erase religion from the earth, strangely left Buddhists alone. He stayed at the temple for about six months without any incident until one day he heard a gunshot. He peeked outside and saw a soldier from the North standing in front of a body that he had just killed. Soon more of them appeared and shot at the monks who came out to see what happened. All of them, including Father Gregory who had remained inside, were found and dragged out. The soldiers were nothing more than young boys, so young that some of them had the fuzzy hair of a child on their faces. They discussed how many they should take as hostages and agreed on five out of the twenty monks. They thought it was such a funny sight to see a foreign monk among the Korean monks, and when they selected the five monks, Father Gregory was among them. They tied up the five of them with one long rope and made them kneel down and watch the rest executed. They went inside seemingly in search for food, and when they came out, some of them were wearing prayer beads around their necks, complaining about the lack of food. They set the temple on fire and dragged the five captive monks in one line. "We'll reeducate you good," a guy said in a thick northern accent. They walked through the woods at night and stayed put during the days. Father Gregory learned why the five of them weren't killed; they would be living proof that the soldiers held authority.

The monks were given a handful of raw beans to eat per day. They were all hungry and cold. Then one day one of the soldiers spotted a pheasant. Excitement broke out; they were so hungry they didn't care that the gunshot might draw attention. The first shot missed the bird, but five or six more frightened birds flew over the tree. The boys, for they were truly no more than boys, started to shoot at the flying birds. They screamed with delight and ran in all directions following the birds, forgetting the prisoners. The monks went to work undoing the rope, which wasn't too difficult. Once free, they ran in various directions without exchanging so much as "good luck."

"I have no idea how many days it had been," Father Gregory said, looking at the cut on his leg that had been stitched by Bongsan. He thanked him again and told him that he'd be off soon.

Bongsan told him that he could stay as long as he needed. "Sam here is a fake monk. He's been here for about ten months. Not many know about this place."

The weather was getting better by the day. Even the rainy days weren't too bad. They took advantage of the good weather and started to work on the vegetable patches and fruit trees. They broke the hardened soil loose and trimmed the trees. Father Gregory was ever so useful. He said he spent more of his life farming than preaching. He grew up on a farm, and when he was placed in the village, he still worked in the fields with the people. It was a treat to watch him go at it. It took a while for Kuju to warm up to him. Suddenly, the small dilapidated temple became crowded, and the four of them lived as if they had been a family together for a long time. There was no tension, no dirty side glances at each other, and no disagreement. The one that touched and endlessly moved Sam was Bongsan. A slow moving, slow talking, gentle heart was always in harmony. Bongsan's sort of harmony seemed to say in any given situation, "It's good because it's good, and it's good also because it's bad." He became a living Buddha in Sam's heart.

One thing Sam noticed was that he never saw Father Gregory praying. It was June, and by then they were quite comfortable with each other. They were tending vegetables when Sam asked him bluntly. "Are you mad at your God or something?"

"What's that all about?" Father Gregory asked back, turning his head to Sam.

"I've never seen you praying. That's why."

"How do you know if I pray or not?"

"Well, do you?"

"All the time, all the time."

"So you're still good with your God?"

"Oh, thank you for checking upon my faith."

"Don't be cross. I thought Catholics prayed in litany, you know, not free-form prayer."

Father Gregory started to laugh. He got up, took off the straw hat, and fanned himself with it, chuckling. "Now I get why you had your doubts. I don't pray like that. As a matter of fact, I much prefer 'free-style,' and that's how I pray all the time." He was still laughing.

This time Sam started to laugh. "It's kind of funny. I'm here with two men who gave their lives to their faiths, and honestly neither of you seems very religious. I'm not laughing at you. Please don't take me the wrong way. I honestly think Bongsan is a living Buddha only not so religious, if that's possible."

"I think it's funnier that a non-religious person like you carries a notion of what a religious person should be like."

Sam got a little embarrassed. He scratched his head and told him, "I guess I was too obnoxious. Forgive me."

"No need to apologize. I enjoy this kind of talk. Innocent inquisition. But one thing I'd like to confess is that it's kind of awkward praying to Jesus in a Buddhist temple wearing their robes." They both laughed until their eyes burned with tears. Kuju, who had been playing with the chickens, heard them laugh and ran toward them. He imitated their English with his raspy voice, which brought out more laughter.

The summer came and went. The sky looked bluer, and the leaves were changing colors. Bongsan went to town more often to obtain enough supplies to pass the winter. Once in a while, Bongsan brought news when he came back from town. Things seemed hopeful, according to the news. He brought back American goods, including more cigarettes for Sam. "You see Americans everywhere. They seem to be a happy tribe. They like to smile."

One day Sam went up the hill with Kuju to gather wood. They decided to start early in preparation for the winter so that they wouldn't have to search for wood as much in the midst of winter. Sam took a cigarette break, squatting and looking down the hill. Kuju sat next to him, humming something. Suddenly, he stood up, pointing his finger towards down below and shouted, "Look, Mr. Sam, there's someone coming."

Sam stretched his neck to see where the small finger was pointing at. He couldn't make out anything. His eyesight wasn't as good as it used to be. His heart started to pound with fear. "Are you sure you can see a person?"

"There, there."

Finally, he could make out a moving figure. He couldn't tell if the figure was a man or woman. All he could tell was that it was a single figure, which lowered the level of fear in him a bit. He sat there for a few minutes with ants of anxiety crawling all over him, his eyes fixed on the figure. Then he saw something like a pink-and-yellow scarf on the person fluttering about. It was definitely a woman. He stood up and slowly walked down, followed by Kuju. "Oh, my God!" He ran down. It was Mrs. Lim.

They held hands, looking at each other with their lips quivering. "Oh, Sam, what a grubby monk you've become. I'd never had thought you could be even thinner," she said, blowing her nose in her scarf. Sam was so choked up he couldn't bring up any sounds from his throat. If human sorrow could give birth to joy, this was it. Together tremendous sadness and tremendous joy made him a temporary mute. Kuju pulled on his sleeve, wanting to know who she was. He couldn't say a word when Mrs. Lim bent down and introduced herself to him.

They walked up to the temple. Kuju wanted to carry one of her bags. She had three with her, two in her hands and one on her back. "Why so many bags?" Sam asked, taking them from her hands. They weren't light.

"Don't worry, I'm not moving in. I brought a few things you might be desperate for."

"You've walked all this way with these by yourself?"

"I had help from someone in the village. He carried this stuff up to the mouth of the hill. I then sent him away, telling him another helper would arrive soon. I didn't want to take a chance in having him see you."

Sam was always impressed by her sharpness. He had so many things he wanted to ask right then, but seeing her sweating in exhaustion, he told himself not to be selfish. Why is the most sacred offering of one's heart to another only recognized in the presence of suffering? he thought, unable to control his shoulders which were heaving from crying, as he walked up the road canopied with mid-October leaves of red and yellow.

She brought food, real food. Rice, dried and canned meat, pickled vegetables, coffee, cigarettes, and dry goods. She also brought some warm clothing for Sam. They had a feast that night. Bongsan and Kuju, who didn't eat meat, had two bowls of rice each, with delicious pickled vegetables. Father Gregory was most excited over the coffee.

After dinner Sam and Mrs. Lim sat in the courtyard looking up the star-studded sky. "You forget there are that many stars in the sky until you come to a place like this," she said. They talked about their lives during the past year and a half. "It's still quite chaotic. People are slowly coming back to their homes, although many of them have to face the fact that their homes were completely ruined by the bombing. Before I came here, I went to Seoul to see for myself if the situation was as improved as people said. I went to your house, and it seemed to be unaffected. Miraculously the entire area, the markets and high street, were untouched although quite bare. The old servant, Huang, and his wife were living in the house. After we 'cremated' you, we boarded up the house. The old couple had no place to go, so they decided to hide there, going in and out through a crawl space. I took Jayu with me to the country where my aunt is. We stayed there until I learned that the situation was getting better."

"How's my boy?" Sam asked.

"It's the third time you're asking about him, and for the third time, I'm telling you that he's doing fine. He lost a bit of weight. He had to eat what was available, just like everybody. But he really likes farm life."

"Judging by the winter clothing you brought me, it looks like I'm going to spend the winter here. If things are better, why do you think I should stay here longer?"

"You know better than me about these things. It's too soon to trust. Let's wait at least until they sign the truce. Don't you think that's wise?" She told him to give it another six months. "If everything goes well, I'll come and get you. You'll be patient and wait for me, right?" she asked like a concerned older sister.

"Life here isn't bad. Not bad at all. It's been hard, but nothing I've experienced in my life has been this rewarding. It's not that I can't wait to get out of here. I learned to live like this, believe or not. There's a simple pleasure here that one can't have from the life I lived before. In the beginning I thought it was just a beginner's excitement, but as time went by, I realized that this is me, too, if you know what I'm saying. The happiness I feel here is healthier, more real. Yet I dream about going back to my previous life, although maybe not the same way it used to be. I guess I want to know what I've learned here will take me when I go back. I really missed you," he said, draping his arm around her shoulder. She leaned her head on his shoulder and said she missed him a lot too.

"It sounds like this exile helped you to grow spiritually. I've never heard you talking like that. You were always a good person, spiritual or not. What I'm wondering is if you ever doubted the person you used to be, if you think of your former self as less of a man. Because that's not true."

"It was strange to meet a stranger in me, who has been with me all along and was yet unknown to me until a drastic change of circumstances came upon my life. Now I'm wondering who else is there. Who am I missing?"

"You must like what you found in yourself. Is it important to find out all the personalities in you; I mean, is it even humanly doable? You might not like all of them. Well, all I can tell you now is that I'm so glad you're still sane. I was worried that the hardships you had to endure here would have me find you deranged. It seems like there is a budding philosopher growing in your head. Please promise me that you won't let it overgrow," she said, slightly concerned that he sounded like a poetic adolescent who questions what is the meaning of life for the first time. If Bongsan and Kuju hadn't been so wonderful, he would probably be singing a different tune, she thought. "You know you've been so lucky."

"Up to the point of guilt and shame."

They sat side by side, catching up with each other's missing time for a while. "What I learned is to respect the power of nature. You must know what I'm talking about as an ex-farm girl. It gives everything then it takes away everything."

"It's the most beautiful, magnificent—as long as I don't have to live in it bare-bottomed. You speak as a bystander, do you realize that?"

"Really?"

"The stupid and arrogant statement of a bystander."

"I've lived in it and with it for a year and a half. I've earned being more than just a bystander."

"I know very well what you must have gone through, I really do. I can see from your hands how much work you had to do, and yet you still tell me you've had a happy time here. I'm quite moved, surprised, but moved. But you don't or can't know what farmers and their hungry children would think of nature. It doesn't give everything. When it gives, it gives slowly and rarely, but when it takes away, it is quick and merciless. You love it when it stands still looking beautiful. I call you a 'bystander' because you know your contact with nature is not permanent. You have a life you'll go back to. This was sort of like camping."

"I see your point, but 'respecting nature' was a flesh-and-blood kind of experience to me, and it was much more than camping in the wilderness. As I said, I see your point, and I meant no disrespect to people whose lives are so much more dependent on the mercy of nature. Maybe you're right; I am being sentimental and romanticizing my experience because back in my mind, although there's no guarantee, I know I would go back to my comfortable life. I must say, you always bring me down to earth in an irritating fashion."

"You're welcome," she said, and they laughed. "Farmers and fishermen fear nature. They don't have the luxury to 'respect' it. That's the point I was making."

"But admit it; you do have a chip on your shoulder."

"I know I do. I don't ever want to lose it."

"Don't, for my sake. It makes you charismatic," he said teasingly. She gently punched him on the shoulder, surprised by the bone she felt against her knuckles. He's become a skeleton, she thought and felt a lump in her throat.

She suddenly clapped as if to catch a bug then got up. "Oh, I forgot. I brought a bottle of Scotch…" She ran in.

Father Gregory, who had returned from his evening stroll, joined Sam when Mrs. Lim came back with the bottle. When he saw the bottle of Scotch, he said, "I don't care if I'm not welcome here, but I won't leave until I have a sip of that."

Sam and Father Gregory passed the bottle back and forth, giggling for no reason. They didn't notice that Mrs. Lim had long gone inside. They sat on the straw mat, consumed by the buzz given by the alcohol. They were talking without listening, murmuring gibberish with curled-up tongues. "Is she your woman?"

"My only woman but not in that way." The streaming chorus of the bugs and frogs soared through the night. When they emptied the bottle, they got up, holding onto each other giggling and went inside. "Oh Danny boy…" Father Gregory sang, making one step forward and two sideways. Sam sang along, "The pipes, the pipes, the pipes…"

She stayed for three days. She had one room to herself, and the four of them squeezed into the other room to sleep at night. Kuju got so excited about the sleepover he wet himself one night. "Has someone spilled hot tea over me?" Bongsan said to the boy, pretending that he knew nothing about Kuju's mapmaking on the sheet at night. Kuju rounded his eyes and threw a threatening look at Bongsan, putting his forefinger on his lips, suggesting him to be quiet. Sam and Father Gregory also pretended that they knew nothing of the event but chuckled later when they were alone.

It was harder than he'd thought it would be. Sam didn't realize how much he'd grown attached to the boy. Leaving him behind felt like abandoning him. He thought about asking Bongsan if he could take him, but in the end, he decided not to. Mrs. Lim came back to get him in May of 1952. When he said good-bye to everyone, Kuju was holding Father Gregory's hand. He didn't seem as affected as Sam, which was both a relief and hurtful at the same time. He gave Bongsan all the gold nuggets he had in his knapsack and bowed deeply to him more than once, promising him that he would visit and urging him to stay well. Sadness and excitement churned together in his chest, blocking his throat and making him feel that he stopped breathing. He was going home.

-47-

A dream woke Miri up, although she couldn't remember anything about it. Nurse Yun was knitting, sitting on the chair under the light of the desk lamp, being looked over by her own huge shadow on the wall behind her, which seemed to be moving as she moved but at a different beat, a bit slower. Her large, round glasses reflected the wool and the needles mechanically moved along with the stubby hands of the pianist. The radio was off.

"Can't sleep?" she asked, seeing Miri sitting up.

"A dream. A dream woke me."

"A nightmare? Do you want to take something to help you go back to sleep?"

"No thanks. I want to remember what I was dreaming. Nurse Yun, you don't have to babysit me every night," she said, watching her fingers moving so efficiently. Miri watched her busy hands thinking that it must feel good to be good at something, even a simple thing like knitting.

"I don't mind. Dr. Min prefers it anyway. Besides, I'd rather be here than in at nurses' station. Is my being here disturbing you?

"No, not at all. Actually, it's comforting." It was a half lie. Sometimes it was comforting but other times annoying. She asked her if she could stay up and talk to her.

Nurse Yun looked at her watch and said, "What's on your mind?"

"You play piano beautifully. I love to listen to your playing."

"Thanks. It's one thing I enjoy. Do you play an instrument?"

"I wish I could."

"You don't wish; you learn to do it. Nobody is born knowing how to play."

"They say you have to start when you're really young, like five or six."

"Nonsense. I started to learn after high school. You're young enough to start learning anything," she said without moving her eyes from her knitting. She was stoic, diligent, and orderly in every way. People made fun of her behind her back, calling her an old virgin or pin cushion (referring to both her prickly personality and her plump bottom). But it was obvious that the people working with her respected her. She was confident and had a presence. She was the type of person that you would step aside from if you ran into her in a hallway and let her pass before you. Miri liked her and her angular way. She wanted to be like her, just a bit.

"Do you like classical music?" Nurse Yun asked.

"I don't know much about it," Miri said, remembering how she and her classmates laughed at a girl who sang an acrobatic, operatic tune. Actually, they were laughing at her facial expressions changing along with the sounds she made. "Is it necessary to wriggle the entire face to come up with the right sound?" one of the girls had said, and they could not hold the laugh in anymore.

Miri continued, "It intimidates me. There are some pieces I find so beautiful, touching, and even magical. Many I find noisy and anxiety-provoking, but whether I like it or not, it intimidates me all the same. No matter how much I feel for the music, I can't feel the intimacy."

Nurse Yun put down her knitting and looked at her and said, "I understand what you're saying. Music should be just music, but classical music, strangely, has a peculiar air about it."

"Do you think it's the music itself or because it represents a certain status symbol?"

"Very good point. At least in our society it has been associated with high-class people. Privileged people. It's possible that classical music became one more thing for them to hold onto to elevate themselves. Some of them really despise pop music."

"I know. They think that if you enjoy pop songs, you are a person with no depth. Ha, ha."

They both laughed, agreeing with each other how full of it human beings were. Nurse Yun added that she liked all sorts of music. "I can say music is the love of my life."

Miri felt there was a whole new person emerging in Nurse Yun. Her love of music made her seemed smart, real, solid, unmovable. Out of the blue, Miri told her about the music teacher in her school.

He was a tall, slinky guy who always had his eyes a little above you when he was talking to you, like they were following a flying bug. He always wore a black suit and black tie that were slightly threadbare and an oxidized-looking, white shirt, all of which Miri suspected to be intentional, to give an appearance of a suffering artist. His jet black hair was combed in such a way that one side of the part was puffed up and draped down so as to cover one eye, precisely. He tossed his head to remove the hair from his eye constantly. At this habit girls joked about a "dandruff shower." He could've been a handsome man, almost exotic, but knowingly or unknowingly, he sacrificed his good looks to perpetual crankiness. When he a threw temper tantrum, it was quite theatrical. He wanted to be an opera singer, a tenor. One time a classmate said after witnessing yet another tantrum of his, "Maybe all those high notes he had to reach by tightening his asshole damaged his nerve system. Not to mention that he obviously didn't make it as a tenor singer." What was obvious to Miri was that he was more into showing off how much he knew than in introducing the beauty of classical music to his students. One time he played the opera *Faust* by whoever it was on a record player through the entire class. Miri decided along with her classmates that classical music was torture. After a semester with him, Miri didn't want to have anything to do with anyone who had a classical tendency.

Nurse Yun laughed with Miri at her story. "I must confess that I've run into people who've claimed to love some classics that were hard for me to listen to. I wondered if they really felt something I couldn't, or if they were more into the idea of having a sophisticated appearance. Of course, I wondered why I wondered, and I still wonder at this minute."

"Do you ever wonder if you might love the pieces you hated someday?"

"That might be it."

"When your emotion, the raw feeling inside of you to which you can't apply any name, is dictated by the ego, we get lost, I think. People feel superior or inferior about what they like or don't like, as if there is a hierarchy according to the rule of nature."

"But it became a rule. We constantly consume ourselves searching for higher standards. Who makes the rule, decides on what is higher or lower, is another matter. It seems to be some kind of social conspiracy, and I know no one who is absolutely free from it. But it changes, the rule or nature of conspiracy, as our frivolous fashion changes. The only thing that's constant is our willingness to join the conspiracy without ever questioning what one would be like if one were to be purely free from this force. It's a movement of both kinetic and potential energy at the end of the day."

"We want to belong to something bigger and stronger because we are dependent. We ride along with a movement because we fear being left behind."

"But it's also human nature to want to be ahead of others, contradicting our tendency of wanting to rely on others. Quite schizophrenic. We envy and desire to possess not only material things but also the hearts of others."

"You mean admiration, the desire to be respected and looked up to. You show off your achievements, but at the same time, you don't want anyone to achieve as much as you do. I guess I'm one of them."

"Oh, yes. We all are. No matter how much we criticize and are unhappy about things going around us, we're encoded with such behavior, including the very doubting of our own thoughts and actions. I'm at ease with it. People in general want to be noticed, admired, and make a name for themselves.

One might do extraordinary things all his life so that even a three-foot-tall toddler can utter his name. His name might live throughout the entire history of humanity on earth, but why would anyone devote his life towards giving his name immortality when he himself is mortal?"

"I guess it's easy for us to judge them. There's something much more powerful in our nature, something that defies the zone of stability."

"What do you mean by 'zone of stability'?"

"You want to feel a certain security, and so you arrive at a place I call a 'zone of stability.' But that isn't enough. You expect extra rewards from the outside: recognition, money, or fame, all of which are unstable and unpredictable. Those expectations seem such a powerful force."

"Do you think cavemen had such problems, or is it something that evolved as a side product of civilization?"

"This is what I think. I think we have an innate quality that makes us desire to get ahead, but at the same time, we're lazy and dependent. Somehow these two sides learn to use each other. They've also learned that if you're more powerful, you gain more access to the usage of other people. Possession, beauty, honor, and physical strength, and so on, if recognized, can expand this possibility. Somehow along the way, they learned 'self-importance': 'I'm good, I'm special, and I deserve to be served accordingly.'

"Therefore, you use that power to make others do things for you. It's the ultimate dependency. That is the nature of hierarchy then. It's so true that human beings don't like to be equal. We are not authentic social animals. What do you think?"

"That's very interesting. We want to belong first then we fight each other to climb up to the top so as to command more labor underneath, so as to reach that perfect plateau of dependency."

"Oh, what do I know? I'm saying things that I have no idea where they come from. I'm in a hypnagogic state.

"What's that?"

"The state between dreaming and being awake."

"Is that a real word?"

"I think so. I read it somewhere, in a psychology journal." She was light-headed, ethereal, and less of body. It was a moment of not feeling anything. It didn't feel good or bad nor strong or weak; it was occupied with selflessness.

Nurse Yun went back to knitting. There were a few moments of silence, only the humming sound of electricity.

Miri looked up at the ceiling and started to hum. "I'm your mother. I'm your merciful mother. Fear is nothing. Aren't you under my shadow, aren't you held in my arms? Drip, drip, drip, let it drip. Drip, drip, drip, let it drip…" She went on, repeating the same thing in different tunes. Nurse Yun looked at her, not knowing how to react to this sudden change in her. She looked serene, no expression on her face. Her eyes were fixed on the ceiling but blank. She kept singing the same thing over and over.

Nurse Yun watched her like a voyeur until she stopped. She looked down at her, and when their eyes met, Nurse Yun said, "That was a soothing sound, I liked it." Then she saw two streams of tears on Miri's face. "Oh, what's the matter?" Nurse Yun said, regretting the talk she had with her. She was worried she might have triggered something in her that she had no authority of. She got up and gave her a tissue. Miri took them but did not use them to wipe her face. She was letting the tears and mucus from her nose drip down to her chin, to her throat, and to her gown. She let it flood, quietly, as if she was afraid of disturbing the stream. Nurse Yun just sat there watching her, feeling her heart pounding, trying to revisit their conversation to see if she could find any clue for this abrupt change. A few minutes felt much longer.

Finally, Miri dried herself, her eyes, nose, chin, and throat. She said, "That felt good. I needed that," with a faint smile.

"Can I do anything for you? Do you need anything, some water, a fresh gown?" Nurse Yun was relieved that she was talking normally.

"No thanks. I'm good. I'm sorry if I worried you. I do this sometimes," she said, pushing her hair back with her fingers. "I'd like to try to go back to sleep now." She crawled back under the cover, closed her eyes, sighed once, and went into a complete silence.

Nurse Yun didn't go back to knitting. She had seen many bizarre behaviors working at the hospital for years. But what she witnessed was something else. She couldn't identify it as a neurotic episode or as eccentric but normal behavior. She decided to inform Dr. Min of what she saw, even though she might get blamed for chatting with a patient. There was something else. It moved her. It was haunting.

While Miri was trying to go back to sleep, out of the blue, the thought of Sohee came into her mind. Beautiful, delicate but cracked. A tyrant, a hypocrite, a volcano of jealousy. One couldn't avoid her negative comments when you were near her; they were aimed at her sisters, female TV personalities, female pop stars. No one asked her opinion, but the woman never quit, and it could get unbearable. One night when they were watching a variety show of young pop stars singing and dancing, Sohee sat among them and started to do what she did best. She criticized them, their looks, their fashion statements, their style of performance, and their low socioeconomic backgrounds. When her comments were ignored, her criticism moved to closer proximity. "You guys are so low class, acting like trash, you know that? Drooling over garbage like this." She went on and on, drowning out the sound from the TV and squeezing a pimple under her chin between her fingers. Now her mother joined her, elevating the criticism to concern for endangered ethics and morality, which clearly indicated that the end of the world was nearby. They were hardly speaking of the same thing, but out of companionship, they aimed at the same target, albeit with different motives. The joined forces gained momentum, making it unbearable for the rest, especially Miri.

Before she made a rational assessment, words flew out of her mouth, but more or less under her breath. "We know your shit smells like morning glory!" A large, familiar hand that Miri had a long relationship with landed on the back of her head, making her fall off the chair. She heard her sisters laughing and her mother's creative curses. She couldn't tell if they were laughing at her falling off the chair or at her mother's artistic cursing words. She got up and walked to her room, thoroughly humiliated once again. Such incidents had happened perhaps ten thousand times in her life, but every time it happened, it produced the same amount of humiliation. She'd never gotten used to it. Familiarity didn't diminish it at all. As she walked towards her room, she heard another roar of laughter and knew the source of that evil joy. One of them must have reenacted the scene behind her. It was like a red card a referee in a soccer game raised, blowing a whistle in his mouth. She saw her reflection in the mirror hung in the hallway, humiliated and defeated. She then burst into laughter. It echoed throughout the high-ceilinged hallway. There was silence for a second or so; they stopped laughing. They resumed it by the time she opened the door to her room. She threw herself on her bed. She recycled what had just happened. Her laughing changed into giggles. When she fell off the chair, she saw Zona taking her seat at the speed of light. That was the best seat for TV viewing. Reviving the scene in her head made the giggling especially delicious. It bore a dark shade, and it totally belonged to her. It was hers only. These episodes stayed in her as many reference points she had accumulated over the years. She learned the wisdom of laughter in tears. She was in it, and yet she was also a spectator. She created a throne for herself to watch the show around her. She thought she was winning at such moments of laughter, but later she recognized the humor she saw was from hostility, not affection.

- 48 -

Miri felt her eyelids getting heavy, and she fell asleep. It felt as if she were sleeping yet fully awake. She saw Nurse Yun scratching her head with the tip of a needle. She was floating a few feet above the bed, and yet she saw her body still tucked in the bed with eyes firmly closed. "Who is this floating above me, is it also me? Nurse Yun can't see me floating. Am I dead, just like that?"

In this confusion she felt something sweep her away. She was out in the open air, floating, and the night sky, with stars and a crescent moon, was looking down on her. "I'm flying," she said to herself. Who is that girl in my bed? he thought, flipping her body to face down below. The hospital looked like a matchbox with miniature lights. I must be dead, she thought without fear. She could hear the whispers of small creatures, but she couldn't see them. She moved her arms as if she were swimming. "I must be dreaming." Another thought passed through her mind without care.

Something grabbed her by the waist, laughing. It was Mr. Goat himself. He let go of her and circled around her with his blue satin coat glistening under the crescent moon's light. He laughed at her clumsy way of moving.

Delighted to see him, Miri shouted, "Where have you been, you old goat?" She hadn't been able to see him on the hill for days.

"I was sitting right next to you in your room."

"Was it you who brought me out here?"

"Yes."

"I thought I was dreaming or dead."

"Dreaming or dead, what difference does it make."

"There is no difference? Dream and death are the same thing?"

"I don't want to talk about it, you wouldn't understand if I told you."

"Try me."

"In order to explain, I have to use a language you have no way of comprehending. Come on, I have a pressing concern regarding your performance these days."

"What do you mean 'my performance'?"

He walked towards her like he was walking on the ground and yanked her by the shoulders. His green eyes had ripples like a flowing river. He hissed at her, "Not enough time left. Neither of us can buy more time. Stop fooling around. I'm not going to be just a surreal memory in your future, that is, if your future survives."

Miri started to laugh and said, "Let go of my shoulder. Your hooves feel funny."

"Gee, didn't I scare you? Just a little?" he said, releasing her shoulders and dropping his head in shame in an exaggerated fashion.

"Now, now. Stop putting on this show and tell me what you want me to do."

He backed away from her a bit and started to dance around like figure skating. Miri tried to follow him, but she couldn't stand up like he did. He came over to her and helped her to sit up in lotus form. "Now, girl, I'm going to be serious. So listen up. I need you. Your ascension is my emancipation, and as I mentioned, we are running out of time. My concern is that you are gaining a taste for this world, which is poisonous to the particular sense you need to nurture in order to grow quickly. The vine of this sense will take you to where you should be, where I need you to be. The vine has to be strong and wholesome. It will serve as an umbilical cord for me to connect to UK."

"United Kingdom?"

"Ultimate Knowledge!"

"How do I make it happen? It's too abstract to me. You have to instruct me specifically."

"Recently you toyed with the idea of death. It's the ultimate test for a person of your ability. You let your garden grow too wild and be out of control. You feel betrayed by your own garden and are thinking about abandoning it altogether. You gave it tremendous freedom, but it lessened your own freedom."

"But you said I'm gaining a taste for this world. Whether you approve of it or not, that means I'm gaining more life in me. Toying with the idea of death or abandoning my garden do not agree with gaining a taste for life. I don't get it."

"Gaining a taste for life is standing face to face with death—the death of your kind, the death of our kind. You start to worry about what to eat, what to wear, and soon life becomes like exile, something fearful and dark, therefore, it's death," he continued, with his right hoof slid between the buttons of his coat and the other held akimbo, his hips tilted. The bottom of the coat moved gently in the breeze, and he looked absolutely magnificent standing among the stars and moonlight.

"You look beautiful!" she said.

"Don't distract me. I'm onto something crucially important." He gave her a scornful look, but his nostrils expanded with pride.

Miri interrupted again. "The pride of looking good must be a universal thing."

"Enough already." Then he struck various poses, and they laughed themselves silly for a while. "Where was I? Yes, yes, here it is. A taste for the world always comes with regrets; it's a pouch full of pus. You're starting to feel regret, and I beg you to turn back. You're beginning to be concerned about being disliked by the new friends you found at this place. You want to impress them, which will teach you shame, and shame is the death of it all. If you continue this pattern, you'll be lost, and I'll be forced to give up on you."

"I've noticed that in me, but I was glad it was happening to me. Slipping into the stream of the ordinary feels relaxing, easy, and honestly right. It dulls my senses, and at the same time, gives me structure, even a vision. Now that you are telling me not to let it happen, I feel suddenly very lonely, but part of me knows what you're telling me. I know I don't belong. I've always known I don't belong. I'm only my shadow."

"I'm sorry. I truly am. You've been so alone you don't even know what loneliness is. But now you learned the pain of being utterly alone. This new-found joy has also taught you to look back with remorse, as if your life has been a series of long blank pages. It might be hard for you to see that the long blank pages are, in fact, overflowing with your true essence, untainted. Your strength is your solitude. When you step outside of solitude, you'll wilt and be slowly and painfully diluted into the murky ocean of insignificance."

"I've already learned loneliness, and the heightened pleasure of being noticed and liked, and frankly, also the feeling of envy, is growing in me too. But not without reservation. Something tells me this newly gained taste isn't solid. Can I enjoy it a little while, just a little while?"

The goat said, "That's not very wise. It's like quicksand; it's serpent's venom to our kind. And I'm running out of time. Pretty soon I won't be able to materialize to you, and the door for you will be closed as well. You'll be trapped in the cycle perhaps for eternity."

"Does my life have to be so bleak, with nothing to look forward to? I don't know why, something tells me that I have to follow you, but it sounds depressing."

"In the beginning you thought I was a fantasy, and you worried that you might be seeing things or hearing things. You thought I was one of the cartoon characters that emerged as an imaginary friend by some psychotic mystery. But I'm real, and you know it, and you are glad, really glad, I've come to you. Let's not waste our time anymore. Once you reach the road I've promised you, you'll have a smashing journey. Not only will it suit you, but you'll also realize you're fortunate. It'll feel right by you no matter what the circumstances call for. Before I leave you for good, I'll see to it; I'll make sure you own that entropy."

"Why does it feel so heavy and impossible?" she asked.

"Good. You've started grieving. Now, before the night is over, I'll give you a tour. Come now." He came over to her, scooped her by the waist, and started to soar. Shooting stars were crisscrossing, making sounds of hissing and crackling. She was surprised how colorful they were. How high up they were, she didn't know. He stopped and drew a large rectangle in the space and knocked. The rectangle opened as a door, and in they went to a room that seemed to be a science lab. There were fish swimming by in the room like birds that greeted them like friendly dogs, making cute squeaky noises of delight with big smiles, showing pointy teeth. An old man sitting behind a desk said hello, standing up. One of the fish came directly to Miri and tried to kiss her. She was unsure of those sharp teeth and shouted, "Does it bite?" She heard them laughing.

"Is she the one?" the old man asked the goat, walking toward her.

"Yes, she's the one," the goat answered proudly.

"What do you want me to do?" he asked, cupping Miri's chin with his gloved hand. Miri stepped back and looked at the goat, who was nodding at her for reassurance.

"I want you to give her a checkup."

The old man invited her to sit on a wooden stool and started to check her head, lifting her hair here and there saying "aha," "um," and "oh, my, my." Fish, small and not so small, all with colorful designs, were swimming by her. She smiled at their smiling faces. When she looked up at the old scientist, who was examining her head like he was looking for lice, he wasn't a man anymore. He was a long-necked bird, ostrich-like with creamy yellowish feathers and a duck bill. He looked more like a stuffed animal that had been washed a hundred times.

"You see me now?"

"Yes."

"Describe what you see."

She did. He turned to the goat and said, "It's working. She has to practice switching on the eye quicker, and the focus is little fuzzy. Of course, I have to run a few tests before I can tell you yes or no, but I must congratulate you.

You did superbly. She has exactly the same hue as you, exactly the same. Finding the same hue is the toughest thing, as you know. And what a jungle she has in her head. Overgrown and messy. She needs a bigger lot soon, but right now I'll clean out some before they tangle too much. Tsk, tsk. Seems like misfiring is already happening."

"You can fix it, can't you?" the goat asked anxiously, almost begging. The scientist crossed his arms and shook his head. "Can it be done now?" the goat asked the old man again.

"If you put her through 'the house of meanwhile' now, and providing that the misfiring is fixable, I can speed it up, really quick. There's no guarantee. But I'll say it again: she's a supreme match to you."

The goat looked happy and concerned at the same time.

The scientist turned to Miri and said, "After I work on you, you'll see a series of small explosions, mostly at night when you close your eyes. This will continue for a while, then when you fall asleep, you'll see fish like you see here now. That's when you are being tuned. You'll see plants in various colors and smell their fragrance, some pleasant, some not so pleasant."

"Does she have the eye?" the goat asked rather petulantly.

"Oh yeah. She's been using it, although she has no idea. So relax. If I'm able to work on those areas, I mentioned you'll be home free."

Miri asked finally, "Is it going to hurt?"

"Not at all. It might startle you a bit here and there, but that's about it."

"What do you mean by 'the eye'?" she asked, concerned about losing control of herself. Mr. Ostrich read her mind, it seemed, and told her, "Not to be concerned. Everything we're talking about is in your realm, including the eye. It's the eye that enables you to see the invisible with those two eyes on your face."

Before she realized it, she and the goat were out in the space once again.

"The next place we're going is quite different from the one we just left," the goat said, putting on an air of caution. The lab they were in a few moments ago had dissolved into thin air. He drew another rectangle with steps in the air. Unlike the first one, this door appeared as a normal entrance to a structure, but it was very rundown and unstable. They walked up the stairs and opened the door to find a neglected, overgrown garden. It was dark and eerie. The air felt chilly, and the trees and bushes were tangled together, covering the opening to the sky. They were swaying, looking down on them ominously. She grabbed his arm and told him she didn't like it. He draped his arm around her shoulder and whispered in her ear, "We can't skip this place. You're to go through that door." He pointed at a wooden door that was covered with gnawing vines of ivy and cobwebs, "alone." There was hesitation, and he tried to say something else, but instead he pushed her towards the door, saying, "Let's just do it." He then vanished.

Someone strange took her over. Normally, Miri would not have done what she was about to do. She pushed the door open using her shoulder. She lifted the vine and stepped inside, not knowing if her foot would find a floor. It was velvety dark. She took one step in front of another, feeling the wall with her hands. Her breathing was shallow and short, her heart was thumping right at her throat, the sound of saliva going down to the esophagus was ringing in her ears, and her eyes were stretching to all directions bigger and bigger. She was scared numb, but there was someone inside of her who owned the determination to face what was ahead of her. And this someone was much too strong to resist. There was something else, a smell, a smell of life, not death.

At the end of the long hallway, a silvery thread of light came on. She walked to the light and found an entrance to her left. She heard something breathing through its mouth, a metallic sound. The next thing she knew, she was face to face with a most hideous creature. When her eyes adjusted to the faint light, she saw that the creature resembled a terribly deformed pig, who was standing upright facing her. It moved, allowing for her to pass, pointing to the interior of the room. When this creature passed her by, brushing his shoulder against hers, she was overwhelmed by sadness and pity. It didn't diminish her fear, not a bit, but now she was crying uncontrollably, as her feet were inching toward the middle of the room. She was startled by small creatures passing by her feet without making any sounds. She screamed, but no sound of her voice reached her ears.

A tiny woman in black was sitting on a chair at the far corner of the room. Her back was hunched, and she seemed to be a thousand years old.

Miri walked over to her carefully but stopped a few feet away. The old woman was sharpening a large knife. Miri held her breath, immobilized at the sight, but tears kept rolling down her face, onto her chin and then to the floor. She couldn't move at all. Then the woman stood up. She was about four feet tall, her jowls stretched down to her chest, her toothless mouth opened like a small but deep cave, and wrinkles deeply buried her eyes. She walked towards Miri with the knife in her hand. Miri screamed, at least, she thought she screamed, but no sound could be heard. There was no sound in the place at all. She was less than two feet away when she raised the knife. She lunged and the knife sliced into her own stomach and fell. Miri screamed and screamed a soundless scream. She reached down to the old woman who just stabbed herself, and she screamed the soundless scream once again when she found the woman was covered with crawly things. She landed on her bottom, screaming muted screams, seeing hideous things in all shapes and sizes coming out of the dark corners of the room. They gathered around the body, which was covered with crawly things. She felt herself being totally disintegrated, but her eyes were so alive as she watched them devouring the old woman. But she was wrong. The creatures raised the old woman, picked up her knife, sat her on her chair, and she began to sharpen the knife again. Then it went dark, charcoal dark. It was a nightmare in a nightmare.

Miri woke up from one nightmare but was still in a nightmare. She sat there for a moment, trying to think. There were no thoughts, as if they had run away from her. She wiped her eyes and moved backward on her butt to the entrance of the room. When she reached the entrance, the deformed pig appeared again, making her cry again with unbearable sadness. He showed a bunch of keys and dropped them on her lap without a sound. He faded away, and her tears stopped immediately. She grabbed the keys and walked down the dark hallway back to the door from which she entered, feeling the wall with her hands and making small shuffles with her feet. When she reached the door, she felt a bit relieved and hopeful. She felt her thoughts were gathering again in her head. She felt the door all over, but there was nothing she could hold onto to pull it open. It was too dark to see. She pushed it frantically, hoping the goat might come to her aid. There were five keys in the key chain, but she couldn't find any key holes. She felt the door with both hands from top to bottom over and over. No keyholes, nothing. She was frantic, her desperation was complete. She banged and kicked the door, feeling her thoughts retreating again. How fear could be so perfect, so complete. The small whimpering sound of a wounded beast was circling in her throat as she started to give up, saturated with fear. Then her own small voice started to pray—the Lord's Prayer, Hail Mary, Psalm 23. She was getting louder and louder to the point of her chest bursting. She knelt down with her knees against the door, repeating the prayer over and over for a miracle, for magic. She said, "I believe, I believe, even when I didn't believe, I believed..." There were no rational or logical thoughts residing in her at that moment. They were fake; they didn't exist. Just her desperate need to hope the Supreme Being had a plan for her and would release her, so that His desired plan involving her could be achieved. She promised, she promised, and she promised. She let out a huge sigh and closed her eyes before she began another set of prayers.

Then the eye the ostrich man had mentioned in the fish room opened. It felt like a miner's headlamp beaming from within. She saw fish and tiny explosions popping, she saw or imagined the keys floating up from her knees, and she heard a click, once, twice, three times. She froze trying not to break the phenomenon, the magic that was real. The door opened after the fifth click. She crawled out to the creepy garden that seemed so friendly and alive now. She kept crawling to the middle part of the garden, thinking the goat would come and get her. She sat on a rock far away from the door, waiting for the goat. The door closed and resumed the appearance of disuse.

As she waited and waited, she remembered the frantic prayer she had recited not long ago. She felt bad about forgetting the comfort it offered already and silently apologized. "But I meant when I promised. I don't know what I promised, but I meant it." She sensed the "fake duo," rationality and logic, slowly moving back into her head. She called them cowards. She remembered the proverb, "If you trust and use rationality and logic, you'll survive a tiger's den." But the experience she just had told her otherwise. They were not real, they don't exist. She then heard children giggling somewhere.

It stopped. She also heard or thought she heard someone sheepishly called her a fool. She immediately realized that it was the voice of the "fake duo." She told them, "I might be a fool, but I'm astronomically braver than you. So hush from now on. I know now to whom I belong, who looks after me, and it's certainly not you. From now on, you work for me, you serve me, and that is that!" She spoke sharply, meaning every word. How useless, powerless they turned out to be; how much they made you laugh at your belief, your faith, and made you feel weak for wanting to own faith. "Now I know your true nature. You are so nothing in front of the power of prayer. How does it feel to be revealed that you're fake, and that you fooled me, fooled everybody. I always thought you were rather dull and boring. You and your fancy excuses." At this, she laughed aloud. It felt good to step on them once.

She heard the children again, a little bit closer. "Where is this goat? Hey, show yourself! I'm done here! If you tried to kill me there, you failed, ha, ha…" She shouted, hearing the sound echoing back. There was a sudden gush of wind shaking the tangled branches above her. A little fear revisited her momentarily. Something grabbed her ankle, and then the next moment it roped around her legs to her waist. Before she could let out any sound of protest, she was being thrown from one branch to another. The vines wrapped her and tossed her around. She heard children's giggling again. Why? She didn't know, but she wasn't terribly threatened. The sound of the children was too innocent and playful. After a few swings she was tossed up in the air with her gown flipped over her head, and she was descending at enormous speed, feet first, her gown over her head in the fashion of a swimming squid. The sound of the children faded. The force of the speed was so tremendous even her feelings shut down.

- 49 -

It was approaching dawn but still dark outside when Miri came to. She was lying in her bed, and Nurse Yun had left. She was lightly trembling, with her knees drawn up to her chest and toes curled down tightly, causing cramps. She reached for her feet and massaged them to release them from the pain. It wasn't a dream, it can't be. It was real, very real, crazy real. What is real and what is not? Everything is real, even dreams, she thought. But I like what I saw, what I experienced, what I didn't hear and what I heard. I was brave, wasn't I? My sympathy was stronger than fear in that horrible place, wasn't it? And I promised. Yes, I promised whatever the promise would be. I'm going to keep it no matter what, no matter what. She got out of the bed and entered into her journal everything that was rushing to be recorded in her head.

While she was writing with fervor, she felt her surroundings become darker. Her desk lamp blinked and went out. It was still dark out, indicating the deepening of autumn and its longer dark hours. But her room was a shade or two darker than it was supposed to be. It was an intentional darkness. She waited, thinking, What now? I'm having a real busy night, aren't

I? Her pen started to move, writing something in her journal. It was too dark to read. She sat and waited, hearing the pen moving fiercely, the pages turning. Some time went by like that, then the lamp light came back on. She began to read. It was written in her own handwriting:

I'm glad you made it back. Pretty smashing stuff, wasn't it? You can thank me the next time you see me. Sorry I couldn't be there when you came out. I stepped out of the garden to have a smoke from my pipe and was locked out. I heard you calling me, and boy, I was so relieved you made it out safely, but you could not hear me replying. Then I saw you flying by over my head, but I couldn't keep up with your speed. Again, I'm not only satisfied with your performance but am sincerely proud of you. What you went through last night was a form of a physical exam. I'm sure you've passed the test. But the real work is to keep yourself alert and sharpened from now on. You'll feel different about yourself. You might find things you previously thought repulsive to be quite agreeable or even see the beauty in them. The ostrich man said he'd fix your receptor to be more flexible. It will now circle instead of being stationary as it has been. Naturally, it will receive more information, and you'll gain tremendous understanding without the danger of falling into the trap of being an average human. You'll like things that you'd never thought you'd like. You'll still despise them, but you'll like them too. You know that song, "Thanks for the little girl…" You'll sing it as "Thanks for the little creeps…" You know what I mean, I'm sure of it, our hues being perfectly identical! I know, I know, I'm getting ahead of myself and aware that you need time to process the vague state of your mind over this adventure. But one thing I'm clear about is that you were super excited about the whole thing. As a matter of fact, you were so excited you felt it ripping out of your chest, didn't you? Oh, Miri, doesn't that feel so marvelous! I remember my feeling, what a fantastic feeling that was. Well, let me go over a few things, things you dread to hear. It's all about finding who you are, not being found by others, custom made to suit their needs. Who am I? One asks. And one answers, "I am so-and-so, son or daughter of another so-and-so. I know this much, my value is such, this is how much I'm respected and needed by my family, neighbors, village, nation, and the world. That is who I am." A custom-made, tailored answer of a bespoke person. You exist only to yourself and for yourself. Deciphering the code embedded in you is the way to obtain a map, a map to the core in you. This exercise is available to every single person, but few travel this way. There's too much noise, too many distractions, and too many suggestions, all forming an army of insecurity. No one says "I really don't know" with ease, with innocent despair. If you stay with "I really don't know" for a while, the door to the journey opens. The door doesn't recognize any other words but "I really don't know." Stay with this state of mind, and you'll be accepted time after time into this door. There will be moments when you want to scream "that's it!," but be very aware the moment when you say it. It belongs to the world that isn't yours. When it happens, immediately be anxious of the next task and toss the excitement to the anxiety. In the universe something new always emerges, and something always dies. Entropy won't let anything stay still. The moment one achieves equilibrium, the deconstruction starts. Destruction being the very beginning of the new. The earth is round and gravity works but for how long? Can you see the possibility that there might not be tomorrow? These endless possibilities and the notion of an ever-changing universe are the reference points you need to go back to from time to time. Picture yourself climbing a ladder. How do you know when you've reached the top of the ladder? You will know for sure when it happens because the number of steps on the ladder increases or decreases on its own. Therefore, there's no need to guess how many more. I'm writing in your notebook so that you can read it regularly. Having said all of the above, you won't be exempted from fear and desire; that is all human. You'll win or lose just like anybody. You will be thrown into despair as well as joy. Most of all, struggles with the unknown will leave you distraught at times. But as I said, your rotating receptor, which is quite ergonomic, will feed you with new aspects constantly. Next time when I see you, I don't know when, it will be our last meeting, and you'll hand me what I need then. I have no doubt you'll be perfectly ready. And I am onto my final residence. As I mentioned, if you remember, you'll replace me when your living in this place is done. If you exceed the expected performance, which is very possible, you will come to directly where I am going. Rejoice, as they sing at churches, ha, ha. By the way, I almost forgot, the way you prayed in the vanity house of Meanwhile was brilliant. Now you've learned all on your own how to channel the eye of your mind. However, next time, which will be our last time seeing each other, you are not to ask any questions about last night, nothing at all. It's all yours and yours to keep and work with. It can be stolen. The only thing we have to wait for is how soon the minor repairs in you will be perfected; otherwise, I have no doubt you've passed the test with distinction. Keep your fingers crossed. Ciao!

PS Don't be frustrated with persisting doubts. They will be forceful and frequent. Denying them is the delay of progress. Just sit with them and listen to what they have to say. One who has to understand must befriend doubts. It's not easy, but you know and I know you wouldn't do anything else, you simply can't.

- 50 -

Miri woke up from Hakyu's morning visit. She didn't remember when she went back to bed. "How come you're not singing this morning?" she asked, sitting up, feeling achy.

"You were singing," he said, stretching his pink blubbery lips into a smile.

"What was I singing, which song?" she asked, not remembering if she had any dreams.

"The one that Christian people sing at a funeral clapping their hands. Something about crossing the Jordan river."

She sang the tune: "We'll meet again someday across the Jordan river…"

"That's it. That's what you were singing. You must've been dreaming of your mom's funeral, ha, ha," he said and laughed, slapping his knee.

In the beginning, Miri heard a rumor from other patients that Hakyu compulsively stole small items like a pen or apple, nothing valuable. But so far none of her belongings had disappeared. The one thing he did that Miri really didn't like was grabbing the nurses' body parts when they were near him, whether they were young or old. They were annoyed but seemed entertained by the little creep. Miri looked at him and abruptly asked him a question that left her mouth before she consolidated it in her head, "Is singing the love of your life? Is it your passion?"

He lifted his eyebrows and rounded his eyes, crossed his legs, then looked up into space, rubbing his chin with his fingers, and slowly said, "What do you mean by 'passion'?"

"You don't know what passion is?"

"Well, red, boiling blood, flamenco dance. Well, I don't know. I've never really thought about it. Let's go have breakfast."

"I'm not hungry. Tell me why you never thought about it. You obviously have some notion about it. You love to sing, and you sing beautifully too. Isn't that a passion?" she asked again.

"My singing has no 'red' in it."

"Bold as red?"

"Hot as red. I love to sing, but there's no burning feeling, no flame."

"So you don't believe it's a passion of yours."

"As I said, sis, I just sing, that's all. I don't need to know why I do."

It was obvious she was making him uncomfortable. She said, "You go ahead and have breakfast. I'll see you later at the hike."

He shuffled out the door, singing with his heart, honoring every note as it was meant to be. He always looked older, more mature when he sang. He transformed into an owner of a secret; perhaps he was the owner of celestial wisdom disguised as a clown. He sang only for himself, as if nothing could come between him and the song. Yet he never seemed to be interested in who wrote the song or why he liked that particular piece. And it was all about melody, the lyrics mattered nothing to him. Somehow Miri believed she saw his passion, which made her envious of him from time to time. She wanted to feel the way he felt when he sang, just once. Does he have to know he has a passion? Do we really need to name it, identify it? Why do I try to fit it into a place when it doesn't quite fit? I'd like to purge what I've learned to be true, and I must. There are too many wrong truths to undo, too little time, she thought, walking to the bathroom.

The weather turned mild and pleasant. The sky was high and the sun was orange, painting the shadows a purplish hue. It had been drizzling at night, dropping the temperature and dressing the leaves into the various colors of autumn. Mrs. Lim came to spend the weekend. Lately, she'd been coming to visit Sam every weekend, sometimes with the dogs, but this time she came alone. They sat together to have lunch. Hakyu became a semi-regular in their gatherings. Every time Miri saw Mrs. Lim, she was amazed at her resemblance to Nurse Yun. The same thick, round eyeglasses, short limbs, large hairdo, and general chubbiness yet neat and confident. Hakyu was slurping soup with incessant humming. Sam and Mrs. Lim were talking business, occasionally looking at Hakyu with affectionate smiles. Mrs. Lim reached over to him and wiped his mouth with her napkin. She was never so warm to Miri, but it warmed her heart to see her being motherly to the little creep. Hakyu reminded them of boys they missed: Kuju for Sam and the young son Mrs. Lim buried long ago. Miri didn't know about the two boys lingering in their hearts, but seeing them treating "Hakyu the clown" kindly pleased her.

On that Sunday morning, Sam called her from his balcony, asking her to join them to see the town. "I've got permission from Dr. Min to take you."

"I'd love to," Miri responded through the window.

Sam hired a taxi for the day. It was waiting for them when Mrs. Lim said to Miri, "Girl, you need a jacket or sweater. It's colder down there."

Miri was wearing a thin pink poplin blouse and a pair of faded black jersey pants. "I'll be alright," she said, getting ready to get into the taxi.

Sam asked, "Do you have an extra jacket, Mrs. Lim?"

"In my room."

"Could you get it for her? As far as I know, this girl has no warm clothing."

Mrs. Lim walked back to her room. Miri asked, "Why do you always call her 'Mrs. Lim'?"

"That's how she demands to be called, that's why," he answered, gently pushing her hair away from her eye.

The taxi rolled down the winding road. They were talking about things Miri had no concern about. She looked out the window, thinking how it looked so different from the day she drove up the road. Some trees had already lost all their leaves and some were still showing off their autumn dress of yellow and ruby. The sky was blue and high, as if moving away from the earth. She wasn't thinking or feeling anything. Tall tree, short tree, tall and fat, tall and skinny, short and fat, short and skinny, unmarked graves here and there. Who could that be buried and forgotten? She narrowed her eyes. The scenery turned into one large canvas of mixed colors sprayed over it.

The fishy smell of the ocean stung her nostrils. The air was thick and salty, and it was low tide. She could see a group of women digging clams squatting on the muddy beach. It wasn't a beach of emerald water with white sand; it was dark and murky in contrast to the sky of translucent blue. The moody, unpredictable melancholy of the ocean seemed contemptuous of the chirpy crisp blue sky. She hadn't decided if she liked the view in front of her. Something wasn't right about it. It was chilly, and she was glad for Mrs. Lim's large sweater. Mrs. Lim draped her hair with a scarf. Sam teased her, "You and your precious hairdo." Mrs. Lim complained the village seemed depressing. "We just got here, woman." They stood at the rundown pier for a while. No one talked. They looked out to the ocean, toward different directions, looking without seeing, as though offering joyless submission to their inner gods. Miri noticed small frowns between their eyebrows. A large seagull flew over them, waking them up.

In silence they left the pier for the street. "Anyone hungry?" Sam asked, leading them to a small pub. The place was dark and damp. A variety of non-appetizing odors could be detected, but there was a good number of people eating and drinking. Mrs. Lim refused to eat but ordered a beer. The lunch Sam and Miri ordered came looking recycled. The food was greasy and extremely salty. Sam asked her if she regretted coming to the village. She said she agreed with Mrs. Lim that the town was depressing, but she didn't regret it. She wasn't being polite. There was something about the village, and she wanted to know what that was before she rated the place. It was neither good nor bad; it was disturbing. It felt ill, cursed, missing a soul. "Good," he said. "This village has a very different meaning to me. By no means am I nostalgic about it. I used to come to this place when I was a young man. It was a bustling place with first-class restaurants, boutiques, shops, casinos, and even geisha houses. It's hard to imagine that this place was once only for the rich and elite. Whenever I stay at the hospital, I come down here at least once. I guess I'm drawn to the strange feelings I get when I come down here."

"What is that?" Miri asked.

"You wouldn't understand. I'm not sure if I can articulate it even."

"Try her. It's your opportunity. She might be able to enlighten you," Mrs. Lim barked at him and sipped her second beer. They laughed.

"Well, it's like, how should I put it, I'm attracted somewhat to things that I dislike. Is that even possible? That's the best I can do." Miri gave him a nod, encouraging him to continue. "I clearly remember how I felt uneasy being here back then, and I feel the same uneasiness whenever I come to this town, even though the difference between then and now is night and day. Yet the uneasiness is the same. The glitzy, almost hedonistic lifestyle the town once offered feels like a dream, a mirage. I remember I had fun here as a cocky young man with money in his pocket. But back in my mind, I condemned the town for soliciting the destructive nature in human beings. To this day, I wonder why and how I participated in things I condemned internally, not to mention having great fun participating." He took a sip of beer, slowly shaking his head.

"That happens to everybody. You like what you shouldn't like. You like it more. Who doesn't know that tug-of-war," Mrs. Lim interjected, which Sam ignored.

He continued, "I don't feel any regret for the demise of this town. I don't feel sorry for their poverty. It's at the same time a very strange emotion to me." He lit a cigarette and blew out the smoke, blinking.

"So would you enlighten me, Miss?" he said, turning to Miri, smiling.

"Do you keep coming here to see if you can put a name on your uneasiness one day, or are you in some perverse way attracted to that feeling?" Miri asked in all seriousness, ignoring Mrs. Lim rolling her eyeballs and letting out a disagreeable nasal sound. Sam elbowed her gently and told her to be more respectable. She apologized mockingly. The two beers in her seemed to edge her into obnoxiousness.

Sam slowly spoke, "That's an interesting point. I don't know. I might never know, but let me think. First of all, as I said, I don't like this place. Not thirty-some years ago and not now. The town turned from glitzy to grungy over night. But my peculiar feelings have stayed unchanged. And I ask myself, 'how come? How come I have the same feelings for two very different pictures of the town?'"

"Tell me, how would you describe this town in one word?"

"Ugly. Ugly then and ugly now."

"But the peculiar feelings you have aren't all that ugly, are they?"

"Right. That's where I get lost."

Miri nodded and folded her arms. Sam waited for her to speak, enjoying having company who paid attention to a matter that most people would dismiss right away. It was a matter of take it or leave it to him, but now that it was being pulled out of the box, it gained momentum. She didn't say anything.

"Well, any opinions?" he asked after a few moments of silence.

"Huh?" Miri looked at him, totally blank.

"Do you have anything to say about that? Aren't we having a conversation here?"

"I thought we were done," she replied, hearing Mrs. Lim chuckling.

"Not me. I'm in the middle of it and so should you be," he said, lifting his eyebrows in disbelief.

"Okay, okay. I'm sorry. My typical bad manners were at play. Now, where were we? Yes, the ugliness, right?" Sam nodded like a little boy. "Perhaps ugly isn't ugly at all to you."

"What do you mean?" he said, resuming his curiosity.

"Meaning that you are attracted to ugliness, that you see beauty in it. It's happened to me before. I know it's possible from personal experience. There's something so repulsive that you cannot take your eyes off it. You keep looking at it, and then something totally unexpected happens to you. It offers you feelings incapable of description but lingers in you."

"I agree. Although I can't be sure if I see beauty in it."

"That depends on your definition of the word 'beauty.' If the word 'beauty' doesn't sit on you right, how about 'art'? You see and feel art from the ugliness that has some kind of hold on you."

"Wow, Miri, Miri, Miri. You should take Dr. Min's seat. That was great, just great." She couldn't tell if he was being patronizing. "What was your experience of seeing beauty or art in an ugly thing?"

"It's happened more than once, although I recognize this to be my opinion and my opinion only. The one that pops in my head is the singer, an American black entertainer." After she named him, Sam nodded and said, "Of course. That tiny man has a voice like a Grand Canyon and can dance as if he were defying gravity."

Miri continued, "When I saw him the first time in a film whose title escapes me, I thought his appearance was rather unfortunate, to put it politely. Then I saw his profile and felt something exquisite, that it was something super artistic like a sculpture done by a master." A burst of loud laughter from Mrs. Lim, who was listening to her, startled Miri. Sam laughed along with her.

She was annoyed and turned her head to the open entrance. A large seagull with snow white feathers and a yellow beak was standing at the doorstep and looking inside. The whiteness of it seemed whiter in contrast to the dark interior of the pub. She pointed at the bird. Sam smiled and said, "I wonder what it's thinking now, if it thinks at all?"

"Food, what else," Mrs. Lim said, a smile spreading on a beer-induced pink complexion. "I'd like to hear what Miss Miri would say. What do you think the bird is thinking?"

"I can really use a drink."

They laughed, but Mrs. Lim had to say, "That was the silliest thing I've ever heard."

When they were leaving, the bird didn't fly away. It simply stepped aside for them to pass and continued to look inside.

The street was windy but quiet. They had a couple of hours to kill before their taxi ride came back. Sam said, "Let's walk around. Come on guys, I'll make it up, I promise." They followed him, walking down the windy and fishy street. Mrs. Lim put the scarf on her head, murmuring something disagreeable. Miri walked next to Mrs. Lim, who was fussing with her scarf. Her double chin seemed doubled up with the unhappiness of having to stay in the village longer. Her face was still rosy from the beer. Miri looked at her and thought with an inner smile that everyone is a child inside. She found that the most likable feature in a human being. She looked around walking slowly behind Sam but with intention, hoping it might give her some understanding of what it was about the place that stirred the man inside. "An abandoned corner of the world." A few people who passed by wore lifeless expressions. It wasn't depression or pain, it was an expression of waiting without hope; waiting was all they knew how to do. Waiting for the punished to be remembered and pardoned. Just waiting. She remembered Sam mentioned that he couldn't feel sorry for these people. She'd been there only for a few hours, but she thought she was able to understand him, if that was possible. You don't feel sympathy when you don't see pain; endurance is a form of honoring life on its own.

They went into a gift shop. There were two old men playing Chinese chess, sitting on a wooden bench in front of the shop. They had their heads buried in the game and were oblivious of them passing by. The window display gift shop was dusty and faded. "How do they stay in business, I wonder," Mrs. Lim whispered. "Why don't you ask him?" Sam joked, pointing with his chin at the man sitting behind the counter in a dark corner, picking his nose with his mouth open. They exchanged malicious smiles with each other at the sight of the cashier. His forefinger was at work busily digging for nuggets from his nostrils, but he seemed like he wouldn't notice if a hundred flies sat on his face. He was a man in his late twenties or early thirties. He sat there as if part of the fixtures. Sam picked out a few things, a hat for Miri, wind chimes for Mrs. Lim, and a beer mug for himself. When Sam paid for the stuff, the man took the money, gave him change, and put the stuff in a bag, all without saying a single word, with a thousand-yard stare. He couldn't wait to be left alone to resume the pleasure of excavation.

When they came out, one of the old men playing chess looked up at them and said hello. His chess buddy turned and showed his face to them, squinting. They were so wrinkly and old they looked like two corpses that escaped from graves. One of them facing Miri directly was so wrinkly she had to search for his eyes buried under loose skin. They weren't friendly when she found them; they were two dark buttons looking for trouble. His voice was surprisingly loud and crisp. "You folks from the city?" he asked with a toothless mouth, "or the crazy house up there?" His attitude demanded payment for the unpleasantness he solicited. In spite of his corpse-like appearance, there was still roughness in him, which was waking up, salivating. Sam turned to him trying to say something diplomatic, blinking his eyes. The old man continued, "That damn loony house! This used to be a nice place. Oh, that was a good time. All those fancy city folks came, pouring money on us…"

The other man added, "Who'd have thought it'd become a loony bin. It ruined us."

"Was it really such a bustling town?" Sam asked, pretending that he had no knowledge of it. Sam offered them cigarettes, which they took greedily.

"Damn yeah, it was the place for unimaginable pleasure," one of them said, lighting his cigarette from Sam's lighter. He took a deep drag, reminiscing.

"Those Japanese loved our fish, raw, boiled, fried, dried, you name it. The whole town had a blast feeding them," the second one said, blowing smoke in a stream.

"Gambling was the best. And there were geisha houses that ran all night long. You had to take a number to get in. There weren't enough whores to serve the demand. There were times that they had to supplement with local girls whose looks could scare sea urchins, ha, ha." He laughed, slapping his knee and swaying his body.

"What did you two gentlemen do for a living, then?" Sam asked.

"We worked for various businesses, kind of like muscle men, you know, taking care of problems," he said, looking at his buddy who nodded.

"What happened?" It was a stupid question Sam asked.

"War happened. It was the saddest day when Japan lost the war. Then that rich asshole whose name was Chum Lee or something bought the hotel all to himself. Once in a while, he would come down and ride his white horse along the shore with his whore. He gave his word to townspeople that he'd make it happen again for us. 'I have a plan,' he used to say. Then he died. After that, no one noticed us until that damn thing up in the hill cursed us." He brought up the phlegm from his throat, turning his wrinkly face red, and spat. The loogie landed right next to Miri's foot. She quickly moved, feeling nauseous at the sight of it. She gave him an extended dirty look. He returned her a threatening once-over. The sunlight found one of his deeply buried eyeballs and gave it a vicious spark.

"Is this your daughter?" he asked Sam, pointing at her in a hostile manner. Before anyone answered him yes or no he continued, "Oh, I see. She is the crazy person who Mom and Dad came to visit. We see your kind from time to time down here. What have you done, young miss? I know it, I know it, you got knocked up." He asked his buddy, "Isn't that what you heard, that young bitches are sent to the loony bin for spreading their legs? To stitch them back?" The hostility rising in the living corpse excited him, gave him a sense of being alive. It was clear that he wasn't going to let go of this delicious moment of feeling alive, which almost never came by his way anymore, without escalating it to a higher level.

Miri stiffened. Mr. Lim pulled her sweater from behind, "Come on, let's go. He's senile." Sam turned his heels, gathering them to move on ahead of him when Miri broke free from Mrs. Lim and stepped toward the old man. Before Sam interfered, she picked an object from the chessboard and threw it hard on the old man's forehead. Without uttering a sound, she reached for the second one when the old man got up, slapped her across the face, and pushed her with both arms, making both Miri and Mrs. Lim fall on the ground. His corpse-like features belied both his height and strength. The force he used was so strong that Mrs. Lim rolled off the sidewalk and Miri hit an electric pole with her head, which momentarily disoriented her. Sam rushed to Mrs. Lim, shouting at Miri to get up quickly, "Get up, get up quickly. Let's get out of here! You fucking old ass!" His scrawny body struggled to help Mrs. Lim get up. The alpha corpse was not finished. His buddy got up too, grinning at the unexpected excitement. He approached Miri, who was sitting up, feeling vomit at her throat ready to be ejaculated, and he kicked one of her legs, laughing. He undid his pants, letting them slip down, revealing the thingy that resembled a worn-out, size-thirteen shoe encircled with grey, wiry onion roots for a beard. The sight encouraged Miri's vomit to move up, and it spilled out of her mouth, making her choke and cough. He held his penis in one hand and started to urinate on her leg when Sam rushed to him and kicked his groin, cursing at him. He screamed in pain cursing with most obscene language possible. His buddy, who was having fun watching the show, went inside the shop and came out with the nose picker. By then Sam pulled her up and the three of them started to walk away, looking back. The nose picker had a stick or a broom in his raised hand and charged after them. They ran but not so well. The nose picker caught up with them and grabbed Sam's jacket with one hand and with the other threatening to strike him with the stick. Sam raised his arms and told him to wait. The nose picker waited when Sam took out his wallet and emptied it out onto the ground. The nose picker grinned at the sight of money and stepped on the bills to keep them from flying away, saying things like, "Wow, wow, ho ho…" Then he said something that none of them could make out. He bent down to pick up the money saying, "Tha—tha—ank, kooo…" with a serious stammer. They turned and walked to the direction where they were to wait for their taxi. Mrs. Lim and Miri started to run, but Sam warned them not to. "Walk, don't run, don't look back. Don't make him think you're still scared." They listened to him and walked with exaggerated confidence. Miri couldn't help feeling the stick being airborne and landing on the back of her head.

They were still too early for the taxi. Miri was smelly from vomit. She didn't want to go in any of the shops or cafes to clean up. She didn't want to run into any villagers. Mrs. Lim gave her a handkerchief, white and starched, when she saw Miri trying to clean the front of her sweater with a large leaf she picked from a tree. "I'm sorry I messed up your pretty sweater," Miri said to her, wiping her face with the handkerchief, wet with her saliva. Miri saw Mrs. Lim limping. "Are you hurt?"

"No, I don't think so. A heel broke off from a shoe." She sat on a stone bench, took off the shoe, and examined it.

Sam was quietly smoking, sitting at the corner of the bench. He looked withdrawn into deep thought. It was the first time Miri saw him being moody, melancholy. Her throat felt dry and scratchy. She was thirsty, but she didn't want to move. She saw Sam lighting up another cigarette. She watched them sitting together facing different directions. One was looking at her shoe in despair, muttering something, the other smoking one cigarette after another with a blank stare, looking rather teary. And she was observing them while smelling barf all over her borrowed sweater. She started to laugh, hard and loud. Through her narrowed eyes, she could see their shoulders waving, then full-blown laughter erupted. Mrs. Lim tilted her head backwards, still holding the shoe with a broken heel, and Sam folded himself in half; they laughed until they couldn't breathe.

The taxi came twenty minutes later. Sam, who sat next to the driver, could not help but tell the driver what had happened. The driver blushed as if it was his shame. He asked Sam to describe the old men, and he did so with the help of Miri, remembering the name of the shop. The driver said, "I'm sure I know who they are. They used to be *yakuza* when they were young, doing dirty work for the Japanese. Even after the war, they continued doing what they were good at, which was harassing people and ripping them off. When they got too old, their sons took over, making it a family tradition. Nasty people, especially the ones you so unfortunately ran into."

"Why didn't the townspeople get together and drive them out?"

"Easier said than done."

Sam didn't press it anymore. Mrs. Lim was massaging her ankle. "Do you think you hurt your ankle?" Miri asked. Sam turned around, concerned.

Mrs. Lim answered, "I don't know. I didn't feel pain before, but now I have a throbbing pain."

"It must be a twisted ankle," Sam said. "As soon as we get back, we'll have a doctor to look at it." He reached his arm to her ankle and rubbed it for her. Miri thought that was sweet and tender. He looked at Miri and asked if she was alright.

"I'm fine. That was the most wonderful adventure I've ever had, and I thank you for inviting me. I mean it." Sam shook his head, smiling in a "what a weirdo you are" way. She began to laugh again and said out loud, "It was more gross than I've ever imagined!" Sam and Mrs. Lim suppressed their laughs, knowing what she meant, the old man's size-thirteen shoe. Miri took over massaging Mrs. Lim's ankle. She was moaning faintly. It looked a little swollen.

Miri asked Sam, "So, did you see ugly beauty in the adventure we've had?"

"If I did, it hadn't registered yet," he answered. Actually, the uneasy feelings he'd had about the town began to form a shape in his mind thanks to the ugly situation that happened that afternoon. It was "sin." It was what he felt thirty-some years ago and every time he went back to the town. Bad feng shui, bad karma, whatever the excuse was, he decided to settle with identifying the uneasiness as sin.

They were quiet for the rest of the ride. Miri looked out the window with one hand massaging Mrs. Lim's ankle. She was facing the same side she had earlier coming down the road, but it looked different. She was looking between the spaces of the leaves and branches this time, which seemed to be a stretched blue fabric connecting leaf to leaf, branch to branch, and tree to tree. Domes of unmarked and abandoned graves underneath the trees and bushes, small and not so small, made her heart skip a beat once or twice, as they reminded her of the truth, the only truth of the inevitable ending that all living creatures had to face. "What are your stories?" she asked the forgotten graves in her mind.

By the time the taxi drove up to the front of the hospital, she felt the side of her face that the old man slapped with the force of ten-pound rice-cake dough go numb. That side of her face felt heavy, like the old man's hand was still on it. "He bruised your face," Mrs. Lim said, examining it after they got out of the car. She clenched her teeth and cursed at the old man. Sam came to her also checking her face, blinking his eyes rapidly with both anger and anxious concern. Miri felt her eye shutting down from the swelling. It was welling up too. She'd never felt loved like that. Strong resistance squeezed her heart at the same time, signaling the danger of invasion. She scolded herself for letting such feelings, which were unreal, a temporary illusion, invade her. She never ever wanted to feel that way again. But it was like fighting against a landslide.

-51-

After Miri came back to her room she rinsed Mrs. Lim's sweater as much as she could. She showered, soaping her body twice, brushed her teeth, and gargled, all through tears. After she dressed in fresh clothes, she looked in the mirror where she saw pity, contempt, and suspicion for affection. "Oh, please. We don't do well with love. Let's not complicate ourselves any further," she warned and comforted her reflection.

She buttoned her blouse, wondering if her family would send her warm clothes soon for the coming season. They never called or visited but periodically sent her pocket money, which suited her fine. Less contact with them was better for her well-being.

Her thoughts moved back to the village, to the scene where the alpha old man revealed his size-thirteen shoe. Various images, some from films she saw and some from her memories of real incidents, zoomed in and out of her mind's vision along with the penis-shoe. The images were all about women being abused. She threw herself on the bed and rubbed the swollen part of her face, letting the images occupy her mind. She had seen a cheesy movie in which a young woman of virtue got raped. She was abandoned by her fiancé after taking a good beating from him. As she was receiving punches and kicks, she kept begging him to kill her because she wasn't pure anymore. She became a whore after she was abandoned, and her life ended in the gutter, blah, blah, blah. The audience generally felt sympathetic for her but didn't seem to disagree with the fiancé. She had disgraced herself, was damaged merchandise, and he had no choice but to abandon the goods that weren't so good anymore. Such films were the most popular at the time. What seemed so peculiar was that no one seemed to care about the rapist, as if he was just obeying a rule of thumb. Society was so definite about what was good or bad without questioning its absurdity. Yet no one raised a voice that the rapist should be punished. Such an objection was missing from their otherwise harsh moral code. Miri then thought of another time when she went to a local hair salon to have her hair trimmed. A woman in her thirties was paying at the cash register when Miri noticed that the cashier was shouting to her the cost of the service. After the woman left, Miri found out she was nearly deaf because the beating she took from her husband damaged her hearing. Women at the shop gossiped about the woman sympathetically, but the conclusion they came up with was that it was her own stupidity. "Why do anything to make your man raise his hand?" was the wisdom those women at the hair salon shared.

One rainy day when Miri was about ten or eleven, her father saw her carrying a red umbrella. "Red is the color of a whore!" he thundered. She cringed but was scared, unable to decide if she should still take the umbrella or step out in the rain without it. It was the last available umbrella that day, and she had to go to school. She stood with her head down for a while, thinking he would make more comments, but he did not. He was just staring at her, full of disappointment in his eyes. She left without an umbrella, feeling the arrows of his disappointment aimed at the back of her head. She cringed at his comment because she knew that was a sick man talking, that her father was a sick man. When she found the red umbrella in the garbage mangled later that day, she felt so sorry for it. She picked it up and saw numerous holes from cigarette burns. That day whatever respect she had for her father vanished, and she promised to the dying red umbrella that she'd never restore the respect in her heart in honor of it.

Another time, when she was older, out of the blue he came to sit with her in the living room and started to talk in an unusually tender tone, as if the day was made for him to do some fatherly caring for his growing girl. He adopted the posture of a man who was about to share profound wisdom with his child. He began with his usual analogy of man being a hungry beast. "Men think of women as a meal," he started. "They eat when they are hungry and forget about it when full. Some food they try and never crave a second time. All these stories about romance or undying love are nothing but fiction. It doesn't exist in real life." Miri listened to him with her eyes lowered, her head tilted politely, as if her father was the wisest man on earth. By then she learned to give him what he wanted, an exaggerated posture of admiration if not worship. It was a self-serving mechanism she had picked up from others. But underneath that subordinating gesture, she was totally free with her thoughts, feelings, and judgments, which could be quite enjoyable if you knew how to play the game well enough. "What a sad creep you are!" her inner self sneered with spittle on its lips, if such an anatomy had been available to it. But the truth was that he was not unique in that way. Men who were good to their women were considered to be wimps and were laughed at, and their women were seen as bitches. That night she sat at her desk studying for a physics exam when she remembered the wisdom her father offered on that day, "A female is nothing more than food to men." I'm just a bowl of rice or soup, why do I bother with physics, chemistry, trigonometry? No one in their right mind tells their bowl of rice or soup to do well in a physics exam, she thought. She had to laugh and went back to her studies, telling herself, "Let's show the world how smart a bowl of rice can be!"

How did it start? Who, in the beginning, said, "Let's treat women as subhuman. They're only a part of men's lives, not a life of their own"? One caveman, Uga, threatened his woman with his fist and accidentally discovered that his physical power was handy in controlling the female species. He gave a lecture about the discovery to his neighbors, and the practice spread like wildfire. This was man's greatest discovery, the use of physical force over the weaker ones. However it started was one thing, but how this practice of sub-humanizing females became a part of the moral sinew of just about every society was bizarre. She knew that even a kind, gentle man who'd never used violence against women carried that sinew of morality within him. And many, many women as well accepted the status of underlings, as if it were God's wish. The virtue and beauty of a woman was to obey and sacrifice. Uga's research proved to be more valuable as time went by. He noticed women fought with their own sex for other cavemen's attention instead of forming a solidarity against them. There was an innate characteristic in females that benefited men, Miri thought, namely, that the bond among females was weak by nature. It boiled down to the law of jungle. Power bred victims, and victims bred parasites. Morality and ethics came along to justify and seal our behavior, to cover up the effluvia of the law of jungle. No great evil and no saints. People didn't let others live, they wouldn't have it.

They had dinner in Sam's room that night. When Miri arrived they had already had a few drinks. Sam offered her a cool beer from the fridge, which she refused, telling him beer reminded her of chilled urine. They checked her face and said the swelling went down, but the bruise had turned darker. Miri asked Mrs. Lim how her ankle was. "It's not too bad. Just a twist I think. The ice pack helped," she said, looking at the bottom of her shoe with its missing heel. Miri asked for a cigarette, which Sam lit for her in spite of Mrs. Lim's disapproving stare.

"Why, Mrs. Lim, why do you think it's wrong?" Miri asked, blowing out the smoke.

"You are a young girl, it's wrong."

Miri interrupted, "Wrong for a girl but not for a boy, right?"

"Well, it just doesn't look good on women, it just doesn't," she said, shrugging with her shoe still in her hand.

"You mean it's not a decent thing that a good woman should do. Only street walkers, barmaids, and prostitutes smoke, and if a regular woman smokes, she would be condemned as a loose woman. Is that it?"

"Well, society associates female smoking in such a way. One can't ignore it."

Miri sensed that Mrs. Lim felt attacked. She heard Sam clearing his throat, getting uncomfortable. She quickly mended the situation by saying, "But you still like me, don't you?" That took care of the atmosphere. Miri apologized if she was antagonistic. She told them that the incident with the old man on that afternoon made her think that being a female wasn't a very nice thing in this world.

Mrs. Lim nodded but said, "I've never felt it was unfair being a woman, though. It's true there's room to improve when it comes to the position of women in general. I see it slowly happening."

"You said that you've never received unfairness being a woman. Don't you think that's because you learned and accepted to live within the limited choices given to you? Like domesticated animals? You've lived in a cage without questioning the possibilities of living outside of it."

"That's true, but how can one question it?"

"How is that possible? Even if injustice didn't happen to you personally, don't you see the awful social injustice being done to those women, and therefore, to you too? I mean, what happened today was an example, wouldn't you say? That old ass could have beaten me up or punched me or kicked me, but instead he chose to show his charcoaled penis and was going to urinate on me. Why, why, did he choose to do that? Because that's what a man is allowed to do when he wants to humiliate a woman, to let her know that her fate is to live with the humiliation."

Mrs. Lim listened to her thoughtfully with a faint smile that bore a tinge of sadness. "I understand. I shouldn't have said I've never felt unfairness. I see a generation gap here. Our generation was much darker than yours. We didn't have the luxury to sit with our thoughts or feelings. Life demanded running around constantly without a break in our time. It took all our blood and soul to be in the here and now, so there was no time to wonder what was fair or not. And such an attitude about life became our fixture. What you're saying is both noble and sad because it's true. But I don't care to think or talk about it. I've had my share of unfairness or injustice done to me throughout my life, yes, as a woman, but I also saw it as a human being. Unfairness can be very fair and indiscriminate. Sam wouldn't disagree, would you, Sam? I can't categorize many unfair things done to me according to gender hierarchy alone. If there weren't gender struggle, there'd be something else. That's how I see it. I understand completely what you are all about on this matter, but I can't share your enthusiasm."

This was the first time Miri thought that Mrs. Lim was deeper than her immaculate hairdo and sarcasm. A small sense of shame for having been rather obnoxious to Mrs. Lim wriggled in her. She actually saw that she might learn something from her. She saw Sam nodding thoughtfully while listening to Mrs. Lim. Miri said, "You're right. What you've just said has given me a different perspective. I guess I was nicked by the incident earlier today. I thank you for sharing your thoughts, and I apologize for my obnoxiousness. What you just said gave me something to think about."

"How so?" Mrs. Lim asked.

"Well, first of all, you helped me realize that youth is blind and that it's wrong to assume others feel the way you do. There can never be two exact same feelings in two separate individuals facing the same event. Every individual should feel what they feel; it's a God-given right. Mrs. Lim, you raised me a notch or two. I can feel my mind expanded a bit." They laughed, not certain if she was being silly or serious. Miri continued, "One thing I'd like to make clear, though, is that I'm no enthusiast. You're looking at a person with no passion, no enthusiasm, and not even a frivolous obsession."

"You could've fooled me there," Mrs. Lim said, feeling elevated by the girl's favorable comments of her.

"Yeah, I have to join Mrs. Lim on that. I thought you were revealing yourself, your passion for social reform." Sam chuckled, patting her shoulder warmly.

"It never crossed my mind. One thing I know about myself is that my thoughts and beliefs change constantly, sometimes more than once in one sitting. My thoughts, judgments, and what not, they flip-flop all the time."

Sam stared at her, disagreeing inwardly with what she had just said.

Dinner came. Sam had put in a special order of Chinese food. Her mouth filled with eager saliva just by smelling it. Every bite made her close her eyes. "This is so good," she kept saying, chewing. She remembered the day she and her buddies, Mun and Ahn, ate at the Chinese restaurant after visiting the shaman with the money she'd stolen from her mom's stash reserved for the priests. She briefly thought about sharing the story with them and decided against it. "There are some things you don't talk about as dinner conversation. You don't share something that is so yours, just yours, and this is that something to you," she heard her say to herself in warning.

Nurse Yun came by to give Mrs. Lim a shot of cortisone in her ankle right after the dinner. "Something smells good," she said, looking at the table.

"Would you like some?" Mrs. Lim offered, seeing her obviously salivating.

Sam interrupted, telling her that it was impolite to offer half-eaten food. But Nurse Yun quickly said, "I don't mind. I'd love some, but let me give you the shot first." After she gave Mrs. Lim the injection, she gobbled up the food that had gone cold. Sam offered a drink, which she refused, saying that she was on duty. Before Sam put down the bottle of Scotch, she said, "Oh, just a drop, just a drop. I guess I don't have anything pressing for the rest of the evening except taking this girl to bed and watching her sleep, ha, ha." A drop meant two glasses on the rocks, and it went down her throat rather quickly.

Miri thought that was funny and uncharacteristic of the nurse. She thought to herself, oh, what do you know! It was another example of how you just never knew about people. So, Nurse Yun was also capable of breaking the rules. Her usual air of stoicism and discipline was transforming in front of Miri's eyes.

"That was so good," Nurse Yun said, wiping her mouth. She held out the empty glass to Sam and asked, "Is it possible to have a drop more?"

Sam got up from the wing chair in which he was sitting, got the bottle, and put it on the table saying, "As long as you know your limit."

"I can take liquor. In my college years, I out drank all the boys. Isn't it funny that now I actually hardly ever drink," she said, helping herself to a third glass.

Sam went back to his chair and turned on the TV. Miri asked Nurse Yun, "I thought Protestants prohibit alcohol and smoking, am I wrong?"

"Oh, they do. They all do. I'm a Christian too, but some of the rules they try to impose have nothing to do with spirituality, at least in my opinion," Mrs. Lim defended Nurse Yun.

Miri looked at Nurse Yun, waiting for what she had to say. "I guess Miri here is under the impression that I'm one of those people who stand in the corner of a street shouting verses from the Bible to passersby," she addressed Mrs. Lim, who let out a laugh or two.

"But you listen to Christian radio every night and carry a Bible." Miri understood, but she wanted to find out more about their religious opinions.

"Yeah, along with many other things, I play piano, I knit, I read. My listening to Christian radio and reading the Bible are basically the same thing. There's something nurturing about it, and they occupy my thoughts in a meditative way. I should say I'm a Christian, an independent one, if you will, ha, ha."

Sam was laughing, but whether he was laughing at the TV or at Nurse Yun was unclear.

"Miri, have you read the Bible at all?" Mrs. Lim asked.

"Yes, I have. You know, in Sunday school and so on." She added, "By the way I wasn't judging you when I asked about Protestants and alcohol. Jesus and his buddies drank." She heard Sam laughing again.

Miri watched the two women sitting side by side on the sofa, undoubtedly intoxicated. Although Mrs. Lim was much older, the resemblance between the two was striking. The two of them were talking about their faith.

Miri listened to them quietly for a while until Sam waved his hand to her to join him on the balcony. The mild autumn night was inviting. She leaned on the railing and looked up the sky. Patches of fog veiled the stars, floating by like wandering souls. "Those two will be engaged for sometime in a Bible marathon," Sam said, offering her a cigarette.

"Have they done that before?"

"A couple of times. Bored me out of my skull."

"You don't have religion, right?"

"No, and I'd like it to stay that way."

"You sound like you despise it."

"It's not my thing. I respect people's faith. My own father, who is no longer with me, took off one day to some remote area of China to be a Taoist monk. He was a bag full of surprises, but I had never thought of him as being spiritual. He was a frighteningly shrewd man. What I remember about him is how focused he was in outsmarting the world around him and how exceptionally good he was at it. I admired him for that. I don't remember seeing him ever being emotional; he always kept an even temper. He was generous and fair but scarce and silent. It was a great shock when he left. I thought it was only a temporary retreat from the time of unrest, but he stayed there till the end of his life."

"Do you know now what was it that made him choose the path?"

"Not a clue."

"Do you feel resentful that he abandoned you?"

"'Abandoned' isn't quite the right word. I was a grown-up, not a boy when he left. In his mind, I believe, he completed his job with me, although he never stopped looking after my welfare."

"What about your mother?"

"When I was born, she wasn't there. I mean, I don't know her. They told me she died giving birth to me, and that was that. I know nothing about her." Sam didn't want to tell Miri the full truth. He gave her the version that he gave most people he knew.

Miri almost said, "Aren't you lucky." Instead, she said, "If you had a mother like mine, you'd be so glad she's gone."

"That's an awful thing to say," he said, even though he and Mrs. Lim already suspected something not so wonderful about her family.

"I know it sounds awful. Mothers are supposed be earth angels. To me, it is a myth. I don't think my relationship with my mother is unique, although I have to say that my mother is way up there on the ladder of maternal delinquency."

"That bad, huh?"

"Frankly, I realized the depth of our conflict after I came here," she sighed, her mind retreating back to her thoughts.

He wanted to hear more about the conflicts, but he didn't feel right asking. He waited, but she didn't volunteer.

"Is she the reason why you came here?"

"I'm not really clear on that. It was she who decided to send me here. I'm sure she is as happy as I am now. Ha, ha."

Her laughing felt odd to him. It was a laugh of defeat, hollow and without hope.

"What happened that she decided to ship you here?" he pressed again.

"Nothing out of the ordinary. We have history from way back that repeats over and over. Maybe this time, as they say, was the straw that broke the camel's back to her. But this is the best thing she's ever done for me."

"Is your father in the picture?" he asked, wanting to fish out more.

"Who knows? Perhaps as a secondary force. Family dynamics is all about the pecking order."

"Let me guess. Your mom and dad don't get along, right?"

"Pooh! The fire of hell wouldn't stand a chance faced with the chill between them."

He sat on the lounge chair and watched her standing at the railing.

"Miri, I'm really curious about your life, about you as a person. This is the first time you've told me anything about yourself. But why do I get the feeling that you try to put yourself in the position of a spectator?"

She didn't respond, going into a meaningful silence. He regretted what he'd said. Leaning on the rail, she took off her left slipper and started to scratch the calf of her other leg with her toes. He was about to ask if he'd said anything that bothered her when she said, "Because I'm not in it."

"What do you mean?"

"I remove myself. Then I can see what's unfolding. It's like infants screaming and crying but unable to explain what they want. Infants cry to communicate their unhappiness and discomfort. They're hurting or unhappy with their situation, whether it's hunger, a dirty diaper, or physical pain. It's all about them. They demand others to take care of them. That's what I see. People like my family are unhappy or miserable with themselves and helpless like infants, overgrown, aging infants. It's all about them: 'You don't give me what I want, you don't make me happy.' Sometime in my life, I don't know when, I must've learned the 'you' they meant in their infantile despair was not me after all. Naturally, I'm not in it."

"How do you feel about having to go back home? I assume that is—" He stopped, seeing her hand making a fist.

"It's not up to me, is it? As long as my parents pay the bill, I can wait for that time. They are good now without me, and it works for all of us. Dr. Min understands, I think. I am not, I don't…"

Nurse Yun came out, looking rather relaxed. "Miri, time to go, girl."

He saw a shadow of remorse on her face. He wanted to end the evening on a better note, but she waved good night at Sam and left the balcony. Mrs. Lim was lying on the sofa without her glasses. Miri shouted good night to her. "Why did you shout like that? You disturbed my serenity. Good night, girl. See you tomorrow." When Miri saw her without her glasses on, she had shouted so that she could hear better. She couldn't help thinking that bad eyesight impaired hearing as well. She had done this before.

She got into bed, and Nurse Yun turned down the light and settled in her chair, getting ready to knit. She said, "I heard what happened in town."

"Are you going to tell Dr. Min?"

"No, but you will."

"If I don't, you will."

"I have to. I can't withhold such knowledge regarding a patient."

"I don't want him to blame Sam."

"That won't happen," she said, pouring a tall glass of water. She drank it in one go.

"That thirsty?!"

"Uh-huh, all that drinking makes me thirsty."

"Have you been to town?"

"A few times. That place is bleak, even on a brilliantly warm sunny day."

"Right. Like Armageddon has happened there already."

"Try to go to sleep," she said. A loud hiccup escaped her throat. She pounded her chest with her fist as if that would stop it. Another one popped out, making her jerk.

Miri looked at her with a mischievous smile on her closed lips. "Drink some more water holding your nose. That will stop it."

She poured another glass of water and drank it, holding her dim-sum nose. It must've gone down to the wrong pipe because she started to cough violently, and a gush of water laced with the contents of her stomach exited the orifices on her face. Miri got out of bed, fetched her a towel, and patted her back. She went on throwing up on the floor, making a beastly sound. When it was all good and done after a few minutes, she went to the sink and washed up, still making beastly sounds. Miri saw her knitting pets helplessly sitting on the chair, blessed with things from their master's stomach. Miri wiped the floor, carefully moving the knitting pets to the basket, and cleaned the chair before she helped the nurse to sit. She looked spent, done for. "I am so fired," she said, trying to control her large head from swiveling.

"Fired for hiccupping?"

"From drinking alcohol on the job, of course. From being drrrrrrunk."

"I thought you said you were an expert drinker."

"Not anymore. I found that out tonight, didn't I? Things don't stay the way they used be. I've learned that, haven't I?" A second projectile was launched machine-gun style this time, blessing Miri with half-digested Chinese food. She managed to sit Nurse Yun in front of the basin to finish the job. Miri washed her face and glasses, noticing that her eyes without glasses were rather sweet, dried her as much as she could, and laid her down on the bed. She had her eyes closed, moaning but obedient. Miri took off her gown, mopped the floor with it, and changed into regular clothes. The room smelled like the garbage bin of a fishmonger. Nurse Yun opened her sweet eyes and asked for her glasses. "You don't need them now, go to sleep." Miri wanted to be with her sweet face without the harsh looking glasses for a while longer.

She turned her head toward Miri, giving her a full view of her eyes. They were dark with long lashes. "I'm so sorry. What a mess I made. I'll be okay in a little while. Oh, my head." She rolled her head on the pillow in agony. She asked Miri to find a bottle of aspirin from her bag. After she found it and gave it to her, Nurse Yun swallowed two aspirins, fluttering her long lashes, then lay her head back down. Miri wet a hand towel with cold water and put it on her eyes. She turned on the radio and found a station that played semi-classical music. Her moaning was replaced with rhythmic breathing, which soon became snoring.

She watched her sleeping for a long while then took out her journal and began to write. She intentionally avoided writing about the day trip to the village. Through the window she had opened to air out the fumes produced by human biochemistry, she heard the soft whistling of the wind in the autumn night, rustling the dry leaves; the sound strangely made her feel that she belonged to life. She looked at the snoring nurse and felt a pang of sorrow. "What is it that we try so hard to forget, what is this incessant need in us to search and wait, what is it that we are giving up?" The deepening night churned with the sorrow, weaving one more insignificant story: that's about it.

In the next room, Sam was dozing off, sitting in the wing chair. He woke up, feeling cold. The door to the balcony had been left open. Mrs. Lim wasn't on the sofa. "She must've gone to her room." He closed the door. "What time is it?" he asked himself, answering with "What do I care?" He climbed into bed. The more comfortable he became, the more active his thoughts. Soon he was on the speedy train of memory, which dropped him off in the past, some years ago.

- 5 2 -

Sam wanted to visit his father many times but could not get a visa to enter China. Finally, in June 1962, he found a way through India, then Nepal, into remote areas. It was an ambiguous place with no position on the map. Mrs. Lim was reluctant to accompany him, but in the end, he was able to persuade her. His father sent him detailed instructions in a letter of how to get there. Once they arrived in India, all of a sudden, Mrs. Lim got all charged up being in a foreign country for the first time in her life and insisted on taking a tour. "We are in the holy land, the land of Buddha. I can't possibly ignore this opportunity," she said. He did not share her enthusiasm, but seeing her happy like a child won him over. Since there was an issue with time, he made her choose one spot that took less than three days. From the various tour packages offered by the hotel, she decided upon Gaya.

Gayasur was some kind of demon, a holy demon. Later they removed the *asur* ("demon" in Sanskrit) and the name Gaya remained in currency. The guide, thinner than a skeleton but an honorably beautiful man with smooth skin that was so dark that it reflected a hue of green or purple from the rays of the sun, started to educate the tourists on the bus. The whites of his large, slightly bulged eyes, in contrast to the smooth dark skin was disconcerting. He had a broadcaster's larynx and spoke in a British accent showing not-so-white teeth with a childlike smile. "Lord Vishnu crushed and killed the holy demon, Gayasur, with his feet. This myth was transformed into the landscape of Gaya, the series of rocky hills which you will witness. Gaya was believed to absolve sins, yours as well as that of your ancestors. Upon his death, the gods and goddesses moved into his body, which became the rocks. Many temples were erected on the hilltops to worship the deities who joined the body of Gayasur. Naturally, it became a place for pilgrimage..." he went on. Sam translated everything to Mrs. Lim halfheartedly.

"Are you sure you picked the right place?" she asked. "So far he hasn't mentioned a word about Buddha."

"That's what the brochure says," he said, thumbing through the brochure. "Here, it's called Bodhgaya, about fifteen kilometers from Gaya town. We are on the right bus," he assured her. He saw her grinning rather mischievously. "What? What's funny?"

She started to laugh, "Didn't you almost marry a girl named Gaya once?"

"Oh yeah. I remember," he said and laughed along. "I never almost married her. It was a fling, somewhat intense I admit, but that was all."

The guide went on educating the tourists about the place's history, mostly mythologies of this god and that goddess, all too much of a mouthful to pronounce. Sam got fed up translating for her. "Do you really have to know everything he's saying?" She scratched him with a sharp glance but gave him permission to take a break. "Tell you what. We'll pick up a book on the subject and study together later."

She didn't say yes or no but turned her head to the window and said, "I never knew Buddha was Hindu." She looked disturbed.

Falgu was the name of the river, a sacred one like the trees and rocks around it. Ghats and temples lined the bank of the sacred river. The imposing architecture of Vishnupadh temple expressed the seriousness of the worshippers, but it failed to move Sam. Groups of women standing in the river, sending messages to their designated deities, looked like corpses erected by the power of the sacred River Falgu. It was impossible for him to feel sacredness standing in the dusty wind. "Something really went wrong in this land" was the thought recycling in his head. Everything he saw there, grand or not so grand, screamed suffering, unnecessary suffering, making him resentful. Judging by the slow pace of Mrs. Lim, who had no particular expression on her face, he was sure that she was bored.

She kept the same expression in front of the ninety-four-foot-tall Vishal Buddha statue in Bodhgaya. When they visited Mahabodhi temple, the site where Gautama Buddha attained Enlightenment, he even detected slight disappointment on her face. She didn't ask for any translation for quite a while.

Then something happened that made the dusty, grueling tour all worthwhile.

It was moving to see her literally weeping at the sight of the place where Buddha meditated for seven years sitting under the Bodhi tree. It was packed with people. The guy truly understood the mystery of laziness, achieved the art of perfect laziness, which was undoubtedly a lot of work, and was able to make a religion out of it. He deserves this worship of fervor, he thought, watching people praying and meditating amid the thick cloud of burning incense and candles, which covered the national odor of curry, cumin, and onions. He loved their food, but the distinctive odor that resided just about wherever he went could be unfriendly. It was in the bedding, in his pillow, and it felt like his own body was soaked in the marinade.

The place was decorated with loud-colored fabrics and heavily engraved gold panels. It must have been a quiet, serene spot when Buddha was seeking Enlightenment, but now it was a market, a constant carnival. He wondered if it'd be annoying to Buddha. "Didn't he say something like, 'accept everything without attachment,'" which translated to Sam as, "everything is nothing and nothing is everything." Stuff no one is supposed to understand. Typical wise man's stuff. They always say things that are so vague and broad, perhaps intentionally, that one can apply them a million different ways. That's the genius, he thought, concluding that Buddha must have been a carefree sort of guy. The ultimate goal of achieving Enlightenment is obtained through being carefree.

The guide called them to get on the bus for the next destination. As soon as they sat down, Mrs. Lim began to fix her makeup. All that crying had discolored her face. "Does this mean you might go back to Buddhism?" he asked. She put down her compact mirror and told him no. He thought about asking why she cried the way she did but decided not to. He didn't want to go there. It was nice to sit down in silence. He leaned his head back on the headrest and closed his eyes, giving her the cue to not bother him, a cue she usually ignored, but this time, she stayed quiet. He dozed off until he felt an elbow on his side.

"The guide is saying something," Mrs. Lim urged him to pay attention. She needed Sam to translate.

"How long have you been taking English lessons, my dear? Years, right?"

"Just pay attention to what he says. I don't want to miss anything important."

The guide was talking about various things; how they had some thirty million different gods, how Buddha expired in 486 BC, and so on. Then he told a story which made Sam lose his irritation. When Alexander the Great came to the place called Punjab, a young man named Chandra-something fell in love with the Macedonian prince and his beautiful army, their brilliant uniforms, their magnificent animals called horses, flying banners, and shiny armories. It was then and there the boy Chandra saw face to face with his fate. His fate called him to be a beautiful warrior like them. Fate was loyal to him through and through, and he eventually became the first king of the land who conquered an enormous amount of territory, making India humongous. Then one day fate showed him the other side of his shining career of conquest: the unspeakable suffering, irreplaceable destructions, and so much bloodshed caused by his sword. He renounced violence and became a guru for Jainism.

"What's that?" a woman asked, chewing gum.

"It's a religion that kills nothing, as much as possible. They only eat vegetables that are wilted and dying. They go the extra length not to step on bugs when they walk. They make sure the place where they sit and sleep is bug free so that they don't squash any. The individual's level of enlightenment is indicated by the number of clothes one puts on. The more clothing you put on, the less enlightened you are. When you see men walking around in diapers, they are considered to be very close to the gate of absolute understanding. The last step ahead of them is to shed the diaper and go completely naked, which is the crowning achievement. It's the 'I got it!' moment, so to speak. It's said that Chandra achieved this goal and lived the rest of his life naked. One more important order Jainism requires is that when you get old and sick, you starve yourself to death and abstain from food and medicine. When it's time to go, go without putting up a fight. This is how Chandra exited his life." People on the bus, mostly Westerners, giggled and some laughed aloud. Some even said that this first king must have gone crazy.

Sam got absorbed in the story the guide was telling and firmly warned the impatient Mrs. Lim that she had to wait in silence until he was ready to translate for her. He wanted to listen without interruption. One thing that annoyed him more than Mrs. Lim poking his ribs, urging him to translate, was the general comments the Westerners made. "How barbaric," "such backward thinking," "how disgusting," "why not outlaw such practice," and so on and so on. They traveled halfway around the world for what? To form an opinion and pass judgment on someone else's culture and history with their limited knowledge or lopsided opinions. But Sam also noticed that the guide showed the general attitude of dismissing his own culture, laughing along with the tourists, eager to make fun of it as if the harder he laughed at it, the less he himself would be associated with it. The world will never be harmonious, Sam thought.

"King Chandra's grandson Ashoka was a warrior like his grandfather," the guide continued, happy that he made people laugh. "It's said that he was born to fight. He was a conqueror like Chandra, but a fate similar to his grandfather's was waiting for him. One day in the midst of a fierce battle, he also saw indescribable pain and suffering caused by the violence. He also renounced all violence, literally in the middle of a battle, and decided to be a sage-king. Unlike his grandfather, he kept the throne and clothes. He ruled with peace on his mind. As a matter of fact, he was the first king who incorporated religious teachings into the social order. He chose diplomacy over war and sent diplomats to the neighboring countries to spread his messages."

Sam was listening to him with his mouth open when Mrs. Lim elbowed him again. He translated what he had heard. She listened to him without interrupting and said at the end, "You never know what you'll learn at any moment in your life."

"Which makes me wonder, how long have you been taking English lessons?"

"Don't talk to me like I'm a schoolgirl."

"I haven't heard a word of English coming out of your mouth on this trip," he said, remembering the silly grin she wore silently whenever someone spoke to her in English.

"I couldn't understand what they were saying. They sounded different from my tutor."

"Didn't I tell you to get an American tutor? Didn't I tell you learning to speak English from a Korean is like the blind leading the blind?"

"Well, I'm not good at languages, period. But haven't you noticed that I could read some signs and order from menus without asking you what they were? And I can say 'I am fine, thank you' politely."

"True. You have been saying 'I am fine, sankyu (thank you)' numerous times. I'm proud of you," he said, starting to smile, which soon turned into a giggle, which turned into a laugh.

"What's so funny?" Mrs. Lim asked, in the midst of the thought that she would hire an American to teach her when she returned.

Sam wiped the spit from his lips with the back of his hand and said, "I just remembered a joke." He continued, still laughing, "There was a Korean man visiting a friend in America. He went to a market one day alone and had a heart attack. When a paramedic came and asked how he was, he answered, in spite of the fact that he was dying, 'I am fine, thank you.'" He heard Mrs. Lim let out a couple of laughing sounds through her nasal cavity, which translated as "it's funnier that you found the joke funny."

During the ride to the next destination, he found himself visualizing Ashoka waving his sword, sitting on a magnificent horse (black or snow white, he couldn't decide) on a chaotic battlefield, his shirtless chest tightly cushioned with enormous muscles upholstered in bronzed skin. And at that very moment he shouted, "No more!" He repeated this image in his head over and over, falling in love with the romantic scene he created in his head. He made a mental note that he would commission an artist to paint the image when he got back home.

It made him so happy to see Mrs. Lim enjoying herself. It surprised him how she tried everything, since he always suspected that she had a touch of hypochondria. The unsanitary situations on the trip, which were rather unavoidable, didn't seem to bother her. It was a new side of her, previously hidden from him, now revealed to his liking. All these years they'd been together, he always believed that she was a creature who had to function in a geometric way. There had to be lines and shapes, bold and clear. She was not a "try anything and everything" sort of person. That was his understanding of her, and oh, how many times he had to depend on this geometric quality of hers. Later, he told her what he observed about her new personality.

She said, "I was just being nostalgic. A little prince like yourself wouldn't know, but the hostile environment we see here is more or less what I and many, many people had to live with when I was growing up. This place reminded me of my childhood, the endless search for your daily meal, no footwear, diseases, being dirty as a chimney sweep, yet we were always so ready to face another day, so prompt for life, willing and ready to be delighted at any moment for any measly gain without prejudice. I guess that's why I'm enjoying being here so much. But not to worry, I'll go back to my stoically corrupted self when we go back home. Nostalgia of such kind is wonderful when it only stays in the head." She said all this as if she possessed perfect control over her life.

They came back to the hotel after a grueling day of sightseeing. Despite the national odor still residing in the bedding and pillows, he felt almost giddy being in an air-conditioned room with a clean toilet that worked. Sipping a cocktail while sitting on a cushy chair in the fabulously decorated lounge transported them to a different world, the world to which they belonged. What they saw and experienced during the tour became just more tales to tell the moment they returned to their pre-tour world. He could kiss the soft toilet paper in the bathroom.

They had a day's rest before the journey to the temple where his father was waiting. The travel agency showed him its approximate location on the map (the place wasn't even marked on the local map). But the agent assured him that it was within a few miles from the town he indicated on the map. "The locals know exactly where it is, sir," he said, dangling his head like there was a spring in place of the thing called "neck." Actually, every Indian he encountered had this spring system in their necks, which Sam found quite amiable. He had anxiety about the journey ahead, but he decided to put his trust in the army of guides he hired.

He was napping before dinner when Mrs. Lim called him from the lobby. "Sam, I need you to come down and translate for me," she said.

"What's the matter?" he asked with alarm in his voice. He warned her never to leave her room without letting him know.

"They have a fortune-teller here in the lobby. I'd like my fortune read."

The fortune-teller that the hotel hired for entertaining the patrons was a man of all ages, with a massive turban and jet black hair covering half of his face. His mustache was waxed and sculpted like the spread wings of a blackbird who was honoring the massive turquoise silk turban. His protruding eyes under the eaves of bushy eyebrows were too unsettling to meet with others. He could be in his twenties or late forties; it was hard to tell until Sam noticed his youthful hands, which were smooth with small knuckles and well manicured. Sam wondered if his facial hair was real. His smooth, hairless hands made him suspicious of him being naturally hairy. He wore a well-tailored suit and an orange-gold-hued silk tie with a tie clip made of a green stone that looked pricey. He also spoke in British English, although his voice wasn't as attractive as that of the tour guide. When it was their turn (for there was a queue), he didn't ask for any personal information like birthdays and so on, which was the crucial information Chinese fortune-tellers needed to have one's fortune read. There wasn't much fortune-telling; it was more like a quiz game. He was more or less telling them of their past, which wasn't fortune-telling in the true sense. They sat in front of this age-deceiving guy who told them triumphantly of their pasts, which they already knew more than him, and charged them for it. For example, he mentioned Mrs. Lim's deceased son, Sam's mother, who wasn't really his mother but was his amah, and his beloved dog, Jayu, and many other things which had nothing to do with telling the future. One thing he said, though, that involved the future was that Sam and Mrs. Lim would be together for a long time. One peculiar thing he said that Sam didn't think anything of was that he had no blood relations alive. He also knew that they weren't a married couple.

"You will decide to marry, although spiritually it won't be necessary. You've been together since the beginning of time."

"What does that mean?" Sam asked.

"It means that in every reincarnation you've experienced you've known each other in one form of a relationship or another," he said with the neck's spring system at work.

"That was rather a waste of money," Sam said to her when they sat in the hotel restaurant to have dinner. She nodded but was quiet. When dinner came, she played with her food and kept ordering cocktails. Sam knew why. She was thinking about her son. He was indignant at the hairy pseudo-fortune-teller who dug out the painful memory. "Are you?" he started after a while.

"Yeah. Sorry…" she said with a wet sigh. He reached over and squeezed her hand. "I'd like to sit in the lounge and listen to the music for a little while," she said, rubbing his hand with her thumb.

"Am I invited? Or you'd rather be alone?"

"Come and sit with me. I'll tell you when to leave me," she said with a faint smile. They sat next to each other in the lounge, listening to the local band playing familiar pop tunes, drinking more. "It's my last tonight," both of them said to each other when they ordered more drinks.

"We have an early morning tomorrow. Are you packed?" Sam asked.

"Yes, my dear," she said, leaning her head on his shoulder. "I'll pack yours later before I go to sleep," she added dutifully.

"It's mostly done, but maybe you want to check anyway," he said to her.

She then responded with a slow, lazy tongue, "Yeah, right…"

A chubby clarinet player with a shiny forehead was doing his solo, accompanied by the rest of the band. There were five of them, no smiles, no tapping feet, just doing their job of producing tunes to earn a living, no need to pretend that they were having fun. The clarinet man finished his solo. It was only about ten o'clock. The song they were playing had not finished, and the rest of the band was still at it except for the clarinet man. He was wrapping up even while his band was still playing. He took out his clarinet case and started to wipe his instrument with a rag, spitting on it here and there. When the cleaning was done, he put the clarinet in the case and closed it loudly, adding an unfriendly sound to the song that was still playing, and casually stepped down from the stage. Sam and Mrs. Lim laughed at this sight. "His part is no more. He is sooo ready to go home." Then they sensed that the beat of the music became faster and faster. The other musicians couldn't wait to join the clarinet player who had left before the end of the song.

The wake-up call was ordered for 6:00 a.m. They had coffee and toast, regretting the amount of drinks they had the night before. Mrs. Lim gave Sam a couple of pills of herbal medicine to ease the headache. A small group would take them in a van to where they needed to go to meet up with another group of guides. The concierge told Sam and Mrs. Lim this would repeat a few times; he also urged them to pack a sufficient supply of toilet paper. "You might have to go in the bush sometimes," they were warned.

The road was hostile. It was so bumpy it vibrated their voices and rattled every bone in their bodies. There were six passengers in the van, all foreigners, businessmen rather than tourists. A man who sat next to them was a medical doctor who came to the region to study local traditional practice for healing. It was hard to tell his ethnic background from his appearance. He could have been African-American or an unusually big Indian. He was a big man, tall and beefy, but not without a certain dignity. He spoke intelligently with a deep but clear voice. He asked Sam where he learned to speak English so well. "I'm from the UK," he introduced himself, this time with a certain formality, laying his large palm on his chest.

Sam introduced himself in turn and asked out of courtesy, "Is there a particular reason for you to pick this region of the world?" Mrs. Lim was sleeping, leaning her head on the window.

"My ancestors were from here. My grandfather is one hundred eight years old. His father also lived to be over a hundred. As far as I remember, my grandfather was never ill. He treated himself with tonics and herbs sent by his relatives from here. When I was in medical school, I used to argue with him about it. I used to call them poison, witchcraft. I've practiced medicine for nearly thirty years. I love medicine. It's the best thing ever when you restore a sick person to health. But sometimes, too many times in my opinion, people don't get well, get worse, or die. That was a tough thing for me to deal with throughout my practice. Whenever a patient of mine died on me, I felt that a little bit of me died too. But it's harder to see them dwindling slowly, hanging onto my empty words of hope. I couldn't take it anymore. I was on the verge of clinical depression. Then one day I noticed how healthy and robust my grandfather was and learned that many of his acquaintances back home shared the same fortune. I started to pay attention to his methods of self-treatment and began to do research on them. So here I am, bewildered but excited."

"You don't look depressed at all."

"Well, this new interest switched the light back on, ha, ha."

Sam told him that back home people trusted traditional medicine more than Western practice. Honestly, he wasn't sure of the fact he stated, but somehow he wanted to say something encouraging to the formerly depressed, good doctor. They chatted through the bumpy ride about this and that regarding diseases and cure. He enthusiastically educated him. Sam wondered about the other members of the good doctor's family, if they'd also enjoyed the same fortune as his over-staying grandfather. He didn't bring up the question in fear of stretching the courtesy talk longer than necessary. Sam was so tired, but he didn't have the heart to dismiss the doctor who was going strong. He listened to him, yawning repeatedly, which the medicine man ignored. Less than half-listening, he politely injected replies like, "huh," "yeah, I know," or "no kidding" in cycles.

By the time he made up his mind to be blunt and tell him that he needed some shut-eye, the good doctor embarked on a bizarre story of his ancestors, which gave Sam's ears a second wind. Sam liked stories, all sorts of stories. The doctor's ancestors were so-called untouchables: "A psycho guru named Manu started a theory that divided the human species into good and bad, meaning useful and useless. To breed the worthy and to eliminate the unworthy was his basis for creating a utopia. Bastards, those born from rape victims, abandoned children, the deformed, and the offspring of these forsaken individuals were condemned as unworthy, the untouchables. Houseflies had more rights than these people. They were kept alive to do the dirtiest work, like cleaning sewage. Things like showing themselves in public, bathing, or drinking clean water, and many more basic human needs were prohibited to them."

"Is it still going on?" Sam saw the medicine man nodding vertically in assent.

"Are your family…"

"They were able to run away a long time ago."

"To England?"

"No, of course not. Not immediately, but eventually yes. After many months of traveling, hiding during the days and moving at night in the most indescribable difficulties, they decided to settle in an area where they felt safe enough. The area where they stopped to rest happened to be in the path of nomads; it was like an oasis. My grandfather, who was a small boy, told me that it was like heaven on earth. The river, abundant green vegetation, and the piercing blue sky were more than anything he could've wished for. It was the only spot with water and greens, miraculously existing away from the rest of the hostile landscape. Slowly nomads and others from unknown origins settled there, eventually forming a small village of their own. Sometime after, English and French archaeologists gathered there, frightening them. The Europeans had come because the area was for them a site of interest; they believed that a large Buddhist temple existed there a thousand years ago and that it was a place for pilgrimage. There was nothing that indicated such a history, according to my grandfather. But the locals were happy that the foreigners stayed, for they employed them in digging, paying them handsomely. It turned out that the archaeologists were looking for buried Buddha statues, one of which was supposed be about fifty feet in length, in a reclining position. Numerous items of priceless value were dug up, confirming the archaeologists' knowledge, but they never found any big lounging Buddha statue," he said, laughing a bit.

"Why don't all the untouchables run away, find a better life?"

"They were like domesticated animals for many generations. They don't think of life other than what they know. Where would they go? Not to mention the severe punishment if they got caught."

"Isn't there a law that protects these people?"

"Such a law would not stand a chance against the thousands of years of tradition, however ill-doing it is. Gandhi legislated 'emancipation of the forsaken people' as a law, but that was just writing on a paper. Coming from a third-world country yourself, you must understand what I am saying. It's the masses that decide which law to abide or not. Pretty democratic in a sense, isn't it?" The doctor gave a sad smile with a far away stare.

Sam was slightly insulted at his "third world" comment. "What does this have to do with 'third world'?" Sam retorted, but with a smile in an attempt to let the doctor know he wasn't being confrontational. "Being economically challenged doesn't necessarily mean a nation has an inhumane culture," he added.

"Oh, I'm sorry. I must've misled you. What I meant was that every society in human history has dark practices. When society struggles for a daily meal, people generally don't have room in them to be concerned with social justice, whether or not something's humane. Justice or concerns about humanity, such things grow wings only after one eats better. You're more likely to see ugly, inhumane traditions perpetuating in the third world."

"I think I understand what you're saying, but I'm not sure I agree. What you're implying is that poverty has no heart."

"No, no. The absence of education due to poverty is my argument. It takes education to reform people, and the promotion of education in a society is proportional to its wealth."

"As I said, I understand what you're saying, but again I disagree. It's much more complicated and deeper, I think. With law enforcement and education, such practices might diminish, but there has to be something more to it, an instinctual affinity, if you will, for darkness and horror that is deeply embedded in the human psyche. You see, it might disappear on the surface in wealthier and more educated societies, but if you dig down in these seemingly more humane societies, you'd find the same disturbing activities in various forms," Sam said, quite satisfied with his statement.

But the good doctor did not give up. "Hold on a second. Didn't you just ask 'isn't there a law to prohibit this practice?' Now you are telling me that law can be powerless in front of the vile nature of humankind," the doctor said, making a quick quarter turn towards Sam, advancing his face with its Russet potato for a nose and using his tongue to intentionally lisp when imitating the question Sam asked earlier.

Seeing the doctor turn into a fifth grader in a schoolyard was almost too hilarious to suppress laughter, but he was able to keep his composure, just barely, though. Sam blinked, realizing the table had turned. Somewhere along the conversation the roles had been switched, just a bit. He also sensed that the good doctor didn't like to lose. When the doctor rotated a quarter turn back to his original position, Sam said, getting in touch with the fifth grader in himself, "I did, didn't I? Although I didn't ask exactly like that. 'Isn't there a law that protects these people' was what I said," he added with an air of stamping on the last word.

"The same thing..." the doctor murmured.

"No, they aren't the same. Prohibit and protect can never be used in place of each other," Sam continued, raising his index finger to stop the doctor whose mouth was open and ready to send out a torrent of words. "Then, as I recall, you brought out the third-world issue. And I disagreed, owning my own opinion. Earlier you said 'such a law wouldn't stand a chance against thousands of years of tradition, it's just a writing on a paper,' right? And I said that the human psyche possessed an affinity for horror. So, wait a minute, we are either saying the same thing all along or debating over apples and oranges. What do you think?"

The doctor was silent for a few seconds as though deep in contemplation. He slid down his seat, folding his arms. Then suddenly, nudging his shoulder on Sam's, he started to chuckle saying, "Which am I, apple or orange?"

Sam chuckled along, pushing the doctor's invasive shoulder playfully with his, which received another push. "Let's settle with the fact that we both belong to the fruit family."

The talk continued. Sam talked about the nature of his trip, about his father's long absence due to his aspiration to be a monk, and so on. In the middle of shooting the breeze with each other, Sam suddenly sat up.

"I remember, we do have a similar, awful tradition." Sam told the doctor about animal slaughtering in Korea. "We called these people 'Baekjung.' They slaughter cows and pigs for butchers. Butchers don't do the actual killing; their business is in carving and slicing. Killing is strictly reserved for Baekjung. They are our version of 'untouchables.' I don't know the details of their lives in terms of what they're allowed to do or not, but they aren't supposed to mix with the public, that much I know. They are what shouldn't have been, so to speak. And, no, we did not produce a great man like Gandhi yet. We haven't produced any writing on paper yet, however meaningless it might be."

The doctor nodded with a knowing air. "They must be in fear of animal spirits, of karma. Superstition is powerful stuff. But when you examine it, there's a practical aspect to it, don't you think? Killing the animals is evil, yet people consume their flesh happily without fear of the curse. Their desire to sink their teeth into flesh was in conflict with the curse of the animal spirits. They must've come to an agreement that as long as you don't lend your hand in the killing you are free from the angry spirits of the animals; it's a manipulation of superstition by biological desire."

"But they hunt and kill chickens. I don't know, maybe it only applies to cows and pigs."

"Koreans eat dogs, right?"

"Some still do, but it's widely rejected. It's a summer delicacy; they believe it has medicinal value for those whose *chi* loses potency by sweating too much. Disgusting! I love dogs. They are, to me, the most perfect creature God ever created. If there's such thing as an angel, I do not hesitate to call a dog one," Sam said, feeling his blood pressure in the temple.

"I'm sorry I brought that up. I'm a dog lover myself," the doctor said, going through the pockets in his jacket. He pulled out a photo of his dog from his wallet, beaming proudly, lovingly. It was a black-and-white shih tzu, glamorously coiffed with its pink tongue peeking out a little. Sam took the photo in his hand and laughed, partly because of the mental image of the glamorous, tiny creature and the big man with a Russet potato nose walking about the town and partly because of the pleasure he felt looking at the animal who surely was living the life. The doctor put the photo back into his wallet saying, "I commissioned an artist to paint a portrait from the photo," letting out a sweet sigh of joy. Sam regretted that he didn't have a photo of Jayu, who had passed away a few years ago from old age. He briefly checked his memory to assure himself of having given his best friend the very best life possible. After his death Sam couldn't bring himself up to get another dog. It seemed like getting married again too soon after losing a partner. Dishonorable.

"Are you superstitious?" the doctor asked, waking Sam up yet again from another daydream, in which he was toying with the idea of getting dogs when he went back home.

"Uh? Oh, not knowingly. I never thought about it. Are you?"

"When I was a young man I was a certified atheist. Everything had to be scientific. It was when I was waiting for an acceptance letter from medical school that I realized I wasn't a pure atheist."

Sam let him continue, rubbing his eyes.

"I was anxious about the letter of admission. That was all I thought about. I began to chew my nails, developed twitches. Then one day I was walking toward an intersection I needed to cross that had a green light. I was still about twenty feet away, and I ran toward the intersection thinking that if the light stayed green until I passed it, it would be a sign that I made it into medical school. And I repeated the ritual over and over. At that time my unusual activity didn't register in my thick head as peculiar or unacceptable or a betrayal of science. I was accepted into medical school, and I kept my position as a certified atheist until one day I noticed that I resumed the 'racing to the green light' activity every time I had to pass an important exam. It became quite crazy. I ran out in the middle of the night just to do the race. I wrote down how many lights I made and how many I didn't. And my expectations for the exam results went up or down according to the chart I created. When the graph was hovering at a low level, I also lost the appetite for studying hard. That was when I began to lose my certification of being an atheist."

"Do you still keep up with the race?" Sam asked, rubbing his eyes again, which had gotten heavier even as his ears were wide awake.

"Ha, ha. Once you get caught, you get caught for good. I tried to lose the damn habit, made another chart to determine success, even cried out of frustration at times, and eventually, the habit died down. No, I didn't ask for the certification of an atheist back."

"You thought you killed it, but it left you after it had successfully changed you. It sounds like the victor was the race, that it won in the end."

"Not only did it win, it returned in mathematical form."

Sam couldn't resist the laugh that exploded out of his mouth, stirring Mrs. Lim who was sleeping next to him. She looked up, momentarily seeing nothing with her open eyes, made a couple of slurping sounds with her tongue as if tasting something, with her hair resembling an abandoned bird's nest. She coiled up against the window again and went back to the business of sleeping.

The good doctor was talking.

"What happened was that I later found myself adding and subtracting numbers on cars' license plates. Strangely it involved only coupes and sedans, never any commercial trucks."

"I bet you made another chart." Sam chuckled.

"No sir, not again. It didn't bother me. It was more random, and since it only required the mental work of simple math, not as taxing as the race, I didn't feel the anguish or urge to fight with it. Although one day I felt something was not quite right, and sure enough, it turned out to be a day I didn't perform the ritual. Yeah, I accepted it as my own personal ritual. I became a believer in a way. Why fight, it doesn't debilitate me in any way, it rather organizes my days, supplies energy, and a sense of readiness. Isn't it the same motive why people attend church and pray? I'm glad there are so many license plates. I feel they are there to give me messages, to look after me."

The doctor, an avid scientist, had confessed that superstition serves him well. Suddenly, Sam felt an enormous laugh rising in his chest, but upon seeing the solemnity of the doctor, Sam had to put a brake on it, regretfully wasting a good laugh. Something about the whole scene and the conversation suddenly seemed hilarious, especially the suddenly solemn but pathetic expression the doctor exhibited. The air from the suppressed laugh blew out his chest and filled up his cheeks like a blowfish, but with strenuous effort, he was able to keep the gate locked. Now he had to do something quickly about his right hand, which was frozen in midair on its way to give his knee a good slap or two in the attempt to enhance his currently incarcerated gas of laughter. The fifth grader in a schoolyard was nowhere to be found. He had to bring out the courteous middle-aged man in him. He brought his suspended hand to his head, ordering his fingers to plow his hair. However, the laugh in him was less controllable than ever; it was about to explode. A high-pitched sound, although barely audible, was already escaping. He had to do something quickly. In the end, he opened his mouth as big as it could possibly stretch out and freed the laugh, passing it off as a combination of a loud yawn and sigh. It didn't end there, though. He had to purge the remaining gas in his chest that was vigorously pushing out for emancipation. At first it came out as a vibrating, whimpering sound, then turned to squeals like a pig being slaughtered, heaving his chest uncontrollably. He reassigned his hand that was plowing his hair to a new position of blocking his mouth with a fist. This allowed him to let out a series of hacking coughs. He was glad of the save but couldn't deny he was upset that such magnificent laughter had to be dishonored and wasted. He had to recover when the good doctor gently pounded his back, asking if he was alright. He nodded, wiping tears from the manufactured coughs. The mental image of him in the near future telling the story to Mrs. Lim, which undoubtedly would allow a second life to the presently murdered laughter, eased the hurt. He wiped his eyes with back of his hand, which had performed superbly at a moment's notice during the ordeal. The doctor offered him water from the canister he had in his bag, telling Sam that it had been boiled three times. Sam drank it at one go, and this time wiped his mouth with his obedient hand.

When the atmosphere returned more or less to normal, the doctor asked Sam, making him utterly nervous, "Surely you must have had a similar experience. I think, I believe, it is universal, ubiquitous." He was still on the same subject.

Sam cleared his throat, feeling a cobweb of mucus and said, "If I have, I don't remember," hearing his voice scratched.

"Oh, I see," the doctor said, sounding disappointed if not betrayed, as though they were supposed to be playing a game of quid pro quo. The good doctor's sensitivity was contagious, and Sam was busily working on his memory to find anything remotely qualified for the nature of the game. He started, "I was raised by my amah, who was very superstitious. I'm sure I must conduct a thing or two in my daily life according to what I learned from her. I just can't put my finger on it at the moment." Saying this he stole a look from the doctor who seemed to be recovering from the hurt.

"What happened to your mother?"

"She died at my birth. My father never remarried."

Sam naturally expected to hear "I'm sorry to hear that" or some such comment from the doctor. Instead he asked, "Was it tough growing up as a partial orphan?" This time Sam didn't hesitate to laugh, as if asking "what kind of question is that?" The doctor continued, "The reason I asked is because when I see you, you emit an aura of ease and confidence, a quality that I so far have only found in people who've grown up in a family of perfect harmony."

"I could say that my childhood belonged to what you call 'perfect harmony,' albeit being a partial orphan. I didn't feel the absence of my mother, thanks to my loving amah. My father was more like a statesman but kind and gentle. He was scarce due to a busy schedule, but to this day, he is the only one who can give me the wisest answer to all my problems. I simply worship him. I always check with him, in my head at times, how he would handle various situations."

"So it was your amah who nurtured you to death and the father who was the ultimate protector. You were a greenhouse boy like exotic plants that can't survive outside of it."

"But I still get to keep the aura of an easy, confident person from a harmonious background, right?"

"I didn't mean to offend you by calling you a 'greenhouse boy.' If anything, it came out of envy. My youth was not easy. Poverty, racism, and a dysfunctional family. I could say I'm a partial orphan too, although not technically. My mother, who was from the Caribbean, ran away when I was a child. Shamefully, I admit that my brother and I were relieved. It was the only noble thing she did. She tormented my father and grandfather. Well, let's not go there. After all, it's nothing but the typical, boring destructive tales of many dysfunctional families. You know what was funny, we all began to laugh again, even making fun of her occasionally after her disappearance. My baby brother had gained weight and noticeably developed a relaxed posture even though our mother's disappearance didn't bring our household economic luck. My father was a window cleaner. He carried a ladder and a bucket, many times with me and my brother, knocking on doors of residential areas asking if they wanted their windows cleaned." The doctor said this with a certain smile in his eyes, bitter and sweet.

"Are you still glad that she left? Do you know if she's still alive?"

He shrugged, pulling the corners of his mouth downward. "If she died, that makes me a full-fledged partial orphan. Ha, ha, ha!" He laughed crudely and said, "One thing she could've given me was her pretty nose. But no, she didn't even do that! Ha, ha, ha!" He laughed, squeezing his Russet potato. Sam felt sorry for him. He could tell it still pained him underneath the crude laughter. He also felt blessed being a greenhouse boy. He didn't want the conversation to drag onto each other's family sagas. Something the doctor mentioned about his father being the ultimate protector was sitting on his chest like indigestion.

"Some ten years ago right before the Korean War, this greenhouse boy had to run away and hide from the communists." Charged by the doctor's enthusiasm, Sam described the series of incidents and actions from around that time: the beatings he took, the distribution of the gold nuggets, weeping farewells at the daybreak of a chilly April, gum chewing, talkative American drivers, a train ride, and circling around in the woods in despair. "The main item of the story is about to come, doctor. As I mentioned, to this day I've never toyed with the idea of God. Such a thing belongs to other people. That's okay with me, meaning, I accept these people as they come, even respect their faith wholeheartedly. When my father left to be a Taoist monk, I absolutely believed it to be one of his clever schemes to avoid the political unrest in the country. Anyway, going back to my story, when I saw the temple where I ended up hiding for two years, I ran down the hill hearing my own voice incessantly saying 'thank you, God, oh, thank you, God.' By the time I arrived at the front step of the temple, I belched out 'Hallelujah!' A Christian exclamation in front of a Buddhist temple. What do you say to that? Does that mean I'm unconsciously a Christian?" He finished the story, rubbing his chin.

The doctor beamed, nodding his head rapidly while blinking his eyes obviously in search of a smart response. "I'm glad you shared that with me. That confirmed my belief that everyone, including the most hardened atheist, has a temple in them. I knew it!" He rubbed his palms together then started cracking his knuckles one after another, still beaming as if his scientific experiment gave him the results he had hoped to achieve.

"How do you define a hardened atheist? According to you, there is none."

"They are the people who believe that God told them that He doesn't exist."

They both had a hearty laugh.

"Aren't we so stupid?"

"Perhaps that's what makes us so amusing to God," Sam murmured, feeling his head dropping on Mrs. Lim's shoulder. A sudden attack of sleep immobilized him. It was like water spiraling down into a pipe. He tried to say "excuse me" to the doctor, but if he did or did not, he couldn't remember. By the time the guide woke him up for a bathroom break, the doctor had gone. His sudden absence made him a tad melancholy. He liked him. After the break, the van started to roll when he began to tell Mrs. Lim about the conversation he had with the doctor, exaggerating the parts that would make her laugh. She laughed in the right places.

"He's right. Just about everyone has a little ritual of superstition, both overtly and covertly, except you. Actually, you know what's strange about you is that you have no opinion when it comes to such things, religion, superstition, ghosts, spirits. I find that weird."

It took three different car rides, which were bumpy and even scary sometimes, two boat rides, and a hike on a mountain with donkeys to get to the temple. It took nearly five days. When they went over the border to Nepal, there was a sudden change in the national odor announcing that they had entered a new realm, proudly welcoming the newcomers with the distinctive scent of animal dung. One of the most important resources of the land was animal dung; it was used as fuel, building material, and in other unimaginably creative ways. Sam and Mrs. Lim didn't mind the scent. The vast landscape, which was dusty and dry with a horizon of flat dirt and sky that could be seen in 360 degrees, seemed neglected like a bastard child of nature. Standing on the soil of this land, Sam felt like he and Mrs. Lim were part of a surrealistic painting, a painting that magically emitted the odor of dung. There was something heartfelt, even beautiful, being in the middle of this hostile terrain, breathing in the dusty air laced with dung perfume. He didn't know why, but he felt honored. Occasionally, they would see old men squatting by the side of the road smoking long pipes, and women wrapped in fabrics carrying baskets on their heads walking with bare feet, the tails of their black fabric undulating. The heat wave from the ground made the scenery blurry and tremulous. "Life is less than temporary, why bother!" was the general ethos Sam gathered from the few people he encountered. They looked neither happy nor unhappy. They seemed to be in full understanding of what "as is" meant. Mrs. Lim gave up on tidying up her hair. Sam's beard felt like a foreign object on his face that itched constantly.

For the first night, the guide put them in the home of a local. The room given to them was more suitable for livestock. Mrs. Lim didn't protest, although the look on her face said otherwise. On the other hand, Sam felt poetry in his heart in spite of his itchy beard. They took turns washing up at a hut by the well behind the house; it was slightly tilted but private enough. The leaning hut of nowhere. After washing up they sat on a wooden bench outside the hut that flipped over if you didn't place the weight of your body on it with precision. It was the first time Sam saw her hair without any work done on it. It was wet in tight balls of curls.

He ran his fingers through her hair asking, "Are these curls yours?"

"What kind of stupid question is that? Of course, they're mine, untreated, all natural." She had resumed her snapping; she was back.

Happy to see her restored, he said, "I thought they were from a frying job, a permanent, as you ladies call it." His fingers played with her hair, which she didn't seem to mind. Those curls between his fingers straightened out when pulled and immediately coiled back with perfect memory when let go, like undercooked ramen noodles. But he made a mental note never to annoy her again about her excessive concern for coiffure. Those tight curls on her head were not her friends. They reminded him of snails, hundreds of them, making a mockery out of his best friend, Mrs. Lim. They made her look terrible to the point of hurting his feelings. It was a wise choice for her to straighten them out incessantly.

"This is really nowhere. So dry, so brown, not a bird," she said, looking out at the rocky desert.

"It's quite empty. Forgotten empty. God must have run out of creativity when he reached this area."

"Perhaps. But I feel closer to Him now," she said, looking pensive.

The sun was setting, tinting the sky pink, orange, and fuchsia as though fruit juices of various kinds had been squeezed over it.

"The room is awfully small."

Here she goes, Sam thought, preparing himself inwardly not to be thrown in a place of defense, which was mostly his domain. I'm too tired. I think my sleep will be sweet anywhere tonight.

"Those beds are bolted to the floor, have you noticed?" Sam then saw that two wooden platforms, a little bigger than the bench they were sitting on, were up against the wall sideways, bolted to the floor. "It would be impossible not to touch the dung-pasted wall while sleeping." She sighed.

"Just try not to lick it, you open-mouth-sleeper. He, he, he."

"Look, what are they doing?"

Sam turned his head to where she was looking and saw the guides pitching a tent for their night lodging. It was a good-sized army tent.

"Sam, let's ask them to switch with us."

"Are you sure? I mean, it's tempting, but are you sure you won't be scared?"

"Oh, no. It'll be fun. Come on, go ask them."

"What if I get scared?" he said, unbalancing the unsteady bench as he got up. Sam approached them, thanked them for everything, and requested that the army tent be his sleeping arrangement for the night. One of the guides scratched the back of his neck showing obvious reluctance, as if he were being asked to break the house rules. Sam knew what the situation called for. He took out his wallet and gave him five dollars, a lot of money in that land of nowhere. He took the money, of course, but still showing a tinge of reluctance, as if he were bending over backward for them.

Two local women came and cooked dinner in an open fire outside. They didn't use dung fuel. All of them except the two local women sat around the fire and had a surprisingly tasty dinner. Sam intentionally didn't ask what they were eating; he didn't want to know if he was chewing on a delicious scorpion. They sampled the local drink, which was a slightly rancid and syrupy liquid that clung to the esophagus. It was enjoyable.

After dinner Sam and Mrs. Lim sat on the bench sipping on the liquor of unknown origin. There were stars, stars, stars mesmerizing, blessing the forsaken land, blushing the moon. Shooting stars crisscrossed one after another, making them wonder if one of them would land in their laps. The inky night sky seemed so close that if you tiptoed up to it, you might touch it. When they turned back to the tent, Sam unzipped the roof. They lay on yak skin.

"Why do they have more stars than back home?" Mrs. Lim asked. He let her muddle in her outstandingly stupid question and ignored it. He had to. He was afraid of uttering any unsavory word that would upset the spell of the reigning stars that seemed so alive and sacred. Mrs. Lim fell silent and went to sleep. He made a pillow with his folded arms, unable to move his eyes from the stars visible through the square of the open roof. Somehow his mind, momentarily separated from his person, turned to baby Jesus, the birth of baby Christ. He tried to stay with baby Jesus, but it faded away.

Mrs. Lim snored gently. He covered her with yak skin. The night air had turned cold. He closed his eyes, and the Russet potato nose of the good doctor was the last image on his mind before the curtains of the day were drawn.

- 5 3 -

"Ever since we received your letter, I've come out here every day waiting for you, and here you are, Botchang!" Mr. Yu, his father's servant, said. He looked surprisingly fit. He was wearing a grey robe like the one Sam used to wear at Bongsan's temple and a wide-brimmed straw hat. He grabbed Sam's hands, "Let me see, let me see you." He greeted Mrs. Lim and led them to the temple. They walked uphill for about a half mile followed by two men, who led the donkeys carrying their luggage, before they reached the top. The temple was situated where hills on the surrounding mountains joined together like the flat bottom of a large bowl. Sam was happily surprised to see how colorfully painted the temple was. It was like a humongous flower arrangement looking down from the hilltop. Mrs. Lim's dusty face lit up at the sight of happy primary colors. Sam had expected to see a dilapidated old temple like Bongsan's. Actually, a few years after he had left Bongsan's temple, he refurbished it for them. The old monk didn't want to change the run-down appearance too much, for he liked the look of ruin. He agreed though that it needed to be reinforced. The new roof and floors were put in along with electricity, running water, and a telephone line, the last there installed behind Bongsan's back. And while Bongsan was hesitating, Sam went ahead and built a five-room guesthouse behind the main temple for overnight or long-term visitors. But no paint, no carved columns, no pagoda...The old monk would have none of that.

Mr. Yu said the people there were like bright colors. Sam's father had the place painted fresh every three to four years. "They are quiet peaceful people with a taste for loud colors."

"Who are these people?" Mrs. Lim asked, looking around.

"There's a village down the other side," he said, pointing with his finger toward the opposite side from where they came. "There were only a few hundred people the first year we came here. This place was barely surviving with a few old monks, a couple of them senile. I didn't want to stay, but your father thought it was perfect. We argued and argued. When I threatened that I'd leave by myself, he didn't care. That really hurt my feelings, but I guess he knew I wouldn't have left him alone all along. The first six months or so we hardly talked to each other. To this day I have no idea what made him decide this is it. Those monks faded away one by one; one of them disappeared, and the rest died within a year. By then we became familiar with some villagers who had spread good words for us. Of course, your father's generosity helped a great deal. The village grew, and now there are easily several thousand people and growing. These people are of different backgrounds: Chinese, Mongolians, Arabs, and a new race they produced among them. Interesting, isn't it? Your father gave them the job of fixing this place. Gradually, this temple became a place to go for these people. Once a month the people bring here whatever they want to sell, making the place a lively market. When we realized that these people worship different gods, your father built more temples so that each faith has their own house of worship. All those four temples have the appearance of a Buddhist temple, but inside they are different churches for different gods. The one at the far end," he continued, pointing at the temple tucked behind a large rock, "is for Christians. And this one right here is for Muslims. Ha, ha, ha." He laughed, clapping his hands.

Sam didn't know what to think. He looked at Mrs. Lim, who was clearly bewildered. "What about the other two?" he asked, pointing at the two remaining unexplained temples.

"Oh, this one here is for Buddhists; it's where we reside. And that one is for those who worship the spirits of nature and ancestors, you know, like shamanic faith. It's the most sought-after one. Do you know why?" He continued without waiting for Sam's reply. He chuckled first and said, "All those Christians, Buddhists, and Moslems visit the temple of shamans when they are in need of quick solutions. Without a doubt, that temple represents the 'here and now' unlike the other three, which promises good things only after death."

They arrived at the bottom of the hills. Two men unloaded their luggage from the donkeys and asked for water for both the animals and themselves. Sam paid them and thanked them for guiding them through a safe journey, which they could not understand without a translator. They smiled, trusting what Sam just told them was a good thing for them. They drank the water Mr. Yu brought. Behind him were two young males in regular clothing carrying wooden buckets with water for the donkeys. They passed right by Sam and Mrs. Lim to the donkeys and lingered around the animals, talking to each other and laughing a little in a very bizarre language. One of the guides showed Sam a piece of paper. He wanted to confirm the date for picking them up. The correct date was written in red ink. They nodded at each other with big smiles and shook hands. Mr. Yu said something to the young men in regular clothing who bowed and took their bags.

"What language is that?" Sam asked, rather impressed by Mr. Yu.

"Who knows? They don't even speak the same language. Everyone communicates one way or another. You know, mix and match. Through the years your father and I were able to pick it up and get by. In a way, it's nice that various languages are being mixed together, making it impossible to know who sounds more intelligent. We talk here for the pure need of simple communication, nothing more. No language snobbism here."

Sam noticed that Mr. Yu did not call his father a master anymore. At the bottom of the stairs leading to his father's quarter, Sam was overcome with a sudden rush of emotion. He lingered, unable to take the first step on the stairs. He took a deep breath and yet another one when Mr. Yu gently pulled his arm. Sam turned to face him and immediately knew what he was going to say. His father was dying. In fact, any day now. He plopped down on the step, leaning his shoulder against the bamboo railing. "You must be awfully tired, honey, why don't you go on up and rest a while. You can see my father later," Sam said to Mrs. Lim, who was about to join him on the step with her jaw dropped, her dusty face turning grey, and her glasses getting foggy. "I need to talk with Mr. Yu about a few things before I see my dad, privately." Mr. Yu quickly told her which room was hers and where to wash up before he sat next to Sam with his head dropped as if he had sinned.

"For how long?" Sam asked after a few deep sighs that carried the faint sound of moaning.

"From about six months ago he started to complain about pain in his lower abdomen with the occasional runs. I was scared that he might have had appendicitis, but he said it was on the left side. Then he seemed to be in good health again until a month or so ago. He began to lose weight rapidly."

"Has he seen a doctor?"

"A couple from the village."

"What kind? Chinese herb doctors?"

"One of them is. And a Polish surgeon."

"Polish?"

"He practices Western medicine. He practiced in Russia before, but he had to leave the country for political reasons, so he came here. The people in the village love him. He's a good man. Your father said so too. Well, they both suspect a problem in his pancreas; they say it's incurable."

"I'm going to take him back to Seoul. No, to America. There has to be treatment," he said, lighting a cigarette in his trembling hands.

"I'm sorry, Botchang. He won't make the journey. You'll know when you see him. If it's any consolation, he's not in pain. Both doctors saw to it."

Sam couldn't control his sobbing. He buried his face in Yu's lap, feeling absolutely defeated, destroyed. "I'm losing my very best friend too, a man who never refused to look after me."

Sam felt drops of Yu's warm tears on the back of neck. "His life here has been a good one, I assure you. He loves it here. One time I complained to him that he was spending too much money for the people in the village. He said that what they gave him back was the knowledge of who he really was. Before he came here, he was a machine, but life here with these people taught him to breathe as a human, taught him to be happy and sad. I think he recaptured the feeling of his youth when he was living in the orphanage."

Inside, the temple was rather modest, unlike the loud appearance of the exterior. The smell of old wood and burning incense had a calming effect on Sam's pounding heart, which had been jumping at the thought of seeing his father after so many years, after the heart-breaking news. His father, sitting on the floor, looked up at Sam and dropped his jaw with wide eyes. His grey, cropped hair and crimson robe was nothing like Sam had imagined. He sat up and held Sam's hands and shook and shook, looking at his face, unable to utter a word. Sam's face was flooded with tears, and choking sounds from his throat replaced any word he tried to utter. Sam noticed how frail he'd become. He gave him three big traditional bows, each ending with his forehead on the floor, where he left puddles of tears. Mrs. Lim, who had caught up to them, came into the room. She bowed once deeply, which Sam's father reciprocated by bowing his head toward her saying, "What an honor to receive your visit here. I'm so indebted to you." She was speechless, overwhelmed by exhaustion and heartache over the news. Everybody was crying for a while, raising the level of humidity in the small room.

"I didn't intend to stay here this long, let alone end up spending the rest of my life here. I don't know if you knew that I left only to avoid the impending nasty political situation back in Korea," he said with a much weakened voice. "Yes, it was an act of voluntary exile."

"Why, what made you stay?"

"Even to this day I don't know. We just did. Yu didn't want to stay in the beginning, then he came around, which he has often said was the best decision he'd ever made. Life is slow and even here. One can be bored to tears, but my mind began to notice things previously inconsequential to me. I can't put my finger on it, what it was, but its presence was firm and captivating. Sometimes I wondered if my childhood as an orphan might have played a role. The most shameful part of my life came back to haunt me, to shame me for being ashamed of it. After all, it was my mentor, my resilience, and strength, and I was ashamed of my master, so to speak. Self-preservation without losing respect for myself had been my religion, and I'd lived by it quite well. My private religion became a map, a secret sign for my life journey. When we learned the situation back home wasn't going to let up anytime soon, I was faced with time that could sit still. Naturally, such a situation forces you to think, and you remember a lot as if your memory were giving birth to a new life. One day I couldn't deny anymore that I had been more alive when I roamed around barefoot as an orphan than as a Western-educated man in a fancy suit. But as I said before, I really don't know why I didn't go back. There was something deeper and stronger, but to this day, I haven't got the faintest idea. So be it. Maybe it's not meant to be. Well, enough of that. Here I am thoughtlessly yapping away. Tell me, tell me how've you been, my son, do tell me everything," he said, holding his hand again and rubbing it with the other hand.

This is my father, but this is not my father, Sam thought. Who is this man I came to see? He'd never talked to him in such a manner, holding his hand, rubbing it. When he was a young boy, the most body contact he had with him was when his father would touch his head with his hand when he was a little tipsy. When they lived together, he was brief in conversation and to the point, never saying more than a couple of sentences. The quantity and the quality of speech coming out of his mouth now were disturbingly foreign. He didn't know how to take it. There always had been a certain formality between them. He was a gentle, kind, and generous father who didn't show heart-sweetening affection. Their interactions had been more like that of a teacher and a pupil. Sam tried to find a trace of that father whom he admired all the same. It truly felt absurd. He was crying inside loudly, for he was dying. But the man sitting across from him, his dying father who was breaking his heart, was a stranger. This stranger who was his dying father, who was holding his hand, rubbing it, who made him insanely upset over the fact of his dying, was asking him to tell him everything about his life. Where is my old man? Where is he? he thought. Sweat beaded on his forehead. Something in him was coming undone. He swayed his upper body sideways, freed his hand, and asked, "May I use the bathroom first?"

He ran out and down the stairs, looking for a place to hide. He didn't know why, but he just wanted to hide for a while from everybody. He went around the temple and found large rocks that looked like heads joined together in the shape of praying hands. He squeezed himself between them and lit a cigarette, one after another. After five cigarettes, he came out nauseous and drenched with sweat that felt chilly against the scorching heat.

This time Sam played with his food during dinner. It felt like he couldn't pass food through his throat. He drank the local brew, which was rather insipid. He kept drinking. Later he suffered from the passive aggression of the insipid, watery drink, which made his stomach feel incendiary. Mrs. Lim had a hearty appetite. The meal wasn't typical Buddhist cuisine. The dishes mainly consisted of things that used to walk the earth on four legs. He smoked and drank and drank some, more playing with his chopsticks. Mrs. Lim noticed this but kept her concern to herself, understanding his grief. She and Mr. Yu, who was spoon-feeding his father, kept the conversation going. He asked and she answered mechanically, talking mostly about their homeland, the political and socioeconomic state that was changing rapidly. Sam observed through his eyes that he was suffering from a profound lethargy from the sobbing earlier. Mr. Yu carefully spoon-fed his father and wiped around his mouth, while his father was processing the porridge in his mouth. This repeated with order and precision. When his father motioned that he had enough, Mr. Yu begged him to take one more bite. For the first time, Sam felt the nature of their relationship was beyond that of a master and a man. His father, although content, didn't participate in the conversation. It took every effort to consume the food forced upon him, which was prepared with a special ingredient, opium powder. Otherwise, his father wouldn't take anything that helped the pain. "This not only eases the pain, it makes him slightly euphoric, even talkative sometimes," Mr. Yu told Sam afterwards. "When he started to refuse to take any medicine, which only caused him more discomfort, we had to figure out something to ease the pain. So far he has no clue. Sometimes he even thinks he's getting better."

Shortly after dinner, his father lay down. He raised his arm, motioning Sam to come near. He knelt down next to the futon. His father looked at him with his yellowed eyes, yellow like pale amber, and held his hand, trembling from atrophy. "You will sleep next to me, won't you, son?"

"Of course, father. You rest now. I'm a snorer, though." A faint smile passed over his lips while he turned his head away, closing his eyes.

Sam sat on the front step and lit a cigarette, feeling the pressure of heaving waves in his chest, the residue of his sobbing. He gulped down the insipid liquor from a jug to push back the possible sobbing that demanded a second appearance. The dark mountains and hills of the night seemed through his blurry eyes to be inching in toward him like monsters, living, breathing, nocturnal. The sky that had touched his body in previous nights was now far away, indifferently looking down, watching him about to be devoured by the night monsters.

By the time Mrs. Lim came out in snail curls, which Sam began to acquire a taste for, he was experiencing the incendiary revenge of the liquor he consumed while treating it as inferior. Every breath he took came right out incinerated. "Did you take a bath?" he said, touching her wet curls with one hand and rubbing his stomach with the other.

"The bathroom is really nice. The entire room was made with bamboo, and they heated the tub with burning wood. Why don't you take a bath, it'll help you relax."

Sam ignored her advice. He bent over, hugging his knees, and let out a few incinerated burps. He was drunk, but his newly gained pain stayed sober.

"I'm sorry, so sorry, Sam."

"How different he is," he murmured.

"He's a dying man, not to mention that you haven't seen him for about fifteen years. Some people's looks change dramatically when they age."

"That's not the difference I'm talking about," he said, resting his chin on his knee. "The crimson drapes, shaven head, tear drops, all that touching and cuddling, calling me 'Botchang,' which he never did when I was a real Botchang."

She listened to him in silence, warned by her intuition that there was something else going on in him other than grieving for his father's demise. She could tell he was quite drunk. He babbled away about how he had cringed when his father touched him all over with tears pouring down his face, how he felt his father was someone he never knew, a stranger. But most of all, the guilt and shame for the awful coldness he felt in himself was tearing him up. This soliloquy took a while, challenging her heartbeat to skip here and there with a prophetic sense of misfortune, even catastrophe. She never saw him like that. A middle-aged man being reduced to a troubled child. Without saying anything, she got up and went inside. A few minutes later, she came back with a canister. Before they left Delhi, she had bought a bottle of Scotch and filled a few canisters at the hotel. She planned to share it in celebration of the reunion and intentionally hid them from Sam. She opened the cap and took a sip, waiting for him to continue.

He turned his head to her and said without lifting it, "What are you drinking?"

She quickly closed the cap, saying, "An elixir to settle my stomach. It's been a virgin to lamb meat until tonight."

He expelled a lethargic giggle and reached for the canister. "I need some too. My tummy isn't happy either." She didn't let go of the canister, telling him the elixir was designed only for females. The last thing he needed was more drinks.

"I don't give a bugger, let me have some." They pushed and pulled over the canister, Sam giggling and Mrs. Lim threatening him.

"Sam, Sam, I don't think it's a good idea. It's Scotch, and you've drank too much already, you shouldn't…"

The canister was already tilted at a forty-five-degree angle in midair, pouring its contents into its holder's mouth. She helplessly watched him then snatched it away from him.

She took a couple large gulps herself when Sam asked, "Mrs. Lim, Mrs. Lim, are they…are they…Do you think they are perhaps, perhaps?"

She didn't catch on right away. Before she dismissed the drunken babble, she realized what he was trying to ask. Momentarily, she thought about playing dumb and drunk like him, but the edginess in her ordered her to push onward at full force. She replied, "Yes, they are, they have been all along."

He giggled with a squeaky, evil sound, shaking his body. He leaned against the bamboo railing and started to laugh aloud, clapping his hands with spit flying out of his mouth. She took a few more gulps looking away, refusing to retain the photographic memory of him being like that. At the same time, she decided that she would be as honest as possible with him. In spite of his loud laughter and shouting that echoed through the night air, she started, "Frankly, I can't believe you never suspected. I can't." His laughter died down and turned to a series of hiccups, which made him lose control of his plumbing. He was peeing on his pants. This made her angry and say vulgar words without regret. Then she said, "Everybody knew, your amah, the servants, the neighbors, everybody except you!" Silence thumped down between them. Their ears began to pick up the sound of the night, which was deafening.

He managed to get up and walked up the stairs, swaying. "I'll take that bath now."

She regretted what she said but didn't want to apologize. She followed him to the bathroom, asked the caretaker to heat the tub for Sam, and brought him a change of clothes. He stood in front of the tub watching with blurry eyes as the water was filling the tub and as the caretaker lit the wood. He began to undress then turned to Mrs. Lim, who was standing at the door. "Are you going to watch me bathe?"

"It will take a while for the water to warm up." She left, closing the door behind her, hearing the water splashing. She thought about staying there until he was done, concerned that he might drown, but she went to her room, unable to ignore the dark clouds circling around her head.

Hunger woke up Sam the next morning. His father was sleeping next to him. He was breathing through his mouth, assuring him. He stared at him for a while, unable to recognize what he was feeling. He slipped out, sensing that his limbs were wobbly. It was only six in the morning. There were a couple of people in meditation, sitting in front of a statue of Buddha encircled with burning candles and incense. He walked down to the courtyard and looked around for the kitchen. Behind the temple he found a young girl of about fifteen or sixteen, washing vegetables. She stood up, startled at the sight of Sam, but then she shyly smiled when she recognized him, wiping her wet hands on her apron. She had a plump, round face that belied her skinny body. Her cheeks were so red as if someone slapped her silly all night long, unable to resist the cherub-like cheeks. She said something he couldn't understand. It took elementary body language to let her know what he wanted. She made a small tray of breakfast, which he took to the steps he christened with his ill-mannered bodily function the previous night. The breakfast the girl with the cherub cheeks gave him was satisfying both in taste and quantity. It resembled a Japanese breakfast.

He decided to take a stroll and visit the temples of different gods. His mind was numb and dull. The numbness sitting on him dulled his senses to uncaring. He started from the shrine at the far end, which was supposed to be a Christian chapel. On the wall was a large wooden cross without Jesus nailed on it. On a long table in front of the cross were several copies of prayer books and nothing else. Similarly, the Muslim temple looked rather unused with its prayer books and square mats in the corner gathering dust. There was no picture of the Prophet, no special writing framed and hung on the wall. The third temple, the one for the spirits of nature, ancestors, and any other deities of the day, was the one Sam found most loved, as Mr. Yu said. The wooden floor looked so much more worn out than the others. Unlike the design of the other two, the floor opened onto a garden with a large, handsome tree and rocks. The tree was decorated with scraps of fabric with writing and homemade wind chimes. Various figures of deities were beautifully painted on the rocks, small and large. "This is it, here and now is what really counts. Forget the afterlife, give me what I want, now!" seemed to be the most heartfelt form of worship. He vaguely hoped those painted deities took a liking to him here and now.

When he returned he found the tray he left on the stairs had been removed. He kept walking until he found himself standing next to the rocks that had offered him a sanctum the day before when he was coming undone after seeing his father. He squeezed his body into the space again and smoked, coming out after five cigarettes. Dizzy and nauseous but successfully numb in the head, he slowly walked back when he ran into Mr. Yu. "Oh, there you are. I've been looking for you all over. I was beginning to worry. Well, your father is waiting for you. He already had breakfast. You should eat something too."

He told him he ate. "Did you see Mrs. Lim yet?" Sam asked, looking at his watch. It was nearly nine.

"She hasn't come out yet," Yu answered, walking ahead of him.

Sam called him, and Mr. Yu turned around, shading his eyes with his hand to block the sunlight. Sam abruptly told him how he found his father disturbingly changed.

Yu walked back toward Sam with his hand still over his brows.

"That's a good thing, a very good thing indeed, isn't it? Change, that is. Otherwise you miss out on a whole lot of life in you. That's what we discovered living here, having all the time to sit with ourselves. We learned to hear our own breathing, converse with our thoughts, pay attention to their wisdom as well as complaints. What you call 'change' is actually a 'return,' a return to your original self. So, Botchang, for now hold off the judgment of your disappointment, however disturbed you are. That's the only proper thing to do now. I'm not asking you to be dishonest; I'm asking you to be kind."

"Stop calling me Botchang, call me Sam." It came out more as a hiss. He didn't mean to say it that way, but the childish hostility in him couldn't stay disguised. There was something about Mr. Yu quite different from the day before. He knew Mr. Yu stayed with his father alone for hours without inviting Sam. He was drunk and not very coherent, but he knew that they were talking.

Yu took another step toward him and said in a stern face with no trace of the submissiveness of an ex-servant, "I'll gladly call you Sam when and if that time arrives, but now, now you are a Botchang, a boy, a middle-aged boy." He turned again to resume the direction he was taking without waiting for Sam's rebuttal. He had none.

Sam felt numb again, but it was a different sensation of numbness than from a short while ago. It was as if Yu had sucked the air out of his lungs. Sam's hostility toward Yu came from the suspicion that Yu corrupted his father. He knew better, but facing such shock and betrayal, he had to blame someone. He couldn't help but wonder about Yu's somewhat angry attitude towards him. As far as he was concerned, nothing unpleasant happened between them until a few minutes ago. Abruptly, the bridge was gone. He stood on the same spot, thinking of his humiliation, staring at the back of his father's lover until he disappeared into the shadow of the temple. His two feet were immobilized, and he stood with one hand in his pocket, the other sacrificing its nails to his teeth in an act of self-mutilation. He looked at his own shadow on the ground, its feet joined to his, short and childlike. He kept his position, unable to hear the chirping of the birds who happened to be the sole witness of the brief but monumental bit of history of this Botchang. His mind was building a temple of humiliation, then it would shrink it to that of embarrassment, again and again, the interval between the two feelings getting shorter and shorter like the shadow of him on the ground. The sunlight needled its way through the thinning hair of a middle-aged man. "He'll come out any moment and apologize, make it all better." No, he didn't, he won't; there was never a bridge.

He started walking, following his shadow and stepping on it so that it became pleated like an accordion as he ascended the stairs. By the time he walked into the room of the temple where his father was, a certain suspicion gathered in his head, warning him to stay sharp.

His father was waiting for him. He was sitting up on the futon, leaning against the wall behind him, propped up with pillows. The room was dark except for a small square area where daylight filtered through the rice-papered window. The smell of staleness and incense seeping in from the main floor seemed to deepen the darkness. Sam knelt down on the floor and gave him a bow.

"Come here, sit next to me, Botchang," his father said in a parched, strained voice. He crawled to him, seeing that his yellowed eyes weren't seeing anything. He raised his trembling arms in search for Sam's hands. He offered his hands for him to rub as much as he wanted, unable to hold back the tears pitter-pattering on their hands. "Forgive me, son, for insisting you take this suffering. This is monstrously selfish behavior of mine. I know that. When you arrived here in time, I took it as a sign that I was allowed a chance to have a clean breast before my departure."

"I know that already. You and Mr. Yu…" Sam told him, hearing a squeal escape his throat.

"Have you known it all along?"

"Pretty much." He lied, remembering Yu's lecture to be kind.

"What else have you known?" he asked, rubbing the teardrops on his hand with his thumb.

"That Yu is not my mother." Squealing laughter came out of both of them this time. His father tried to laugh, joining that of Sam's in an agonizing metallic sound.

Sam took his hands back to wipe his face and blow his nose with his shirt. The rough edges of his fingernails, which had been chewed up by his teeth, caught the threads of his shirt.

"I'm comforted by your knowledge of me, that you can joke about it. But what I had in mind, the stuff that required cleansing, involves the both of us. Go on, light your cigarette." He read his mind. Sam obeyed.

The first puff went right into his head, giving him a pang of dizziness. He couldn't smell the smoke due to the heavy invasion of mucus in his nose from crying. "No, please no," the Botchang in him begged. "I don't need to know more secrets, yours, mine or even God's." Either his father didn't read his mind this time, or he ignored it with the tangential force of selfishness to save himself, forsaking his little Botchang's already troubled heart.

"Your knowledge and kind understanding of my relationship with Yu gave me the courage to say what I'm about to say. Wait a minute, you might know this already…" he said, searching for his hand again. Sam gave him one.

"No, sir. I have no idea," Sam said, feeling the skin on his body tightening, his physiognomy hardening.

"It's about your birth."

Sam held his breath, being strangled by the suspense.

"I'm not your biological father. I found you crying in a basket at the gate. You were nicely and carefully wrapped. Whoever left you there obviously cared about you. They were likely heartbroken but decided to give you a chance for life. I could feel it. At that harsh time, especially for women, it wasn't shocking to find newborn babies naked, left to die with their umbilical cords still attached to their protruding belly buttons, their tiny bodies lying about in ditches. I'm sure that you are aware of such sadness existing around, although it's diminishing. The reason why I'm telling you such things of a tragic nature is because I want you to know that whoever it was who dropped you off, your mother I assume, clearly suffered having to do so. You were about three or four months old. She kept you with her and probably did everything possible to hold onto you until then. At first we looked for her, but all we could find was your biological father, who was serving time. By then you had become a part of my life, and I didn't want to be apart from you. We didn't contact your biological father and decided to adopt you. We intentionally spread the word around the neighborhood that a woman I slept with gave birth to you and that I claimed my son after a legal battle." He sighed, a sigh of selfish relief.

Sam lit another cigarette, and the rush of dizziness returned. "A trite concoction of a senile, dying man" was one conclusion. "Fishing out profound gratitude from a basket boy he saved and raised in style" was another. Time to be honest, he thought, which was dishonest in of itself but seemingly honest in regard to his psychological need.

"Nothing new about that. I mean, I knew it all along deep down although no one told me," he said to his father, not wanting to hear anymore. He brought out Sam, urging Botchang to stay put inside. This time he held the old man's hands with a gentle chuckle. "Come on now, rest your heart. You've suffered unnecessarily. You're the only father I have and a good one too. You need your rest. Let me help you to lie down." The old man, the gay ex-father of his, obeyed with his mouth quivering, which could have been his attempt for a large smile of triumph. Sam lay down the pillows and helped his cracking body to lie down, gently and lovingly. The old man couldn't see the hardened eyes of his ex-son.

Sam came out, wanting to leave the place immediately. He looked for Mr. Yu who was sitting on the step. He walked down and sat next to him who was looking down on the ground.

"Nice day, isn't it?"

Sam started, turning his head around in an exaggerated motion. "Uh-huh, we need more rain, though."

Yu received him nonchalantly. "How was your visit with your father?"

"Good. Very good, indeed. He suffered for nothing, nothing whatsoever. I knew it all along." He was Sam, a professional Sam, a successful businessman who could be shrewd and smoothly calculating.

"You're wrong about that, my dear fellow."

Was that a promotion? From Botchang to dear fellow?

"What am I wrong about, Mr. Yu?"

"He didn't suffer keeping the secret. Why should he? He gave you a good life, constantly looked after your well-being. He could've gone to his grave with it without telling you, which you already knew. No, he didn't suffer, I assure you."

"That's a relief. My only regret is that he didn't give me a chance to pay him back." His hardened eyes started to twitch.

"He decided to tell you to leave with you the suffering that is yours. But it seems like it's already taken care of." Yu's speaking tone was mild but distant.

Sam thought, What happened between now and yesterday? Hadn't he received him, waited for him for days on the hill, as good old Mr. Yu?

"I don't understand what you mean by 'leaving me the suffering that is mine'?"

"You're not going to have that gift anymore, are you?"

Oh yeah, he gave me the gift alright, Sam thought, his hardened twitching eyes turning cold and narrow. He said, "But still, you know I could be dim. I beg you to enlighten me. Please what suffering are you talking about and why? Why does he want me to suffer?"

He laughed, turning his upper body towards Sam. Sam lowered his eyes, not wanting him to see them steel cold.

"Yeah, you could be a dimwit, endearing, though, as your father used to say." He patted his back laughing, clearly enjoying it. Sam laughed along still looking down, making his laugh sweet and docile.

"First of all, let me ask you when did you find out?"

"Which one?"

"Both."

"I used to be teased by the kids in the neighborhood about both regarding your questions. My suspicion about my birth started when I was old enough to compare the stark differences between his appearance and mine. We were too different to be even remotely related. I put two and two together. But here comes the definite conclusion, at least to me. I saw you two together...Well, let's stop there." His fluent lie renewed his energy somewhat.

"Did you know what that was at that young age?"

"I learned about such thing from history books. King Gongmin of the Koryo Dynasty was one. His wife died a virgin. Kids do know more stuff than you think."

"I see." He lowered his head thoughtfully. "Okay. The gift of suffering, which you missed by the way, meant that it is suffering that eventually makes you whole; it's a chance to build yourself up and open the gate to self-imposed realization."

"So, when you make someone suffer, you're actually giving them a precious gift. Did I get it right?"

"Right. No money can buy that."

"I must've disappointed father for being unable to receive the best gift he had saved for me. I guess I'll suffer for not being able to suffer the way he wished."

Sam's sarcasm in the guise of a dimwit didn't seem to register with Yu.

"You'll suffer anyway. Without his finger pointing where to go, what to do; you'll be like a boy on a broken ship in the middle of the ocean. Yes, you'll suffer alright," he said, smacking his lips as if what he was saying was so tasty.

Mrs. Lim showed up in her troubled hair. Yu stood up and said hello to her as his former self. "Did you get a good rest?"

"Yes, thank you. It was very comfortable."

This phony exchange of asking about each other's well-being went on, oblivious to Sam, whose body was rigid and whose inflamed eyes were cast down; they were so hot they could combust at any moment in their sockets. He couldn't tell if it was Sam or Botchang. In the attempt to resist the force in him that desired to kick and punch the guy—his ex-father's lover, a servant turned philosopher, a man who clearly harbored hatred for him seemingly for eons, who looked younger and rejuvenated after successfully stepping on Sam—he started to count the number of steps repeatedly, thankfully coming out with different numbers each time so that he could focus his mind on attaining the correct number. Their conversation about the weather in different regions of the world, the indigenous plants and birds of the area, and so on began to blur in his ears that had had to endure abuse from this indecent man. While doing his counting therapy, his eyes cooled down and returned back to their normal housing.

"Would Botchang like to join us to see the village after lunch?" The voice he despised currently with all his might startled his poor ears. He looked at them, shading his eyes from the sun with his hand. He pumped up the cheerfulness in his voice and said, "You two go ahead. It's tempting, but I'd rather be with father."

Mrs. Lim didn't insist and agreed to spend the afternoon in the village with Mr. Yu. She sensed something unsavory was going on inside the man she had known for decades. As soon as Yu left for the kitchen to sort out lunch, she sat next to Sam. Before she struck her vocal chords, he struck his.

"Don't worry. I'm fine. I'm really sorry about last night."

"It's okay. I'm your family, you know that," she said calmly, laying her hand on his. The sound of her mature voice and sensible tone, rare but always genuine, dissolved the heat in his eyes into steam, which moved into his nose. "Try to enjoy yourself at the village and tell me all about it later.

I need to be alone to think and plan about a few things. I wouldn't be surprised if he passes in the next few days. I'd like to talk with him in case he wants things done in special ways after his death," he said, laying his hand on top of hers. "You don't know how glad I am that you came with me."

He stayed with his father after lunch and fell asleep. He suddenly heard Mrs. Lim screaming and ran out. He couldn't believe his eyes. A beautiful carriage with a midnight black horse decorated with flowers was waiting to take her to the village. Yu was sitting in the driver's seat dressed in what seemed to be brilliantly starched organza. Sitting on his small head was a traditional black hat for a nobleman fashioned in the shape of a foot-long upside down pagoda. Sam walked down to have a closer look at him. He helped Mrs. Lim to her seat, who was giggling with delight, with his eyes fixed on Yu. Is that rouge I see on his cheeks? he thought. Yu immediately opened a lavender satin parasol with gold fringe for her with a majestic gesture. Seeing her in delight like a child helped his smile to be more sincere. He wished them a good time, hearing his heartbeat ticking and tocking.

He went to Yu's room to search through it, but at the door, he changed his mind and went to his father's. He was sleeping, breathing through the mouth. He went straight to the wardrobe at the far end of the room. It wasn't locked. He found nothing but crimson robes, a couple of shoes, and linens in the drawer. He opened the wooden trunk next to the wardrobe and failed to find what he was looking for. Disappointed, he came to the conclusion that he would have to search Yu's room after all, half regretting not telling Mrs. Lim to take her time, as long a time in the village as possible. Suddenly, he realized the trunk he just searched seemed more shallow on the inside than indicated by the height on the outside. He flipped it over and found a secret compartment. At first he thought it was a regular panel firmly secured, but something told him this was it. He was sure something paper like was moving about when he flipped the trunk. It took a while for him to understand the mechanics. He was sweating profusely, but the excitement was dreamy. He started to press all the ornamental carvings at the bottom. He heard a click, and a piece of the ornamental carving popped out, loosening the bottom panel. He jiggled it with his hands, and it fanned out effortlessly. Inside he found what he was looking for. With his heart beating excitedly, hopefully, anxiously, he went through the papers. First his father's bank books from various accounts in America, then his *chap*— his name seal— and finally his will and deeds for his real estate in Korea and the temple. He read the will quickly. He felt fortunate, even happy, but was trembling uncontrollably. When he opened the will, the paper shook from his violently trembling hands. He took a deep breath silently, warning his mind to calm down. The will was in his father's handwriting in two languages, English and Korean, signed and sealed as well. It was also notarized with a witness's signature whose name he could not figure out. When he saw the date the document was signed, his jaw dropped and he stopped shaking. It was prepared before he left Korea. He looked through the chest thoroughly again and again, thinking there must have been a new one hidden somewhere. He found none. One thing Sam knew about his father was that he kept certain things close to him, never to be shared with others. His love and devotion for Yu could have been out of this world, but Sam knew that his bank books, his property, and his wealth were whom he was, his spine. Sam was quite sure Yu didn't have a chance to peek at it, but perhaps he didn't need to. Everything he left back home still bore his name as the owner, including the business Sam built, which became one of the most successful real estate companies in the country. Sam never claimed even a partial ownership, being his father's only child. All the wealth he built, which he had sadly believed was because of his father's unbeatable wisdom and guidance, had been accumulated in banks and stocks under his father's name, nearly tripling in amount. Sam was the power of attorney with access to the funds. Sam never doubted this was for his own good. Once his father said to him that keeping everything under his name would save him from the thievery of the government. He might have been telling him the truth. So far Sam was totally free with his money. Being a hoarder of bank books and property deeds didn't make his father unkind and cheap. He had been always generous, kind, and loved by everyone who worked and served him. Sam wouldn't have thought about doing what he did if it hadn't been the sudden change in

Yu. But even when he was engaged in the search for the documents, a large part of him dismissed his suspicion. He just wanted to be overly sure. And he smelled something went on between the lovers during the night when he was out on the step with a bad stomach. His actions were too dramatic for his liking, but he had to know. His father must have shared important information with Yu, information that empowered the small man enough to stiffen his posture. If Yu had kept the same demeanor as the first day they arrived, Sam wouldn't have come to the suspicion. "Now who's the dimwit? How fate laid her finger on everything!"

The will said that after his father's passing the firm that Sam had successfully built would be left to Sam, but the rest went to Yu. The firm that was awarded to Sam was next to nothing at the time his father prepared the will, but the land his father owned in Korea had skyrocketed in the value. This would make Yu one of the wealthiest men in the country. Sam laughed inwardly, feeling absolutely drained. He trembled, his teeth chattered, and his eyes steamed up with hot tears of devastating hurt and anger. But he didn't let this moment last longer. He quickly hid the bank books, his father's important *chap*, and property deeds. He briefly thought about leaving the files in the temple but changed his mind and put everything into his suitcase, which had been silently observing its owner's criminal activity from the dark corner of the room. After he zipped it up, he gave it a pat and ordered his suitcase, still trembling with his face mixed with sweat, tears, and mucus, "Guard them with your life."

Before he came out of his room, he looked down at his sleeping father. He couldn't tell what he was feeling— contempt, betrayal, perhaps, but hadn't he been a good father also? How could he deny that! Hadn't he been the fortress that protected him all his life? That must be love, wasn't it? He couldn't bring up the hatred, maybe anger. But he couldn't escape the thought that they played him all along. He went out and smoked, feeling his shirt sticking to his body with sweat. It's done, he thought. In his passing thoughts of this and that, which were traveling fast in agitation, he had a glimpse of his biological father as one of the passengers.

They came back near dinnertime. When Sam heard the horse, he quickly went into the room and sat next to his father, whose eyes were still closed and was breathing through his mouth as if a thin tread were being pulled from a worn-out fabric.

Mrs. Lim came in and sat next to him. "How is he?"

"The same. Did you have a good time?" he asked.

She rolled her eyes twice and said, "It was an experience. Definitely weird."

"Tell me later." He put his index finger on his lips, warning her not to go on. She caught on and nodded in affirmation. He put his mouth to her ear and whispered, "I'll explain later. We shouldn't leave my father alone with Yu."

She nodded, pushing her glasses up to her nose bridge. "I'll wash up before dinner." She got up and left.

A few minutes later Yu came in, wearing his humble grey robe without a trace of rouge. "Has he been sleeping all this time?" he asked, sitting close to his father, feeling his forehead.

"Pretty much. The girl in the kitchen came to spoon-feed him some water and changed his undergarments, but he didn't open his eyes at all," Sam reported, using a voice that would suggest he was intimidated by Yu.

Yu fussed around his sleeping or unconscious father for a while. Sam could not tell if it was sincere or not. It didn't matter. His confusion about how to judge them was over, at least then. "How was the village? Mrs. Lim said she had a blast."

"Oh, indeed. The weather was perfect, people were friendly. She said it was the most friendly, peaceful place she'd ever been to."

"I'm glad to hear that. I thank you. I've been feeling bad about dragging her on this trip. You might've made it worthwhile for her."

Yu threw a side glance at Sam somewhat shrewdly. Sam realized that he might have been overly friendly, which could have alarmed Yu. Sam changed the subject. "Should we wake him up for supper?"

"We should try. He should take his pain medicine."

Mrs. Lim came in freshened up, smelling of soap. The dinner was brought in immediately after by the kitchen staff. His father managed to get up and took a few spoonfuls of the porridge without opening his eyes, and lay back down. Sam ate more than he wanted, as if he were a warrior getting ready for a fight.

"Botchang, how about I stay with him tonight?"

"I need to be with him. I'll sleep here, next to him."

"It doesn't look. Someone has to keep vigil tonight. I'm used to it. I'll, of course, let you know if anything changes." He broke into tears saying that.

Sam felt something in his heart. Maybe regret, sorrow, or fatigue, he'd never know, but he felt something painfully confusing, a mixture of love and hatred, desire to be in the place of trust but in the presence of unmovable suspicion. "You've been doing that all this time. Allow me the privilege to stay with him, please," Sam asked, giving Yu a slight bow. "But I'll come and get you in case of anything, please."

Yu tilted his head, let out a sigh, and agreed reluctantly but made the mistake of shooting a sharp glance at the wooden trunk. It was a mistake that deepened Sam's suspicion. He turned to Mrs. Lim who was quietly finishing dinner and said, "Please tell me you have more Scotch."

"A little," she said, showing her thumb and index finger separated by an inch.

"Can I have it?"

She left the room to get him some. Sam didn't drink any of the local liquor at dinner, which Yu had been insisting him to consume. "I can take just about any alcohol except that one. It turned into firebugs in my belly." He refused more than once. It seemed like Yu was going to linger as long as allowed. He was massaging his father's legs when Sam started to tell him how much he appreciated all the things he had done for his father.

"What I did for him, he would do the same for me. But I'm glad you're aware of it. I don't know what I'll do after he's gone."

"Are you planning on staying here?"

"I don't know. I miss back home, though, from time to time. I don't know. My grieving will guide me where to be." He lifted his chin to keep the tears from flowing down. Sam didn't miss his eyes darting to the wooden trunk one more time.

Sam intentionally lowered his head to the floor and said, "You know, Mr. Yu, you can always ask me if you need any help." Sam meant what he said. Mr. Yu didn't reply to Sam's offer. The despise, distrust, and betrayal, even hatred he felt for the man wasn't big enough to want to see him suffer or to deny the love he and his father shared through their lives. He didn't want to disown what he believed to be his father's love for Yu. What Sam had done on that afternoon was not from greed but strictly to have control. He trusted himself to be the only fair party. Mrs. Lim came back with the Scotch in the canister, shaking it to inform him that there was very little left.

It was a balmy night. The sound of frogs ribbitting, some in baritone, some in tenor, calling for their mates, was getting louder as the night deepened.

"Did you know frogs hear only the sound of their own kind?" Mrs. Lim said, yawning. They were sitting out on the step after Yu finally retired to his room.

The first large sip of Scotch was an elixir sent by God. "What's going on?" she asked, taking the canister from his hand. The moment she took a sip the canister was snatched away by Sam.

"Tell me about the day in the village first," he said, almost in a whisper.

She started, "I couldn't believe my eyes when I saw the carriage, the horse, his clothes, and that ridiculous hat…Anyway, the village was a village. There was a strange mix of people, some Mongolian- or Chinese-looking people with green or piercing blue eyes. Poor and backwards, but the people seemed to be lively. They treated Yu like some kind of demigod. They bowed at him with their hands in prayer calling him 'Sonsaengnim'(Enlightened One). It was embarrassing and nauseating. But what a sight he was to look at!" Sam had to motion to her to keep her voice down. She continued, lowering her voice but with intensity. "We went into a house for refreshments. It was a regular, small house on the outside, but inside was more like a bar. It was decorated nicely, though, in a Western style, I think. Two young men, very pretty, came out and served us Russian cake and tea."

Sam interrupted and said, "I know what you're going to say. They were his lovers, right?"

"No doubt whatsoever," she said, hammering the air with her fist.

"When I saw him dressed like that with rouge on his cheeks, the thought crossed my mind."

"I didn't know him very well in Korea, and you used to tell me wonderful things about him, but from what I saw today, he will remain in my memory as a creepy guy."

"He's nothing like the man I thought I knew." Sam told her the conversation they had on the steps before lunch that day.

"How old is he?"

"He's about ten years younger than my father." And he told her what he did while she was visiting the village, literally pressing his mouth to her ear.

"The will?"

"And everything else regarding…"

"He has it with him? He didn't keep them with you?"

"You know my father, obsessive about holding onto stuff." He quickly added in a whisper, "The main thing is that I found it. After my run-in with Yu this morning, witnessing his puzzling attitude toward me, I had a strong suspicion that my father must've revealed something to him the other night, something that empowered him. I don't know for sure, and that's not important. His attitude toward me did a 180 overnight, as if he had waited for that sweet moment all along, which I consider a deadly mistake on his part. When he said I've always been a dimwit, there was spittle on his lips. Such hatred! It was like an angel turning into a demon that could no longer resist the delicious delight of revealing himself to me."

"But you said they're in your hands now."

"Practicality first" having been the supreme motto in her life, she wanted to be reassured. Sam nodded, pursing his lips. The story of him being a basket boy couldn't leave his lips.

His father slept all the next day. Sam and Mrs. Lim took turns watching him. Yu was clearly agitated and went in and out of the room frequently. When Mrs. Lim took over, Sam visited the rock sisters, smoked five cigarettes, got dizzy, and went back to the room. This continued and re-peated for a few more days. Then he expired.

On the night of his passing, Sam was lying on the futon next to his father. He wanted to think, sort things out in his head, organize them to reach a sensible plan. He couldn't wrestle with his head anymore and fell asleep, seeing a faint image of someone pulling the plug out of the socket in his brain.

In his dream that night, he was walking on a narrow isthmus. The ocean on his left was frighteningly dark and choppy, but the one on the right was sunny and the water was an inviting emerald green. Halfway through the isthmus, he changed his mind and turned to go back. But the narrow road he had walked on was being covered with the water from both sides of the ocean and moving slowly toward him. He started to run in the direction he didn't wish to go, and his feet, although running, wouldn't gain an inch. The water behind him caught up with him and hit his back with a giant wave. He woke up and found his father's knee was pressing against his back. He got up and immediately knew that his father was gone. It was three in the morning.

Two days after his death, the two guides with donkeys arrived late in the morning. Streams of people from the village came to pay their last respects to his father, who had been laid out in the main temple hall. He was to be cremated in a few days. Sam decided to leave as scheduled, which Yu not only agreed with but encouraged. Sam knew for sure Yu hadn't had a chance to go near the wooden chest yet.

He was achy and incoherent. He sat on the steps for one last time waiting for Mrs. Lim to be ready. The lusciousness of the surroundings under the strong sunlight seemed to depersonalize him. It seemed like the place rejuvenated itself overnight. Even the sun looked younger, immature. He lit a cigarette and blew out the smoke in a long stream, waiting for the coherency to return without rushing him. He felt his heart thump once, followed by a series of darting rhythms like ducklings running after their mom. "Another day, just another day. A man became a corpse and ashes to ashes…just another day of giving birth and surrendering to death." The image of his father he'd carried in him was swallowed and expelled to the uneven heartbeat.

He had been the guiding light, a symbol of invincibility, a crystal ball that showed him what to do next. Now, he was a dead man in a pathetic crimson robe receiving respects from people he had spent a lot of money on. Sam had a good cry, alone, on the night he woke up and found that his father was gone. It was involuntary, a blank sorrow. It was from the loss of something that he never had, not from disappointment. It was the loss of something, something quite massive that was just a mirage.

Mrs. Lim came out with a cup of tea for him. "The donkey men have finished loading already. They can wait a few more minutes" she said, handing him the cup.

"I can't wait to have a decent cup of coffee." He took a sip, complaining about his aches. She gave him two aspirins from her purse, which he swallowed.

She spread her arms wide toward the view in front of her and exclaimed, "The quality of the air here is incredible, it feels like every breath cleans out the toxins in me." She took a deep breath, ballooning her already inflated stomach.

He stood up and took another look at the surroundings, turning his head all around. It was beautiful, but it wasn't friendly. It was too strong, arrogant and seductive with the random passion of youth. Could his father have been seduced and mutated by this force he felt? Beautiful yet ominous, sinister and diabolic. It wants you, it wants to devour you…

- 54 -

As soon as Sam came back, he sent a large sum of money to Yu with a letter encouraging him not to hesitate to ask when in need of help. He didn't receive any reply.

Six months or so after he came back, Sam began to vacillate between his normal and not-so-normal self. Mrs. Lim thought he might have picked up an unusual bug from the trip, for he had a low-grade fever and often broke into a cold sweat ever since they came back. Numerous trips to doctors and every possible test didn't indicate anything abnormal, and the barbiturates the doctors gave him didn't help. This worrisome situation lasted a few months. Psychological evaluations were not widely advised at that time unless one suffered from obvious mental incapacitation. Mrs. Lim was gravely worried, noticing the cycle of his irrational behavior where he worked and worked for three or four days without sleep then collapsed into a comatose sleep for a couple of days.

When a monstrous energy occupied him, he liked to use abusive language and laughed aloud for nothing. There was a moment or two when she wondered if something really had possessed him at the temple. She was

desperate for help. Thankfully there were rare moments that he acknowledged the problem as being psychological and showed an intention to get
help. Then he would go through a period of denial. Mrs. Lim asked around
to have a reputable psychiatrist ready for the rare moment that he wished for
help. She waited patiently without forcing or arguing until his want of help
took a leap. Dr. Min was introduced and the treatment started. There was a
stretch of stabilization during which period he was healthy and normal, but
when triggered by God knows what, he relapsed, sometimes badly.

Well into the ten months of treatment, when he had already been hospitalized twice, he became perceptive enough to recognize the subtle change
in his mood, and when it happened, he would go off to the island, to his
reserved room, to Dr. Min. "I feel like Dr. Jekyll and Mr. Hyde," he admitted
to Dr. Min, who kindly told him, "We all are to a degree. In your case, the
war broke out between them. That's all."

Dr. Min suspected from the first interview that Sam's problem was tied
to the visit to his father. In the first couple of weeks of Sam's admission to
the hospital, Dr. Min devoted his time and effort to him; the board suggested, or rather ordered, him to do so. Just like anything else in life, it was
all about money. Sam's enormous wealth made the board pant like a dog.
Endowments, large donations, the hospital's reputation…Dr. Min didn't
mind, although he had to endure the extra scrutiny by the board.

They talked and talked and talked in his room at meals and during
their afternoon strolls and sometimes over drinks in the evening. Sam ping-
ponged from hyper to hypo in one sitting. Sometimes while strolling together, he would be calm and peaceful, walking leisurely with his hands on
his lower back then suddenly he would get jumpy, clicking his heels in the
air, all ten fingers wriggling separately. He used vulgar language, laughing
at his own words and repeating them over and over. During the first week
or so, Dr. Min mostly observed him, making notes and conversing with him
when possible. Sam seldom sat in the chair during the office sessions. He
paced the room from one end to the other, talking incessantly. When pacing
in a straight line back and forth became less stimulating, he weaved through
the furniture.

One time while pacing, he asked for a cold drink. Dr. Min offered him a glass of ice coffee. He drank it at one go, although he said he never drank coffee cold. A few minutes later, his speech became slower and more coherent, and eventually, he sat down on the chair. The rest of the session went without another episode of pacing around with motor mouth or lying on the floor with his lips glued shut. Dr. Min noted that one of the most amazing things about this particular patient was that he switched from one state to another without any noticeable transition. He remembered one day when they were walking in the garden like two friendly gentlemen. Suddenly, Sam decided to lie down on the dirt and would not move, his glazed eyeballs fixed on the sky. He was a scrawny guy, but it still wasn't easy for Dr. Min to carry him alone. After that incident, which repeated a few more times, Dr. Min had an orderly always nearby. When he was calm, occasionally, he was like a nice next-door neighbor.

"Would you like another glass?" Dr. Min asked.

"Yes, yes, I'm still thirsty."

He gave him another tall glass. After he gulped it down and wiped his mouth, he went silent with his eyes turning dreamy. He's thinking, Dr. Min observed and waited. Sam took out a handkerchief from his pants pocket and started to wipe his forehead, his neck, and then the large drops of tears that were rushing down his bony face. He covered his face with his hands, his shoulders shaking. This lasted for a while. Dr. Min waited. Finally, Sam drew up a breath of air, which carried an involuntary bodily sound that resembled that of a barking seal. He blew his nose in a handkerchief and said, looking at the doctor's eyes directly for the first time ever, "What's happening to me? I want it to stop, stop. Please, please make it stop. I'll try any treatment, any." This was also the first time Sam expressed how desperately he wanted it to stop. Dr. Min cancelled his other engagements and spent the whole day with Sam. In his mind it was a breakthrough, a minor improvement, a small a possibility to work with that gave him a window of hope.

"Let's talk about what is happening to you now," Dr. Min started cautiously. "Psychiatry is not an exact science. Frankly, I hesitate to call it a science. I can name the variety of a patient's symptoms according to the manual we use as our bible, but my experience tells me that two individuals suffering from the same symptoms don't necessarily require the same prescription. What I will promise you is that as long as you pursue help you can count on me to do everything I can. I don't like experimenting with drugs, and I don't necessarily believe that all mental illnesses, even the hardcore ones, are somatic. I might be proven wrong someday, but I know I take a safe approach. You mentioned Dr. Jekyll and Mr. Hyde, and I remember telling you something like 'we all have that quality.' In our psyche, there are mechanisms of inertia and momentum just like in nature around us. I think one learns to control this balance rather than being born with it. When this control is solely yours, even though it was learned, you function within the realm of so-called normality. Knowing when to pull back and when to charge is very important in terms of survival or self-preservation. However, in my opinion, this control can be overly artificial, too unnatural for an individual's system. We lose the balance between the two mechanisms of inertia and momentum by overusing one and laming the other. That's how breakdown occurs, in my educated opinion. Together we'll find out how to make it work for you again." He checked if Sam's attention was with him. Pleased to see that Sam seemed comfortable, he continued, "We don't expect our bodies to fly like a bird, but we make such impossible demands of our minds, imagine that!" He raised his arms in the air, seeing his patient sitting in front of him like an obedient child. "How do you feel now?"

"Like myself, but that feels strange."

"Did what I said make any sense to you?"

"I don't know, but it was comforting."

"When you have an episode, you're quite aware of your action or non-action, right?"

"Every inch of it. Even the struggle inside of me that tries to stop it. But the force is too strong to resist."

"So you're suffering even when you have excessive energy. I mean, you don't experience a euphoric state of mind. Am I right?"

"Oh, no, it's painful, to put it mildly. It's like being pushed and pulled nonstop, randomly thrown about. I beg it to stop, watching myself doing strange things."

Later that day Dr. Min wrote a letter to Dr. Morita thanking him for sharing his most amazing discovery. Dr. Morita was avant-garde in the field of psychiatry, where many of his colleagues dismissed him as a psychotic himself. But Dr. Min respected his absolute devotion to his patients, ignoring the criticism, and at times, severe attacks by fellow practitioners. Some time ago Dr. Min had called him, hoping that he could share any useful information concerning a case like Sam's. After he listened to Dr. Min's description of Sam's situation, he said, "Try caffeine, strong caffeine, when he acts like a machine gun."

"Wouldn't that stimulate him even more?"

"If it does, then you know it doesn't work, right? A pretty harmless experiment, don't you think?"

"Is it real knowledge from your experience?"

"Yes, although success was not one hundred percent. But when it works, it works."

"But you are not saying that caffeine is the cure."

"Oh no. No, no, no. But then again, what do we know about cures? All we have been doing is a temporary treatment of symptoms, putting out the immediate fire, so to speak."

"How did you come up…"

"My caffeine theory?"

"Yeah."

"I noticed that these particular sufferers seemed more exhausted than energetic when they were in a manic state. Like babies and toddlers who become impossibly active when they are exhausted, they fight to stay up not because they want to stay up, but because it's too hard to turn off what is on. So I wondered if maybe it isn't sympathetic nerves pumping energy into these babies but rather parasympathetic ones that went berserk with exhaustion. When the nerve system that helps or commands us to rest gets disoriented, the normal sleep-wake cycle loses its regularity. You see tremors and shakes in normal healthy people when they are weakened or overly tired. They become agitated and hostile. Rest and relaxation are the work of nerves, as you know. Somehow, for some individuals, exhaustion causes stimulation in the brain, making it hard to shut down. Have you experienced that it's harder to fall asleep when you're too tired? One needs energy to relax, to go to sleep. One has to invite the sleep politely. So the caffeine, in such cases, is for the parasympathetic nerves not for the sympathetic. Give it a try. But of course, it's not a solution to rely on. But it calms them down when you need them to be."

"So wake them up instead of knocking them down, brilliant, just brilliant. I assume you tried it on your patients and saw positive results."

"I was my first guinea pig. Well, it was more of a coincidence. Once I went on without sleeping for a couple of days, I don't remember why, and I was supposed to be exhausted the more I felt the rush of incoherent pseudo-energy, up to the point that all I wished was to fly out of my body. It was impossible to reside in my body. I wasn't able to relax, something inside fought the idea of much needed sleep by then. The most unbearable thing was the sensation throughout my body. First, I tried a sleep aid which made it worse, much worse. It was like your body was asleep, but the mind was wide awake. One night purely out of frustration and anger I drank a strong cup of coffee instead of taking a sleep aid. I thought I might as well stay awake more if I could not sleep."

"And it worked."

"It worked for me, and later on, I tried my hypothesis on patients with manic episodes. The outcomes proved to me that it could be a helpful method."

"Maybe this isn't the right thing to compare it to, but it reminds me of people with high blood pressure who sometimes show symptoms of low blood pressure."

"Correct, also in thyroid disease. You can't rely on the blood numbers; a patient's demeanor can be more accurate. The blood number of an obviously depressed patient could show hyperthyroidism and vice versa. As you know, hyperthyroidism causes hyperactivity. By the way, speaking of thyroid disease, I have had several female patients who suffered from mild to severe depression. I noticed from their blood screenings that they all had mild hypothyroidism, hovering around the low-normal range."

"Did you treat them with Synthroid? Did it help the depression?"

"It was trickier. Synthroid noticeably brought them out of a state of physical lethargy, and they started to talk, which was a good thing, but mentally it was still hard to tell. My suspicion is that those women, having lived with low levels of thyroid hormones for a long time, if not all their lives, already trained their brains to form depressive personalities. Generally they become more energetic and showed more willingness to participate in life but sadly wouldn't know what to do with the new gain. Interesting, isn't it?"

"It is, indeed. I'm curious, though, what did they talk about when they started to talk? The material, physical, social, spiritual? Is there a common theme?" Dr. Min asked, envious of Morita's undying zeal.

"Well, it's more or less the same as any patient suffering from depression who starts to talk. They talked about all of the items you've listed, but what was unique about this group of women was their severe judgment and criticism. Blame was the common emotion I observed. Bitterness of various natures, some heart-wrenching but some ludicrous. And this is the interesting part: they all believe in endurance. In their mind they had to endure whatever they had to endure because 'they are better.' But enduring and more enduring is their supporting mechanism. Their frail self-esteem relies on this mechanism, as you already know."

"A self-appointed holy disposition to save the ego."

"And to take pleasure from pain. A tinge of masochism, so to speak."

"You enjoy and suffer simultaneously."

"That's a good way to put it. The bottom line is that they unequivocally crave an unreasonable amount of praise, acknowledgement, and even admiration. It might sound too generalized and doesn't have scientific merit, but to me, it was startling and provoked my curiosity."

"One thing I can tell you is that ever since I've met you, a million years ago, I've never seen you slowing down. A person like me is only so glad that you don't stop."

"I know I'm driven," he said with a laugh.

"I'm curious…Did any of the women in that special group come out of that chain of judgmental bitterness?" Dr. Min asked, remembering a few of his female patients whose problems fit the description of Dr. Morita's special group of female patients. Dr. Min simply wanted to compare notes.

"I'm glad you asked. First of all, I'm always drawn to the opposite or underside of things that manifest. Same with these cases. A manifestation of one extremity always has the tail of the opposite extremity."

"What would be the opposite in this case?"

"The birth of tyranny. When they seemed to be improving, they became bullies, tyrants from the seat of an endurer. The trouble is that when they reach that point, they don't think they need any more help. They believe they're home free."

"Ha, ha, ha. I think I know what you mean."

"You remember I have been a true believer of Yin-Yang physics."

"Of course, I remember we had some nasty arguments about it in college. Remember your shadow theory? 'Shadows bear tremendous power and answers to many mysteries. It's the true color of light.' Ha, ha." Dr. Min remembered that the shadows Dr. Morita was referring to weren't metaphorical or analogical. He meant it literally, shadows drawn by real objects.

"And you said that I should've been a poet, not a scientist."

"How is that hypothesis going? I tell you now, my friend, you have a gift."

"I do know I have that gift. God didn't create me to be easy on the eyes, but he gave me something special, special enough to erase my dilemma of being not so beautiful."

"Well, my friend, I thank you again, and I'll let you know soon enough how it goes. Look after yourself. You are very pleasing to my eyes, ha, ha. I mean it too."

"Likewise, likewise, darling."

"What? 'Darling'? You called me 'darling'?"

"No offense intended, my darling. Well, sometime ago I saw a cheesy Hollywood film. Everyone in the movie called each other 'darling,' even to their enemies. I hated it. But what do you know, it landed on my own tongue ever since. It's on the tip of my tongue ready to shoot out of my mouth indiscriminately. It's embarrassing, but I decided to ignore it. Who knows, it might be because something new is brewing in me. I decided to give it freedom. Let's see what'll become of it."

The call ended with loud laughter on both ends of the phone.

-55-

D r. Min put Sam on caffeine pills for a short period without entering it in
the chart. It controlled the manic episodes temporarily, unveiling the
deep depression. Sam told him he felt so much better even though he was sad
and didn't have any appetite for anything.

"It's more manageable. I'm able to rest," he said one day. "My thoughts
are dark and negative, but I'm glad I'm thinking, which was impossible before. Although I'm not hardly who I used to be, I mostly accept this down-
time as a resting period."

"How's your recent restfulness different from the times when you would
collapse flat after a manic episode?"

"I'm depressed, sad but not without feelings. When I collapsed flat before, I felt nothing, everything stopped; I was catatonic. It was like I was in
a coffin, dead."

"Have you ever been depressed before?"

"I can't say that I have. I rarely got sad. I'm not a bubbly person but am
generally content; that's the word, 'content' is how I would describe myself,
how I used to be, that is…"

"I'm glad to hear that you accept this period, albeit difficult, as a resting period. That's a very positive sign, not to mention this courageous point of view of yours. Now we have work to do, real work to do."

"It might sound strange, but to tell you the truth, I sort of like this sadness I feel."

"I understand. It gives you a sense of broad and nameless understanding. You told me a little bit about your visit to your father, which you and I both believe to be the onset of your illness. I think it's essential that we explore that step by step. Are you up to it?"

"I am. I am indeed."

"Tell me the first thing that comes to your mind when you think about your father."

"A carnivore."

"Next?"

"An herbivore."

"This is good, very good. Can you explain how and why these two words came about in relation to your father?"

"All my life I've listened to him; he was the ultimate sign for me to follow. He was strong, decisive, and in my opinion, a man with incredible foresight. He ruled without ruling. If you had known him, you'd follow him without a hint of doubt. He was a dragon breathing fire, and he was my protector. During the time I was hiding from the communists, there wasn't a day that passed without me thinking what my father would do if he had been in my situation. I constantly compared myself to him with pride, with a sense of achievement. But I wasn't competing with him. It was more than good enough that I had a father like him, as if he was residing in me. He was the one and only. That's my explanation for describing him as a carnivore. He was quick, powerful, and sly as a fox without compromising dignity."

"You idolized him."

"Even when he was physically absent for many years, I relied on his long arm to reach over and pluck me out of a hole. But when I saw him after many years, that man wasn't there anymore. He was a stranger, a basket-weaving, melancholy homosexual, a weepy man, an herbivore."

"But he was dying. You saw him when he was weakened, losing his grip on life. He sounded like a man with a great deal of regrets. You told me that you were initially upset, tormented, and shocked at the revelation of his homosexuality, but you were able to reconcile with it relatively quickly."

"Other than being totally out in the dark, the truth of his sexual orientation didn't alter my opinion of him after I got over the initial shock. It's really okay with me." Sam sighed, looking sleepy. "He was touching me all over, calling me Botchang, which he never did before, sobbing in that awful crimson robe…I cringed, turned cold inside, and later felt hellishly guilty but unable to warm up to him until the end."

"Was he physically affectionate before?"

"The only physical contact I'd had with him was shaking hands or him rubbing his hand on my head when I was a boy."

"Did you long for physical affection when you were a young boy?"

"I don't think so, I don't remember. Don't get me wrong. I felt plenty loved by him. He was kind, gentle, and I always knew my well-being was the most important thing to him."

"Let's investigate this more. I need you to tell me as accurately as possible the emotions that went through you during this time."

Before Dr. Min finished his sentence, Sam started moving away from his previous calmness, alarming the doctor.

"Do you know what he did? He begged for my forgiveness for misguiding my life. He said, 'I sheltered you too much, robbing you of your life along the way. It wasn't intentional by any means. It was from my own weakness of fear; it was from my own ego that I thought you wouldn't do well on your own. I had decided for you, and on top of that, I made you believe that my way is the only way you wanted to be. I've never shown you anger, said harsh words, or given a cold glance, because I didn't want to give you any reason to rebel. I sinned, my son, I sinned. I stole your free thinking, your free will to judge me, to correct me, to put me in my place, to show me the other side of everything.' So as atonement he decided to return to me the gift of suffering, which was rightfully mine to begin with. I mean, I understand to a degree about his regrets, which were absurd, but seeing how his life must've been in that isolated place for so long, wearing that crimson robe, listening to that slimy fellow day in and day out articulating his bullshit as a form of deep philosophy…" Heat flashed in his eyes. He stood up and started to pace around. Dr. Min knew what was coming, but he didn't interfere. It was too important, he thought, not to interrupt. He paced back and forth in a straight line but continued to talk, addressing Dr. Min in normal sentences instead of the telegraphic way he used to murmur before the caffeine treatment. Dr. Min waited; he felt something crucial would be revealed any second. He chewed his lips, hoping that Sam would not crack before the session took a leap.

But he cracked, he cracked badly. There was blood.

By the time Dr. Min was able to get help from outside, his left arm, from the palm to the elbow, was cut by the mail knife on the desk. The last thing Sam heard when he attacked Dr. Min was a screeching falsetto, illegible.

He didn't see Sam for two days. Sam called him and apologized. Dr. Min told him that he was an immature spoiled brat who could not handle the truth, which was also a calculated assertion like his refusal to see him for two days. "You are not insane, far from it. You can't bear to live with yourself; you are no one you want to recognize anymore. Acting crazy suits you, right? So that someone else decides your fate again like your father did yours." In contrast to the hostile, juvenile nature of the words of the verbal assault, Dr. Min used a calm monotone, mature voice. It was a calculated professional advance he had to try in order to give Sam a sense that he was actually dealing with a human being, a regular ordinary person, instead of a machine-like professional.

"Does it hurt?"

"What do you think!"

"When will I see you?"

"What made you think I'd see you?"

Silence from the other end of the phone.

"Tomorrow at ten in the morning, my office. There will be an orderly present."

"Thanks." Sam lingered on the phone, but Dr. Min hung up.

- 5 6 -

"Everything I know about myself belongs to my father."

"Not true."

"True."

"Who were you when you cut me? It certainly wasn't the characteristic of your father's. I have to tell you something I noticed when you attacked me. You were hesitating, you could have gone for my throat, my eye, but you chose my arm. You know what I think? It was a scheme of unsteady mind to avoid what is inevitable to face. You want to be denounced, to be left alone, so that you don't get pushed into revealing the fear; you want to deny its existence."

"Do you know what it is?" Sam asked timidly.

"No. You have to talk to me in more direct terms."

"I've been direct with you."

"I know you've tried. When trying isn't good enough to jump over resistance but only scratches its surface, resistance gets annoyed, so to speak, and acts out to stop the annoyance, sometimes at any cost. What I'm saying is that I believe you don't consciously withhold from me, but your mind decides what's important to tell and what's not. I need you to drop that. You don't have to sound intelligent, grown up. In circumstances such as this, such a barrier only betrays you. I know it's hard to ignore the built-up ego, which is more or less second nature to intelligent, well-learned people, including myself. I'm not here to judge if you are a refined intellectual or a gaucho, if you are a holy man or scum. Between the two of us, there's no winning or losing here. We want the same thing."

There was a long silence.

"Would you like some coffee?" the doctor asked, seeing Sam nodding with a faint smile.

"That's what I'm saying. A controlled smile with definite gauging."

"Gauging? What?"

The doctor ignored his question with an air of "you don't need to know" and asked back in return, "Hot or cold?"

"Hot, black."

Dr. Min called the secretary for two hot cups of coffee. Then he remembered the orderly, his bouncer of the day who was sitting on the sofa at the far corner of the room reading a magazine.

"Coffee?" he shouted at him.

"Iced, lots of cream and sugar please!" the orderly shouted back, with his eyes still on the magazine.

He called the secretary once again for an extra creamy, sugary iced coffee for the orderly, all the while, looking at him and exchanging a knowing silly smile. Sam liked what he saw, a brief scene from an average workday between two people of different ranks taking a moment to ensure each other's humanness.

Sam began to talk about his birth in relation to his father's precious gift of suffering. He dropped the shame and let his tongue lead.

"When I was a little boy, I was teased, not often, by kids in the neighborhood who said that I was born to a whore and a murderer. I ran to my amah who embraced me and told me that wasn't true at all. She said she knew for sure that my mother died when giving birth to me. 'Those kids are jealous of your good fortune. You live in a big house, you wear nice clothes, and everybody loves you. Don't mind them.' Of course, I could not ask my father. I was afraid that he would think that I was not man enough. Several days later my amah showed me a photo of my father and mother. Until then I hadn't seen any photos of her in the house. 'It makes your father too sad,' Amah explained. In the photo that she showed me, my father and mother were sitting on a bench in a park looking happy. It wasn't of good quality; there was too much exposure, and the faces were small. The man in the photo resembled my father and that's about it. And that was that. I never harbored the doubt anymore. I can't imagine to this day that my real mother would have been better than my amah. I clearly remember how I didn't feel any emotion for the woman in the picture. She was a stranger. I'd rather be with my amah at any cost. No way would I replace my love for Amah with anyone, mother or not."

"So no more doubts after that. But you are, you were a—"

"Basket baby. You don't know how embarrassing and silly I feel now talking about it. A middle-aged man who hardly knows any serious tragedy—a fact of which I'm slightly ashamed—telling another middle-aged man the sorrow of being a 'basket baby.' It feels unbearably shameful the way I let it trouble me."

"You're doing very well. Middle-aged or not, one shouldn't doubt or shame the pain he feels just because the pain doesn't match his age. When it comes to trouble in the heart, trust me, it has no age, and that is universal. There's no such thing as a right problem for the right age. Don't belittle your pain. Why add more pain to already existing pain? One shouldn't grade his pain because there's no such thing as a 'more justifiable' pain or sorrow. If it is you who suffers, no matter how ludicrous the pain seems, you owe it to yourself to honor it."

"How do I honor it?

"It will come to you."

"So I just wait until it comes?"

"There are several ways to approach it. The very first step is to lose the shame."

"Right. That's easy. Like throwing away a pair of old shoes." Sam's sarcastic tone gave Dr. Min encouragement that he was truly participating in the talk.

"Easy peasy, lemon squeezy," Dr. Min said in English and laughed, seeing Sam chuckling like a healthy man.

"Let me put it this way. What if there's a small innocent child inside you, and another you, a grown-up, is observing the child in you? All of us are born with the faculty of meta-cognition, whose function is to notice what we are thinking as if there were a third intelligence in us." Sam tilted his head in confusion. The doctor continued. "You must've experienced thinking of something while at the same time someone inside wondered why you were engaged in such a thought."

"I think so."

"Be aware of this faculty and use it for self-observation in the absence of judgment and criticism. Just accept what you observe as a loving parent accepts their child no matter what. You have to imagine this picture I just described and make a mental picture of it. Instead of treating the shame with contempt, treat it with kindness and sympathy for being misunderstood, neglected. Talk to it, comfort it, apologize to it, have a pity party with it. Be a friend to your wound. As Nietzsche said, 'it is the wound that heals you.'"

Sam looked up the ceiling scratching his chin and blinking, wondering why the coffee was taking so long. Then the light came on in his head. Someone inside of him noticed that he was thinking about coffee on top of other thoughts. He immediately shared that with the doctor.

"I had this German shepherd I loved dearly. He was lovingly spoiled and did some naughty things now and then, but there was no way I would've treated him any differently for that. I taught him to correct the bad behavior patiently and lovingly, taking delight for every small step he took towards improvement, actually having fun with him in the process."

"There you go. I'm glad you remembered that. That's the approach I've been telling you about. It might sound like manipulating our minds using an unnatural method, but after all, it's for relearning how to love ourselves."

"So proper love for yourself leads you to the knowledge of yourself."

"Yes. You said the key word, proper love. Love is a very complicated thing isn't it? It can be black, white, and every possible shade in between."

"How does one know when it is proper?"

"I'm telling you this as an ordinary human being, but I think that when it's right, it gives you a sense of freedom and peace. You feel that all's good so long as you have yourself."

The coffee came, and the orderly took the tray and served them, mixing cream and a mound of sugar in his own, whistling. A few pimples as big as lentils on his cheeks looked painful. "You have to treat them, young man. They look infected," Dr. Min told him, sipping his coffee.

"Well sir, as they say, 'God must be jealous of my beauty.' I can't fight it." He took his cup and went back to his seat. Sam wanted to smoke, and they had a coffee-and-cigarette break.

"We have to touch upon the incident, the attack, in depth. I don't know if you're ready. If you aren't, we'll wait until then."

"I think about that incident almost every moment these days with a great deal of shame and horror. I've never even clenched my fists over any-one in my life," he said, blushing with quivering lips.

"Please go on."

Sam moved his head with his eyes looking up at the ceiling, as if what he was about to say was written up there. At one point he shook his head and jerked it backwards, still looking up and said, "I think I need you to give me a starting point."

"You screamed in a high-pitched voice when you attacked. I couldn't make out the words. Do you know, do you remember what you said?"

Sam shook his head. "No, I don't. It could've been utterances of profanity."

"As I said before, I saw in your eyes that you didn't want to hurt me badly. There was a nanosecond's hesitation in which I saw clearly that you were scanning for where you were going to strike me. I've had my share of violent patients, and I think I know who is real and who is an impostor."

"Impostor?" Sam let out a nervous laugh.

"Before I go on, I want to tell you to tell me 'yay' or 'nay' about the assess-ment I'm making," Dr. Min said, crossing his arms.

"Uh, hmm..." Sam crossed his arms and legs, swiveling the chair he was sitting in.

"No rush. Take as much time you need, just no filtering." Dr. Min started to swivel his chair too.

Sam started, "I don't know if it makes any sense. I don't know the man who attacked you, but it had to be me all the same. All I remember is that the moment was unbearable, mentally and physically. It wasn't pain. It was more like a coup, a coup of saints, a coup of evil, neither winning nor losing…no sense of consequences…"

"And?"

"And the thought of my birth father, him being a—"

"A violent man. So in the moment of violent confusion you, perhaps unconsciously, identified with him, the man of whom you have no hands-on knowledge other than his incarceration, which was only hearsay? You desperately wanted to stop the chaos in you, but there was no controller, so to speak, because you were no longer you without your adoptive father, who you believed deceived you and maybe even used you but also cared for you, made you love him, admire him. Someone had to put a stop to the chaos, and you let the fiction of your birth father take over. But part of you was there, even though you could not feel its presence, which made you hesitate. That nanosecond of hesitation is you, the real you, believe that. You were in control even when you were out of control."

"Why do we have to be so goddamn complicated?"

"Indeed we are. One thing I have to caution you is that my role here is not to give you mathematical answers. I'm just being an extra voice. At the end of the day, it is you and you alone who decides to jump over this hurdle."

"That kind of makes sense to me. Frankly, my birth father is irrelevant to me. At the same time, it bothers me, him being irrelevant. I have no desire to search for my biological parents or curiosity about who they are. But it bothers me, my moral fiber. What troubles me and makes me ill comes in many folds, all concerning my late father. One side of my brain tells me to forget about it, which I'd like to more than anything at this point. But I can't go there, no matter how I try."

"Our minds like to play tug-of-war. It doesn't necessarily look out for you. Tell me about the time you overdosed."

"The botched attempt. I just wanted to stop the thoughts. If I can't forget, that is the sure way to forget."

"Do you think about trying it again?"

"Yes, but as you know, I come here instead." He told the doctor of the rock sisters and the five cigarettes at his father's temple. "Strangely, I get a similar feeling of being between the rocks by being here on the island."

"Many suicidal people happen to be trapped in helplessness. The idea of helplessness is still a component of life not death."

"Does anyone kill himself for the pure reason of not wanting to have anything to do with life, even though his life is good?"

"Perhaps, I really don't know. Most people with suicidal tendencies that I've dealt with had problems that they wanted to avoid or were overwhelmed by sadness or thought they had nothing to look forward to or were deadly bored with life, which is very rare. Perhaps that 'very rare' group of suicidal people I mentioned answers your question. But all of them take time to get there, as if something in them still wanted to see what's ahead of them in life. I remember a line in a novel written by Goethe. It says that 'being suicidal is a terminal illness.' I interpreted that particular line as a somatic illness where the individual's brain is wired in such a way that he can't help it. I don't know. He might have meant something else altogether, but the line stuck in my mind to this day." Something in Dr. Min was nudging him to stop such talk with a patient. It was too late.

"I like that. I've heard his name somewhere. Therefore, a truly honest suicide is from illness, a somatic illness like cancer. Anything else is acting out due to entrapment in helplessness. That's what he's saying."

"No, that's what *I* am saying. As a man, not as a doctor, mind you." The doctor started to chuckle and said, "You know why I remember the line? I memorized it to impress girls in college. Ha, ha. It's strange, though, at that time my only intention was to use it for my superficial ego, but it turned out that wasn't all after all. I found myself, occasionally, regurgitating it in my mind."

Sam laughed, liking the doctor's openness. "Who is this guy, Goethe? I heard the name somewhere, as I said." Sam asked, feeling ignorant.

"Some German poet. That's all I know. I read his book only because during my foolish youth that was the thing to do in order to belong. I couldn't understand what he was saying for the most part," he said then laughed, pounding the desk. They laughed together like two school chums, reminiscing over the foolish days of youth. When they were done, Dr. Min asked if Sam wanted to end the session for the day.

"I'd like to continue, if that's possible."

"I'm more than happy to continue."

"Tell me more about this identity stuff. For some reason it hit a spot in me, like a lightbulb flickering."

Dr. Min took a piece of tissue, scrunched it into a ball, and threw it at the orderly. He looked up and said, "What's the matter?" shaking the ice in his glass before taking another sip.

"Stop that ice-shaking thing, it's distracting. And easy with the page turning of whatever you're reading."

The orderly looked back at him with an expression of wonder at how was he to manage such an impossible task. "The papers are too crispy," he said, but seeing the doctor getting up with the intention of snatching away the magazine, he quickly smiled and said, "Sorry, sorry."

"Now, let's tackle the issue of identity, shall we?" Dr. Min sat down and turned his attention to Sam, who was beaming from amusement at the interaction between the doctor and the orderly.

Dr. Min continued, "It's my suspicion that you believed you were your father, who raised you, in the making. You loved him, of course, but he was more than that to you. You liked who he was. Following in his footsteps became the meaning of your life. And you followed him successfully, which made you believe that you were becoming him in your mind. You could've continued your life contentedly if you hadn't witnessed the great change in him, not to mention the revelations which are quite shocking to anyone at any age. The shrine you had built crumbled, and you felt your life was stolen by deception. But you know your life had been good, very good. So you feel guilty and are angry for not being able to move on as a grown, well-experienced, and confident man. You couldn't come to terms with the angry, rebellious adolescent in you, and you began to doubt that you were not who you believed yourself to be. All the trust in yourself was destroyed as if you had to start all over again at your age. Before this bomb had fallen in your lap, you could've laughed at such a story if it happened to others. Perhaps you'd have thought that suffering from such a thing as a grown man was ludicrous. But the laughable suffering of others isn't that laughable when it happens to you. You try and try to laugh it away, but the effort only shrinks you smaller, creating a land of suspicion in yourself. You see your life's history as blank pages. Hard stuff for a person who lived in harmony with himself all his life. Were you angry with him?"

"I must've been. I kept calling him an ex-father in my head, with the image of him in that crimson robe. More heavy stuff followed. When Mrs. Lim told me that Yu and my father were lovers and that she had thought I knew just like everyone, and when Yu suddenly changed his treatment of me, which drew a dark shadow, I remember that I felt I had been played. When my father told me about my birth, I was so shocked but didn't show him any such sign. I guess that could be an act of anger."

"What made you lie to your father that you knew everything about his secret?"

"As I said, I began to feel that I had been played. I didn't want to give him the satisfaction of a game well played. But it was like an ectoplasmic being took over me."

"You blame him for telling you the truth?"

"What's the use? I think I question the motive behind his doing so."

"Has there been any time in your life when you did anything without your father's voice in your head?"

Sam rubbed his eyes with both hands and said, "I've been asking the same thing myself."

"And?"

"One incident that comes to mind is the time when I ran away to the mountain I told you about, right before the war broke out, when I was in the woods alone searching for the temple. Now, I want make it clear that the day in the woods didn't traumatize me. If anything, it's a sweet memory. So by no means was the situation I'm telling you about a big deal. True, I was frightened with a good dose of shame, but there was a clear moment when I heard my own voice, mine alone. It wasn't a voice of a grown man but that of a young boy who was excited and ready to face the unknown. I almost wanted to be up against some dangerous situation. Why? I don't know. I clearly remember someone in me warned me not to be foolish, but strangely my excitement was so heightened, I wanted to test myself. I felt like there wasn't anything I couldn't handle. I almost wished a hideous monster would show up so that I could show myself the hidden Sam, Sam the hero...ha, ha... pretty childish! Actually, when I found the temple after hours and hours of wandering in the woods, I was ecstatic but part of it was anticlimactic. In a way, I felt let down for having been saved again. That's the only time I didn't hear my father's voice in the background, the one and only time. Although actually I imagined my father being proud of me then too...ha, ha." Here he lowered his head with a smile on his lips, reconstructing the day in the woods. Then he lifted his head, looked straight into the doctor's round eyes and said, "That isn't all true, partly yes, but now I remember I kept thinking, 'What would my father do? What would he tell me to do now?'"

"But you heard a different voice, not your father's. The new voice that encouraged you to think you could handle anything. It's no doubt all you, and I gather you liked the new voice."

Dr. Min saw color appearing on his cheeks.

"I must confess, though, that I'm fond of that memory," Sam said with a wide smile.

"A couple of things are happening here. After you saw your father for the last time, you put the brakes on everything because you could no longer accept your father's way. That's clearly your choice, your decision. You made that choice without your father's instructions. True, you are bewildered, and at the same time, deeply ashamed. It makes you feel tiny and insignificant, which is a brand new emotion to you. It caused you to disintegrate. You said you didn't know who you were anymore. You are who you are now, as you've always have been. Your father was just an emotional crutch, like a lucky charm. You weren't made by him or your biological father. It just happened that your late father's way and yours were in sync in some aspects. You know the academic argument of 'nature versus nurture?' In my opinion, it's a stupid argument. Nature and nurture are just two drops of water in the ocean of an astronomical number of things that influence the making of us. Let me put it this way. If I grew up in your environment, would I be me? Not likely and vice versa. No matter what, you are you through and through. That is when the question of the soul comes in. One can become a saint in spite of a harsh life or a criminal even though he had everything going for him. If a bear in Alaska and a bear in a zoo switched their environments at birth, would they have lived the exact life of their counterpart? I don't think so. When your father said that he had stolen your life, that was his problem not yours. You followed his way all your life, as you say, but you chose to follow because you decided it worked for you. It clicked with you. As one philosopher—I think it is Schopenhauer, I'm not sure—said, 'Life happens.'

"My life happens as does yours and everyone's who's landed on this planet. We seem to live in a controlled, organized world, but that is an illusion. The fact is that every moment is an adventure through a whirlpool of chaos. It's hard, especially when you believe that you can control life as if it made sense like mathematics. Controlling becomes a state of mind, making one's being unbelievably dull. When you begin to hear an unhappy cry from within as you face another day devoted to controlling, inner war begins."

There was a veil of serenity over Sam's face, Dr. Min thought, as Sam cast his eyes down, examining his thoughts with the corners of his mouth slightly curled up.

"I like that. 'Life happens'…Indeed, life happens…" He looked up as if waking from a sweet dream and said, "Is that what you believe, or is it your trained professional mind talking?"

"Does it matter to you?"

"Yes it does."

"In what way?"

"Because I feel like I'm becoming your friend."

"That's flattering, but I beg you to pay attention to the development that just surfaced in your mind."

"Well, okay, let me see." He looked a little embarrassed, rejected perhaps.

Dr. Min forbade his tongue to say anything to ease Sam's embarrassment because what he was about to discuss with him was crucial. Sam moved his eyes slowly from one side to the other, back and forth, rubbing his chin that was pushed out, making his bottom teeth touch his upper lip. His eyes sleepily moved to the window behind the doctor. The issue that the doctor wanted to touch upon had to wait for another day. He knew he should not break the mood Sam was sinking in.

-57-

A series of similar conversations as described above went on, day in, day out. After his first stay of several months on the island, Sam went back to the city to resume his life. They carried on weekly meetings at the doctor's office in the city, but he brought himself to the island every now and then to his reserved room, sometimes just for a weekend and other times for a whole week or so. As time went on, they started to have meals together in the city, becoming closer. There were no more violent episodes or frantic revving of the motor in him, but there was a dark cloud that once in a while made him deeply sad. He didn't want to call it 'depression' because he felt the word to be too clinical for the quality of his sadness. He said jokingly that his sadness was way too poetic to be dumped in the category of clinical terminology. But when his poetic sadness weighed him down and was no longer so enjoyable, he came to the island. He called it 'the island,' never the hospital. Dr. Min wrestled many times over whether to be a professional or a human being who knew a thing or two when it came to Sam. For the most part, he chose to be neutral, a caring citizen, so to speak.

The longer Dr. Min practiced in his field and the more success he enjoyed, his suffering, which used to be a tiny speck of irritation that he could cover up easily, grew to be something else, a shadow of his own. He poured his heart and soul to some of his patients. But the more sincere he became, the more his own imperfections protruded, creating a fault line of hypocrisy. Silently, he turned into a sufferer himself. If there was any merit to it, it made him feel closer to honesty. In the end, the knowledge of his imperfections deepened his understanding for others in pain. A small shrine of compassion (he liked to visualize it as a fountain with a statue of a cherub with lotus flowers) resided in his heart, telling him that he was also in the making of a better person. "Perfection is a stupid thing, it's a dead end. It's a ridiculous practice we get ourselves trapped into to darken our suffering," the statue of the cherub whispered to him by the fountain of compassion.

Sam wasn't interested in finding out who he was. It was not too difficult for Dr. Min to come to that conclusion. Sam was always needing someone to depend on; it was essential to him like a religion. He couldn't believe that he didn't really need anyone to depend on; he didn't want to. He had to have someone to replace his father. Dr. Min tried to make him see it, face it, and eventually lose it. When Sam told him he was becoming Dr. Min's friend, he got somewhat irritated and felt tired of Sam. Another time Sam said, "I'm being saved yet again, this time by you."

"Are you okay with that, or is it a letdown to you? I mean, in your mind, it's always been someone else other than yourself who has saved you, according to your assessment of your life. But what about the time when you found the temple and felt a little anticlimactic? Didn't you feel that anticlimactic because you were a bit disappointed at being saved too easily once again?" he asked.

Sam answered, "But I also felt like a puppy who found a home."

Dr. Min was heading for a dilemma. He was very uncomfortable over the fact that he was becoming the replacement of Sam's savior. The first couple of years they went through intense psychological muscle work over the issue. Although his melancholy was less frequent, Sam's dependency on the doctor wouldn't let up. Eventually, the doctor let it go, allowing their interactions to evolve and have a different angle. He found himself getting less and less un-comfortable, which alarmed him although not too much. By no means was Sam a dependent person. He was nothing like that. But he had this need to cling to a security blanket; he needed a thumb to suck on. Dr. Min began to think, "All of us need that, either consciously or unconsciously. This is how he serves his primordial longing for peace and comfort. Who am I to tell him to destroy it? After all, don't I have my own little something? The fountain of compassion? Isn't it true that I sort of worship my imperfections?" He was very happy on the day he came to this realization. "There is no true atheist. Everyone has a secret shrine in them. How humbling, how innocent this behavior of men." Naturally, he became a friend to a man named Sam.

- 5 8 -

Miri fell asleep on the chair while watching Nurse Yun sleeping on her bed, but she woke up mid-morning the next day in her bed. She didn't remember when Nurse Yun had put her to bed. It was raining. She got up and went to the sink to brush her teeth. She saw a blue circle around her left eye although the bruise on her cheek had diminished. She pressed the blue area with her finger. It registered pain, shooting down to her teeth. She pressed it again and again, feeling the pain shooting down to her teeth every time without fail. She located the teeth that received the shooting pain and pressed them with her fingers. They didn't reciprocate the pain up to the eye area. "What do you know," she said to herself, smiling at her reflection. The blue mark seemed rather becoming. Physical pain always put her in touch with someone she liked in herself. That someone calmed her, enveloping her with a humble but gently euphoric cloud. She felt a secret wisdom flowing into her, temporarily expanding the horizon of her understanding and melting down her naughty judgment into benevolence. In other words, she felt beautiful, besotted with herself.

The rain turned to hail, hitting the windowpane like dried beans. She went down to the lobby and saw a rice man worming through the furniture and people with bowls of rice. Lunchtime, she thought, feeling hungry. She sat with her usual three elderly munchkins, who were already engaged in their daily argument. Miri could tell they had finished their meal but were carrying on the verbal exercise. The topic of their argument had something to do with a plane crash in Osaka some years ago. "How many were killed?" "Over five hundred." "There's no plane big enough to take that many people." "Yes, there is." "No, there isn't."

She finished a bowl of soup with rice at the speed of light and stared at a red apple on her tray. When she took the apple from the food stand, she was still in the fantasy of feeling beautiful. She felt like being a pretty girl eating a pretty apple, like in a commercial. But the fantasy faded. She was her real self again. She was not a fan of fruit, and apples were her least favorite. She thought fruits were generally deceiving. Her opinion of the fruit family was that the fruits are beautiful and look so delicious but are mostly sour and too crunchy in the mouth. She also noticed that she generally didn't get along with fruit-loving people, her mom, sisters. She couldn't bring herself to eat it, but she felt stress from the apple sitting on her tray. It was judging her. She left it there and walked away, feeling slightly betrayed by herself again, fully aware that she would repeat the act again.

She explained to Dr. Min the source of the dark circle around her eye. They talked of this and that about the village. The rain became steady, evenly vertical. The trees began to show more branches, losing leaves of autumn colors more and more every day. "Do you know that less rain during the year makes the color of autumn leaves more brilliant, but they don't stay as long as the ones that lived through the year with more rain?"

"So the more rain, the less color, but they live longer, right?" he said indifferently. He sensed that she wasn't going to talk much that day. He got used to her various moods.

"Okay, Miri, let's do some work, shall we?" She shrugged, still looking out the window.

"If I send you home, and I know you don't want that, but think about it for a second, what is the first resistance that comes to your mind? Straight answer, please."

"Can we talk about something else?"

"Not today." He started tapping the table with a pen with the intention of showing her that he was getting impatient. Her eyes landed on the tapping pen.

"You already know the answer, it's my mother."

Her demeanor was changing noticeably. It was like bringing down a child who was sitting in a tree daydreaming to do a chore.

"There must be something you miss about home."

"My grandma. I worry about her loneliness more than missing her. I didn't have a chance to say good-bye to her before I came here. She was visiting a relative in the country. And I miss my room."

"What do you miss about your room?" He didn't want to bring her grandma into the session in fear that it would turn toward an unplanned direction.

"Small, a single bed, a desk facing a large window with a view of the woods leading up to the mountain, a little cocoon of mine..."

"What's on your desk?" He saw her throwing a side glance to his tapping pen. He stopped and clasped his hands on the desk.

"School stuff, candles. Is this a memory test?"

"Of course not. You told me about your relationship with your mother in our numerous sittings. Is your hatred for her such that you would spend an important time in your life in a mental hospital? Have you thought about that?" He immediately regretted the tone he took.

"I don't hate her."

"How would you call it?"

"Pure dislike. She hates me. That I know."

"Has she ever told you that?"

"In various, colorful ways, and yes, she's said she hated me many, many times."

"What distinguishes between 'pure dislike' and 'hatred'?"

"When you hate, you suffer more, a lot more, but when you dislike, well, it's like an 'out of sight, out of mind thing.' You don't suffer as much. But I learned to feel sorry for her hatred. It's like 'dislike' seems superior to 'hate.' But to tell the truth, I would still dislike her even if she was a decent mother."

"How so?"

"My bodily chemistry changes in her presence. She has a peculiar odor that I can't describe, and sometimes at mealtime, when her foot accidentally touches mine under the table, my entire body reacts like I stepped on a snake. I flinched noticeably and moved my feet away. I'm sure she felt it."

She continued, "I felt bad, really bad and guilty," shaking her head, facing down.

"Did she appear to be hurt?"

"She doesn't know how to get hurt; she only gets mad. She doesn't necessarily react right away. She takes her time to plan her attack. But I felt so bad I could've cried feeling sorry for her. Suddenly, I became the villain in my mind, knowing fully that wasn't so. It was painfully confusing at that moment."

"I'd like to hear more of that, please go on."

"The word I can use to describe what went through my mind at that moment is 'guilt,' but later on I realized it was something totally different. That moment threw me down into an abyss of absolute sorrow, and how absolute it was, my breath rattled. You see doctor, it seems trauma can come in a most subtle way. I can say it was traumatic, at least, to me."

"You said you realized that its nature was totally different from your initial thought of guilt, what was it?"

"I can't stand the fact that there's a human being, my mother in this case, whom I'd rather love but find it impossible. Can you fathom the idea of feeling guilty for not being able to love someone who you dislike causally, who you know in your heart hates you? It was such a helpless feeling. I felt suspended in a dark, disused well, neither going up nor falling down." She sighed, scrunching her body.

"I assume that didn't change anything, though."

"Nothing on the outside, but a great deal had changed on my part. It took many sittings on my own with my thoughts, reliving the moment over and over. The accidental contact of our feet under the table while having a boring lunch with the family eventually gave me a scientific interpretation to our relationship. The immediate electromagnetic field around me repels that of hers and perhaps vice versa."

"That's a unique, original…" the doctor started to say, clearing his throat to erase the laugh slipping out. "But she didn't flinch or pull her feet away like you did. How come?"

"My electromagnetic field is more sensitive to hers because it's weaker than hers. That's not all. There was information, rather edifying, humanistic information."

"And what was the information?" he asked, making a few notes just so he could lower his head to hide his laughing eyes.

"I started to try to put myself in her shoes, so to speak. It wasn't a conscious attempt. Sometimes I found myself staring at her from behind, watching her doing whatever she was doing. 'What if I were her' was the voice I heard in me whenever I watched her like that. That's what I meant by 'edifying information,' being in touch with what's human in me."

"Would you be any different from her if you had been her?"

"You see, that's the confusing part. If I were her, how could I be different from her? I am her. At the same time, I was glad I wasn't her."

"You began to pity her."

"Perhaps I pitied her unnecessary suffering."

"What's so unnecessary about it?"

"Unnecessary in terms of another person's point of view, I should have said. Her life could be a good one, but she can't accept it because she loves anger. She doesn't give a second look at anything, as if it's her duty to God to be loyal to her initial hatred. I've never seen her—this I say in clear conscience—being at peace. Even when she prays, she looks like she's simmering in a soup of anger."

"You think her life is actually much better than she believes it to be?"

"That is where my pity is."

"What do you do when you feel pity for her?"

"Nothing. Her anger is too toxic for my infantile pity."

"I'm not sure I understand."

"Me either. Sometimes I say things I don't understand. Well, let me try again. My pity for her is still too puny, but her anger is Mount Vesuvius. Then my dislike…That is a whole other story." She described the size of her mother's anger by holding out the tip of her finger, winking an eye, and drawing a big pyramid in the air, puffing her cheeks. He had to laugh; she did too.

"I wish we could go on, but I have to stop for today. Can you hold onto your thoughts of what we talked about today? I'd like to continue this discussion in the next session."

She nodded indifferently. She stood up, looking outside through the window behind him and said, "Oh, look, foxes are getting married," which meant that it's sunny and rainy at the same time. He didn't know how that phrase came about except that everyone, including small children, knew what it meant.

"You might see a rainbow," he said, getting up.

"The first time I saw a rainbow I was disappointed."

"I agree. I thought it was overrated," he said, opening the door for her. She bowed politely and left. He made a note to pay a visit to her parents. He'd been sending progress reports to them regularly but received no response.

-59-

The following week Miri's father agreed to meet with Dr. Min at his office in the city. It was mid-morning when Dr. Min found himself sitting in the waiting room outside of Miri's father's office. The meeting was delayed. Half an hour later from the appointed time, a secretary, a young, skinny girl in a tight dress and high heels, came to fetch him. He adjusted his tie, smoothed his hair with his palm, and buttoned his jacket before he entered. The huge office he stepped into was dimly lit. It was on the seventh floor with windows that could have provided natural light and a nice view. However, all the windows, which were wall to wall, were covered with heavy curtains. The darkness of the room and its size made him search for her father as if he were buried somewhere in there. He heard a voice, clear and manly, come from the far end of the room where there was a large desk with a small lamp. "Please have a seat" was what he heard. He found his way to a leather sofa and sat down, feeling rather like a country simpleton. The leather beneath him felt like butter. His eyes gradually adjusted to the dark room when Miri's father came over to him and turned on the lamp next to another large leather sofa across from him. He sat down on this sofa and precisely crossed his legs, showing an expensive-looking shoe above the coffee table between them.

"Sorry about the darkness. I think so much better in the dark."

Dr. Min stretched out his hand, which the other man touched with his soft but cold fingers. He looked freshly groomed with not a hair out of place. During their phantom-like handshake, he noticed fancy cufflinks, onyx with gold trim, he thought. Miri's father was also wearing an expensive watch with a narrow black face and gold band but no ring. The dark blue suit he had on had the sheen of pure silk. These fancy, pricey vanity items strangely worked well with him, making him look stylish and charismatic to Dr. Min's displeasure, instead of vulgar, which would have been more satisfying. He had a strong face with hard eyes that matched his voice. He was a very handsome man, reminding Dr. Min of James Bond, or a Korean version of him, a James Bond wannabe. Dr. Min felt a bit shabby and got a little pissed off at his feet, embarrassed of his discolored brown shoes. A different girl from the one who fetched him came in with a tray with both coffee and tea. Unlike the other girl, this one had curvy body, but she wore the same style of a tight two-piece dress suit and pointy high heels. When she was pouring coffee for them into cups deserving of an emperor and empress, Dr. Min noticed she had sensuous lips but the eyes of a brainwashed mouse.

Against his will, he turned his neck and looked around the office before he took a sip of hot coffee. Behind the humongous desk was a wall-to-wall glass cabinet with taxidermy animals, mostly birds, large and small. Mr. Bond caught Dr. Min looking at his collection and said proudly that he was a born hunter.

"Very nice." A polite lie escaped his mouth but not without indifference.

James Bond put down the emperor's cup on the saucer, wiped his mouth meticulously with a snow-shaming white handkerchief, and said, "I gather you are here to talk about Miri. How is she?"

Dr. Min detected a slight defensiveness. Mr. Bond uncrossed his legs, lifted his chin, and raised his eyebrows, giving the look that he was in charge. Dr. Min felt like a hired help being asked by his master, "What do you want?" Dr. Min took a sip of coffee, wanting to cross his leg but then quickly went against the impulse in fear of exhibiting his sad shoe. But he spoke with a controlled, "gentle aristocratic" voice. "It's hard to say." He didn't want to say she was doing well. He began to think coming here was not a productive thing. He was getting warm inside with anger but decided to make the best out of the visit. "She's physically sound. A clever girl she is. But she's not an average teenage girl. She seemed to have a hard time assimilating to her environment."

"What was wrong with her environment? Having too much is the cause of all this."

Dr. Min was quite sure by then that he had made a mistake in coming here. The fancy man continued, "Young kids these days are so self centered. All they care about is if they are happy or unhappy." He offered a cigarette to the doctor, which fanned out of an object that resembled an umbrella, highly decorated with enamel painted on gold, by lifting a knob on the top. He lit the American cigarettes, which were only available on the black market, for the both of them. Dr. Min smoked one, half regretting his visit but still half curious. Part of his mind had already went out the door. Mr. Bond blew out the smoke at a forty-five-degree angle toward the ceiling, shaking his head in disapproval. "Happy, unhappy, such words don't exist in my book. They belong to lazy bums, parasites." He looked down, uncrossing his legs, took a brief, thoughtful moment, and added, "I always thought she was the sturdy one. It would've been better if she were a boy. As a matter of fact, there were times I wondered if she were all female."

"What do you mean?" Dr. Min asked, moving his upper body toward the table thinking to himself, by nature females desire to please others. Not her. She doesn't care about pleasing others. She's vacant of the most essential component of being a female. A feigned sadness passed on her father's face, Dr. Min thought. "I assume it isn't your intention to keep her there indefinitely."

"Certainly not. But she became such a scandalous shame to the family. No one half decent would marry her. That part of her future is rubbed off, erased, gone. One thing for sure, and I pray you understand, that I can't live with an arsonist under the same roof. I have a deep suspicion that it is calculated behavior. Not because her head is cracked, I know that, I do. She has this look about her that can strangle you. She's not crazy. She's playing with evil thoughts. That's worse than being crazy."

Arsonist? Dr. Min thought with great confusion but didn't bring the curiosity to his lips. He took three calm breaths in and out to disguise his shock. Eventually, he decided to get more information about the arson. "She told me about what she did, but I hope you can fill me in with your facts, your side of the story, the evil things she did," he said, making an attempt to sound clinical, professional.

Bond raised his eyebrows, sighed, and said, "She might not have told you the whole truth, knowing her." He moved his lower lip sideways then bit it with his upper teeth, flaring his nostrils. He looked up, hardening his already hard eyes even more. Whatever he was about to say next clearly caused this facial activity that made him look not so James Bondish. "I travel a lot on business. I wasn't home when it happened. Her mother told me that she had to commit Miri, which was your advice. She set fire to my taxidermy collection one night. Fortunately, a member of the house staff caught her in time. She was caught soon enough, but fire had already singed the tails of some animals. Then her mother confessed that it wasn't the first time. She was caught setting fire to other things." He smacked his lips, leaned back, and continued, "I'm telling you that her mother and sisters are scared of her. They fear her coming back home. Have you ever administered electric shock treatment to her? I heard that is very effective."

"No. We stopped using that treatment. And you heard it wrong; it's not effective but much more destructive." The doctor abruptly got up, put his hands in his pockets, and said, "Thank you for your time. For any reason, give me a call. You know where I am." With a slight bow, Dr. Min left Miri's father, who didn't bother to get up, without waiting for his final words. By the time he left the room, his impression of the simulation of James Bond dissolved into that of a malignant creep. Without having gained anything, he felt triumphant. Miri, a pyromaniac, he thought. While he was going down on the elevator, he burst into laughter, imagining Miri scorching the tails of the taxidermy animals one by one in the wee hours of the night.

-60-

Dr. Min was early for his lunch date with Mrs. Lim but happily found her having beer while waiting for him. It always amazed him to see her looking like a hardcore business woman whenever he saw her in the city. Her demeanor, even her voice, was that of an admiral. But then on the island, she became a regular, pudgy middle-aged woman. It'd been nearly five years since she took care of Sam's business affairs, but she still called herself "Sam's secretary," just as she insisted on being addressed as "Mrs. Lim." They greeted each other like two good old friends. "Beer?" she asked.

"No need to ask," he replied, sitting across from her.

"You look a little pinkish."

"Do I?" he said, looking into the mirrored panel along the wall next to the table. When the waiter came, Mrs. Lim ordered beer and the usual spaghetti with meat sauce for the both of them. They talked about politics, the climbing cost of this and that, all the usual good stuff.

He drank the cold beer and took a mouthful of pasta, which was so satisfying. "I just had a meeting with Miri's father."

"Really? Did I tell you that I know him? I mean, Sam and I know of him. Sam wanted to find out who her family was. But don't tell her we know."

Dr. Min shook his head, slurping his noodles.

"I don't know him apart from the fact that he is one of the pioneer industrialists in this country, that he's hugely successful, totally self made. They say he doesn't owe a penny to a bank. Sam told me that he and the owner of Jinsung Construction fathered half of the illegitimate children in town. The rumor is that the two became close by sharing the same women. But according to Sam, they're comfortable with each other because they both have an enormous complex about being under educated."

"People have to have something that makes them unhappy. It's the rule of thumb for being human. Educated or not, he must be smart to be so successful. He could be charismatic, if not intimidating, and what a spiffy dog!"

"Yeah, he must have something extraordinary to achieve such success. Sam said that he's tight lipped but unbelievably shrewd. He said it's impossible to guess what he thinks. But why say 'spiffy dog'?"

"Oh, that," he said, wiping his mouth with a paper napkin. Mrs. Lim guided him to the sauce remaining on his lower right cheek by pointing to the area on her face.

"No, no, the other side," she said.

"I thought you were being my mirror image. Anyway, the guy looked like a mannequin in a department store."

"A vain man, is he? Like Sam?"

"Sam enjoys nice things, a bit loud for my taste, but this man is something else."

"How so?"

"His insecurity and desperate attempt to hide it."

"In Sam's case, his father taught him to pay the utmost attention to his appearance because he was scrawny. Anyway, I'm not wrong to conclude that you don't like him, right?"

He answered her by pursing his lips and raising his eyebrows.

"Actually, Sam and I were surprised when we found out who Miri's father is. Now that you told me about his obsession with his appearance, it's more surprising. As you must have noticed, the girl looks so shabby."

"Maybe that's her style. I thought it rather suits her."

As soon as he got back to his office, he called his wife, who shrieked on the phone, telling him what she was cooking for him for dinner. He told her that he'd take them out for spaghetti. "Best in town, honey." After briefly exchanging news with each other, he hung up feeling loved and important, shabby shoes or not. Every time he called she shrieked with delight, as if he had been missing for a long time. Some time ago he guessed that her affair with the horny young son of a fishmonger had ended. He didn't pursue it any further to confirm. He could feel it from her, and he didn't find his name in her schedule book for piano lessons. He left it at that. The kids didn't complain anymore about too much seafood either. She called him more when he was on the island, and he made sure to tell her how much she meant to him in the most possibly romantic way that his ability allowed, which sometimes made them giggle, feeling sweet and silly. Even though it felt corny and made him blush, he meant every word, and with practice it was getting easier. He knew she was the gatekeeper to his shrine. After he ended the affair with Sohee, he didn't venture for another girl, which he was proud of. He still caught himself daydreaming about it, but the hardest thing to resist was seduction. He never was an initiator, maybe a passive one, but never an eager participant. But the warm presence of that irresistible mist, the fragrant taste of sin on the tips of his senses made him feel oh so good! Seduced by seduction. He described the sensual emotion on a piece of paper when he was captured by those weak moments. He liked what he wrote and saved the paper in his desk drawer. Many months later he saw the note in his drawer: "Warm presence...irresistible mist...taste of sin...oh so good..."

He felt his ears on fire with shame. Something had changed. He tore it up, thinking that it was a lie, it was never that good.

The second spaghetti of the day was as enjoyable as the first one. He sat sandwiched between the boys, who insisted on sitting next to him. His wife reached over to his plate, mixing the sauce and pasta for him. After dinner they took a walk in the mild, chilly autumn evening, his hand holding that of his wife's, feeling saved, renewed, and glad. When they happened to pass a hotel newly refurbished, he remembered the ice cream he had there.

"Hey, what do you say we have some ice cream?"

"It's not summer anymore, Dad," his younger son said, showing his missing front teeth, the rim of his mouth still a bit orange from the spaghetti sauce.

"This place has ice cream all year round."

So the boys both had chocolate ice cream, his wife strawberry, and coffee for him. They were all so quiet. They didn't want to miss out on any bite. The verdict was that it was the best ice cream they'd ever had! He promised them that they'd repeat the same course of the evening again very, very soon.

That night in bed after a sumptuous session of honest sex, his wife said, "Dr. Min." She always called him that when she wanted something. He turned to her, feeling the rolls around her bare waist with his fingers.

"What is it that you want, porky?"

Laughing a little, she said, "I want a nose job." He laughed, his fingers still kneading the rolls.

"Well, what do you say?" she asked, putting her hand on his.

"You always do what you want in the end. It doesn't matter what I say."

"As you know, I have no bridge on my nose. I have to push up my glasses constantly."

"You don't need an excuse. I understand, although I like your nose. God must have forgotten to put one on you and suddenly realized that right before he sent you out. All He could manage at that late stage was to pull out the dough in the middle of your nose-less face and poke two holes for nostrils." He was giggling at his joke.

She pinched his hand and said, "You must know a good surgeon, right?"

"Cosmetic surgery is still in an embryonic phase in this country. I've heard some horror stories, but you can do it in Tokyo. They are masters in the field."

"But how am I going to get a passport?" There was a severe governmental restriction on traveling abroad.

"I know just a person who could arrange that," he said, thinking of Sam. He added, "How about you join me at the conference I have to go to in Tokyo? I think it's in late January or early February." He hadn't planned to attend the conference, but now it seemed like a good idea.

She got excited. "Oh, oh, oh…Dr. Min! I get to go to a foreign country and get a nose job by a master!" She started to count her blessings like counting stars. He could not keep his eyes open anymore. The last thing he heard or thought he heard was, "Maybe I'll have my eyes done too as long as I'm there. They might give a discount."

- 61 -

"What is this?" Miri asked, receiving a large package from Sam.

"Mrs. Lim sent it to you. Dr. Min picked it up when he went to the city. Open it."

"Clothes, for me?" She didn't know what to say. She was touched, embarrassed, and slightly angry. They were warm winter clothes and looked pricey. She was quiet looking at them, feeling them between her fingers.

"Why, you don't like them?" Sam asked, unsure of her silence.

"Of course I like them. They're very nice," she said with her head lowered.

Sam thought he heard a tremor in her voice. He sat next to her on the sofa and realized that she was crying. "What's the matter?" He put his arm around her shoulder, not knowing what to say.

They stayed a few minutes in silence. She tore up the paper from the package and blew her nose. She lifted her head and laid it on his shoulder. "Thank you," she said. "But why am I so embarrassed?" She buried her head in her palms and cried again.

"You don't have to wear them. They're just a gift. Why the embarrassment?" he said soothingly, knowing fully the nature of her embarrassment.

After a while she asked if she could smoke. He gave her a cigarette and closed the door in case anyone should pop in. She didn't say a word until she finished it. She blew out the last smoke, putting out the cigarette in the ashtray. "I'm sorry, Sam. I was being dramatic, being stupid."

"No apology needed," he said, frustrated by the limited talent he had with words. But a force in him pushed him to say what was on his mind this time, talented or not. "You took it as charity, am I right? Well, you don't have to answer that. It's true that I feel sorry for you. If it offended you, so be it. We thought you could use some warm clothes." Then he saw she was smiling with her eyes, her nose pink from crying. "Now you are smiling. I'm totally confused."

"I can use warm clothes. You didn't offend me. Quite the opposite. I guess it's not a secret how little I mean to my family. I didn't realize until now how seriously I'm embarrassed about that. And frankly I was angry at myself for being embarrassed, can you understand that? I always believed that I wasn't bothered by it, but that's not true. I'm not being sarcastic. I thank you for being a kind, generous friend. Frankly, I used to get angry at myself whenever kindness touched me. I still have a lot of work to do on myself, which is a letdown, humbling, but still a letdown."

"Miri, you haven't told me why you're here. I understand if you don't want to tell me, but I would very much like to hear it from you," he said, remembering what Dr. Min told him after he came back from the city. They had talked about Miri's father; it was tasteless gossip they both took delight in. They were having a few drinks in the evening at his quarters. "One thing I'm deeply troubled by is that he believed Miri was an arsonist." The doctor shared the news as a friend not as a professional, which irked him from time to time.

"What? Arsonist? Is she? I mean, I can see that's not the—"

"No, that's not why she was sent here."

"Are you sure you interviewed the right father?" Sam said, lifting his upper body from the back of the wing chair, spilling his drink on his pants. Dr. Min told him the story of the taxidermy collection, which made them double up with laughter. But before the laughter died down, Dr. Min took a somber tone and said, "I don't think they want her back any time soon."

"Do you think her father might believe that to be true, the arson thing?"

"Quite possible. Her mother, obviously, concocted the story."

"Why would she do that?"

"I suspect, no, I am sure that she wants her to stay here as long as possible. You know, they don't get along, to put it mildly. She had to involve him to have it her way."

"You aren't going to tell me why she is here, though."

Dr. Min shook his head.

"I understand," Sam said, nodding his head. He then asked, "Why not tell her father the whole story?"

"I couldn't. You should have been there and seen him. Besides, I have to work it out with the mother first. If I told him, it would only be shaking the hornet's nest, and I would lose control. I have to think about the girl's welfare first."

"What are you going to do?"

"I don't know. Not yet."

That night Sam found himself saying "poor girl, poor girl" over and over under his breath. He didn't understand why, but the more he knew her, the more he wanted to take care of her. He wanted to save her!

He moved to a chair across from the sofa where she was sitting. She was looking out the window with her typical blank stare, showing her profile just like the first time he had seen her sitting at his writing desk on the day she stole his cigarettes. He wished her to stay that way for a while longer when she started to speak.

"Maybe there are better places somewhere out there for me, but so far this place happens to be the happiest place I've ever been to. My being here also works for my mother's happiness, which she deserves." She spoke with the voice of a mature woman, nothing like the crying girl a few moments ago. "But I can tell you how it happened if you want to hear it."

"I want to hear it."

She told him about her night ventures, her fainting, and the small run-in with her mother. And now she became obsolete, forgotten, a déjà vu to anyone she had known before. There were so many questions he wanted to ask, but he kept them inside. He couldn't dare.

- 6 2 -

It snowed for two days straight. The first snow of the year cheered up the people, patients and staff alike. Pretty soon this beautiful gift of nature would be blamed; there was too much of it. It caused bad traffic, wet, muddy roads...until the first snow of the next year.

After the snow, the weather got unusually warm and bright. The warm temperature erased any trace of snow on the ground. "If this weather continues, we might see spring flowers in the middle of winter," so said one of the three members of the argument club who shared the same dining table with Miri, a comment which met immediate opposition. And the ritual began.

"There'll be a hike in the afternoon. Are you up for it?" Miri asked Sam, who was sitting next to her pulling up his socks that kept sliding down. She looked down at his socks. Sam's fashion statement, Miri thought, was rather flamboyant. Unlike many men, especially middle-aged men, he had no problem showing up in colorfully printed or accessorized attire in public. He carried a leather purse in which were his fancy platinum cigarette case, a gold lighter, an alligator wallet, and a beautifully carved ivory case for his toothpicks. Miri never teased him about it but giggled behind his back now and then. "These socks have got to go," he said, frowning, noticing Miri's eyes paying attention to them. She smiled rascally. "What? That's a mean smile."

"Is it?"

"Yes, it is. I know it, and you know it. That's not a smile of admiration."

"Your socks, are those a man's?" she asked. His dark blue socks had orange flowers printed around the ankle. All of his socks had some kind of flowery design on them.

He gave her a side glance of annoyance.

"Sorry, but I'm a bit bored, and I decided to poke fun at your darling socks."

"They are rather nice, aren't they?" he said, lifting his foot to give her a better view.

"In the beginning when I met you, I thought you were secretly a cross-dresser."

"You must be really bored. You sound like you are out to emasculate me," he said pouting, but letting her know he didn't care one way or another. He added, "What changed your opinion?"

"Who said it did?" she said, laughing and clapping.

It was nice to see her like that, a spoiled high school girl acting silly.

"Now that it's out in the open, not to mention the humiliation you've showered me with, you owe me the history of your suspicion."

"Okay. Do you realize how loud your clothes are, from top to bottom? No man I know carries a purse like you or wears a gold chain around your neck. When I saw you for the first time in your regular clothes—remember that black chiffon blouse with large yellow orchids? And the—"

He stopped her by saying, "By the way, it's called a 'shirt,' not a blouse."

"Are you getting pissed?"

"A bit. It's not as much fun as I thought it would be."

Miri motioned as if she were zipping up her mouth. Then she said she really like the perfume he used.

"It's aftershave lotion, not perfume," he grumbled, crossing his arms.

One time she had a chance to peek inside of his closet. In it were a garden variety of colorful shirts. She thought she could smell a potpourri of flowers and perhaps even hear birds singing. Although she strongly disagreed with his sense of fashion, she looked at these clothes with affection.

"Are you done?"

"Yes, sir."

"It's my turn then."

"Be kind."

But he said instead, "Well, on second thought, I'll reserve the right to critique your fashion someday. It's not a fair game. You have to wear what is given to you to wear." He wondered if this came out diplomatically.

"I'll stay anxious for that someday. Better yet, I promise I'll let you know when I'm ready." She then thought to herself, what is someday? Someday was a blank page to her, opaque and flat. In such a blank place called "someday," where could she send a promise to wait for her?

- 6 3 -

"Sam, how come you never married?" Miri asked, walking a few feet in front of him during their afternoon group hike. It was a mild day for the winter month even though the crisp air felt freezing on the tip of nose.

"I just never did."

"Just like that?"

"Just like that." He caught up with her and said, "Have you noticed that you are into ordinary stuff today, unlike your usual abstract, atmospheric, and super egotistical stuff?"

"Am I?" she said, turning her head to him.

He gave her a look of shock.

"You're bleeding by your left eye." He grabbed her arm and was ready to go back down, but she pulled back and said, "It's nothing. I get this once in a while. It's a sty that popped, nothing to worry about. Actually, it feels good when it pops, gross, ha!"

"Are you sure?" He offered his handkerchief, concerned.

"Yes, I'm sure. Don't worry." She turned back to follow the group. By the time they reached the resting point, the bleeding had stopped, leaving her left eye puffy and red.

As always, Miri headed to her spot near the edge of the cliff where the large rock stood in a shape of an open palm as if to warn about the cliff ahead. The cliff dropped about thirty to forty feet easily and at the base of the cliff extended ocean of vegetation. On a good day one could see the silver of the sea waves behind the outline of the vegetation. Sam joined the circle of people gathering under a pine tree. They were talking about the rice man. "They moved him to the fifth floor," a woman said, shaking her head. Another woman volunteered to tell him what had happened. "For a while he was doing so well," the woman said, seeing everybody nodding their heads in agreement. Some days he had even been good enough to join the hike. The woman said, "I'm not sure how much of it is true. I heard it from someone who said that he showed up at the lounge the other night naked, covered with steamed rice. He approached the people there and ordered them to eat it. He was quickly removed and now I heard he is on the fifth floor."

"Oh, that's too bad." Sam expressed his sympathy but wasn't able to remember who he was. He looked up to see where Miri was standing, with her chin tucked in the collar of her coat. The wool coat in teal green that Mrs. Lim chose agreed with her. She looked like a sophisticated young lady. She was standing there talking to the rock, it seemed, occasionally pushing her hair from her forehead.

She spotted the blue satin coat tail behind the rock, gently waltzing to the breeze. "There you are!" she said, happy to see him again.

"Yes, here I am," he said, leaning his shoulder on the rock, looking pensive.

"What's the matter? I detect melancholy, am I right?"

"It's just the weather. I don't do well with the change of weather."

"It's not too cold today," she said, sensing the goat being evasive.

"We had some fun," he said, ignoring her weather comment, looking out at the horizon with narrowed eyes. Then he closed his eyes tightly as if he were trying to force himself to forget something.

"What is it? You act like a scolded child."

"Not scolded. Disappointed." He turned to her opening his eyes and spoke slowly. "I have to move on without you. Your ego stays with you. You turned out to be a wrong match. I received the test results from the ostrich man. Your performance at the 'house of meanwhile' showed startlingly different results from what I had expected. I was wrong…" He stopped her when she was about to speak.

"Listen, listen up. The following is the best explanation I can give, that is, in your language. Your world is built on buying and selling. Even the truth has its grade, price, and value. Morality, ethics, the Ten Commandments, the Gospels, mother's love, child's innocence, compassion, and on and on. These so-called truths in your world wear the appearance of truth to promote buying and selling. Truth is a solid package, both seen and unseen. You can't customize it. But your world is designed in such a way that a solid truth has no place in it. In order to obtain what I wanted from you, an earth person, I purchased a scheme that is understood easily in your world. Buying and selling. But the clever scheme that I thought it would be wouldn't work in this case." He was about to go on when she let out a single laugh that sounded like a metallic scraping.

"What's so funny?" he asked quizzically.

"Sorry, please take no offense. I wasn't laughing at what you were saying. Please go on, I beg you," she said politely but without being able to clear the laughter in her eyes.

"I'd like to know, tell me what was so funny?" he insisted, moving his head toward hers. She noticed that his large green eyes were rather dull, and there were no ripples of a flowing river like before.

"I laughed because what you said reminded me of something. I'd rather not say it, but I'll show you the image. Surely you can read from the image in my head, right?"

"No, I can't. You have to verbalize and describe as you do with people, except, as you know, do it in your head."

"Oh, I see. Well, what you said made me remember something I saw or I thought I had seen. It was from this fashion show I watched on TV. The beautiful models were walking on the catwalk one after another, arrogantly, and probably marveling in the belief that everyone who was watching them would be drooling over their beauty. No one walking on the catwalk smiled, as if a smile were an ugly thing to wear. Anyway I saw, or thought I saw, through their bodies to their intestines and the stuff in them, in their bowels. That's why I laughed. I don't know why, but when you said 'the truth is a solid package, seen and unseen,' the scene I mentioned popped in my head."

"Rrriightt," he said, dragging the word, annoyed, "and people still drool over their beauty. Therefore, perfecting hypocrisy is the right thing to do, rather than opening up the box of truth. I get it."

"But please continue what you were saying."

"Forget it. I lost my train of thought. I'm pressed with time too. So I'll sum it up," he said, adjusting his coat. "You never had the intention of passing it on to me to begin with." He turned to the view of the horizon as if he were tired of her.

She blinked rapidly, thinking but unable to catch what she was thinking about. After a few moments of drilling her head in silence, she started feeling odd about the anxiety growing in her at the same time,

"How can I have such an intention? This is a dream, a hallucination…I mean, I couldn't discount that possibility. You are a phenomenon that my mind manufactured." Pell-mell speech flew out from her head, surprising her more than anything. She couldn't recall when she had ever separated the activities of her mind from reality. All she knew was that she didn't want him to leave her even though he might only be a figment of the play thing in her mind. This figment, possibly her own creation, was hurting her feelings by telling her that she was of no use to him.

"Ha, ha, ha. Ah, the alter ego thingy. Oh, please. So you're saying that I am your creation?" He laughed pejoratively and continued. "Listen, I have no interest whatsoever in relationships, fantasy or not. To me it is all about, as you people say, business, and I must say you won."

"Okay, alright. Can you at least give me the courtesy of telling me what happened?"

"Fair enough. I'll give you the courtesy. Your ego is a part of your spiritual repository. I had misread it as innocence, dumb, and lazy but with independent innocence. I was wrong. It is unreachable for me. How you unlocked the door of the house of meanwhile proved it."

"But you wrote in my journal—"

"Hush, let me finish. I don't have much time left," he hissed rudely. "When I read in your journal that you prayed repeatedly at that desperate moment, I thought it was a natural human response, a response of the ego, a pure will to survive. But when the ostrich man reported your test results, I was disappointed to learn that it wasn't your ego that opened the door. It was the spirit of yours who did the work. You weren't supposed to see the old lady in the 'house of meanwhile' as a symbol of compassion. You were scared to death in there, but all your cries and screams originated largely from feeling sorry for everyone, not only for the old lady but for every creature you encountered."

"I don't recall feeling such an emotion. I was too scared, too frightened to feel anything else."

"But you did. You let your spirit take over. And guess who was taking a ride on the spirit! Your ego! What a surprise! You might not remember, but you let your heart open widely. You, to my disappointment, learned the true nature of compassion, which formed a covalent bond between the spirit and the ego. As you know now, having become the owner of this knowledge, compassion lives off hurt, pain, tears, and misery. It also keeps the parasites flourishing."

This time it was Miri who looked out at the horizon, vaguely listening to him, simmering in thoughts, thoughts that had no attached images. Finally, she interrupted the goat. "That is sufficient, Mr. Goat. I no longer want to understand you. Whatever you are saying with such an air of authority is just words. You or anyone can't distort what I saw, what I experienced. And you don't possess the answers for me anymore. It's obvious that you don't know what you're saying or doing. No, I'm not angry. But I won't listen to you until you tell me the truth. I can sense that you're hiding something. Actually, don't bother, I don't have to know."

He stepped into the air with his arms behind him, then turned his heels to face her, lifted his chin, and was about to say something. He hesitated at the sudden sound of cheering and clapping from the hikers. She turned to the group, some sitting on the rocks and some standing, waiting for Hakyu to sing. She hadn't seen him earlier in the group. He was wearing a red wool hat and oversized grey overcoat. He clasped his hands on his chest and started, "Oh mio babbino caro..." in falsetto. Anyone with their eyes closed would've believed it was a female voice. "What a beautiful gift he has..." Humming words of admiration and the warm affection of fellowship weaved throughout the tune, like butterflies in slow motion on a warm spring day, reigning over a moment of stillness, giving gentle permission to forget and to forgive. She turned her eyes to the goat. He was watching the singer intensely. It appeared that the river in his green eyes was flowing again.

- 6 4 -

I t snowed almost endlessly through early December. A tall Christmas tree was up in the lounge where Christmas carols played constantly. One snowy day Miri was chatting with Hakyu in her room about his skin problem, for there was an eruption of painful-looking pimples on his face. "Don't they have something to clear them?" Miri asked when he complained about the pain they caused, especially when he sang and tried to hit higher notes. "I'm sorry, but I have to laugh," she said, covering her mouth with one hand to be modest. He started to laugh too, even while protesting that she was rude. Then he said that laughing hurt the area with pimples just as badly, which made them go on laughing.

"Some might pop if I laugh harder."

"Give it a try. I'd like to see."

Then he lowered his voice almost to the level of a whisper and looked around to see if anyone was nearby. He said, "Sis, is it true that…that frequent masturbation, you know, cures acne?"

"Where did you hear that?"

"Oh, from here and there."

"I've never heard about it, but it wouldn't hurt to try, would it?"

"I'd give it a go if I had a private room like you. That fart who I share the room with complains a lot about me already."

"We got to figure out where you could…" Seeing a gross grin spreading across his face, she quickly said, "Don't even dream about it! Not in my room!"

A nurse came in and informed her that she had a visitor waiting in the lounge.

"Who is it?"

"I don't know. I just got a call from downstairs," she said, leaving the door.

The last person she would have expected to visit her was waiting for her. It was Father Mark. He was standing in the middle of the lounge awkwardly with flakes of snow on his hat and the shoulders of his long, black coat. They shook hands.

"How have you been?"

"How…why…" She could not think of anything proper to say.

"Is there any place we could talk quietly?" he asked, removing his hat.

"We can talk in there," she said, pointing and leading him to the music room.

"Wait, wait. I have to tell someone where I'll be. Do you remember Father Gregory? He's here with me, and what do you know, he ran into a man he used to know a long time ago. They're in the dining room."

The man was Sam. He and Father Gregory were holding hands as if their four hands were tied together. It seemed to be a joyous reunion. What's happening today? Why is it so weird? she thought, squinting her eyes toward the table where the two men were massaging each other's hands. Father Mark walked over to them, and Sam jerked his head in surprise seeing Miri standing near the door in surprise and waved at her. She waved back, feeling her heart pounding.

- 6 5 -

"Would you like something warm to drink? They have all kinds of winter tea," Miri asked Father Mark when he returned.

"A piping hot cup of coffee would be nice." Miri poured two cups of coffee and led Father Mark to the music room.

They sat together on the sofa facing the fireplace with burning wood. The room was dimly lit as always, but she could tell there was no one but them. "Had I known you were here...I only found out right before your grandma's passing," Father Mark said apologetically, bringing the cup of coffee to his lips.

"She what? She died?"

Father Mark sat up and turned to her looking absolutely puzzled.

"You didn't know?" he said, lifting his eyes and deepening the line between his brows, shaking his head from side to side in disbelief of Miri's ignorance of the fact. Her eyes stayed on his, looking through him. A gush of tears flooded her cheeks and landed on her lap. She wiped her face with the bottom of her shirt.

"When, when did she go?" she managed to ask, with her rounded shoulders heaving.

"About ten days ago. I'm so sorry. You knew she suffered from hardening arteries." After a long while, her crying became less violent, but she moaned like a wounded beast. "I didn't know until the very end. I hadn't seen her at church for a while, for a month or so. When I ran into your mother one day, I asked about your grandmother, and she told me that she was under the weather. 'Because of her age, it will take longer for her to fully recover,' was what she said. About two weeks after, the nurse who was taking care of your grandma came to see me and told me she was gravely ill, but she refused to go to the hospital. I guess she knew that her time was near and wished to die at home. I heard that she had to stay sitting up on a chair day and night because she couldn't breathe lying down. The nurse told me that she asked for me to hear her last confession. I went to see her right away. She was very weak, but her mind was still crisp. Before anything else, she told me about you. She was so worried about you. It seemed as though she was delaying her death until she found someone who would help you. I gave her my promise that I'd do my best to help you. She passed away a few days after my visit."

So Father Mark had come to see Miri not only to keep his promise to the old lady, but he wanted, personally, to see the lugubrious girl who had come to see him on that cold winter afternoon. He had forgotten about her. But when he finally remembered her, he remembered everything of that afternoon with her, of what they talked about, how lugubrious she seemed, how at times she scared him, and later how the talk they shared stirred his mind. At that time he was troubled with his faith in relation to the Church, and once again he was thinking about leaving it. And once again Father Gregory told him, "It's my church too, nothing will remove me. The Vatican isn't the enemy; it's just architecture to me. A long time ago I read Fyodor Dostoyevsky's *Demons* in which a man said 'the Vatican was the Antichrist, the kingdom the devil conjured to try to seduce Jesus during his forty days in the desert.' It troubled me a great deal. I must say I was upset. Much later I realized the source of my trouble was fear. I feared that part of me agreed with this man's argument that the Vatican was the Antichrist. But Jesus taught us the order of spirituality, not the order of society. His words are simple, but in truth they are metaphors that could be explained in many ways, perhaps as many as there are people. He showed his way of faith in the most courageous way. We'd like to follow in his footsteps, but what he tried to teach us was that one should know his own faith and sit with it firmly and courageously. It demands free thinking, which can be bitterly painful, and it should be done without prejudice. You have to give an equal voice to everything from 'good' to 'bad.' You'll see many perfidious elements, but they give meaning to our suffering. Leaving the Church wouldn't change anything. That's nothing but a form of aggression. Why blame anything when it's a matter between you and your personal God? What does anything else got to do with it? Why let anything irritate your faith in God?"

Father Mark sat quietly next to Miri, who was blankly staring at the burning wood in the fireplace. Her face was red and shiny from tears. The sound of popping wood and the occasional hiccups from her throat were the only things that seemed to be alive in this immobile time.

Time moved again when they heard the door open. Father Gregory and Sam walked in. Miri got up and moved to a darker corner of the room. Sam was about to follow her, but Father Mark pulled his sleeve to stop him. He whispered to them, "She didn't know of her grandma's passing. I didn't know she didn't know."

They joined Father Mark on the sofa. Sam kept looking at the dark corner where she was sitting alone.

"Did you two catch up a little? What a tremendous coincidence!" Father Mark said quietly.

"Indeed. In spite of the bad weather, something in me couldn't refuse your offer to come with you," Father Gregory said, facing the same direction as Sam, his large eyes sad and concerned.

- 66 -

"Have you ever gone back there?" Father Gregory asked Sam while sitting in the dining room.

"I go there regularly. The place has become a part of my life ever since."

"Are they still there? The old monk and the boy."

"Believe it or not, the old man is still there, frail and carrying a cane but sharp as ever. I always called him an old monk, but I have no idea how old he is. He could be younger than he has led me to believe or over a hundred years old, ha, ha. The boy is another story. He's a grown-up, nice-looking young man but in physical appearance only. He has some kind of 'phrenia.' His mind stopped growing. He remained as a bright six-year-old in a twenty-five-year-old young man's body. Have you been in Seoul all this time?" Sam said.

"Mostly. After I left the temple, which was sometime after the war. I couldn't move in haste. As you know, I don't blend in with the population. I had to make sure this alien face would be accepted. Oh, how much I owe you and those two. And I've never gone back to the temple."

Sam didn't ask why. The old monk had once said to Sam that Father Gregory had serious issues regarding his faith by the time he left the temple. In the end the old monk had to persuade him to go back to where he came from. Father Gregory had doubts about the God he chose to devote his life to.

One day near his departure, he had a heart-to-heart talk with Bongsan.

"My god seems to be angry and even violent. But your god is peaceful, warm, understanding, free of judgment. Most of all, his teaching is to ease the pain and suffering whereas mine glorifies it."

"Buddha isn't a god. He's a human being who became a sign pointing to enlightenment. Every one of us has Buddha consciousness. We are all in the making of Buddha," the old monk said to Father Gregory.

"I'm drawn to your god, I mean, Buddha consciousness, and I find myself utterly torn. I don't think I can face my god the way I used to."

"Yes, you can, and you will. As I said, Buddhism is not a god-worshipping religion. Although I must say, there's too much corruption in our world of Buddhism too. When a religion becomes a business, the leaders modify the original teaching to suit the needs of their customers. People are short-sighted. They need to believe that the supernatural power is working for them to improve their immediate worldly concerns. Any religious group you pick, you'll find them offering this supernatural quality one way or another to stay in business, so to speak. Having said that, religious practice is a habit that becomes a part of one's skin, meaning once a Christian, always a Christian. You might decide to be a Buddhist monk like me, but you would find yourself making the sign of the cross in a desperate situation. It's like superstition. You break a mirror, and you fear seven years of bad luck. That's why you are torn and agonizing."

"I see your point. I'm a Catholic priest who follows the teaching of the Church word by word. In olden times, my telling you about my doubt would be a sin deserving of death on a stake. My head tells me how ridiculous that is, but I childishly struggle with the fear of hell all the same. I'm a simple man, always have been. Something plucked me out of the pool of simpletons, and now I find myself bewildered in a desert. I'm afraid I can't put my faith in catechism as blindly as before, so I don't know what kind of priest I'm going to be."

"I don't see the problem. As I said, everybody has a Buddha consciousness including you, a Catholic priest, and some shaman who believes that he will fly like a bird someday. Once you drop that rigid idea of 'one belief and one belief only,' you will be free from your trouble."

"It won't be that simple."

"It's lots of work, of course. If I can advise you, the first thing you should work on is to be critical about what you've learned about God. And this criticism should be made by the human that you are, the human who you love. Others' interpretations you've learned to believe to be the words of God have to be examined one by one. Have the conviction that you will find a God of your own. Be more gracious of the freedom God gave you. You're not a simple man. You chose to be simple to avoid thinking, to avoid the fear of facing insecurity. Do think, enjoy thinking; it's calling you to pay attention. The more you learn about yourself, of body as well as mind, the more you'll understand who God is to you, not who you are to God."

"Knowing God is tied to knowing myself?"

"It's the same thing. Buddha said to people when they asked him to teach, 'It's not teachable, I can only show you the way,' meaning that you have to sit with your thoughts, let them brew and simmer until they become quiet. You hold all the answers within yourself. I think there was one mistake Jesus made. He used social metaphors in attempt to explain the unexplainable, which gave room for his good words to be distorted and misused."

"Are you familiar with Christian teaching?"

"I read the Bible; as a matter of fact, I still own a copy. It seems man made. But I also found parts that revealed Buddha consciousness that were deeply moving. But Christian teaching is not consistent in my opinion. 'Love your enemy,' Jesus said. But then he also said, 'The wicked will be thrown into the eternal burning hell.' Also he didn't describe how one goes about loving his enemy, how to forgive, what is love and forgiveness. Isn't it the most difficult thing to understand? He didn't mention that. He just said 'do it' or else. As I said before, parts of his words seemed distorted and manipulated by the hands of others. You see such a thing in every organized religion. But he moved me. I do like him. One thing I'm puzzled about is the death of Jesus. Why did he do that?"

"He died for our sins; it's in the Scriptures."

"What I'm saying is doesn't that make you question? Simple-minded or not, I highly doubt that you believe everything written in the Scriptures is what he truly said and did. Don't you find some of it is too out of Jesus's character? After all, weren't they written by human hands?"

"They were written during the age of the Emperor Constantine after he converted to Christianity."

"When was this?"

"In the fourth century AD"

"During the Japanese occupation, we were forced to speak Japanese only, to change our names to Japanese names, as you are well aware, and they tried to convert people's religion to Shintoism, their national religion. It wasn't very successful, but the intention of this attempt was clear. Putting people under the same roof of worship and language is one way to control them. This Roman emperor understood, it seems, that side of human psychology."

"If you told me to go back to my god, then why all this criticism? You're confusing me. Well, frankly, you're succeeding in making me feel like a fool."

"Let me ask you something. You mentioned the unsavory, insincere, hypocritical elements existing in all religions including yours. So why?"

"Why am I here, in this monk's robe? Just like you are where you are, that's all. It is what it is. We are both stuck in our personal imagination, ha, ha. But tell me, you said I made you feel like a fool, but isn't it because you were already feeling foolish yourself on your own? Aren't you actually defending your foolishness of a private nature by blaming me to be the cause of your discomfort? I'm telling you this to point out how one refuses to see what truly lies in them. You couldn't perceive the fact that I respect your imaginary God, although I don't share your loyalty to him."

"Imaginary God?" Father Gregory was getting offended.

"Mine, yours, and everybody else's. Two devout Christians wouldn't have the same idea of the supposedly same God they worship. They are more likely a universe apart. Isn't it the true nature of us, keeping one's God close to your heart? No one shares their God with others. And I think that you misunderstood my meaning of 'imaginary God.' Imagination is one of the most powerful entities we carry, in my opinion, but it is very real. In it one can do the most impossible things. But we don't know anything about our imagination. Is it from the body, spirit, or soul or something totally else? And it's always there in us. One can't turn it on and off at will. This is what Jesus meant by saying God is omnipresent. 'Imaginary God' doesn't mean He's not real. God is as real as the imagination."

"That's too hard for me to fathom, almost bizarre," Father Gregory said, feeling strong resistance emerging, fighting its way to express itself against a brand new force that desired to understand, honestly and courageously. He murmured under his breath, "I feel so defeated."

The monk heard it and said almost mockingly, "How could you be defeated when no one claimed victory? Look, we can talk and talk until our tongues break apart about things we know nothing about. That's the truth, that we know nothing, is it not?

"Creatures like you and I are hopelessly in love with the mystery, knowing fully that the possibility of unveiling it, even a tiny bit of it, is an impossible thing. Then why? Why are we the way we are? The only answer I can give myself is that this is what I do, like birds fly and fish swim. We only feel right taking this path along the mystery called faith. Who knows, we might be comedians created to entertain the Creator. So here I am telling you this and that, committing a sin by hurting you. Oh, what do I know about God, or the spirit, or the soul, or nirvana, or anything at all?"

"Life was simple until I came here. It will never be the same."

"Life, if it is alive, should never stay the same," he said and laughed, slapping his knees.

Father Gregory, who wasn't a young man himself, felt green behind the ears. But something took him over entirely at that moment. The old monk's hearty, almost obnoxious laughter echoing through the valley and the hills in front of him perhaps cracked open something in him. He began to laugh himself, looking down at his feet in miserable-looking shoes made of straw, woven by the man sitting next to him who was laughing his heart out. Giggles with a slight shaking of the shoulders became a full-blown Irish style (if there was such thing) belly laugh. It lasted for a while. It was as if they had seen a great monster that momentarily scared them to death suddenly shrink down to a cute, tiny creature right in front of their eyes. "Isn't being nothing blissful?" the old monk said, still laughing.

- 67 -

While Father Mark was talking quietly with Father Gregory, Sam got up and walked over to Miri in the dark corner, taking out a handkerchief from his pocket. He stood behind her and gently squeezed her shoulder, offering her the handkerchief. She turned her head without looking at him but took the handkerchief. He went around the sofa and sat next to her.

"Would you rather be alone?"

"Yes, I'll find you when I'm ready. Thank you." She returned the handkerchief after dabbing the tears from her eyes. Reluctantly, he got up, squeezed her shoulder one more time, and returned to the priests.

Father Mark then got up and asked the two men to leave him alone with Miri. Her grandmother hadn't told him why Miri was there. She had simply said that her parents sent her to this place. A situation like that made him embarrassed of his black suit and the white collar around his neck indicating that he was the man of answers, a man of calling, a man who would lead them to a safe, comforting place. He tried hard, and that was all he could hold on to—trying his hardest.

Miri's face was red and shiny, her hair disheveled. She sat on the far end of the sofa and combed her hair with her fingers, blankly gazing at the fire while breathing through her mouth. She turned to Father Mark, who was sitting up and facing her, showing all his willingness and readiness for her.

"How come they didn't tell you?" he asked.

"We don't communicate at all. Not them, not me."

"Not at all?"

"Not once since I've come here.

"Why are you here?" He didn't want to beat around the bush.

She told him of her quarrel with her mother over her night walking.

"To tell you the truth, this is the best thing they've ever done for me."

"I thought you looked surprisingly well." When he saw her in the lounge, he thought she looked her age, not like a thousand-year-old girl as when he had met her in his office that winter day.

"This might sound thoughtless, but do you have any plans?"

"It'll come when it comes. I spend my time here thinking. I think a lot, which I couldn't do as much as I wanted to before I came here. Here I have time to get acquainted with my thoughts." Her voice was hoarse, but she wasn't crying anymore. There was a certain firmness in her attitude as if she had tied a knot of broken strings.

He noticed this "I'll go on" attitude, which gave him a bit of relief. He decided to be bold and direct, not knowing when the next chance of sitting and talking with her would come again. "Don't you think that your night walking would be alarming behavior to others?"

"People go hiking all the time. I happened to like it at night. It was a valuable time for me. Up there at night, I felt glad just being me, all of me. There was no good or bad; being me was sufficient. That feeling readjusted something in me that would get warped a bit during the day."

"Did you feel a presence when you were up there? I promise you that I'm not asking as a priest, I promise. You can say I am selfishly curious."

She turned her face toward him, frowning and smiling at the same time.

"You mean, a ghost?"

"No, not necessarily. Just a presence, a feeling that you are not alone."

"Unfortunately, that didn't happen."

"Were you expecting or looking for such phenomena?"

"No, but I must admit that would've been something."

"Have you always been like that, not easily getting scared?"

"I'm scared of people. Perhaps the word 'scared' isn't quite right. I should say I 'fear' instead." She let out a deep sigh, blowing through her mouth. "Come to think of it, I've never heard myself saying that I fear people."

"Oh, Lord, I share that fear. People make me anxious, and I do fear them sometime, although unlike you, I'm scared of other things. This might make you laugh, but I'm scared of being alone in the church." He laughed, and seeing her laugh along he continued, "Maybe we have a similar reason why we fear people." A part of him didn't feel right carrying on this talk, but another part of him that was glad that she was talking not crying was more forceful.

"I don't know if I can describe my fear for people accurately. People behave according to society's manual of dos and don'ts or right and wrong. Some people are comfortable with such guidance like trained animals, but many have to battle with the don'ts and wrongs in private. But it seems that many are unable to keep their feelings completely locked away, and they unleash them because they're too overwhelming or feel really good. They skillfully pick safe victims and inject venom in them; watching them suffer relieves their own suffering. The victims learn this behavior, and the chain reaction begins."

"Are you a victim?"

"Both, I think. Both a perpetrator and victim, just like most of us. Isn't everyone to a degree?"

"But people in general don't examine themselves that deeply. People tend to see themselves as either weak or strong."

"I fear people, and I wrestle with the anxiety of facing them. Family, teachers, neighbors, classmates...they come in all different colors and shapes in terms of the poison in them. Oh, Father Mark, I don't know what I'm talking about now. I'm exhausted, and right now nothing I think or say makes any sense." Father Mark closed his eyes and nodded when she spoke again. "Where do I go after here? What do I do when I'm ready to leave here?

The things I took for granted, having a home to go back to, food and shelter mainly, things I believed to be my right, all of a sudden, it seems that I don't have the right to them at all. I'm a bit ashamed to have believed that I hold such rights over people who'd rather erase me from their lives."

"That sounds like the exhaustion talking. Of course, you have a home to go back to; you'll continue your education and plan a sound future ahead."

"Funny, though, I do like life. I like myself, I always have. It defies my own theory. I always trusted naively that I have a right to my life. I was wrong. I don't own that right, it was never there. But I like life. I want to go on living." She was mumbling at this point, talking to herself. Her eyes were wide but blank.

Finally, when she stopped, Father Mark said, "Of course, you have the right. You are a strong person. Don't you give up that right of being you. You owe it to yourself."

"Everything is changing rapidly, too rapidly. I see my right, whatever it is, flying out of me."

"Nonsense. Give it time, and you'll see that it never left you. It will turn up stronger and wiser. It seems that you need to allow for your right to be selfish." Whenever he had to comfort people who were in despair but found himself lacking in proper words, he simply, but not without shame, asked them to pray with him. That always offered a safe exit. This made him feel guilty, but Father Gregory had given him permission. He said, "It's a better choice to feel guilty than lie to them, giving them false hope, telling them things we don't even know to be true. Listen to them quietly so that they can hear their own voice, and wrap it up with a nice prayer. Your problem is that you somehow believe you have a God-given gift that enables you to fix things. Come down from that arrogance, and try to be their neighbor, a fellow passenger sharing a seat on a bus. Be a sincere listener, but drop the idea that you have to be the main tool to fix their problems."

She rambled away as if he weren't there. He let her go on without interruption. She was talking about her grandmother without tears but with great emotion. How her grandmother carried her as an infant to one nursemaid after another when her mother disappeared, often for a whole day without feeding her. How she had to watch her mother when Miri was alone with her from the day she found the infant lying alone, her head covered with a blanket, struggling for air.

Father Mark vaguely remembered hearing such rumors. It was, if his memory was correct, on Easter. The bishop held Easter Mass, and a fancy lunch for a large group of people was to follow. As usual, on such occasions, Miri's mother made herself a leader of the event, making a fuss, correcting, criticizing, and ordering nuns, annoying the heck out of them. After the event, an elderly nun who had to endure Miri's mother for years couldn't keep inside the accumulated frustration and called her a hypocrite of the worst kind. And she happened to mention the above story of Miri's birth and traumatic infancy. "If it weren't for your mother-in-law, the child could've been murdered." Her fellow nuns and the staff stopped and hushed her.

He heard the door open quietly and saw Sam coming in. He walked towards them, trying to be soundless. He sensed that his presence should have been minimal and stood behind the sofa like a shadow. Miri kept talking to herself without noticing him. "I was a boy. I was dressed as a boy for a few years. You know, those country folks dress their girls believing that will increase the chance of having a boy the next time. I didn't enjoy that. I didn't enjoy having a boy's haircut done at the barber shop. Where was my father? Who knows? I had never seen him until I was three or four. I didn't like the look of him. And that was that. That first impression saved me from expecting him to be like other fathers in the neighborhood who picked up their children by the underarms and swung them around, making them shriek with delight. I watched them, but I didn't envy them. I only wondered how it felt. Certain criticisms in the neighborhood about my mother's unmotherly behavior reached her ears. It was a scary day. She cornered me in a dark room and pinched me black and blue, hissing at me, accusing me of going around and spreading lies about her. But after that day, she became more attentive to me."

It was clear to Father Mark that she wasn't aware of him, and for that matter, anything around at all. It was a dry narration; it was a stream of incoherent thoughts voicing itself, a soliloquy of self-pity that had been thirsty for her attention. He couldn't ignore the feeling that she was searching through self-pity, and it was this searching to which his attention was directed. Father Gregory's words that "it's arrogance that makes you believe you should be able to fix others' problem" were ringing in his head, but this time he felt the urge was too strong to avoid participation.

"...I wonder, I wonder to this day how you had been a funny child." He went back to her narration, noticing that she was addressing herself in the second person. "What did you get out of making people laugh at that young age? I remember you dancing like a monkey wearing green-striped long johns to the music from the radio in the evening, making people laugh, enjoying it yourself. Who were you? Did you feel that they were happy with you for that moment? Or was it you and your inarticulate pain inside acting out? You still do show that side of you from time to time, clowning around silly. Was it the form of payment to survive? Paying your dues? No. No, you didn't do that to make them happy, I know it, because you never expected to collect anything from them, although I can't help but suspect that your acts were emotional panhandling from time to time. One's sense of dignity comes with your birth. You adore dignity more than anything. We don't bow unless our dignity allows it. We don't."

Her lips were parched, and she kept wetting them with her tongue.

Almost in a whisper, Father Mark asked if she would like some water. When she turned to him, he saw two clear, sane eyes looking into his. Sam, who was standing behind her, said also in a whisper, "I'll get it. Would you like something to drink, Father Mark?"

"I'd like some more coffee, black, if it's not too much trouble. Where's Father Gregory?" he asked, seeing Sam already heading toward the door. He turned and said that Father Gregory was in his room watching TV.

The fire was dying down. Father Mark got up and added a couple of logs. He returned to his seat and saw her leaning back on the sofa, looking more relaxed. She clasped her hands behind her head, gazing at the fire, and started to speak. She was back. "Father Mark, I want to be able to face all the misery coming my way as my friends. I'll take up residence in this world among these friends."

Is this determination of some kind? An epiphany? Wisdom from anger? Or a plan for masochistic revenge? These words are too equivocal, he thought.

"Do you have God in this residence?" he asked with a sinking sensation in his heart, regretting his hastiness. His selfishness wanted to compare notes with her.

"Yes, there is a God who is funny, sad, full of mistakes, nonsense, and even weakness at times, but whose intention is always kind and gentle." She showed a sheepish smile when saying this.

"Do you feel love for this god?" he asked unable to disguise the enthusiasm hearing the door open. Sam came in with a tray in his hands.

"Yes, I do. How can you not?"

How purely simple and beautiful, he thought, watching Sam putting down the tray on the table in front of the sofa. Sam said quietly, "Please don't mind me," handing her a glass of water and a cup of coffee to Father Mark. He took the cup thanking him mostly with his eyes. This time Sam didn't leave but sat on a chair next to Father Mark with his cup of coffee. Father Mark took a sip of black coffee that tasted sweet to his stale mouth. She finished the water in one go. Father Mark was a little concerned that Sam's presence might break the trail of their conversation. She must be very comfortable with him, he thought when he realized the trail wasn't broken. She continued, "You've asked me if I felt a presence. Actually I do."

"Up in the mountain?"

"Everywhere, actually. I mean I feel someone kind and gentle is with me even now. I feel love for this presence, a god if you will, but I feel sad for the presence. My god is perhaps sad and depressed. I don't have a heart to ask him to help me, protect me. It seems as though he is asking me to help him."

"What would you say if I ask you to describe the relationship between you and the god?" The question came from the curiosity not from a concern.

"Constant companionship."

"Has being raised as Catholic played any part in it?" he asked feeling a bit embarrassed for his curiosity that stepped in front of his righteous role.

"That, I don't know. I'd never liked going to church. It reminded me of the dark public bathhouse, naked people dripping water from their hair, squatting here and there exfoliating their skin. But I think I told you at the time I visited you that I like Jesus. So maybe I am influenced by my religious upbringing no matter what."

"What do you like about him?" He was sure that she told him about her opinion of Jesus, but he forgot what that was. But she answered without embracing his ill-behaving memory.

"It is just a feeling. I feel sorry for him and that feeling makes me want to be closer to him. He tried to teach the un-teachable, and I think I can share such helplessness. Sometimes I wish I could hold his hand and tell him that I won't ever leave him."

Father Mark had many questions about her god, or her constant companion, but he knew better. He was there to lend her his hand, but his mind was stuck in childish and selfish desperation of wanting to match her god with his. But she continued as if she had read his mind.

"How does one know whom he is serving? How does anyone know that? Your god, my god, either they are the same one or not, does it matter? One chooses to believe his god to be almighty who possesses the supreme power of shutting down the sun if he wants to, but the other sees his god who needs help and wishes to assist him through the faith. There is a mythology of creation that I like. It says that God created humans to garden his world. We are his gardeners according to the mythology. I thought that was lovely. After all whether one belongs to a church or not, it is an affair of the hearts. One who wonders can never deny that at the end of the day."

"I agree. We tend to form a group being an insecure animal who is petrified of standing alone, but each one of them, in fact, carries an individual affair of the heart with the god. And they, at the same time, fear anyone who could stand alone."

At this point Father Mark felt something changing places, one rising up and the other going down finding a balance. "I must confess that I am embarrassed as a man of the cloth. I came here with an idea that I would be useful to you, but I am sitting here totally being useless." He let out an apologetic laugh or two.

"Please don't say that. You came here to see me, to help me, and I am deeply touched. Isn't that what really counts? I am sorry if I sound patronizing. I mean what I said. Please don't take it the wrong way," she said, throwing a glance at Sam who was sitting on the chair watching them like an audience who was deeply involved with the show. Miri smiled at him with affection. The thought of her grandmother's passing stuck in her throat for a moment, but she didn't want to go there. She wanted to give her grieving a solemn respect in solitude. "Did you know my grandma never touched the phone in her life? It frightened her so. No radio, no TV, and no phone. She couldn't read or write either. Sometime I wrote letters for her to her relatives in the country. I giggled when writing down what she was dictating, full of country dialects and primitive expressions."

Sam cleared his throat to draw attention to him said, "How about I order the chef to cook something for us and we dine together in my room?"

"Thank you. It is tempting, but we should head out," Father Mark said, laying his clasped hands on his knees.

"I don't think you can make it back today. The weather turned nasty. I already talked to Father Gregory about staying for the night earlier, and he was willing if you are. But now the weather has gotten much worse. I don't think there is any transportation available either."

"If there is a room available for us here…"

"I've taken care of that. So Chinese like last time, Miri?"

- 6 8 -

D r. Min was scheduled to be in the city that evening but was stranded on
the island due to the weather, so he gladly joined the dinner in Sam's
room. Miri left right after the meal for her room to rest. Four men sat around
drinking and chatting about this and that through the night. The darkness
covered the monstrous snowfall, but it was coming down with such force
that it hissed and occasionally made the windowpanes tremor as if it was
desperately looking for a way to come inside.

"What weather!" Father Gregory said, looking out the glass door with a
glass of brandy in one hand and a cigar in the other. Dr. Min carefully asked
Father Mark what kind of ties he had with Miri's family. "My ties with them
are, were, mainly through her grandmother. Ever since I was posted at my
church, she took a liking to me and brought me sweets she baked. Other
than that, the family has been the main support for the church."

Dr. Min had already been informed by Sam of her grandma's death. "No
one in her family told her," Sam had told him when he invited him to dinner
on the phone.

Dr. Min sensed that Father Mark was not so keen about the rest of the family. His mind was playing ping-pong with some questions he had about Miri's family. "Ping" told him to go for it, but "pong" reminded him of his past experiences with clergymen, that they were trained or brainwashed to believe their own lies, like his own father. In the end, the few drinks he had supported the "ping." By engaging the priest in mundane talk, he was able to form a basic opinion in his alcohol-soaked mind about Father Mark. The guard he put up was dissolving, and he already liked Father Gregory. But it was Father Mark, after all, who started to talk about Miri's problem.

"Dr. Min, please allow me to ask you to help me understand a few things about Miri. I know you are bound by professional ethics."

"The patient comes first. Please feel free. I myself want to hear what you can share," he said, seeing Sam moving his seat closer to them from the corner of his eyes.

"Father Mark has a psychology degree," Sam joined in, smiling while slightly facing the priest. "Oh, Father Gregory mentioned it."

"It's not anything more than reading a few books," Father Mark said, sending a look of disapproval to Father Gregory, who was still standing by the glass door looking out at the dark, snowy night.

"Is there something in her clinically wrong?" Father Mark started.

"Not until 'free thinking' makes its way into the Diagnostic and Statistical Manual of Mental Disorders, the DSM."

"When I first saw her today, she looked so different from a year ago. She looked her age, young and even happy. I should be happy for her but am dreadfully concerned that this place agrees with her too much."

"She's not on any medication, if that's what you are implying.

"Not at all. Forgive me if I gave you such an impression. What I meant to say is that she looked blossoming, in tune with life. And I know no drugs can induce that."

"Can you tell me your observations from when you had seen her before?"

"Oh, I knew she was a high school girl, but there was something so old about her. I mean, at times she spoke as if she were a thousand years old. Honestly, she managed to drag out the blasphemies in me against my church, my personal dilemma regarding God and faith, which startled me."

A big voice near the glass door roared with a laugh and said, "Startled? You were frightened. Remember you came to see me all upset? Remember? Well, I do, drunk or not." Father Gregory continued quietly, as if chewing his words with a closed mouth.

Father Mark flat-out ignored him. "I don't know if I am making any sense here, but she appeared to be more than one person in one sitting," he explained, looking at his drink blinking in search for words.

"I've noticed that myself, that she has an old woman in her," Sam interjected. "But I also noticed that there is a side of her so infantile, innocent, and rascally and mean too."

"Sam here is like her shadow," Dr. Min said, extending his index finger to him. He chuckled and added, "In the beginning I was a bit concerned when you two became friends rapidly."

"You thought I was a dirty old man, is that what you are saying?" Sam raised his voice bending over towards Dr. Min.

"Well, yes! Not anymore, though. It's my job to consider every aspect for my patient, isn't it?" Clearly they were tipsy, but the chumminess between them made Father Mark feel he was with the warmth of human beings. Father Gregory had briefly told him about Sam. But he kept the information that Sam was an inmate at the hospital, which Sam had shared with him in the dining room, to himself. He only told Father Mark that Sam liked the place so much he reserved a room so that he could come and stay anytime he wanted.

"Hear me out, my good fellow, hear me out first," Dr. Min said, waving his hand to Sam who was protesting against Dr. Min's confession of his past suspicions over the budding friendship between Sam and Miri.

Sam poured more drink in Dr. Min's glass and that of Father Mark, who was slowly feeling the effect of the alcohol that released carelessness. He asked for a cigar, feeling that boldness was happily in charge. When was the last time his heart was filled with such ease, carefree-ness. If feeling so good and happy like a monkey eating a banana lounging in a tree is a sin, let me embrace this lovely sin a while longer. This is a peccadillo at most, he thought, laughing to himself, lighting his cigar and feeling like a gangster in a movie. "I don't even smoke, it's my first time smoking a cigar," he said sheepishly, seeing Father Gregory returning to the sofa after helping himself to a generous refill of brandy. Father Gregory was in a zone of his own, his face showing absolute harmony as if he had finally come home.

With a lightly curled-up tongue, Dr. Min continued his defensive apology or explanation to Sam. "After I observed you two being together all the time, to my annoyance, I came to the conclusion that you two were good for each other. I came to appreciate it. If you require my apology, here it is, I apologize." The two men shook hands comically and laughed. Then they simultaneously turned to Father Mark, who was enjoying the taste of his cigar, picking bits of tobacco on his tongue. Not a single cough issued from his mouth, even though he was a virgin to cigars.

"Oh yeah." He sat up and tried to resume the conversation, but he could not remember. "Where was I?" he said, blinking and shifting his eyes side to side in vain.

"Oh yeah. We were talking about Miri. What about her, though," he said, scratching his chin. He got no response from his audience.

"It was about her being a thousand years old," said Father Gregory, half lying on the sofa like a centerfold in a *Playboy* magazine, his shoes off, his drink in his hand with his elbow resting on the arm of the sofa. His droopy eyes blankly gazed at the glass that was glowing with the seductive amber of brandy from the lamplight beside him.

"She scared me," Father Mark remembered. "Why, I don't know. I felt I was being tested by an ominous supernatural creature. Remember I went to you to talk about it?" he turned to ask Father Gregory.

"I told you that already. If I remembered correctly, I had told you that she might have been a shaman, a real one, not like you and I."

By then all of them spoke with the tips of their tongues curled up. For a while it seemed that all four of them were talking over each other, and none were listening. But the doctor managed to ask, "Did she talk about any supernatural experiences? Seeing or hearing things, for example."

"It wasn't anything she said or did, I am quite sure. Well, she's an unusual teen, as we know. At first I thought she came to challenge me, but there was something more than that. I'll try to describe what gave me goose bumps. It was something like she was transgressing a certain sadness so that her sadness didn't seem to be sad at all. Sadness that doesn't weep, that is so solid and dignifying. But I felt the transgression nevertheless."

"That's not what you said," Father Gregory interjected, which Father Mark ignored and continued. "It seemed that she gained profundity through sadness. She was so comfortable in it."

"So you didn't witness anything out of the ordinary," Dr. Min said, trying hard to make his speech as crisp as possible.

"'Out of the ordinary' was all she was at the first meeting. But she never came back. All I can tell you is that she made a strong impression on me."

"What was the nature of the conversation?"

"Mostly about God, Jesus, and the Bible. But if any devout Catholic would have heard us, we both could have been excommunicated. It was different, refreshing but frightening at the same time. Sam was there with us for a while when she and I talked today." Seeing Sam nodding without saying anything, he continued, "I feel awkward talking like I know her, though. I'm just sharing with you the brief encounters I've had with her. What she told me this afternoon troubles me a great deal. She didn't believe she could go back home."

"What do you mean?" Sam asked, leaning towards Father Mark, drawing a deep line between his brows over his glassy eyes.

Dr. Min took over and said with a deep sigh, "That's the dilemma I'm facing too. She doesn't want to go back home. But I think she suspects that her family, especially her mom, would be happier in her absence. She told me once that her presence tormented her mother. I'm pretty sure that it was her mother who lied to her husband, Miri's father, that Miri is an arsonist. I have no doubt."

"An arsonist?" Father Mark asked with disbelief in his eyes. Father Gregory, who seemed to be oblivious to his surroundings, struggled to sit his heavy body upright to hear better.

"It was her mother who did it to set her up, no doubt. What a bitch," Sam said, sitting up, pushing the hair on his forehead up and back, twisting his mouth in disgust.

"I haven't talked about it with Miri, but I'm not sure if I should. It'll only confirm her suspicion that they want to lose her, I'm afraid."

"It isn't a suspicion anymore, Dr. Min. In her mind she no longer has the luxury of suspicion. It became real to her. When she found out that they didn't even bother to let her know of her grandmother's passing, she seemed like she gave up all her rights over them." Father Mark then told the doctor how she murmured for some time about bits and pieces of her history, as if the murmuring was only for her ears. "Then all of sudden, she began to talk about God, her God, my God. She talked to herself as a second person. It was like a mother talking gently to a child." He looked at Sam, then at the doctor, moving his head back and forth a couple of times waiting for their responses, unaware that the cigar in his hand went cold.

"Sam, is it possible that you make some coffee?" Dr. Min asked, stretching his arms over his head.

"I only have instant coffee."

"Instant is good."

Sam got up, feeling a little unsteady on his feet. One by one they got up to use the bathroom with their wobbly legs and then took the instant coffee Sam had mixed with hot water, with un-dissolved bits floating on the top.

Dr Min struggled to clear his head so that he could think or remember what he was thinking. Father Mark sipped his coffee, thinking that he would miss this night when he went back to his church life where the human quality was so lacking. Looking through the Church's dictionary of sins, he thought of how many of them aren't sins at all in the real human world. Father Gregory poured more brandy into his coffee cup and walked over to Sam, who was standing at the glass door looking out at the darkness. The snow was still strong.

"Sam, would you let me join you the next time you visit the temple? I think I'm ready to face it."

Sam turned to him, took a sip of his coffee, making a sweet-and-sour face and said, "Sure thing, my good friend," draping his arm around his round shoulders, feeling moisture gathering in his glassy eyes. The plentiful affection lingering in that very room was both sad and deeply touching. The hissing sound of the snow-blowing wind falling took him back to the winters at the temple. "How is it that one misses the harsh time one had…"

- 69 -

Nurse Yun found Miri already sleeping when she came in that evening. She was a light sleeper, and even though a slight noise would normally wake her up, that night she slept deeply. Even in her sleep, she looked exhausted. Other than her chest rising and descending to the faint rhythm of her breathing, she looked like a rag doll tucked in under a cover. She had the radio on softly for Nurse Yun.

In the dark woods of somnolence, she was wide awake dreaming, watching herself looking this way and that way, observing the particles of minds, hers and others, floating about, incapable of communicating with each other, just staring at one another, while the almost strangers sitting in the next room were consuming the stormy night with the story of her life.

The next morning she woke up with a pounding headache. She sat on the bed, staring at the white wall. The window was caked with frost. She stayed like that for some time, her thoughts still asleep. They will wake up like noisy children soon, she said to herself. She went to the basin, turned on the water, and looked into the mirror. Her eyelids were swollen from crying, and there was a line of dried blood on her left jaw. She turned her face to see the source of blood and found that it was from her left ear. When she returned to her bed, she saw a blood stain on her pillow. She stood there looking at the blood stain. It didn't inform her of anything. She went back to the basin and washed off the blood, not at all concerned. Maybe all that crying popped something inside of my ear, she thought, but the headache was another matter. It felt like her eyes were being pushed out from their sockets.

She changed into her day clothes, wondering why Hakyu, her personal alarm clock, hadn't shown up. For a reason unknown to her, he was the only one she wanted to be with at that moment.

He wasn't in his room. She asked a nurse at the station if she knew where he was.

"Didn't you know? He had an accident yesterday. He's at the clinic."

"What kind of accident?"

"He fell in the snow. That's all I know," the nurse answered.

Miri thought about asking for a couple of aspirins for her headache but decided not to. She didn't feel strong enough to push through the nurse's indifference. Instead, she went back to her room and fetched her coat, passing by Sam's closed door, and went downstairs. She drank a cup of coffee at the counter in the dining room and then passed through the crowded, overheated lounge, throwing a dirty glance at the tall Christmas tree, and stepped out to the hair-icicling chill. The grey sky hung low, but it wasn't snowing. Everything was covered with white snow like a Christmas card.

The icy air made her nostrils stick and her eyes watery, but it felt good for her achy head. She walked toward the clinic, hearing the new boots that Sam had bought for her at the hospital shop making squeaky sounds on the snow.

Hakyu was lying on the bed, working his mouth with a nurse. Miri was relieved to see him being his usual obnoxious self. He had a broken foot, a twisted elbow joint, and some head injury that was superficial.

"What happened?"

"I fell, skiing in the snow."

"You went out yesterday, in that awful weather?"

"After you went downstairs to see your visitor, I got bored," he said, adding that when he went out the snow wasn't too heavy. He had gotten two rulers made out of bamboo from the nurse's station and tried to ski on them.

"How did you walk back, you idiot?"

"It was strange. I knew I was hurt, all bloody and stuff, but I was so cold and partially frozen that I couldn't feel the pain. One of my ears was half torn off and dangling, bleeding badly, but I couldn't feel any pain. So I made it back like nothing. But once my body melted down the pain was..." he trailed off, showing the stitches behind his ear.

The nurse, a fat middle-aged woman with whom he was talking when Miri found him, interrupted and ordered him to peel off his pants to receive a shot on his behind. "This will make the pain go away." She slapped the upper part of his bottom hard in an attempt to counter the pain of the needle when it pierced through the skin. Miri thought about asking her for aspirin, but she didn't. Every faculty in her system seemed to be intimidated. The pain was shooting down to her neck, and she felt her left thumb was jerking on its own. Miri asked him if he wanted her to stay.

"Please," he said, playing with one of the many pimples on his cheeks with the fingers of his good arm.

"Stop playing with it. It'll get infected," the fat nurse yelped. Before she left, she told him that the injection would make him drowsy. They looked at the nurse's behind when she was walking to the door and giggled.

"Huge."

"Huge, indeed."

"Monumental."

"Colossal."

They went on taking turns with words to describe the size of her butt. "We both can fit in her underpants and still have room for a pet," he said and laughed hard. He didn't forget to moan here and there while laughing from the pain. Afterwards he asked, "Who was your visitor?"

"A priest from the church." Miri didn't want to tell him more. They went on gossiping about the boys and girls in the west wing.

"I hope it snows heavily for about a month."

"It might. But why?"

"When my family hears that I had an accident, they'll come as soon as possible, but I don't want to see them. I need peace and quiet."

"You? You want peace and quiet? Those words don't belong to you, I mean, those words don't know you. Ha, ha. Peace and quiet, bullshit!"

"Sis, you don't know them. I am the most quiet and peaceful among the bunch. When they come to see me, they come as an army. They constantly argue about things that are totally irrelevant to me. By the time they leave, they get so pissed off at each other that they can't pretend to say a decent good-bye to me."

"Does your father come too?"

"Always. We're better now. I think he feels very badly about the beating. Last time he was here he shook my hand, you know, like two gentlemen."

Miri could tell the injection was taking its effect. He was sliding down, unable to keep his head up, his eyelids were heavy, and his speech was slowing down.

Miri pulled the cover up to his chin and told him to go to sleep.

"Sis."

"What?"

"Who were you talking to the other day at the hike?"

"Who?"

"He, I think it was a he, was wearing a blue thing, shimmering fabric. I couldn't see his face, but he was wearing a white wool hat or something…"

Miri went silent. In a while his eyes were closed. He murmured something she couldn't make out and then soon after, nothing. He was asleep.

She left the clinic and was back out into the snow-covered world. She started to walk towards the main building, her boots resuming their squeaking, her hands in her pockets and chin tucked into her chest. The pain in her head was dreadful and the thumbs in her pocket jerked. She stopped, took a deep breath, then another one. The icy air needled her throat. She felt the sadness, the kind she liked, deepening in her mind, inviting the pain in her head as a guest. She walked slowly, not wanting to go back to the main building. She didn't care to see anyone that day. She wanted to be left alone in her solitude with her pain, with her sadness. She owed them her undivided attention, realizing she had neglected them for a long time. For a long time, she had ignored and almost denied their existence, their undying friendship, ever since she came to the island. These friends reminded her of the truth that she was once again in the middle of a passage, nothing more.

These friends had sat with her time after time, tutoring and drilling her, even locking her up in a box until she could not wring her thoughts anymore, until she sank down on her knees, surrendering before the road of understanding. She felt a sorrow that was immature yet aging, that was flowing through her veins and slowing down her heartbeat, softening her breathing and revealing the color of her spirit, making her queen once again.

A thought interrupted her image of being the queen of sorrow, reminding her of what Hakyu had asked. "Who were you talking to the other day at the hike?"

"Does that mean the goat is real? Or did Hakyu just happen to witness my own imagination in the flesh, in a blue satin coat and white wool cap?" Strangely, it wasn't important to her.

She was about halfway back to the main building when she saw a drop of blood on the snow and felt warm, red liquid on her cheek. Her left eye was bleeding; she wiped it with a glove and kept walking, but it wouldn't stop like before. The blood was dripping down her neck, and her ear was bleeding too. She stood there looking at the dripping blood violating the snow. She turned back to the clinic, thinking of the line from the Gospel, "Take this in memory of me. This is the blood I have given up for you." The pounding pain in her head shrilled inwardly, and when she walked into the clinic in a bloody mess, she collapsed, violently vomiting.

-70-

Dr. Min got up late that morning. He was scheduled to be in the city but was stranded due to the bad weather, so he didn't have any patients to attend to that day. He had a hangover, and it was rather enjoyable. He couldn't remember the last time he was hungover like that. Every pore of his body participated in producing the redolence of sewage. He made himself coffee and popped two aspirins in his mouth. He showered while drinking coffee at the same time, planning for the day of no plans. But he ended up getting dressed and decided to go to his office to catch up with some delayed paperwork. He swiveled on his chair, drinking another cup of coffee and smoking mindlessly, looking at the piles of paper on his desk.

Then he decided to pull out Miri's file. There was a binder containing her psychological evaluation from when she was admitted to the hospital. It was just a formality administered by the hospital staff. Since Dr. Min was very skeptical of any such tests, he never bothered to examine them.

He secretly believed all those tests—Stanford-Binet's IQ test, Rorschach's ink blots, and so on—were borderline superstitions sadly sheltered in the bastion of science. Her IQ wasn't that high, only a bit higher than average, which made him smile affectionately. He flipped the pages, wetting his thumb with his tongue. Then unexpectedly something caught his eye. Miri had addressed every single Rorschach ink blot by the name Hans. "Hans is fishing; Hans is looking in a mirror; Hans is sitting on a riverbank under a willow tree." Who is this Hans, he wondered, tilting his head, still rather heavy from the persistent hangover. "It's a German name, isn't it?" He closed the file and turned his chair to face the window behind him, puzzled but intrigued. He decided to talk with her in the afternoon and called his secretary to have her in at around three or four, and he left for an early lunch which his abused stomach demanded badly.

When he came back to the office, his secretary told him that she just got a call from the clinic. "After you left I tried to get hold of her, but she was nowhere to be found. Then I just received a call from the clinic."

"What happened, what did they say?" he asked impatiently.

"The nurse said she apparently fainted or something."

Before she finished he was on the phone with the clinic.

"This is Dr. Min. What was she doing there? Um, um. Has the bleeding stopped?" He waved at the secretary, who had been standing there seemingly awaiting instructions, to leave the room. He hung up the phone and headed out to the clinic.

He was met by a young doctor when he walked in the clinic. He told him how she was and what had been done. "I checked her ear and eye, and they seemed to be fine. No infection, nothing. The bleeding stopped after a while. I suspect that there must have been a rupture in the capillaries. And the vomiting could be from the excitement of seeing herself bleeding. Oh, she mentioned that she woke up with a terrible headache and had bloody discharge from her ear overnight."

"Did you give her anything?"

"Just aspirin for her headache. I didn't want to give her anything else without consulting you."

Doctor Min thanked him and went to see her.

She was sitting on the bed, leaning her back against the pillow and staring at the ceiling. She looked like the first time he saw her in the city, old and disheveled, seeming as if she were seeing something only available to her eyes. He approached her and squeezed her toes, "How are you, kiddo?"

She turned to him and parted her parched lips to say something. No words came out. She closed them and looked down on the sheet. He sat at the bottom of the bed trying to follow her eyes with his. They sat like that for a while in silence. Finally, she peeled apart her parched lips and said, "Dr. Min, I think it's time for me to go home." Her voice was hoarse and low as if someone else was speaking for her.

"Why so suddenly?"

"I told you I would know when I'm ready."

"It was only a few days ago you said you could not go back."

"That was then. A long time has passed between then and now, for my mind." She looked into his wondering eyes, her own eyes telling him "this is it!"

"Okay, we'll talk about it more later, but first things first. What happened today?"

She told him about the blood stain on her pillow, her headache, more blood, vomiting, her knees buckling up.

"Oh, one more thing. It stopped now, but my left thumb was twitching involuntarily," she said, showing her thumb that was displaying a tremor. The sight alarmed him, for the twitching of the thumb was usually a sign of trouble in the central nervous system.

He asked her to make a gentle fist and pressed her fingers one by one with his fingers. The thumb started to jerk like wipers on a windshield. Oh, my lord, he thought. But he said, "It moves like it has a mind of its own," putting on a cheery air, but at the same time, checking every medical knowledge he could summon, rolling through his head like a film reel. He let go of her hand and checked her eyes and ears with a small flashlight he carried in his pocket. They were slightly reddened, but as the young doctor said, the bleeding could have been from broken capillaries. It was her headache and the jerking thumb that alarmed him, raising his heartbeat.

"Are they still here?" she asked about the priests.

"I'm pretty sure. The road hasn't opened up yet. Miri, I think we have to run some tests on you. That means you have to be in the city. We don't have the proper equipment here."

"Might as well. From there I'll go straight home," she concluded without giving him any room to debate.

He simply nodded and said, "We'll see, we'll see." He got up and told her to rest. "I'll check back with you later." He had to resist his question about "Hans" and left her.

Being slapped around by the cold air that he earlier cursed as "bitch of a weather" felt good. He started to walk faster when the slapping of the icy air no longer felt good. Then a sudden feeling of foolishness—his foolishness, the foolishness of the entire population in the world, young and old, learned and ignorant, blessed and cursed, saints and demons—flooded into his mind, commanding him to surrender to the tidal wave of melancholy that began to engulf him.

-71-

When he walked into the lounge of the main building, he spotted the two priests sitting among the hospital tenants. Father Mark had the typical posture of the perfect modesty of a career priest, sitting on the edge of the sofa listening to an aging patient next to him. Father Gregory was sitting on the loveseat angled towards the sofa, looking at his nails. He ignored them and headed to the office when he saw Sam at the reception desk.

"Oh, I was just about to call you."

Dr. Min kept walking towards his office saying, "Not now, Sam. I've got something to take care of."

Sam followed him, saying, "Wait a minute, is something wrong?"

He kept walking and snapped at him.

"I am a doctor. I have a doctor's job to do." He took two more steps then turned around. Sam was standing in the middle of the dark hallway, perplexed. "I'm sorry, Sam," he said, throwing his sad glance on the floor with his hands in the pockets of his heavy overcoat. He stayed liked that for a moment or two, then turned his heels decisively and said, "Come on, Sam, into my office. Let's talk there," directing him with his right shoulder.

By the time he finished telling Sam what had happened, what he suspected about Miri's present condition, Sam looked shrunken in his chair, pale and expressionless. He took a deep breath several times in a row. For the reason, only God knew why, that he really cared about her, Dr. Min thought.

"Are you sure it's a tumor? I mean, is it…"

"I'm pretty sure. I hope I'm wrong, but…And no, there is no cure, not yet, not for some time. That field of medical science is still in the dark ages."

"You could be wrong, though."

"I could. We'll know better after the test."

Sam lowered his eyes and said,

"I didn't think anything of it. She said it was a sty in her eye."

"You saw her bleeding?"

"Just the other day on the hike. She said she had a sty inside of her eyelid that popped. Then, yesterday I gave her my handkerchief when she was crying after the news of her grandma's death, and I saw blood on it again when I emptied my pocket this morning. What do we do now?"

Sam had said "we" instead of "you." It was touching and helped Dr. Min to push the fog of melancholy out of him. This good soul sitting across from him jumped on his boat to accompany him. They both lit cigarettes. Dr. Min said, "First of all, I have to talk to neurologists and take it from there."

"What about her parents?"

"That too." Dr. Min blew out the smoke with force to the ceiling.

"Boy, I wish I didn't feel so sorry for her, Sam, my friend." He puffed his cigarette in agitation and said, "As your doctor, I have to worry about your attachment to her too. I fear that you might break down again." Dr. Min knew how involved Sam was with the girl, how he wanted to be the savior this time instead of the one who was saved.

"Um…one thing at a time, one thing at a time. Oh, it's snowing again," Sam murmured, putting out his cigarette. "I have to go back to the priests." He got up and asked him if she would be brought back to her room on that day.

"She'll stay at the clinic today."

"Do you think I should tell them?"

"I think at least Father Mark should know."

They dissuaded Father Gregory from accompanying them to the clinic. "It's started to snow again, not to mention the road's slippery. If you fell, we'd have to leave you there to freeze to death. You're too heavy for us to carry." Father Mark told him.

"I heard that dying by freezing is a rather pleasurable experience."

"Has anyone come back from such a death to tell you that?" Father Mark said, pushing him down on the loveseat by the shoulders. He obeyed, shaking his head. "Do some rosary or something." Father Mark said it a little loud, causing some of the fellow loungers to look at Father Gregory, whose face was reddening with embarrassment. He threw a sharp glance at Father Mark, picked up the newspaper on the table, and screened his red face with it, leaning on the back of the seat.

By the time they arrived at the clinic, the snow was coming down, curtaining everything around them. When Miri saw them, she seemed neither happy nor unhappy. Her expression was emotionless, as if seeing strangers passing by. Sam hesitated and stood at the doorway. Father Mark approached her and said, "If you want to be left alone…" She shook her head then gave a smile to Sam and waved her hand. She didn't want to see anyone, especially Sam, but she could not show that to the only kind person she'd ever known in her life. She didn't want to see him because she would burden his heart, worrying about her. Friendship isn't always a sweet thing, she thought.

"No, not at all, I'm glad you've come. I was getting so bored I was going to wake Hakyu up. He's been sleeping for hours."

"He's here too?" Just mentioning his name made Sam smile widely. Then, catching himself, he said, "Nothing serious, I hope."

Miri told him what happened to him the other day. All of them laughed.

Sam noticed she squinted her left eye when she laughed. She looked like an old lady. Her face was colorless with a dried layer of skin on her lips that looked wrinkled, and there were two vertical lines between her eyebrows that were new, but the lights in her swollen eyes were strong as if they were engaged in matters of importance.

"Seems like you're stranded here today. How's your pain?" Sam asked gently.

"It's there. It hurts," she said, smiling a social smile.

"I'll leave you two alone for a while. I'll be with Hakyu if you need me."

"He's two rooms down the hall on the opposite side," Miri directed him.

Dr. Min was too upset to sit through their conversation about God and faith and what not, which he was pretty sure they would be having.

Father Mark pulled up a chair and sat next to her bed.

"I'm going home," she started.

"That's a frightfully quick decision. Did you ask Dr. Min?"

"He said we'll talk later."

"Why do I get the sense that you're giving up something?"

"I'm giving up avoidance. Being here was a gift, a long holiday that indulged my lazy nature to its maximum potential."

Father Mark listened to her silently, pressing down questions in his larynx while listening to her.

"The sudden charge I felt from being challenged and the rise of an impulse to challenge back, it was like the return of life itself, only more mature. It feels right, a 'this is it' kind of simple thought, encouraged by what feels like primordial courage." She made a warrior-like expression, pressing her lips and flaring her nostrils, with her gaze fixed on the blank ceiling.

"Primordial courage?" He was thinking and asking at the same time.

"You know, the force that comes out of you and acts before your mind starts to consider logic and reasons, which are mainly concerned with negative outcomes or possible disasters that might be revealed ahead, like the weather forecast. I call that primordial courage."

He listened to her carefully and thought how she seemed to be alive when she described her inner self. But at the same time, his mind was circling around the practical reality that she was only sixteen. Her ideas and experience were largely limited to her head, however profound she might have sounded. With his unsuitable knowledge of psychology, he suspected "grandiosity." Her life seemed to have been an invisible, inaudible one, and she'd never fought to be noticed. And this sudden courage, a collective accumulated force of deep anger and pain, was manifesting as a glorious banner. But he could not come up with anything remotely useful thing to say. He imagined himself standing in the middle of a desert, not knowing in which direction to go.

"Do you believe in prayer?"

"Yes, I pray," she said, remembering her night in the house of meanwhile, how she prayed trying to open the door in that suffocating, dark hallway. How the prayers she learned from church that previously bore no meaning for her, the very prayers that she used to sneer at, took over her entire being at that horrifying moment, rushing out of her mouth as her only savior. She thought, didn't I really believe with all my heart and soul that it was the only thing I could rely on?

She then corrected herself and said again, "Yes, I believe in prayer, very much so."

"So it helps you."

"It saves me too."

"Do you pray to the one you told me about yesterday, your constant companion?"

"I say simple prayers in the absence of intelligence, like the Lord's prayer, Hail Mary, and the rosary."

This surprised him, and he had to say, "I thought you might have your own set of prayers."

"I've thought numerous times that I should invent my own prayers, but to tell you the truth, when I feel like praying, it always starts with those I mentioned. Isn't it funny? 'Once a Catholic, always a Catholic.' I experience that in me over and over. But I reconciled with the Catholic in me. I respect any style of faith, their own way of worship. Forever mysterious, forever teaching; this faith stuff is the shadow you can't get rid of. It's there in me, and it talks to me in a language that my brain can't decipher, yet my mind understands. There's an entity in us that understands before your brain does. The Trinity in us can't communicate with each other, unlike that of Jesus Christ."

"What's your idea of the Trinity?"

"The Church says they are the Father, Son, and Holy Ghost. I think they are our mind, spirit, and body."

Father Mark looked into her eyes, tenderly thinking how wonderfully her mind was spinning.

"There were a few times I almost took off these clothes I'm wearing. But every time I had a crisis, it was that very thing you've just said that haunted me, that 'once a Catholic, always a Catholic.' Whether or not I'm a man of the cloth, I knew I could never get away from it."

"Have you reconciled with yourself?"

"More or less. Father Gregory played a crucial role during my struggles. One thing he told me, which I remind myself of over and over, is that the Church I despise is my Church too. Whether you worship your God wearing a black robe or butt naked, it really doesn't matter. It's God who chooses you, not the other way around. I wondered and worried about being brainwashed too. But with the help of Father Gregory again, I settled with the idea that one doesn't get brainwashed. Instead, something in you already recognized the information, as if they were messages from home. Have you noticed that it's really hard to make a person stop wanting to eat his most favorite food? Or to teach them to eat what they absolutely hate? There's a sad and funny story I heard. During the French Revolution, King Louis–the-something fled for his life. But when he saw a shop selling his favorite cheese, he had to stop to sample it. Well, that was the death of him. He got caught. There must be a component in us that issues an uncontrollable desire, however ridiculous, that makes you take most obvious risk."

"Father Mark, I think we should let her rest."

Sam was standing in the doorway. He approached her and asked if he could do anything for her. She gave him a loving smile that almost made his eyes moisten and shook her head. "We'll leave you alone. You need to rest, however boring it is. Be a good girl. I'll check on you later," he said, pulling Father Mark's jacket to get up. Sam really didn't like the conversation Father Mark had brought up. Such talk belongs to a dying person, he thought, resenting Father Mark's insensitivity. Actually, Sam had withheld the information from Father Mark that she might have a tumor in her brain or central nervous system. Then again, it could be totally nothing. He braved his heart and left the clinic with the reluctant priest. The snow was furious, like angry ghosts dancing menacingly in white shrouds. They walked holding each other's arms tightly through the macabre snow. The poor visibility made it impossible for them to see beyond a few feet, and the trip back to the main building took twice as long as normal.

-72-

After Sam and Father Mark left, Miri tried to go to sleep, but she was too hungry yet nauseous. She thought about asking for some food but decided against it. The thickness of the stillness in the room, with its white walls and white ceiling, seemed to be moving closer to her with every blink of her eyes. She thought she heard a high-pitched screeching sound. The more she imagined it, the more real it became. The whiteness turned an opaque iridescent, alive and liquidizing. Panic moved her heartbeat up to her throat. She got out of bed and walked toward the door, tiptoeing in fear of being noticed and swallowed by the iridescent monster. In the hallway, she stood thinking over which way to go, to the nurse's station or to Hakyu.

On the bed next to Hakyu's sleeping head was the goat, sitting up, resting against the headboard with his gloved hooves on the sleeping boy's head. She stood in the doorway, gaping.

"Come on in," he said, waving his arm. Her feet moved toward him in spite of herself. Although he told her to come in, she still felt like she was intruding. "Sit down," he said, pointing at the chair next to the bed. "This is an unexpected development for both of us," he said, looking at her directly with large green eyes that shone like headlights. They looked different indoors, unreadable and cold. She couldn't help feeling betrayed, but strangely there was a sense of relief, as if one of her mysterious burdens was leaving. "You are not responding, Miri. Hello, hello?" She shifted her eyes to the sleeping boy. He was covered with the sheet up to his chin, his eyelids fluttering, indicating the movement of his eyes under the lids. His asymmetrical head looked like a deflated football.

She finally spoke. "Where is he now?"

"It's not for you to know," he said nonchalantly.

"So, this is what you meant about moving on."

"Oh, be glad that I found him. Weren't you a little sorry for me when I found out you weren't it?"

"I don't know if I feel sorry for you that I'm not your 'it.' Part of me still insisted on the notion that you are—"

"I know. A part of the imagination, some fragment of an entertaining fantasy. That was and is who I am to you. And I thought I almost completed my mission. The only thing left was the need for your firm conviction. But now even your conviction has no value to me," he said, clicking his tongue. "You don't seem to care much either way. Well, I have to start all over again with this guy. I guess I'm still lucky to have found him before I ventured on endlessly to somewhere else."

"You'll be kind to him," she said, rubbing her achy head that was causing her to screw up her face in pain.

"Are you talking to your imaginary friend, or am I real to you now?"

"It doesn't matter, either way," she said, wanting to leave the room.

"Have I ever been unkind to you?"

"Not at all. But you are selfish." She managed to smile at him as her way of saying good-bye and good luck. She began to turn around when the goat called out her name. She stopped without turning to him.

"Miri, I lied to you. Your ego being part of a spiritual repository was bullshit. I'm sorry. You got ill. The ostrich man alerted me of your illness. You are spoken for already. I need a person with your kind of ego but with a healthy body."

"I'm dying, is that what you're saying?" The pain in her head wouldn't allow her to feel the shock. The question came out as if she were concerned with someone else, a distant acquaintance.

She stood there hearing him but not listening. She continued for the door again. The pain was worse than what she had just heard, much worse.

"Miri, wait. I had good times with you. You've been a good pupil, but I must tell you that you're much more beguiling than I had thought. I'm sorry if I harmed you in any way."

"No harm done. But can't you help me with this pain, don't you have a magic potion or something?" she asked, turning to him.

He looked down and shook his head.

"I'm miserably sorry, but I can't. Meddling with such forces is against the code."

She left the room and walked down the hallway to the nurse's station. "Please, give me something, my head hurts, it hurts so much."

The nurse, young and skinny, gave her a once-over and slowly picked up the phone.

"I have Dr. Min's patient asking for a painkiller. Can you page him and have him call me?" Then she looked down at the paper on which she was working and said, "You've got to wait." Miri stood there, her head pounding, when the nurse said without moving her eyes from the paper, "Go back to your room and wait there. There's nothing I can do until he calls."

Miri then jumped over the counter, grabbed the nurse's cap and hair, knocked her down on her back with her fist, and pressed her chest with her knee, screaming. She screamed and screamed, the scream she had held inside for sixteen years. The nurse underneath her was screaming too. A volcanic eruption of anger that took over her was intoxicating, somewhat counteracting the pain in her head. She put one hand on her neck and raised the other in a fist, ready to have it land on the nurse's small screaming face when she heard footsteps running down the hallway towards the station. The phone rang, and Miri picked it up, leaving her foot on the screaming nurse's chest.

"This is Dr. Min, what's going on?" he asked in an alarmed voice, hearing the screaming nurse in the background. A couple of older nurses had come to rescue the young one on the floor. One of them tried to grab the phone from Miri as she was screaming into the phone, "My pain is killing me! I can't stand it anymore, not a second more! Don't send me to the room here. It'll devour me."

By then a male nurse showed up, still chewing his dinner in his mouth. He yanked the phone and gave it to the old nurse who started to explain to him what was going on. The young nurse was hysterical. She cried aloud, "She was gonna kill me."

Was I? Was I really, could I have? Miri thought, looking at her white uniform moving up and down from heavy breathing. A wedge of tissue paper the nurse had stuffed in her bra was crawling upwardly over an exposed bit of chest where a couple of buttons had been torn off. Whatever was passing through her mind didn't succeed in bothering her conscience, it felt exceedingly good at that moment.

The male nurse restrained her with a leather strap. A few minutes went by after she was strapped and forced to sit down in a chair. The pain started to reappear. The old nurse came and gave her an injection, which Dr. Min had ordered on the phone.

She was strapped on a gurney this time and transported to the main building through the heavy snow, which landed on her face in the darkening winter afternoon. Two orderlies with whom she was familiar with moved the gurney. The one that did the pushing, right by her head, started to giggle. "Miri, I thought you wouldn't hurt a fly."

"She wasn't a fly." she answered, making them both laugh.

The injection she received warmed her body, made her eyelids droopy. Lying on the gurney made her imagine being a corpse. The thought didn't bother her. She opened her mouth wide to receive the falling snow. She didn't believe a word of what the goat had said to her.

-73-

Dr. Min was late. She sat in the waiting room where his secretary was typing away. For all those months of seeing her regularly, she and Miri had barely exchanged a few words. She noticed new pictures hanging on the wall. They were drawings of Dr. Min's sons, nicely framed. A few days had gone by since the episode in the clinic. The grey sky with falling snow turned to a harsh winter blue. The priests had gone back to the city, and she was mostly staying in bed, drugged with painkillers. She was drowsy, felt almost airy.

"Sorry I'm late." He rushed in. She could feel the cold air from his coat. He opened the door to his office for her, ignoring the secretary who was bowing at him deeply. He changed into his white robe and sat behind the desk, pointing at the chair in front of it for Miri to sit. He looked preoccupied. He looked both old and young, for his face was rather gloomy, but the cold air added a youthful pink to his cheeks, and there was a rushed energy about him.

"How's the pain?" he asked, fussing with the stuff on his desk.

"Much better, just a dull sensation."

He nodded, clasping his hands on the desk and looking at her meaningfully in the eyes. Something else seemed different about him. His posture of authoritarianism was not there. In spite of the fussy energy, there was a calmness, perhaps a touch of sadness in those round eyes. He looked peaceful but defeated. But there was an honest willfulness in his demeanor at the same time.

"I just came back from the city. It seems like we have to wait for the tests. It'll be after Christmas and New Year's...a few more weeks. We can wait, right?" He then asked, "Do you still want to go back home?"

"I don't know anymore, I don't know why I said that, but even now I'm not totally against it. What I want to say, what I realized, is that I don't trust myself."

"There's nothing wrong with you. Being different isn't an illness. Another thing is that I can't change you to make you fit in with others. I think it's wrong, a sin, and a crime in my book. In the end you have to decide because I have no right to guide you toward which direction you should go. And you don't look for guidance or help," he said, shaking his head. He looked at the pen that he had been twirling between his fingers. "Miri, I can see why people think you are odd, although not to me, I assure you. I think it's refreshing. But people in general feel safer in uniformity, and when they face oddness, they tend to avoid it or destroy it. Funny though, as you pointed out, once a character like Madam Yumla becomes popular, these same people enjoy odd personalities as long as they belong to the world of fiction. What I'm saying is that oddness to one can be a unique blessing to others, a gift." He continued, ignoring the blankness in her eyes, "I'm telling you this as a fellow human being, not as your doctor. I've seen so many people in misery. The strange thing is most of them don't want to work hard to get out of it. They want their surroundings to change. They want to blame something for their misery and want to be compensated. I'm not belittling their misery. Some of the cases I've dealt with were truly heart wrenching. The point I want to make is that people go about the wrong way to relieve their pain. It's so hard for them to see that the pain and hurt they are facing can be an important cue to them to move on. Time to change, so to speak.

By no means am I being cynical. God knows our minds are not that simple. One noticeable thing is that people really have a hard time letting go of their hurt. They almost seem to be fatally attached to it, and they enslave themselves to it. And it's so hard for them to see what prevents them from having a good day."

She was actually listening to him carefully, but she could not help but wonder if he was giving up on her, if he decided to send her home. He sounded like a man who was disappointed.

"Am I making any sense to you?" he asked, lighting a cigarette.

"Yes, I think so. But who do you have in your mind when you said 'they'?"

"Oh, no one in particular. Suffering people in general, I guess."

She didn't believe him all the way but decided not to pressure him. Instead she carried on the subject of the conversation, if it was indeed a conversation.

"Probably what 'they' really want is to be avenged. Being avenged should be the beginning of healing or the only thing that heals. Without that out of the way, nothing can move. Because just letting go of the hurt is defeat, a form of surrender and betrayal to oneself. Giving in is like killing a part of yourself."

"But how does one avenge life? One only prolongs his hurt, and the hurt kills too."

"True. But some use their hurt to elevate themselves, which is a kind of attempt to avenge themselves. When it works, it's a blessing. That's the cue they'd like to hold on to, the cue from the angry hurt that shouts "move on." But those who can't summon their hurt to the level of energetic anger sit in the box of suffering, slowly disintegrating themselves. I've seen it myself. I am with you about moving on in terms of philosophically and psychologically. But to do that, one needs a mind that innately aspires for actualization. To most it's impossible even to imagine such a state of mind; it would be easier for them to move a mountain overnight."

He looked at her drowsy eyes with a smile, rather impressed.

"Does your hurt give you any meaning of life to speak of?"

"Yes, to a degree. But my hurt is healthy," she answered promptly.

"Ah, a healthy hurt. Share that with me," he said then sighing and laughing at the same time, putting out his cigarette.

"The hurt I carry in me, old or not so old, knows how to do the math. It calculates pros and cons. This way I can control the balance. We work together. Frankly, I would feel like an empty shell without it."

"I don't quite understand," he said, wanting to hear more.

"Let's see...I get hurt, and I cry sometimes, then the hurt unfolds the incident that caused the hurt, step by step, and encourages me to consult with my brain. While I'm doing so, the hurt nurses the wound until I return from my brain with instructions over whether or not I should act out from pain. The more I practice the method, the easier it is to see the humor in the cause and effect of the hurt process. But mind you, the memory of it never fades. Well, that's the best I can explain."

"So you've learned to laugh at it."

"It's a good, clean, and hearty laughter. I enjoy the dramas with me in them. Being able to see the humor has taught me pity, to see that the situation is laughable but not without pity."

"Do you realize how differently you sound from several months ago?"

"Really? Perhaps the time I've spent here has given me the opportunity to be with my thoughts. Before I came here, they were all over the place, but now I have them better organized. Perhaps that's why I might sound different."

"You haven't talked about Madam Yumla for some time. Have you abandoned her?"

"No, sir. She is still with me, and she always will be."

"Has she taught you any tips on how to be willful?"

"I don't think I can ever be as solid as the master herself. What I clearly learned is the beauty of will."

"Did you consider will an ugly thing before?"

"In a way. The individuals I've encountered who seemed to be willful didn't appear to be at peace with themselves. They seemed to be in constant battle, whether or not they like it. Thanks to the teachings of the master,

Madam Yumla, I figured out that what I had perceived to be the willfulness in those individuals wasn't true will at all. It is diseased ambition. That's why they appeared to be not at ease."

"This Yumla woman, isn't she antisocial?"

"To be sure. She doesn't dance around other's opinions."

"But she makes others miserable?"

"She didn't make them. They chose to be. She wouldn't care if they were just like her."

"I don't know, Miri. I thumbed through the copy because of you, but she seemed to be too much. Obnoxious, to put it mildly."

"After all, it is a comic book; she's supposed to be overacting."

He inwardly laughed at her comment, at her defending a cartoon character and calling her a master. He thought, what is the use of all this talk anymore? This young one, barely a bud, might be facing death. The thought he had been fighting inside was floating in bits, making him tired all of a sudden. He wanted to lay his head on the desk and go to sleep. He thought about wrapping up the session for the day but instead decided to continue the talk with the girl. Her chattiness, most likely drug induced, made her look as innocent as they came, making him feel dreadfully guilty. All they had been talking about would be a matter of absolute irrelevance to her before she turned seventeen. He knew what she had in her brain. He was sure. He could not doubt that he might be wrong if he tried.

"The other day you said you decided to go back home. I'm curious what brought you to the decision so suddenly. Does your grandmother's passing have anything to do it?"

"I'm not clear about that anymore, as I told you. I just felt like, as we talked about earlier, moving on, changing. I don't really know, but clearly it wasn't a comforting thought."

"But you haven't abandoned the thought."

"No. It's like being trapped in an orbit, going round and round and round," she said, drawing circles in the air. "The other day I was so sure that I was ready, like I was sure of *not* wanting to go back several days ago. I guess I'm becoming impulsive."

"It depends on how you'd coexist with your mother, am I right?"

"Come to think of it, that could be it. Perhaps I'm ready to cause her pain, to hurt her."

"And yet you say you don't hate her."

"She's not well. She belongs here more than me. I'll tell you one thing, though. I know I'd dislike her even if she was a total stranger, sick or not."

"Oh, the electromagnetic field theory."

"That's the only reasonable explanation to me. It's a good one too, scientific. Only, there's no way I can make her understand."

"You said her feelings for you are that of hatred. How do you distinguish hatred and dislike in terms of electromagnetic theory?"

"Hatred has a hot temperature, whereas dislike is rather cold. Totally different physio-chemical forms of entropy. Her hatred being much hotter than my orbit of dislike, she can't be hurt by me, whereas her heat can burn me. I feel rings of heat waves around her. But I can tell she suffers, she really does."

"Do you enjoy seeing her suffering?"

"No, not at all. I think such an emotion belongs to hatred. I don't know."

"I'm sure I said it before, but you do have a great mind, one of a kind."

"But insecure—insecure in my own orbit?"

"You can put it that way."

"Wrong."

"Oh?" He was startled.

"I'm distracted rather than insecure."

"Right. That makes sense too. Allow me to correct you a bit. Your distraction comes from insecurity. I don't think you belong to any orbit. I think you are a freelancer. Maybe that's why you feel distracted and insecure. You don't look for guidance. As a matter of fact, you might get offended by any friendly attempt to guide you because you want to be totally, absolutely left alone, undisturbed. Then a thought dawns on you, and you follow the thought, putting all your faith in it, knowing that it can change at any moment."

"What's the nature of my insecurity? I never thought of me being insecure."

"Well, let me see. Insecurity comes from everything you've learned that is in conflict with something in you, something strong. It rises from disagreement in your own self. The moment we are born, we have to rely on someone. This someone teaches you a thing or two to survive. You behave according to what has been taught to you, becoming a product of the teaching you received. What we call a success story is if you become what they want, the one that pleases, the one that works. If an individual has doubts over or inner conflict with what has been taught, trouble starts. I said 'trouble' for lack of a better word. You go underground, losing self-value. You feel doomed and unworthy in your own skin."

"That's sad and unflattering. I thought I was okay, strong enough, despite the unpleasantness in my life."

"It's your affinity for solitude and being quite at home with it that prevents you from recognizing the insecurity. Don't misunderstand me. We all live with a certain amount of insecurity. Just as you described 'hurt' as a potent energy, so is insecurity. It wears you out and wastes you away."

She asked, "Can I be more distracted than insecure? You succeeded in portraying me as a man on the moon. I like that. A single distracted figure on the moon."

He laughed and said, "I must insist on the issue. It's true that your insecurity has different characteristics in comparison to the general public. You don't know why your existence isn't pleasing to others. And you don't care. You have to be you as much as possible and being you disagrees with others, which you are aware of, but it still shrinks the horizon of your freedom. This shrinkage is the source of insecurity. Do I make sense?"

"Sorry, not at all. I'm still with the picture of me being alone on the moon."

"When are you coming back to Earth?" he said, chuckling.

"Not for a while, I'm afraid," she said, holding her nose.

"Come right back down at the speed of light." Not knowing how many more times he'd have with her, he had to make her continue. Why? He just had to.

"Why should I be insecure if I don't care about pleasing others?"

"You don't care, but you are well aware of it. You're depriving yourself of a chance to meet people who might be well pleased by you. You're missing out on them and them of you. I'm one example. You please me as you are. I became fond of you from the very first time. You didn't catch on to that."

"Thanks. Too many people I've known would throw stones at me, for no apparent reason." Dr. Min had expected a different response, like "what is it that you like about me?" Then she fell silent altogether.

Dr. Min waited and waited. "I'd like some coffee, would you like a cup?" She nodded without looking at him, and her lips seemed to be quivering. He called the secretary and asked for coffee, seeing two streams of tears on her face drawing lines on her cheeks.

"It's true, Dr. Min, I don't remember any time I've ever tried to please anyone."

He gave her tissues and asked, "Why the tears?"

"You're trying to make me see your truth, which I don't, can't."

"What is this truth I'm forcing on you, dear?"

She wiped her tears, her thumb twitching a little, which reminded him of her dire situation of which she was still unaware, reviving the tremor in his heart. They sat quietly for a while. He was glad when coffee arrived. She cupped the mug with both of her hands, then immediately retreated the left one with the twitching thumb back to her lap.

"You're trying to implant the idea in me that I am better off without trying to please others. Maybe, maybe not. I don't know, and I don't see what good it would do for me. I don't blame my upbringing. Yes, it was bleak, and I disagree that people should live in bleakness as such. What for? I'm good with myself; I don't want to be anyone else but me, even in my next life. I'm not denying that my upbringing played a big part in making me the person who I am. I fully understand you. I live with memories all the time. They are good memories, references to consult with at times and reminders of the blessing I was born with."

"What is this blessing?" he asked, motioning her to drink the coffee, taking a sip himself.

"Being me." She took the mug to her lips and drank it all up in one go.

"In the end, those who intentionally hurt me or tried to edify me for my own good brought out my true nature. In a way, I should thank those who ended up helping me to know myself better, to like myself more. As I mentioned, I fully understand where you're coming from, the cause and effect that could be the constant force of building and destruction. My story isn't of the destructive kind. One story that comes to my mind that involves the issue of pleasing others..." Seeing him nodding with his eyes glued on hers, she carried on, "I was in the third grade, when I joined the school choir. We sang at various places like hospitals, army bases, and even in radio stations. I liked it because we got to go places and were treated to lunches afterwards. There were about twenty to thirty kids, all girls. One day after the performance, we were taken to a Chinese lunch. Everybody ordered chow mein with bean paste sauce. In the middle of the meal, I had to go to the bathroom. After returning, I simply resumed eating until I cleaned the bowl. Laughter broke out among the kids, calling me a pig. What happened was that the kids piled up my bowl with their unwanted noodles, which I didn't notice. Mind you, I wasn't embarrassed or hurt. Two things in relation to that incident stayed in me for a while. I found myself wondering if I would do the same thing to them. The answer was no."

"And the other thing?"

"I saw the similarity between them and my family. The world is full of them."

"And where did it take you?"

"I think that incident perhaps played a crucial role in forming my worldview. The point is that I don't necessarily believe a bad experience causes a bad effect. It could be quite the contrary."

The thought of Sohee, her sister zoomed by him. She blamed anything and everything for her problems. Everyone was a villain one way or another, and yet she wanted those villains to pay homage to her. The dichotomy of the two sisters was startling.

"Kids do such stuff, you know that," he said, smiling, imagining her digging into a triple serving of the chow mein.

"I know, of course. But I tend to believe that such behavior comes from hostility, like any practical joke. Anyway, that was probably the beginning of why I don't engage in the game of trying to please others."

"You think it's a game?"

"Most of it. An attempt to disguise insincerity, even as one wants to belong.

"But that wasn't the case with your grandmother, right?"

"She was real but a dying breed. One doesn't encounter a person like her anymore. I don't know much about her life before my birth. She was a person who would protect her young at any cost and expected nothing back from them. I thought that quality in her was most beautiful. I used to comb her hair, oil it, braid it, and make a bun on her nape, just the way she liked. It pleased her. She would close her eyes and hum a tune, swaying her body gently."

"So, there you go. You tried to please someone, your grandma, after all."

"No, not at all, you got it wrong. I did it because it pleased *me*."

Dr. Min leaned back, chuckling. He looked at the clock. "It's close to lunchtime. We can continue later if you're hungry."

"I'm not. But if you are…"

He shook his head and pulled his chair closer to the desk.

"If it's okay, I'd like some more coffee," she said, showing him the empty cup. He ordered a pot this time, telling her, "I noticed you are a coffee drinker."

She replied, "Only when someone makes it for me. Ha, ha." She laughed, showing no trace of tears anymore. Then out of the blue she said she didn't get along with tea drinkers. "Even though I used to go to the teahouse with the boys I used to hang out with and drink cup after another." She looked at him vaguely, as if waiting for an explanation from him as to that irregularity.

"Who are these boys? You've never said anything about friends?" he jumped in, like he found a missing link. She always referred to her school friends as classmates. She made that distinction clearly.

"Oh, there were these boys I became quite chummy with for a while."

Sensing that she wasn't going to continue, he quickly asked, "Tell me about them. You've got me interested."

She threw a glance at him as if saying, "Really?"

"From top to bottom, yes?"

"It might bore you to death," she said, turning her head to the door where the secretary had shown up with a pot of coffee.

After she filled up Miri's cup and left, he said, "I'll be the judge of that. Besides, I'm trained to sit through the thick and thin of boredom. Every insignificant thing can be crucial at times. But more so, I enjoy talking with you, truthfully."

She drank the coffee, reminiscing over the time with the boys. It seemed so long ago. She told him everything including their trip to the shaman on that early spring Sunday. She told him in detail the vision she had had after smoking the pipe and also how she stole money from her mother to pay for the visit and the Chinese lunch that followed.

He asked, "What are their names?"

She looked at him funny, as if saying, "What for?" but she told him their names. Neither of them were Hans, although he didn't think any Korean would give their boy a German name. Still, he had to give it a try. He decided to ask about Hans later.

"I think it's a charming experience. I wasn't bored at all. But why the abrupt disconnection? Did anything happen?"

"Well, as I already told you, Mun moved to Tokyo and Ahn just disappeared. Ahn was Mun's shadow. When the object disappears, so does the shadow...ha, ha. Mun and I wrote letters to each other, just a couple to be more accurate, but our relationship faded away. I'm terrible at keeping in touch with people."

"You don't want them to know what's going on with your life or are curious about theirs?"

"Not at all. It's like an out of sight, out of mind kind of thing. It has to be face to face in person for me to feel that it's real."

"But judging by your story, you must miss them, no?"

"I miss that time and what we did together but not the individuals per se."

"That sounds almost cold." He didn't believe her. She didn't open up to anybody in fear of remembering her hurt, the hurt of missing someone, which she saw as weakness, a humiliation to herself, no matter how much she boasted about her "healthy hurt." This strategy worked for her throughout her life; perhaps she became to believe that it was her strength.

But the next statement she made surprised him. "Dr. Min, I know what you're thinking, tell me if I'm wrong. You think I don't let myself be vulnerable, especially in human relationships."

"Yes and no. Only it puzzles me how you can open and close your mind at command. To me that is humanly impossible. You said 'out of sight, out of mind.' Do you know all infants go through that stage?"

"Then I must be stuck there. But allow me to romanticize it a bit, because I really like that part of me. I call it having a 'nomadic personality,' where one has to be on the run constantly...ha, ha. There's no time for attachments."

He wasn't convinced but let her continue. He felt his skin shrinking with chills, imagining the abyss of loneliness this young creature had to wander through. She found a defense mechanism that worked for her. Who was he to tell her that she was wrong? Only he hoped this self-deception was kind to her.

"You know, I see it like people sharing a bench at a train station. Sometime you enjoy each other's company while waiting for your train. At that moment you become transitional objects for each other, a toy, a plaything...until the train comes, and we go our separate ways."

"Do you mind if I wrote that down in my notes and used it sometime? It's beautiful, the way you put it." He exaggerated his praise to disguise the sadness deepening in his heart. She put her feet up on the chair, drew her knees up, and started to rub her forehead on them. "Is the pain coming back?"

"It's not time for the shot yet. I want to lie down."

"Okay. Go on back to your room. I'll tell them to give you the shot now."

"Sorry, but I'll wait for my regular schedule," she said, getting up. She bowed and walked to the door when he asked her, "One more thing before I forget. Who is Hans?"

She had her hand on the doorknob and said without looking back, "Who?"

"Hans? Remember the psychological test you took when you first came here? You mentioned the name."

She turned to him, giving him a look indicating that she was beginning to remember. "Oh, yeah, I remember. Hans…yeah." A mischievous smile appeared on her lips, then she said, "He's a hero in one of Hermann Hesse's novels called *Under the Wheel.*"

She turned to the door when he asked again, "Who is he to you?"

"A character in the book. I had just finished the book, and I decided to use his name over and over to try to speed up the boring test. That's all." She left.

He opened the drawer on the desk, took out a cigarette, and lit it. He turned his chair to face the window, blowing out a long stream of smoke and said to himself, "What a joke of a profession I'm in! Dr. Min, you have no business in laughing at Father Mark's profession as the most ludicrous one. You, sir, are very much in the circus."

-74-

Dr. Min ordered lunch and ate it in his office, catching up with paperwork when the phone rang. "Send her in."

Miri came back. He gave her a quizzical stare but motioned her to sit.

"If it's not a good time, I can come back."

"Anything wrong?" he asked, looking at his wristwatch. It was three in the afternoon.

"No, I'm fine. I had my shot and am without pain. I wanted to—I have to ask you something that you must answer me with the truth."

"Let's do it then," he said, putting away his papers. He saw her eyes deeply involved with her inner dialogue.

"My life at the moment is a bit angry. I sense something odd is going on but am left in the dark. I need to know."

He propped his elbows on the desk and made a pyramid with his hands touching the tip of his nose with his fingers, wondering where to aim his eyes, which eventually parked on her arms that were rather tightly crossed in a threatening manner.

"First of all, give me a moment to think this through. Can you do that?" he said, noticing her sitting firmly. He took out a cigarette and lit it with his eyes fixed on her crossed arms. It was the first time he saw her looking so defiant.

"Can I have one?" she asked. He walked to the door and locked it. He lit a cigarette for her saying, "If anyone saw me giving a minor a cigarette, I would be unemployed. But what the heck, if it helps you from beating me up, I have a good excuse." He laughed nervously. She laughed back, sticking to her defiant mode. They finished their cigarettes in silence, he looking blankly at his desk and she at the floor with her head tilted. He noticed she wasn't simply inhaling the smoke but sucking on the cigarette, holding it between her fore and middle fingers tightly. After finishing the cigarette, her arms resumed crossing over her chest.

"I wouldn't know until the necessary tests are done."

"Then tell me what you suspect."

"It might be nothing. It's irresponsible of me to—"

"Just tell me." She stood up, leaning over the desk with her head nearly touching his. He looked up to meet her eyes.

He ordered her to sit back down.

"As I said, it's just my suspicion." As he told her about his suspicion, he noticed no change in her. She was silent for a full minute or two. Her face began to soften, her eyes turned dreamy, and there was even a faint smile on her lips. She got up and said, "Thank you," and was about to leave when he ordered her a second time to sit back down. She obeyed.

"You should at least tell me what this information means to you."

"I have nothing more to do except wait for that time."

"Which might not happen if I'm wrong."

"I'm pretty sure you're right, don't ask why and how I know," she said, remembering what the goat told her. "From now on I'd like to spend my time concentrating on one thing. There's much work to do."

How peculiar! Where are the tears, where's the shouting of 'Oh, my God, it can't be true, it's not fair.' The usual stuff, he thought, intrigued.

"There's nothing more to do, you said, but much work to do at the same time?"

"'Nothing more to do' means I'm free of expectations and obligations. I don't belong to dreadful hope. Frankly, this news takes care of many things in my case. But at the same time I have to prepare myself to accept this, which is a lot of work. Did I explain myself to you?"

He simply nodded.

"Have you ever thought about cutting your life short?" He could kick himself hard for letting the question materialize.

"Suicide? No, I would never do that. Speaking of suicide, that's the middle name of my sister Sohee."

"Don't you think she suffers? You sound sarcastic."

"Maybe so. I don't know about other people who are suicidal, but in my sister's case the word 'suicide' belongs to the world of life, not the world of the hereafter."

"It's not that simple. Suffering is suffering. As a matter of fact, isn't that what you said once?"

"You're right. I don't feel like being kind at the moment. And I would never kill myself, if that's your concern."

"As long as we're on the subject, let's be blunt and brutally honest about death, shall we?"

"Why, I'd like that more than anything now."

"What does death mean to you?"

"What does it mean to you?"

"I asked first."

"You answer first."

They both laughed, both waiting for the other to answer. He went first.

"When I was a little boy growing up in a Christian household—my father was a minister—I decided to believe anything else but Christianity. What a bore! I told myself that if heaven is for these boring people, I didn't want to go there. I was a nature boy top to bottom. One day when I was observing nature, as I always spent my free time, I decided to believe that life is constant, that it continues without end. Death was just a resting period, like plants in the winter, to be renewed for the next round. But that was then. It was a rather sweet thought, I must say."

"I like that. What changed you?"

"I haven't had a chance to think about my change, to tell the truth. My belief just dissipated, evaporated without replacement." He started to doodle again.

"I thought the same thing. I didn't want to be in heaven if all these people at the church would go there. But I suffered from the idea of a burning hell, eternal fire, and so on. When I was thinking about it, I suffered like I was already in hell. I was extremely sensitive to ghost stories, let alone horror films. I couldn't even look at a skeleton drawing in a comic book without my heartbeat accelerating uncontrollably. When I was eight or nine, it was during summer, I overheard people saying the world might end on that night because a large comet was heading to Earth. It was a hot night, but I covered myself with a blanket from head to toe, waiting for it to be over, so alone, so scared."

"I remember that. People didn't think anything of it, and it didn't happen. I mean, the comet was real, it just happened to miss Earth."

"I remember wondering why other people were so much braver than I was." She giggled.

"You know now that people didn't believe because they didn't want to. On the other hand, you believed. So please continue."

"My head tells me one thing, but my heart says another when it comes to the idea of my own death. The gap between the head and the heart is immeasurable."

"Do you know the phrase: live a life of 'short but thick' rather than 'long and thin'?"

She nodded.

"People use that phrase often. Is that supposed be comforting?"

"We glorify a persona that has no fear of death. I call it a 'persona' because it is nothing but that. People play that role because it sounds strong."

"I'd like to think of death as the reward of life, that you get a 'life well-lived award' no matter how one's life has been. You leave the stage and go home. Then again, when I think how it will be a reality to me someday, the romantic idea of death being well-earned rest after a grueling performance turns into a bleak, airless, eternal darkness. I really don't like the notion of an afterlife. I want it to be over when it's over. No more me, no more anything."

"Does that idea comfort you? Most people I know choose to believe otherwise."

"Dust to dust. Why ask more? But am I being honest with myself when I say that? I have no idea. I believe in a Creator. Then I wonder if the Creator is kind and loving or vicious and psychotic or all of the above, like us. In the end, it doesn't matter; you can't be choosy with an unknown thing."

"Do you see this Creator as your God?"

"I can't say. I remember learning about Darwinian theory in science class. After that class I found myself paying attention to things in nature. I was so blown away with the design, its mechanisms as well as its beauty, as if everything were individually and lovingly painted with a brush, so carefully and perfectly. That day I became a believer that someone had great fun in creating all creatures. But He also let them be crushed mercilessly."

"But I get the feeling you don't include humans in God's careful, loving, and perfect design."

"We don't have much aesthetic properties compared to the rest of nature, in my opinion. But on the inside, we are the most colorful creatures that God created. His abstract work, if you will."

He laughed, saying, "I like that."

She suddenly changed her posture to be more erect and energetic. "There's one other thing. I think this world overlaps with different dimensions."

"You mean aliens?"

"No, entities who are here very much like us but invisible. Sometimes you're alone, vegetating, but you can't help sensing something else is happening right where you are."

"Sixth sense, intuition?"

"I don't know. But to me it's more than that. It feels like physical properties, such as temperature and the magnetic field around me suddenly change; sometimes I can even smell it."

"What does it smell like?"

"You can laugh at me as much as you want, but please not now, after I leave."

"Do you see me laughing?"

They both laughed.

"Sometimes it smelled like jasmine or a bouquet of some kind, other times man's cologne or even rotten fish."

"These are ordinary odors of the dimension to which you and I belong." He then observed to himself, this is what she loves the most. Playing with her thoughts, which are fluid and ever ready to change their direction. He could see she was full of opinions but not opinionated. She had a tendency of starting to say something about, for example, an elephant, and before he realized it, she would be on the subject of zebras. But time after time, he was impressed by the great mind she owned. Only the world she lived in had no heart to offer a place for such a mind, and she knew it too, he was sure of it.

"Let's go back to where we started," he said in an attempt to bring her back to the moment when he was forced to tell her about the possibility of her grave illness. However disheartening, he thought it was important. She looked like she'd forgotten about it. He was wrong.

She said, "Suppose I am terminally ill and have to face the end." She lowered her head, hugging her torso and rocking a bit.

He felt ashamed. He lowered his eyes, feeling a mixture of anger and humbleness. "I'm so sorry. I really am so sorry."

"Don't be, please. You're gonna make me sad, doctor."

"I feel like the ass of the century," he said, tapping his desk with his fingers, trying to disguise the tremor in his voice. He knew what the young girl would face, the excruciating pain that was inoperable, that there was no treatment to prolong her stay. He felt like a criminal.

"Let's talk hypothetically about…"

"My exit plan?" she asked, seeing him nodding his head. "How long do I have?"

"That depends. The test will give a better idea."

"Six months? A year?"

"Can't say…"

"Will I be in a lot of pain?"

"The painkillers you're on seem to be working."

"I don't like pain. It turns me into a beast."

"I know, like the other day at the clinic," he said and chuckled.

"But, boy, Dr. Min, it felt marvelous, unbelievably satisfying. Did I mention that the pain disappeared when I was exercising my right?"

He laughed aloud this time, but at the same time, felt totally weird.

"I do know for a fact that some people fix their migraine pain by reminding themselves of situations that made them furious. They claim the pain goes away miraculously when they induce anger in themselves."

Silence fell between them for a while, as if they had forgotten each other's presence. Her keeping up a normal appearance confused him. It would have been easier for him if she went hysterical, in which case he had plenty of training and experience, but this?

"If I could be of any help with anything, you'll let me know, right? Can I count on you in doing that?" He looked at her helplessly.

"I'll be okay, and yes, you can count on me."

"I feel so inadequately equipped as a medical doctor; I feel stupid. Forgive me," he said, reaching for her hands. She offered them to him, with her twitching thumbs tucked under her palms. They held hands, not looking at each other.

"Am I going to lose my mind?" she asked, almost in a whisper.

"No, honey. No, you won't," he lied, gently shaking her hands in his.

"I've never felt that I was truly in this world. I never felt I was living, never fully awake. The funny thing is that I like life, I really do."

Dr. Min thought to himself, oh what have I done! What have I done! His heart was sinking, sinking to lower than the bottom of all the stupidity in the world. Oh, what have I done?

- 7 5 -

In 1969 the spring came late and didn't last long, so the spring flowers had to share the stage with misguided summer blossoms. It was late April, and people were saying "April is last year's June." Miri was sitting on the steps made of old stones in front of the temple. Her hair had grown back a little from when it was shaved for her surgery. It didn't do her any good. It wasn't surgery to remove the tumor; the fluid building up in her head needed to be drained.

She lit a cigarette and blew the smoke out to the morning sunlight veiled with lingering fog. The green of the trees was already deep in shade like those of midsummer. Two swallows were jetting back and forth to feed their young, who were popping their heads out of a nest tucked underneath the eaves of the temple, screaming for more food. "Pretty soon they will practice flying, the sweetest thing to watch," the old monk said the other day with a toothless smile, placing a large basket filled with leaves underneath the nest in case any of them fell.

It had been nearly two months since she came to the temple. The moment she arrived there, she knew her ending would be perfect. She wept a lot alone, walking up the hill, walking down the hill, sitting among the bushes and listening to birds chirping, waking up in the wee hours of the night looking at the moving shadows of rustling trees on the rice-papered window, caused by the lonely wind. The soft snoring of the nurse who was sleeping next to her made her sob. She was a quiet middle-aged woman whose world didn't demand much of her by way of speech but allowed her the gift of maximum laughter. She laughed like a frightened chicken, startling everyone around her every time.

In early February Miri was moved to the city hospital. She was in and out of consciousness from being heavily drugged when her mother and Sohee came to see her. She opened her eyes at one point and thought that she was unhappily dreaming of them standing next to her bed. Later she found out that they were real. "Oh, your poor mother, she couldn't stop crying," said a woman who changed her sheets. The next day her father showed up with a priest, his childhood friend. He even brought bananas, which were rare and expensive even in summer, let alone in the winter. He didn't come near her bed. The entire ten minutes of his visit he sat on a chair next to the door with his priest friend. At first she thought the priest came to listen to her final confession, but he sat next to her father with a polite smile without saying a word. It seemed he came to give his father moral support. "You'll receive the best care money can buy," her father said, stretching the corners of his mouth downward showing his bottom teeth perfectly lined up.

A series of tests occupied the next week or so. By then every orifice of her body was taking turns in bleeding, a little drizzle here and there, stopped for a day or so then came back. Her mother visited her regularly, and Miri pretended that she was incoherent whenever she showed up. Sometimes she opened her eyes and saw her reciting the rosary sitting on the chair next to the door. Another time she sprinkled holy water on Miri, praying, "Save this poor soul from the eternal fire." "Please show a miracle for my daughter," wasn't one of the prayers. Miri stayed with her dislike of her mother. When she spooned the holy water into her mouth, pulling down her chin, her body cringed. Around the third week of being there, her visits became less frequent, which Miri welcomed with a laugh, "Maybe I'm not dying soon enough. It became a bit anticlimactic, perhaps."

Dr. Min came back from his trip to Tokyo with his wife, who had successfully gained a new high-rise nose. Sam licked a few pair of shoes to get a passport for the doctor's wife. It was late February when the doctor came to see her. He noticed her face was more asymmetrical and that she had the appearance of a palsy victim. The left side of her face was concave with a droopy eye, and the right side, which was retaining fluid, puffed up her cheek and pushed her eye to a slit. It was like two different faces were merging. He squeezed her toes and sat at the bottom of her bed.

"Hi, Dr. Min." She moved her lips to smile, which was distorted. "How was your trip?" He just nodded. "How's her new nose?" she asked, startling him.

"Sam told you that?" he asked, seeing her nodding. "That guy can't keep his mouth shut," he complained. He was thoroughly embarrassed. He acted like he was really pissed off at Sam for a few seconds and said, "It's still bruised and swollen, but she's happy with it."

She gave him that distorted smile again and said, "So good to see you."

It pained him right in the chest when she said that. "Have they been treating you well?"

"I wouldn't know if they mistreated me. I've been doing nothing but sleeping, it seems."

"We have to do some procedures on you. First of all, we have to drain fluid."

"Yes, yes. Just make sure I don't have any pain."

"There won't be any pain, I promise."

"Dr. Min, I have a favor to ask."

"What is it?"

"After this procedure, I would like to go to Sam's temple and spend my last days there. The favor I want to ask is…"

"To talk to your folks, right?

"Yes. Could you?"

"Of course. I'll do better than just asking. I'll make them give you all the comfort you want, even if I have to beat them up." They laughed, and it made him feel a little better. He tried hard not to sigh in despair.

"Have you been to the temple?"

"Yes, several times. Sam and Mrs. Lim fixed it up so nicely. You'd like it. It has all the modern conveniences but kept the old charm," he said with dreamy eyes, drawing lines in the air with his hand.

His first visit to the temple was some years ago. Sam asked him to have a look at Kuju, a happy young man with the mind of a young boy. He was painfully shy. "That's what I noticed. He wasn't a shy boy before," Sam told him. The only people Kuju was comfortable with were the old monk and Sam, as well as his animals. By then he not only had various pets roaming around the temple but found a true love for the stuffed animals that Sam brought for him, with which he filled his room. Seeing him take a special interest in toy animals, Sam brought him a whole bunch one day. Bongsan and Sam once talked about Kuju's affection for the toy animals. "He loves the live ones like he always has, but there's something very special he feels for the toy animals." Sam agreed.

After the doctor examined Kuju, who was trembling and sweating from shyness, he said to Sam, "There are too many things we don't know. When people shout what is scientific and what isn't, I want to throw a brick at them. What we know in terms of science is a fraction of the tip of the iceberg. Even the things we claim to be scientific fact could turn out to be wrong someday. All I can tell you is that he is physically healthy and strong. We know of cases like his, but that's about it."

"Do they regress further down?"

"Sometimes. They regress as though shedding years. The curious thing about Kuju is that it seems he enjoys life, unlike the few cases I've encountered. There was definite suffering in them, which exploded at times even to the point of violence."

"Oh, not my Kuju. He lives like a sunflower."

"My guess is that his environment suits him, and he's not pressured to change. He's lucky to have the old monk and you. He seems to be happy, a ton happier than normal people."

"I know. I found myself being envious of that sometimes. Ha, ha."

"One thing, though, they have a relatively short life."

"How short?"

"Between now and middle age. They rarely pass middle age."

"But why such shyness? It's uncharacteristic of him. He was such an outgoing, chatty boy.

"I don't know. He still is that way with you and Bongsan, as you said. Maybe that's all he needs. People like him are similar to the mentally disabled, but unlike them, they develop shyness as if part of them were aware of the fact that they aren't ordinary."

"Isn't it possible to train his mind? For example, show him the dos and don'ts of the adult world. He's a bright boy."

"You're comparing him to normal immaturity. What he has is totally different. It's an organic disorder like schizophrenia. He's not only stopped mental growth, but he's regressing. You wouldn't expect a little child to understand calculus by teaching him."

"I didn't know schizophrenia is a physical disorder."

"Some theories still assert that the disorder stems from environment or trauma, etc. Circumstances may contribute in detonating the bomb that was already there. Someday we'll know more. But I have no doubt that it has something to do with the physical-chemistry of the body."

"In my opinion, every single one of us is a bit sour in the head."

"Boy, don't I know it! Well, you sir, are one who owns hands-on experience," Dr. Min said and giggled, gently pushing Sam with his fist. Sam nodded, looking down, joining him with a semi-giggle.

"When you get to have this many years in my field, you really get confused about what's normal. The word 'normal' becomes the most mysterious, most bizarre term."

"Do you think people would be healthier and happier if they could roam around freely, you know, like cavemen?"

Dr. Min said, "If that worked, we would not be where we are now. I think we are hopelessly in love with the idea that things should be better. We search endlessly, miserably, for that 'better,' dismissing what was 'better' before as not good enough anymore. I'm not discounting the fact that such behavior of ours contributed to the comforts we now couldn't do without. Then again, we lost something on the way to civilization so that we could never be able to go back to the way our ancestors were. We became weak, calling a little nuisance suffering. Animals know pain but without any cognition of 'why me?' But we humans know how to pity ourselves. Maybe God wasn't feeling well or was drunk when He was creating us and ended up poorly wiring us."

"And why didn't He correct his mistake?"

"He liked the result of His mistake better than the original draft. We, His mistake, turned out to be better than He Himself had planned."

Sam said, "When I took a trip to Africa…"

"You never told me you'd been to Africa?"

"Now you know. I went there once when I was studying in America. My university had the summer programs abroad."

"It must have been something else."

"Stop interrupting, you're making me forget what I want to say. I was an immature, cocky young man who insisted on wearing a suit and tie in spite of the professor who led our group's urging me not to. Ha, ha, pretty stupid. I wasn't aware of other kids laughing at me. I regretted having chosen to spend my summer there when I got there. When I first saw the natives, I shuddered at the sight of them even though I'd seen pictures of them before. Their lifestyle made me think they must've been slow, very slow in general. Towards the end of the trip, something happened to me, to my empty brain. I had more respect for the natives living in the huts, almost naked, with sticks and spears than those who converted to the Western lifestyle in the city. The city people seemed to me to be fish out of water. They didn't seem as noble as the ones in loincloths. I tried to picture Manhattan in that land. I couldn't, as though it wasn't meant to be. It saddened me to know that the land, that magnificent, powerful soil on earth with these noble people was being violated by what we call 'civilization.' This is why I asked you about happy cavemen."

"So you came back as a changed man who would be less formal, less cocky, perhaps?"

"Not really. As soon as I returned, I resumed my most comfortable—insufferable to others perhaps—old ways. Until one evening, when I went to see a movie with a few guys. The film was about aristocrats in Victorian times. I found myself comparing the characters with the African natives. Their self-imposed importance, their spiffy outfits that looked uncomfortable with their top hats, canes, and white gloves, the women next to them decorated as if they were competing with garden flowers, seemed so stupid, consumed with outdoing others. I guess that was the first time I thought that civilization was leading humankind in the wrong direction.

"It taught us to be ashamed of our natural self. The sad thing is that we don't even know how to dislike it. It became us. Civilization is becoming a question of to be or not be."

"Too true."

"There's no such thing as 'too true.'"

Sam gave him a dirty look and said, "Have you noticed that you're cursed with correcting others?"

"Too true," Dr. Min said.

-76-

"My daughter wants to die in Buddhist temple? I won't allow it. If she doesn't want to stay at the hospital, she should either come home or go to a Catholic convalescent home. I won't let her die as a heathen." Miri's mother was vehement when Dr. Min told her about Miri's wish. They were sitting in the hospital cafeteria. He hardened his eyes and stared at her in silence. She stared back. He didn't move, and neither did she. A ridiculously long time passed, up to the point that his eyes began to water. Eventually, she lowered her eyes and took a sip of cold coffee, turning her face away from him and tightening her lips. However silly the staring match was, he felt he won a small victory over the scary woman. In the end he thought it was a waste of time and ended the meeting cordially.

"What do I do? I promised her," Dr. Min said to Sam, who was pacing around listening to him.

"Maybe we should just kidnap her. I'll pay for her medical needs," he said, sharing his frustration, almost angrily. Lately, Dr. Min was concerned that something about Sam was different. Miri's situation could have affected him and caused a setback. But he looked good; he seemed bigger and his complexion was brighter, healthy. His boyish eyes bore the sadness of a mature man but with acceptance. The guy is finally growing up, he thought with cautious optimism. He could not gauge the depth of Sam's affection for Miri, but he knew he was in pain. Perhaps being on the giving end rather than the receiving, which had been the history of his life, brought out the change. Dr. Min himself had never been as involved with his patients as he was with both Miri and Sam. He couldn't deny the feeling that he was among friends, among good people helping a friend in trouble. The feeling was both sweet and tender, rekindling what he had once hoped for in life but long forgotten, the feeling of why he chose the profession as a young man. Sadly, before he realized what had happened to him, it became a living. More and more he put on layers of the armor of rules and regulations, like others in the field who he used to sneered at. The belief in himself, the conviction of a spiritually noble person was long gone, and he became a darling boy in the industry, efficiently going along with the flow. "After all, this is a business like anything else in this world," was what the chief administrator told him when he was a young resident eager to put the patients ahead of anything. His initial frustration and dis-appointment faded, and the phrase "it's a living" became his guiding voice. True, he had to take a deep breath now and then and sighed as if he would have purged his conscience out of him.

"Have you rearranged the furniture? It looks different," Dr. Min said, giving a look around, sitting on the sofa.

"I got rid of a few things after I last came back from the island."

"Oh? What made you to do that? You had some beautiful things, price-less things." Sam was a knickknack junky. He collected antiques and un-usual items, all valuable. Dr. Min got up and walked around the spacious office and noticed them gone. He saw the window coverings were gone too.

"I realized that I had no attachment to those. It all seemed silly, espe-cially the price tags they came with."

"You didn't dump them in the trash bins, though," Dr. Min said, tast-ing regret in his mouth. Something in him was hurting, as if they were his belongings.

"I donated them to a university museum."

"That was a noble gesture. Why not give them to people? Valuable items like that can be useful when they need money."

"I thought about it. But in the end I decided not to. You look hurt that I didn't consult with you."

"No, no. Not at all. I salute you, honestly. I am…It's just that my head is bombarded with the dollar amount you gave up. Although for a rich man like you…"

"You are wrong there. Rich people have a stronger attachment to a dollar bill than people with not much money. Wealth comes with money sickness. A single dollar means so much more to a rich man. I bet you that it's a lot easier to make poor people give up their change than extracting a dollar from a rich man."

"Well, it will take some reconciliation in me to process this. Isn't it so weird that I have nothing to do with those knickknacks whatsoever, but it still hurts me? I didn't even care for them." They both laughed.

"Anyway, going back to Miri, can you give me any suggestion other than kidnapping her?" he asked, lying on the sofa with his feet on its arm.

"Why not speak directly with her father? Isn't he the final voice in that family?"

"But I noticed that he leaves it up to his wife when it comes to a matter of religion."

"I thought he was the tyrant of the family."

"He is, I believe, when it comes to money and other creepy matters, but when it involves the girls and church, she is the domineering one." He added, "Trust me, she isn't a willow." He told Sam about the staring match with her, which doubled them up with laughter like two little boys.

"Is she good looking?"

"Unfortunately, yes. She must have been striking when she was young, except for her eyes. They're hard. They reminded me of those of a crocodile. She dressed less than modestly, which I think she takes great pride in as a God-fearing woman. Oh, but you should see her hands. They're easily a size bigger than mine. My hands are rather large too, as you see." He fanned out his hands to Sam and continued, "…huge knuckles and seriously abused nails."

"Miri told me that she was into hard labor."

"I know, a constant cleaner. You met her father before, Sam."

"Just in a large group situation."

"But you must've noticed his appearance. He looked like he stepped right out of a fashion magazine." Sam nodded in agreement, remembering how Miri mocked him as a latent cross-dresser.

"What a contrast, he and his wife are."

"How about this for an idea," Sam started, ignoring Dr. Min's comment. "We send Father Gregory to her. He carries significant weight in that church, not to mention that he himself was a tenant at that temple where he was saved from near death by Buddhists. I think that will work."

-77-

"It's done." Father Gregory's voice roared on the phone.

"Great! How did you pull it off? I heard the woman was some kind of a reptile."

"It took two long sittings with her. Father Mark played an important role. I played a saintly holy man and Father Mark a punisher, ha, ha, he, he."

"Did she agree reluctantly or willingly?" Sam asked, puzzled by his own curiosity.

"She's all willing now. When you gave me this job, I couldn't quite understand your interference. Father Mark filled me in. But when I saw her and talked with her at length, I realized that it's my duty to make the girl's passing as peaceful as possible, I mean, away from that woman."

"I'm curious. What made her to be 'willing'?"

"First of all, Father Mark scared her by using flashcards of heaven and hell, so to speak. He said, 'Even the most pious kind fall into the flames of hell because they're too consumed in loving God, so they ignore or even hurt the people around them. Faith and hope give you transportation to the gate of heaven, but it is only love that will let you pass through the gate. This 'love' is a very complicated thing and too easy to misunderstand. The only kind of love God truly enjoys is the love powerful enough to make one feel cold in hell. In other words, He wants to know how willingly you are to go to hell for your loved one. Just think about it for a moment, what a beautiful sacrifice that is, that would be, in His eyes. Just imagining such love gives me goose bumps. After all, isn't it what our Lord, Jesus did for us? He died for us, and it took him three days to resurrect. Where do you think he had been during those three days? He was in hell.' It was a brilliant performance!"

"That did it then?"

"No, numerous quotes from the Scriptures had to be used, mostly frightening stuff. The woman is spiritually retarded. I felt sorry for her in the end."

"Why?"

"Because she carries the worst curse."

"Which is?"

"Not able to love. Isn't that hell?"

"I owe you big time."

"Reserve a room for me in the temple when my turn comes."

"You don't have to wait for that. It's there for you any time, any time at all, my good friend." He was about to hang up when he heard Father Gregory from the other end saying, "One more thing. It's kind of funny. After she agreed to grant the girl's dying wish, she demanded an absolution in writing, signed by both me and Father Mark."

They laughed hard. Strangely, Sam saw a tinge of Miri in her mother in that last statement Father Gregory made. After he hung up the phone, he thought about what Father Gregory had said. "The worst curse of all is not being able to love." He remembered Miri once said how she could never hate her mother. "Whenever I'm warming up to hatred, the pity I feel for her always blocks it, overwhelming me. I strongly dislike her sometimes, but in the end, it's pity that takes me over, making me feel guilty. Not an easy combination of emotions to feel simultaneously."

-78-

Sitting on the stone step smoking, Miri tilted her head this way and that way, trying to remember something. It didn't come to her. A loud belch escaped her mouth, frightening the sparrow sitting on a branch. She laughed, watching the bird flying away.

Her mother was to visit her that day. She came once a week with food she had prepared. Her sisters had also come one time but got freaked out by Kuju's pets, among them chickens, pigs, goats, and two raccoons that he raised after he had found them next to their dead mother. Her sisters locked themselves in her room and didn't come out until it was time to leave. Her mother never stayed overnight, which was a relief to her. Sam stayed, keeping her company, but he went away during her mother's visits. Mrs. Lim also came during the weekends with her dogs, who, like Miri's sisters, were also afraid of Kuju's pets.

Nurse Chan came out with a bowl of porridge. She squatted down next to her and began to spoon-feed her. "Nice day," she said with a thick southeastern accent. She spoke so rarely and softly, which was at odds with her thunderous laughter. Miri turned her face to her, opening her crooked mouth to receive another bite. Nurse Chan wiped her mouth with a tissue before she drizzled another half spoonful of porridge into Miri's mouth, opening her own mouth widely in the process. It made Miri laugh, causing her to spill out more goop. Without saying anything, Nurse Chan wiped the goop around her mouth and chin and gave her another bite of porridge.

It was midday when Miri's mother came with Mr. Yu, who walked behind her carrying a bag. They were sweaty. Nurse Chan brought them iced barley tea and then sat next to Miri to help her drink her tea. They moved to a bench underneath a large pine tree. Mr. Yu quickly came to help Miri to the bench. She was able to walk alone, slowly and wobbly, but she still managed. He said into her ear that she was a brave girl. He sat her down on the bench next to her mother, murmuring something in her ear that she could not make out. It was something like "She won't stay long." Miri turned her face to him and thanked him, squeezing his skinny arm with her trembling hand. "I've always liked you. You're a good man and a happy man." He touched her trembling hand and walked away. As usual her mother put the bag she brought with her in between them and started to tell her what they were, item by item, in detail, how the porridge was prepared this time, how she pounded the meat extra to tenderize it so that Miri could chew easier, and so on. Her next injection time wasn't till two hours later, but she began to feel the pain coming. She could tell her mother was nervous. She talked and talked, looking at the view in front of her. She didn't seem to notice that Miri hadn't said a word. "God gave us this beautiful world. Imagine how heaven must be like. You know, honestly, there wasn't a day that passed in my life without dreaming about going there. I'm truly looking forward to it." She walked to the edge where the land dropped to a slope with her hands behind her and looked out at the expansive view that was half encircling her head. In her white cotton blouse and black trousers, she looked rather dignified. She talked about the clean life she'd had, so much work she had to do without complaining. "I pray for your grandmother day and night so that her poor soul can be admitted into the Kingdom. As you know, she and I didn't see eye to eye for a long time. But I forgave her, and I beg Jesus to forgive her too." While she was rambling away, Miri lit a cigarette and looked at the custom-designed lighter Sam got for her that popped open and was lit by pressing a button on the side. Her mother turned around and frowned seeing her smoking. "Where did you get the cigarette?"

"What difference does it make?" Miri said, seeing her mother sharply turn her head back to the view and spit, tarnishing the dignified appearance she was able to forge a few moments ago.

"Well, you always have been my 'blue frog.'"

Before a child reached three feet in height, she or he learned about the story of 'the blue frog.' There was once a frog who was blue all over, unlike his mom who was green. He had a mind of his own, which put his mom in despair all the time. "Go east," his mom said, and he would head out west, and so on. Every time his mom told him one thing, he did the opposite. In her dying bed, the mother asked him to bury her near the shore, thinking he would do the opposite. She wanted to be buried in a hill. The blue frog felt terrible and sad that he didn't obey his mom all his life, so he decided to respect her last wish and buried her near the shore. Whenever Miri heard the story as a little girl, she felt sorry for the blue frog. "Why did his mom never give him a chance? Why did he have to repeat his mother's experience to be a good son? He was a bad son because he was different. And he had to live the rest of his life in guilt, labeled as a bad son."

"Yes, I am your blue frog. Only in our case, *you'll* bury *me*," she said, staring at her back. The pain began to pound. It felt like she was both hot and cold.

Oblivious of Miri's stabbing stare, her mother started, "I'm sure you're full of regrets. When I heard that you were dying, I thought deeply and hard why God sent you to me. Then I realized with the help of the Holy Spirit, who kindly felt sympathy for my anguish, that you were my cross. You are my personal cross."

"I hope so," she said, knowing her idea of the cross had a different meaning from her mother's. She saw her mother broadening her chest, her hands on her back, looking up at the sky. She looked full of hope.

She returned to the bench and sat with the bag in the middle and handed Miri a rosary. As she always did when she came to see her, she offered to say a series of prayers with her. First, the whole circle of fifty and more beads of the rosary, then reading liturgy from the *Book of Mass*, specially written for the dying.

After the round of rosary in which Miri had to participate, her mother began to read the creepy liturgy: burning hell, eternal flame, poor vanished souls in exile, the sinner, the sinner, the sinner. She was reading away, occasionally pounding her chest with her fist as the book instructed.

Death always wins, though, Miri thought, remembering the photo of a painting in an art history book at school. She forgot the title and the artist of the painting. It was an oil painting of a skull and some morbid items arranged around it. In front of the skull was a scroll with writings in Latin whose words translated into "Death always wins."

"Mother, I need to lie down," she said when her mother was finished.

"Already?" she asked but didn't look disappointed. She moved closer, removing the bag to the other end of the bench, touching her knees. She grabbed her hands, with her eyes looking over her head and said, "Please forgive me if I unknowingly, unintentionally hurt you." It probably was the hardest thing for her to say, ever. Miri felt a fireball stuck in her throat, noticing her pain losing its intensity. She slowly pulled her hands back, closed her eyes, and said, "You didn't do anything that requires my forgiveness. I was not hurt by you. I was never hurt by you." She said this more for her own ears than those of her mother. She opened her eyes and met with a smile on her mother's lips.

"I want you to know I've forgiven you already."

"So we are in good ways," Miri said, wanting her to leave, to disappear right away before she expelled flames from the fireball stuck in her throat.

Then her mother called out to Mr. Yu who was sitting on a rock down below and told him to fetch the nurse. "She said she needs to lie down."

When the nurse came, Miri stood up, said good-bye, and watched her mother and Mr. Yu walk down the stairs leading back to the road. At the bottom of the steps, Mr. Yu turned to her and waved. She waved back.

-79-

Dr. Min came with his family only a few times, but he called frequently. When the priests and Nurse Yun came to see Miri, spending weekends at the temple, she enjoyed their visits but outdid herself. After their visit she had to stay in bed for several days. The dark room with her solitary futon bed was the most comfortable place. She cried now and then without any thoughts. Her thoughts would not talk to her, leaving her in utter loneliness. Waiting began to be worse than the pain. Sam came by a couple times a day, but she pretended she was asleep. His presence burdened her heart.

She must have been asleep for a while; she couldn't tell. The light filtering through the rice-papered window told her it was afternoon. "I'm still here. It hasn't happened yet." She vaguely sensed movement in the room, a human sound, a sob? She listened, thinking it might be Sam. She moved her head on the pillow to make out who it was. A man was sitting in the corner of the room. She adjusted her eyes to the dark silhouette, which was surely that of a male. It was her father, and in front of him, was what seemed to be a fruit basket. He was crying silently, his head buried in his drawn knees, his shoulders heaving. She listened to the sound of her father's sobbing, squeezing the edge of the covers with her hands, wetting the pillow with her tears, not wanting to break their silent crying.

He left afterwards, leaving behind the fruit basket without coming near her bed, without the knowledge that his child had soaked her pillow with tears for him, without knowing that her eyes were following him, watching him leave for the last time.

- 8 0 -

After the day of her father's visit, she was able to get out of the bed, feeling a little more energy. Mrs. Lim came that weekend with the dogs, prepared for a cookout. The evening was warm and sweet. Miri sat on the straw mat watching the people, animals, and the fire. The popping sound of burning wood, the flying embers against the darkening sky, the dancing flame of blue, green, orange, and yellow, with all of them talking, laughing, eating, and drinking; the only thing missing in the scene was Hakyu's aria. Kuju seemed to be having the best time, giving the empty plates to the raccoons who sat on their butts licking the plates clean, holding them up to their noses. He never approached her, not even once since she came to the temple. Her crooked appearance might have scared him off, she thought. Although he was a child in a grown body, he never looked goofy or undignified. Somehow his pride was intact in him, and just being himself was plenty good enough for him. The old monk was lovingly petting the dogs who glued their bodies to him, petrified by the animals around them. She heard the nuns giggling, drinking the beer Sam made them try. Mrs. Lim tried to feed Miri the meat, which took a long time for her to chew. She made her laugh, because whenever she was with Miri, she would always tell her, "You've got to eat more, otherwise you won't get strong."

It was a good cookout. The smell of meat being cooked on the fire, the nuns drinking beer, all in a Buddhist temple...

- 81 -

She woke up. It was early but still light out. She could hear the birds chirping and smelled the incense coming from the main hall. Bongsan must be praying, she thought. Nurse Chan was sleeping, softly snoring. She got up and went out to the front of the temple, making sure that each step would hold her up. Her wobbly legs cooperated. She carefully passed through the corridor with its open archway to the main hall where the good monk was meditating. She went out to the courtyard and stood there, gazing at the wonderful greens in front of her, getting ready to receive another day. The air felt warm and gentle, and the edge of the sky was turning pink with the rising sun. She took one look at the swallow's nest below the eaves and slowly walked down to the stream where Sam and Kuju had washed clothes and caught sweet shrimps. She heard the birds chirping noisily, flying from one branch to another. It took a long while before she heard the shallow stream down below making its way among the pebbles and rocks. When she arrived at the stream, the top arch of the sun was hanging above the hill. Pink blossoms of cherry and peach trees along the water blew out their petals to the soft breeze that danced with them, twirling and bouncing before they reached the flowing water. She stepped into the water and stood there, looking around as if she were determined to count how many pink-flowered trees were there. A sudden brief wind snowed the petals of the blossoms to the water. They floated, turning round and round before they joined the chatty stream to be where they would be.

A large peach blossom plopped down on the water by a bird jumping through the branches. She bent over trying to reach the flower circling round and round on the water. She slipped on a rock, seeing the flower flowing away with the stream, and away it went.

She was lying in the stream facing the sky, unable to feel if the water was cold or wet. The water passing by her gently swayed her body, lifting and tugging her gown. She saw, through the water running over her face, a sparrow sitting on a branch that hung lazily over the stream. Suddenly, it flew away, bouncing the branch and making the petals fall like butterflies.

"Death always wins. It must win to take me home."

-END-

www.ingramcontent.com/pod-product-compliance
Lightning Source LLC
Chambersburg PA
CBHW020244030726
47499CB00001B/43